SHADOWS OF THE SKY

SEAN CURTIS

Shadows of the Sky
Book One of The Leyline Trilogy

Written by Sean Curtis

Story by Sean Curtis & Patrick Stephens

Edited by Clara Abigail

Map Design by Patrick Stephens

Cover Art by Leonning

Iconography by Anna Maslennikova

SeanCurtisBooks.com

Sean Curtis
Honolulu, Hawai'i USA

GALEDUL
OROMI
Vetrel
ARTANI
Soulos Sea
THE LANDS BELOW

North
Duskward
Dawnward
South
EYENDOR
ODISIA
THE DAWNWARD REACH
BANEHÛL

CONTENTS

Prologue // The Waterfall // 1
Chapter 1 // Life in Shae Glen // 11
Chapter 2 // The Desqen Forge // 25
Chapter 3 // Under the Rug // 38
Chapter 4 // The Warped Glass // 45
Chapter 5 // Secrets // 54
Chapter 6 // An Oath in An Empty Home // 64
Chapter 7 // Two Strangers // 79
Chapter 8 // The Cave // 93
Chapter 9 // Nicol's Wood // 104
Chapter 10 // Monster Hunters // 119
Chapter 11 // Into the Jungle // 130
Chapter 12 // Lone Wanderer // 140
Chapter 13 // Not Lost, Just Looking // 152
Chapter 14 // Deep Water // 158
Chapter 15 // Anger of the Jungle // 173
Chapter 16 // In the Dark // 184
Chapter 17 // The Last of the Jiye // 199
Chapter 18 // The Maiden Rhiannon // 212
Chapter 19 // Strife in Shae Glen // 228
Chapter 20 // The Land of Shadows // 235
Chapter 21 // The Night Blades // 249
Chapter 22 // Blood In the Streets // 260
Chapter 23 // The Fifth Day // 272
Chapter 24 // After the Fall // 279
Chapter 25 // Once More Into The Ruins // 297
Chapter 26 // The Governors' Council // 312
Chapter 27 // Cages // 327
Chapter 28 // A Warning // 340
Chapter 29 // Battle In The Shadow // 354
Chapter 30 // The Golden Forge // 376
Chapter 31 // For Helanái // 385
Chapter 32 // Fires of Rebirth // 395
Chapter 33 // Shadows of the Sky // 408

"The power in one life lives in the lives of all it touches. That power is then imparted to each being, forevermore, flowing in a constant state of renewal."

The Preachings of The Eagle

Prologue

THE WATERFALL

The twins walked down the bustling street of Shae Glen, eager to return home. Tylanna Desqen clutched the bundle she held in her small hands as her brother, Tahnir, gripped her shirt sleeve and led them through the oncoming swarms of people. The flow of the crowd moved against the two children, but Tahnir blocked most of those passing by from bumping into his sister. The pair shuffled their way through the throng as fast as they could. The village of Shae Glen was raucous, with shouting and cheerful music, but the twins did not share in the cheer.

All of the bustling villagers would be heading to the Rebirth Festival in the large field that sat next to the village center. It was an annual celebration of the new children that were born in the past year. Most of the village would be gathered until dawn, with performers and merchants traveling from distant lands to partake in the festivities.

As her brother forced their way out of a large knot of cheery villagers, Tylanna stumbled and dropped what she was carrying onto the dirt road before them. She fell to her knees and scrambled to return the spilled contents to the bag. It was medicine she carried. Medicine for their mother, who had fallen ill a few months ago and seemed to grow weaker and weaker with each passing day.

The twins' mother was the village healer, but as her condition worsened her apprentice had been forced to take over. The apprentice would visit their home once a week to check in on their mother and deliver medicine, but their mother had sent them to get the coming week's delivery a few days early.

Once she had placed everything back in the bag, Tylanna rose to her feet and dusted off her short pants. Tahnir stood a few paces ahead of her, his eyes looking back at her with a strange mix of gentleness and urgency. She strode over to him and grabbed his hand. Together, now free from the bustling crowds, they ran back to their home.

The pair of children looked nearly identical, with light brown hair and soft green eyes. They were at the age of ten, just before they would start to look more and more different as the years passed.

Tylanna slowed her run as they approached their home. It was a pleasant house made of wood and stone, with their father's forge attached on the right-hand side. It was not the largest house in Shae Glen, nor the smallest. They had lived in the house for the twins' entire lives, and their father had built the home sometime before they were born.

Surrounding the simple home was a large field of swaying green grass that led into the forest that bordered the village. Due to the twins' adventurous nature, their father had warned them many times not to venture too far into the forest without him, but they rarely listen. The house was built on the outskirts of the village, but in recent years, more and more homes began to crop up around theirs.

Tylanna pulled Tahnir onto the front porch and flung the door open. They dashed inside and through the front hallway until they stood together, hand in hand, in the doorway of their parents' bedroom.

Their father, a massive man, knelt hunched at the side of the bed while deep sobs wracked his form. His large, calloused hands gripped their mother's dainty one which hung limply from the side of the bed.

Tylanna dropped the bag she carried and stared. Their father only seemed to notice the twins at the sound of the bag falling. He wiped tears from his eyes and shook his head sadly. His huge hands gently placed their mother's hand on the bed, and he moved across the room to wrap the children in a mighty embrace.

Tahnir fell into his father's arms, but Tylanna squirmed away and ran out of the house. Once she was outside, she ignored cries from her brother and father and just kept running. She didn't know where her feet were taking her, but she knew that she had to get away.

Tahnir stood on the front porch with his father. Tylanna was already out of sight, but he had a pretty good idea of where she was heading. After briefly shouting to his father that he would bring his sister back, he started to run towards the forest, his father shouting objections until Tahnir could no longer hear him. Already Tylanna was much faster than Tahnir, so he didn't figure he would catch up with her until she reached their spot. Still, he pressed on, knowing that they both had to be there for their father. They were all he had now.

Tears flowed from Tahnir's eyes as he ran, and he momentarily struggled to see the forest unfolding before him. After nearly losing his footing on a large fallen branch, he wiped the tears free from his eyes. There would be time later to grieve, now he had to make sure Tylanna was okay.

As he exploded into a clearing, he saw Tylanna facing away from him, her legs dangling over the edge of the waterfall. The waterfall was the result of a river that carved its way along the southern edge of Shae Glen, or so their mother had told them. Though the river leading into the falls did not have a particularly strong current, the water crashing from the top of the formation crashed and churned into a collision of white water at the rocky base.

Wordlessly, Tahnir eased himself down next to Tylanna. Even though he had always found his sister to be the better climber and adventurer, he still found that he was able to clamber over to their spot without difficulty. They had never told their parents that they climbed out to the ledge, primarily because they knew that they would never approve of the potentially dangerous location.

As he settled into a seated position, he let the water wash over his hanging feet as the burden of caring for his sister weighed heavily on his shoulders. The stillness of the forest was all around them, leaving them completely alone with their thoughts, aside from the noise of the water crashing on the rocks below.

Tylanna was the first to speak up.

"I can't believe she's gone." Her voice was quiet, each word forced between whimpers.

He thought long and hard about how to answer her. He was sure the same emotions that flooded through her were doing the same to him, but he also knew in this moment that he had to be strong.

"I know. She told us this may eventually happen, but I didn't believe her. Even when she kept getting sicker, I always thought she would do something to make herself better, as she did with everyone in Shae Glen whenever they got sick."

Tylanna seemed to busy herself with moving her feet in and out of the water that flowed beneath them, the way Tahnir had when he first sat. There were a few more levels of rocky surfaces they could climb down to, but they always just sat on their ledge at the top of the waterfall.

After a short silence, she finally asked, "What do you think will happen to her?"

Tahnir let out a deep breath before answering. "I really don't know. She's not here anymore, I know that. But what will happen to her next? I've heard Father say that when someone passes on, their spirit is rejoined with the energy of the world, where we all came from in the first place. Maybe she'll be a spirit that wanders around the world forever. I don't know, Tyl."

"That doesn't sound so bad," Tylanna replied. As she sat, she gently wiped a trickle of water that had splashed onto her leg with her free hand. "I think I would like to travel forever, not be held down to anything. If only I could trade myself for Mother."

"Don't say that, Tyl. Mother wouldn't want that. She was always saying how happy she was that she had us and couldn't wait to see the great lives we would lead. We still have to do that for her."

Tylanna nodded and fell silent. Tahnir decided to match her and just sit, taking in the majesty of the forest around them.

Soon, the silence was interrupted by the chirps of a small bird flying down from the treetops. Tahnir noticed the bird first and saw that it was their mother's favorite: a blue sparrow. They were common, especially in the forest. When their mother walked through the forest with the twins, they would see who could spot the most blue sparrows before they returned home.

Presently, the bird fluttered down to one of the rock ledges below them and came to a rest. Tahnir saw Tylanna's eyes grow wide when she noticed the bird, and he already knew what she was about to do.

He saw her swing her small body around and climbing down. The bird sat on a very small ledge about three rungs below where she was now.

"Tylanna, stop! There isn't enough room!"

But she didn't stop. Tahnir had seen this determined look in her eyes many times before, and he knew whatever he said, she was going to do what she had set out to do.

With little trouble, he saw her drop to the next ledge, now only two away from the blue sparrow. The bird seemed to be staring at her warily.

Tahnir rose to his feet to get a better view. She skillfully worked herself down to the ledge just above where the bird sat, which was the last one that could fit a person, albeit a small child such as his sister. He saw her squat to stare deeply at the bird. They made direct eye contact before she lifted herself down so she hung from only her hands on the ledge with the bird. Her legs dangled freely, with nothing below her but water colliding with the rocks.

Tahnir shouted to her again to come back, but she didn't even seem to hear him, her focus devoted to the blue sparrow.

Tahnir found it odd that the bird wasn't flying away. It seemed to just stare intently at Tylanna. She came to a stop an arm's length away from the bird, and, supporting herself with just one hand, reached her free hand towards it.

As Tylanna's hand made its final grab, the bird darted into the air.

She slipped, and before he could do anything, she was falling.

Her brown hair billowed around her face, but he saw a slight smile cross her lips as her eyes followed the bird flying away from her. She hung there, for a moment, untethered to anything in this world.

And in the next moment, she lay at the base of the waterfall, sprawled over the rocks.

Tahnir sprinted towards the forest. When he reached the base, Tylanna still hadn't moved. As he approached, the water around her was turning red, and her eyes were closed. The slight smile she had flashed him was gone, and her face was limp.

He knelt next to her and lifted her head. Something warm and wet sluiced over his skin, and even before he looked, he knew it was blood.

"Tyl. Tyl, wake up."

Tylanna said nothing.

"You have to wake up, Tyl. I can't do this alone."

Nothing

Tahnir shook her. "Tylanna! I need you! Please wake up!"

Just then, a hand rested on his shoulder. He spun his head around to see the old man Nara, a hermit who lived outside the village, standing over him. Tahnir had never officially met him, but their father always said he was a man who could be trusted; he was just an odd fellow who preferred to live by himself.

As Nara stared at the twins, Tahnir noticed that he had bright, golden eyes.

Tahnir wiped tears from his eyes and tried to collect himself. "She slipped! She fell from almost the top of the waterfall, and I can't get her to wake up! Can you help her?"

The hand Nara had placed on Tahnir's shoulder began pulling him away from Tylanna. He resisted at first, but after he had set her head down, he moved aside for Nara. The hermit kneeled gracefully, the robes he wore seamlessly flowing around him. He looked over Tylanna once and then gently placed his hand on her cold forehead. Nara remained in that position for quite some time before rising back to his feet.

With a gasp, Tylanna sat up, her eyes darting wildly. She looked to Nara and then Tahnir, and only then did Tahnir notice. The iris of her right eye was now golden, just like Nara's.

Tahnir jumped forward and embraced his sister. He could feel her heart beating loudly and rapidly against her chest. She hugged him back, and then Tahnir helped her to her feet.

"Where did Nara go? I wanted to thank him," she said as her hand brushed over the back of her head absentmindedly.

Tahnir spun around to see that the hermit was nowhere to be seen. Assuming he had gone back to wherever he lived, Tahnir grabbed Tylanna's hand. "It doesn't matter. We can thank him later. We need to go home before anything else happens."

Together, the twins rushed into the forest. Tahnir spared one last look at the waterfall, where he could still see the scarlet stain of his sister's blood being washed from the rocks where she died.

CHAPTER 1
LIFE IN SHAE GLEN

The late spring air whipped through her flowing hair as she rode along the shaded trail, a beaten dirt path that had been trodden into place by the footsteps of her fellow Shae Glenners in years past. Small pockets of light appeared to rip through the canopy above her and illuminate the forest. Shades of green, yellow, and red bloomed all around her.

The land around Shae Glen had an abundance of vegetation, and she had been sent to gather several of the native plants for her instructor, Xelina Marcs. Carrot, her trusty steed, handled the uneven land beneath her with ease. Carrot was an old mare who had been a member of the family for as long as she could remember. Though she always remembered the horse as being old, Carrot never seemed to slow in her duties for their family. Tylanna had ridden her through these lands often, though never too far from Shae Glen. The adventurous spirit she had possessed as a youth had died with her that fateful day ten years ago.

Since the accident, Tylanna had been far more withdrawn than she ever was in her youth. The dreams she had once had of leaving Shae Glen for a life of adventure now only lived in her nightmares.

A few weeks after the twins returned to their home on that day, they went together with their father to visit Nara and thank him for his help. They found his small home abandoned, and Nara nowhere to be found. He never again appeared around the village after that, according to the rest of the people of Shae Glen.

The family had decided to keep the secret of her resurrection between them. Tylanna still received questions about her strange golden eye, but they had explained it away by saying it was a symptom of a family condition that sometimes manifested during puberty. Their father was not originally from Shae Glen, so the village had no reason not to believe her when she told them this.

When she had become old enough to begin study, she had become one of Xelina's apprentices. Tahnir had chosen to support their father's work in the forge. Xelina, who was only six years Tylanna's senior, had flourished as an incredible healer renowned throughout not just Shae Glen, but most of Eodisia. Would-be healers from several surrounding villages now came to study under her, giving Tylanna several classmates. She did her best to stand out from amongst the crowd, and she did find that she had a natural aptitude for learning, especially when it came to studying the written word. Tylanna saw studying to become a healer as a way of preserving her mother's legacy, as well as save as many people as possible from death's icy grasp.

She often had strange dreams, sometimes of wandering through the forest alone and seeing herself fall from the ledge of the waterfall. If the memories and dreams were not enough to remind her of that day, she also had her right eye to serve as a permanent reminder.

Presently, she was returning from gathering medical herbs from the wild area to the duskward side of Shae Glen. She and Carrot had left the village yesterday and camped beneath the stars overnight. Tylanna quite enjoyed camping, when she was close of enough to the village to return whenever she wanted. Her brother or her fellow students would often accompany her, but Xelina had sent her on this trip as a personal favor. Now she and Carrot returned with Tylanna's bag filled to the brim with the herbs she had been tasked with finding.

As they exited the shaded trail, the sprawling village of Shae Glen lay before them. Shae Glen was a relatively small village nestled in a valley between a large forest and the wild area she had just left in a particularly sylvan region of Eodisia. The village was relatively young, having only been founded about sixty years ago by Eodisians who sheltered refugees fleeing from a series of foreign wars. This had led to a wonderful blend of different cultures that weaved an intricate tapestry of tradition and festivities.

Many of the structures in the village center of the village remained from the original construction of Shae Glen, such as the Mayoral Palace, the sanitarium, and several large buildings that offered small living spaces to many families. The southern district of village, where the Desqen's home was located, was all built as a later addition to Shae Glen's borders, which came as the result of a formal request to the High Chair of Eodisia for more land to support the surge of refugees from the terribleness of the world. This left the Desqen home just outside of the village center.

Their father had come to Shae Glen from some other land, though where that was, he had never mentioned to Tylanna or Tahnir, often saying that he did not wish to discuss it. He had built the home they would come to inhabit himself and quickly found work in the growing village as a forge master.

Her parents had met when their father injured himself in his forge and visited the sanitarium for treatment. They had felt an intense connection instantly and were married just a year later. The twins arrived sometime later, and for ten years the four of them had a peaceful, quiet life, safely nestled in the arms of a village that had been created to provide a safe haven from the evil of the world around it.

Tylanna descended from the hill at the duskward side of the village and rode into the village square. As the beaten dirt path transitioned to a firm cobblestone street, she slid off of Carrot's back, giving the old mare a firm pat once she was back on the ground. She slung her bag of herbs over her shoulder and pulled at Carrot's reins to lead her through the streets that would very soon be teeming with denizens of the village getting their day started.

They walked through the quiet village together, with little but the sound of Carrot's hooves sounding off of the cobblestone. After only a few moments Tylanna caught sight of one of her fellow apprentice healers, Akiye Komoto, and her parents. She gave Carrot's reigns a tug and walked over to greet them.

Akiye was a tall girl with a slender frame who moved in very refined and controlled movements. She was quiet and highly intelligent, a few of the many reasons why Tylanna was so fond of her. She had her beautiful black hair cut short, which she claimed was better for not getting in the way of her work. Though she was a little over a year younger than Tylanna, the two of them together were each poised to be completing their training soon.

Her village, Nagashi and Ghanai'm Komoto, had arrived in the village around the same time as the twins' father. During the days, they worked together as wine merchants, and Ghanai'm also served as a member of

Shae Glen's watchmen. Tylanna's father was also a volunteer for the watch, having pledged to keep the village safe long ago. The family greeted her with smiles.

"Hello, Aki. Lady Komoto, Ghanai'm, nice to see that you two are well."

Akiye's eyes drifted to the bag Tylanna had slung over her shoulder. "I see the trip for Lady Marcs went well? Unless you have stuffed that bag full of something else."

"Yes, yes. Xelina was correct again about where the herbs could be found. I found everything she needed to concoct that medical paste she read about, which should help with the outbreak of fevers we have seen lately. This should lighten our workload a fair bit at the sanitarium, should it prove successful. I'm heading to drop these off with her and then get some much-needed rest. Being outside of the village for any time at all seems to drain me of all my energy."

"I know precisely what you mean," Nagashi chimed in. "There is no greater comfort than the comfort of home. Please give our love to your family for us."

Tylanna nodded pleasantly. Just as she did, she saw her brother approaching from behind Akiye and her family. Tahnir had finally grown to be taller than Tylanna, by nearly his entire head. His time working in the forge had served to widen his already stocky frame, and his shoulders were almost twice as wide as hers. He had cut his hair short some time ago, but now it grew to a shaggy length that would soon require cutting once more.

It would now be nearly impossible to confuse either of the two twins for the other, a fact Tylanna felt somewhat melancholy about.

“Tyl! You’re back already. I was wondering when you would return.” Tahnir greeted Akiye and her family with a smile and a nod before turning back to his sister. Tylanna noticed Akiye grow slightly red when Tahnir had looked at her, a fact which amused Tylanna greatly. “I was just heading to the field for some early Derby-Ball before I help Father. I can walk with you to see Xelina if you’d like.”

Derby-Ball was a popular game played by the locals of Shae-Glen, that Tylanna generally considered herself too old for. Tahnir, however, never seemed to tire of running about on a field, trying, but often failing, to impress the girls that would play. It involved several teams of three kicking and throwing about a leather ball and attempting to knock out the other teams by hitting them with the ball and then grabbing the ball before anyone from their team could take it back. It was all a little intense for Tylanna, who preferred to sit quietly with a nice book while the more enthusiastic young ones, including her brother, who to most could not be called a young one anymore, could blow off some steam.

Tylanna agreed and said farewell to Akiye and her family as they all set about their day. Tahnir took Carrot’s reins from Tylanna and gave the horse a few pats on the head as the twins set off together for the sanitarium.

“How did Carrot do on the trail?”

“Fine, just as usual. You would never guess her age seeing her run at full speed. What have I missed in my time away?”

“You must have been gone far too long if you expect there to be some exciting news from Shae Glen after only one day away,” Tahnir said with a lighthearted chuckle. “It was the same as always, except Father was up all night, pacing through the house with worry. He still wishes you would let him, or I come with you on these supply-gathering trips.”

Tahnir gave Carrot’s reigns a light tug as the mare had become distracted by a group of children playing in the street. The mare snorted and lumbered on behind them.

“I know, but if I ever want to become my own person, I’ll need to be able to take care of myself.” Tylanna readjusted the bag slung over her shoulder. It was not that she wouldn’t like to have the company, but she wanted to push herself. “Just wait out here while I go give these to Lady Marcs.”

They had already arrived outside the sanitarium, Shae Glen being the small village that it was.

“And miss the chance to see Xelina? I think not.”

Tahnir dashed ahead of Tylanna and pushed the doors open excitedly. Inside, many young apprentices ran about tending to the few patients that were scattered about the facility. Many were gathered around Xelina Marcs, who was talking with a patient who appeared to have severely injured his leg. After speaking for a while with the patient, she turned to the apprentices around her and gave a long list of instructions, which they immediately set about following.

Once the apprentices had dispersed, she turned to the Desqen twins, and a radiant smile lit up her face. Her curly black hair bounced softly as she skipped over to them, wrapping them each in a tender embrace.

"Welcome back, Tylanna! And great to see you again, stranger! It looks like you've grown even more since the last time you came to see me, Tahnir." Xelina's voice always had a bright and cheery quality, which was beyond helpful in easing the worries of troubled patients of the sanitarium.

Tahnir laughed bashfully before replying, "Well, I see you look even better than ever, Xelina. If only I could have fallen ill more often so that I may have soaked in the light of your smile just a few more times."

Tylanna released a dismissive snort as she unburdened the bag from her shoulder and passed it to Xelina, who accepted it gratefully.

"You are too much, Tahnir. And thank you so much, Tyl. Did you find everything all right? Did the almanac I gave you help?" Xelina turned her attention from Tahnir to Tylanna. Her expression grew slightly more serious, though for Xelina that was not saying much.

"Yes, absolutely. It was extremely detailed in how to locate the right herbs, and which to avoid. It helped tremendously," Tylanna replied shortly. Though she and Xelina had a close relationship, Tylanna could not help but revert to the role of a student eager to please whenever she was discussing anything relating to her studies.

"Good, well, I want you to hold onto it. Consider it an early graduation present. Look at the two of you!" Xelina clapped a hand on each of the twin's shoulders. "It seems like just yesterday Tritelle took me in as an apprentice when I had nowhere else to go and I met her two new babies. Now you're each becoming such independent adults, I know that somewhere she is smiling at how far you have come."

The twins each smiled but fell silent at the mention of their mother. Their father never visited the sanitarium unless it was absolutely necessary; he said it reminded him too much of their mother. They once had to nearly drag the man there when he had come down with a fever that Tylanna couldn't seem to heal on her own.

"Thank you, Lady Marcs - Xelina," Tylanna responded, stumbling on Xelina's formal title. "I couldn't have come this far if it wasn't for you. I'll use the almanac to help any way I can."

The healer gave them one last smile before turning back to her sanitarium, where her apprentices still ran about the space, scrambling to do whatever she had asked. As she returned to orchestrating the organized chaos, the twins took their leave.

When they stepped out of the sanitarium and into the warm morning air, Tahnir spun around to face Tylanna.

"So, what will you do? Do you want to play the game with us, or are you still too scared?"

Tylanna weighed her options for a moment before deciding that she was fine just watching the revelry. The pair wandered over to the large grassy field that lay beside the village center, Tahnir pulling Carrot along behind them. He wore a goofy grin that he always seemed to have after visiting the sanitarium.

The ball ricocheted away, but Tahnir's friend Greguh just barely was able to clip it with his foot, sending it flying high over Tahnir's head. Keeping his eye on the ball, he began to sprint at his full speed towards where he thought the ball would land, knowing that catching this would eliminate the last team, winning the game for him and his partners. He pumped his arms madly as the ball began to drop right above him, he was nearly there, just a few more steps and-

Tahnir came to a crashing halt as he collided with something massive and fell to the ground hard. As soon as his head stopped spinning he raised himself up, only to see his father, Rynestian, standing before him, seemingly unfazed by Tahnir crashing into him at full speed. He also calmly held the ball in his upraised right hand.

His father laughed in the full-bellied voice he used when he found something truly amusing and then offered his free hand to help Tahnir up to his feet. The man was a giant, nearly a head taller than Tahnir still. His hair was almost completely gray, with a few splashes of the red hair he used to sport. He wore a thick mustache on his upper lip, which he often stroked when he was stressed or nervous.

Tahnir graciously accepted the hand, though he felt a little embarrassed that his father had not even budged an inch and easily caught the ball. Tahnir often mused to himself that he was an unstoppable force on the Derby-Ball field, but really he was just glad his father had never stepped onto the field with him.

His father threw the ball back out onto the field while pulling Tahnir up and towards him, still giggling in a voice that barely seemed suitable for a man so large. "I guess you need to learn to focus on two things at once, my boy. One must be able to see their goal while maintaining themselves in the present."

"I'll try to keep that in mind," Tahnir replied, rubbing his hand over his head. He was sure there would be a lump where he had hit his father, and the old man didn't seem to have a scratch on him.

"Is your sister here as well? I just received quite a large order, and I need both of your help with it."

Still running his hand through his hair, definitely feeling the beginnings of swelling, he pointed with his free hand to Tylanna, who was already striding, with Carrot in tow, across the field, all the while remaining away from the other villagers who had resumed playing without Tahnir; they had most likely assumed him injured after crashing into Rynestian.

The forge master was known all through the village as being a towering and hard man, but as the twins and a few others knew, the man seemed barely able to hurt a fly. He even disliked crafting weaponry in his forge, though the better-paying jobs were usually for tools of war. He much preferred creating tools that could be useful in helping the people of Shae Glen build up their homes, or to make farming easier for those who worked in the fields.

As Tylanna approached, their father pulled her in for a large embrace that pulled the girl off her feet.

“Aye, I’ve only been gone one day!” she shouted, urging her father to let her down. “And I’ll be going on much more trips like this once I finish my training with Xelina.”

“I know, I know. I do worry, is all.” Rynestian laughed as he eased Tylanna back down to her feet. “Come, we have an order at the forge I’ll need your help with as well as your brother. Must be some trouble in the Eodisian capital for them to send an order all the way out to Shae Glen.”

Tahnir took Carrot's reins from his sister and patted the mare's head, allowing Tylanna to walk with their father.

"I'm sure they just seek your fine craftsmanship. No better steelwork in all of Eodisia than at the Desqen Forge," Tahnir chimed in.

Their father sighed, putting an arm around both of them. "Ahh, I don't know about all that, but we'll do the best we can. It really is a large order, though. We better be off."

With one last look back at his friends running around on the field, Tahnir gave Carrot's reins a tug and followed along with his father and sister. Games were fun and all, but his responsibility was to the forge, and to his family.

Chapter 2

THE DESQEN FORGE

Night had already begun to fall by the time they reached their home just outside the village. Tahnir rushed to settle Carrot down into their small stable. The family all shared the one horse, who was getting on in years but still handled all the work they needed of her well.

After he had given her some feed and locked the stable door, Tahnir ran over to the forge, where Tylanna had already gotten the fires started. Their father had already donned his thick leather apron and was rolling up his shirtsleeves to slide into his long leather gloves. Tahnir followed suit and began gathering his necessary equipment, as his sister ran about the forge trying to find where she had left her gloves and apron.

The forge next to the Desqen home was not gigantic, nor was it flashy. The small building was constructed basically, with four walls and a chimney venting out the smoke. The inside of the forge was designed for maximum efficiency. Each tool and structure were arranged with a master's mind guiding each decision. Their father had constructed the forge at the same time as their family home, apparently using it to craft tools for the home when he could not find them in Shae Glen. With all three of them inside, working together, the room was nearly filled to capacity.

Primarily, it was just Tahnir that worked the forge with their father, but Tylanna had helped out enough that Rynestian had given them both their own forging outfits. Tahnir believed that if their father had his way, they would both live at home and work in the forge with him forever, though he would never come out and say that directly. As for Tahnir, he liked the work and found that he had a natural aptitude for it. He could easily see himself working the forge for the rest of his life, enjoying a nice quiet life in Shae Glen, and maybe starting a family of his own. Tahnir hoped that one day he could surpass his father's legendary skill with the craft.

Though earlier he had jested to Rynestian about their forge having the best steel in the country, he genuinely believed that his father had to be one of the best craftsmen. He was constantly creating new tools that no one had ever seen or conceived of before, and even though the material they acquired was not always the finest, he seemed to make tools that outlasted the tools of any other master. Even while Tahnir finished getting into his apron and gloves, his father had already begun laying out the preparations for their order. He was not joking when he had said it was a large one.

When Tahnir and his sister were both ready, they approached the large workbench where their father was already deftly arranging materials and tools, seeming to have slipped into a world of his own, as he often did when they were all working together. As they got closer, he startled before he looked up, as if he had forgotten they were there.

"Ah, all right then. The order comes straight from the Eodisian General-Master, apparently. They have heard of our work and wanted us to craft some weaponry for their armies. Now I know this is not the sort of crafting we be normally doing, but the coin from this job will set us up to put in some major upgrades to the forge, which will help us help the people of Shae Glen, so I decided to take the offer. I will be running the forge. Tahn, you'll be handling the hammer and anvil, and Tyl, you can help me at the forge and then be in charge of the quenching at the end. You both know what you're doing, so let's get to work. The order is for fifty sword blades, fifty spear points, and two hundred arrowheads. We'll start with the blades as they'll be the most difficult and handle the points when we're finished."

The Desqens went right to work. In no time at all Rynestian was plunging the rods of steel into the fire as Tylanna worked the bellows to keep the flames at the right height and temperature, a practice she and her brother could probably do while they slept at this point. Tahnir and his father had become so accustomed to working with just the two of them that having an extra set of hands was extremely helpful, and the work went quickly.

As his father passed the heated steel rods, Tahnir went right to work with his trusty hammer, the leather wrapped around the hilt grooved perfectly for his hand's grip, and began to craft the heated metal into shape with precision and ease. Though they did not craft swords and other tools of war very often, they did make scythes and other farm tools with sharp blades, so crafting these was not too much of a departure for them.

Tahnir usually found that when crafting something he had not made before, or he had not made very often, as was the case with sword blades, he usually found the shape as he went along. Since the order was so large and not looking for uniquely styled swords, just fifty of the same, he would find the shape with the first steel rod and then try to emulate that form the best he could.

The rod was quite long, and the heat had given it a slight curve. Deciding he would go along with the natural shape that had presented itself to him, he began to hammer out the metal. He found that he had quite a bit of metal to work with as he hammered, so he folded the steel over once to give it an extra sharp edge on the side that curved out. He worked the steel until it he found the blade's shape: about three and a half feet long with a generous curve, only edged on the one side, but he felt the speed would make up for that.

Once he felt he had finished, he passed the blade to Tylanna, who was standing ready to slowly ease it into their quenching liquid. Their father had devised the recipe, as every forge master had their own. Even Tahnir did not know it as Rynestian protected the secret very closely. After passing the first blade off to Tylanna, he began work on the second that his father passed him.

An order of this size would take a few weeks of all of them working late nights, but they figured they should get as much done as they could right away. Tahnir and Rynestian both often lost track of time when they were working in the forge, often needing to be reminded to eat or take breaks by Tylanna when she came home from studying at the sanitarium.

After placing another sword blade on the cooling rack after quenching, Tylanna returned to the bellows and began talking to their father as they worked.

"So with all these weapons being made for the Eodisian army, do you think there will be war soon?"

Their father didn't react at all to the question, his eyes fixed on the flames of the forge, for so much time that Tylanna began to repeat her question just before he spoke up.

"There may be, there may not be. Whispers of war always run through the lands, though Eodisia itself has not been involved in a war in a long time. Eyendor always seems to take some issue with their shared border with Eodisia, Artani and Helanái are constantly bickering over their shared land, and religious cults and uprisings keep popping up all over the nations. Who is to say why Eodisia is arming its military? They may be simply training their standing army or supplying new weapons just in case there do be an attack someday. It never hurts to be prepared for the worst."

Tylanna seemed unsatisfied with the answer, so she pressed on, "Do you think war will reach Shae Glen?"

Rynestian took another long pause, the reflection of sparks from the forge dancing in his large green eyes. "I hope not, Tylanna. I came to Shae Glen with hopes of never having to see war or violence again, to start a new life of peace. Many of the other villagers who have come here have the same idea as me, so I believe we will do all it takes to stay out of any coming conflict. That being said, we have worked too hard building up this village to let it be destroyed by invaders, so if it came down to it, I am sure the villagers would rise up to defend it."

"I'm sure we would send anyone packing no problem, if they ever tried to mess with our home," Tahnir added encouragingly. "No one has more pride in their homes than the people of Shae Glen."

"Aye, that do be true." Their father nodded absentmindedly as he pulled another steel rod and passed it to Tahnir without ever pulling his eyes from the flames of the forge.

Much later into the night, their father finally agreed with Tylanna that it was about time to finish up, though she practically had to drag him and her brother away from their workstations by force. Darkness had long since covered the land, and they had not yet eaten dinner, though they had been working for several hours in the hot forge.

Tylanna readied the water to dose the flames while the two men cleaned up their areas, leaving most of their tools out so that they could easily resume their work in the morning. After they stripped out of their working clothes, the men staggered back to the house behind Tylanna, only now seeming to notice how hard they had worked their bodies.

Once she had opened their front door and kicked her boots free of her feet, she took a long deep breath through her nose. Even after only being gone for one night, the smell of home always had a way of comforting her.

She strode directly to the kitchen, Tahnir and Rynestian both stumbling behind her. Their house was not gigantic on the outside, but it was incredibly roomy with very high ceilings built close to the roof. She always believed that their father did this to compensate for his ridiculous height, but it made most people that visited, and herself, feel quite small. The kitchen and dining room were an open concept separated only by a large wooden countertop. The floor of the dining room was decorated with a wool rug that had been there for as long as Tylanna could remember, with their large and ornately crafted wooden table resting on top of it. The walls were constructed from wood, all handcrafted by their father some twenty-odd years ago.

There were enough rooms for each of them. She and her brother had shared a room for a long time; after the accident and losing their mother, they could not bring themselves to sleep in different rooms for a few years. But now, they all had their own space. Her room served as a study, various books strewn all about the room, so much so that she usually had to shove a few of them to the side just to sleep. Both her brother's and father's room were very bare, with only the essentials neatly organized to maximize space. The only decoration that hung in her father's room was a small painting of the entire family, including their mother, done a few years before she passed.

Together, she, her brother, and her father all set about their various tasks in the kitchen. Once dinner was ready, a simple mixture of a few vegetables gathered on her trek outside the village along with some soup, the family gathered around their sturdy wooden table and went right about eating. The exhaustion from riding all morning and working all night had begun to creep through Tylanna's muscles and joints, though the food did seem to bring a sudden burst of energy back to her.

"So," she asked, "have you ever been part of a war, Father?"

Tahnir choked on his soup.. Their father had never told them much of his past and usually would avoid questions about it altogether. Rynestian set down his utensils and soup bowl and gave a long sigh before answering.

"Aye, when I was very young. Before you two came along, and before I ever met your mother. One of the many reasons I left my homeland, and how I ended up coming to Shae Glen. While I was fighting, I heard of a small village in Eodisia that was created as a haven for refugees of war, and I decided to run away from my post and travel all the way here, and I never looked back. I do not like to discuss it not only because I abhor the man I was when I was doling out violence, but also because I left my homeland in shame."

Tylanna looked down at her food before speaking again. "Sorry to bring it up. It's just you tell us so little about your past and your home, I cannot help but be curious."

"I know, and for that I am sorry. One day I swear to you, both of you, that I will tell you everything you wish about my past. But as for my home, Shae Glen will always be my home. It does not matter where you are born – home is where you make it, and where your family is."

"Did you have any other family?" Tahnir asked.

Rynestian stared down at his soup , clearly eager to get back to eating. "I did, but my parents both died when I was very young. I had one older brother, who I have not spoken to since I left all those years ago. I do not know what has become of him. I doubt I will ever see him again."

After replying, Rynestian picked up his bowl and began loudly slurping, an indication that both Tylanna and Tahnir picked up on right away.

They ate the remainder of their meals in relative silence, with a few comments here and there about their schedules for the coming days. Tylanna was returning to her studies at the sanitarium in the morning tomorrow, and Tahnir and Rynestian would return to completing the order in the forge. She suspected that she would have to drag them out of the forge once again tomorrow evening.

After cleaning up the table and kitchen, she decided to go to sleep early. She bid goodnight to her brother and father, who stood in the kitchen discussing the plan for the forging in the morning and retired to her room.

As she swung the large wooden door shut behind her, she sighed to herself about the pile of books and papers scattered over her bed. Too exhausted to do anything about it now, she dove over the pile and used her feet to push the books to the edge. Reorganizing the books would be tomorrow's problem. Once her head had rested on the pillow for a few moments, she felt herself slipping into unconsciousness.

She found herself standing on a large island clear of any trees or vegetation at all. The land seemed to be made of a sort of polished stone she had not seen before. Around her stood several beings that looked vaguely human, but their bodies did not seem to hold a permanent shape. Each figure's form seemed to be a tight collection of multicolored flames wrapping in on themselves, but she could detect no heat coming from any of them.

Tylanna recognized this as one of the dreams she often had. She did not know where the inspiration for these figures had come from, but every time she dreamt of these strange images, she always awoke confused and poorly rested. The figures seemed to be conversing with each other in a language that she did not understand, but from the tone and rate of speech, she could tell they were arguing. When they spoke, instead of moving their form where a mouth would normally be, the sound seemed to emanate from their entire form, and the matter comprising them seemed to shift and change color more frequently.

Including herself, there were twelve figures in all, all of them scattered about the small smooth isle in a strange semi-circle, with two of the figures standing before the rest, seeming to guide the majority of the conversation. From all she could tell, these two were on opposite sides of the argument and trying to convince the rest of the gathering of their positions.

All of a sudden, one of the two figures addressing the others made a loud declaration of some kind and pushed the other figure away. When the two figures touched, their forms emanated bright lights where their matter had connected. The figure who had pushed the other turned around and moved what must be its hands in front of it and dragged the air before it down. As its hands fell, so did the space before it.

It seemed to Tylanna to form some sort of passageway. The area on the other side seemed similar except the water level was much higher and there were many other islands jutting around the small isle the other figures stood on. The figure who had opened the door slipped through the passageway, and there was an extremely bright flash of light.

Tylanna threw her arms up to cover her eyes, and just before she was completely shrouded in light, she noticed that the same coursing energy of multicolored flame made up her form.

As the light encapsulated her, she heard a familiar voice sternly whisper to her, “Wake up, child.”

Chapter 3

UNDER THE RUG

"Wake up, Tylanna!"

Tylanna woke with a start to find her father shaking her shoulders. There was a panicked look in his eyes as he practically lifted her up out of bed and onto her feet.

"Follow me, hurry!" he panted out. She could hear the desperation in his voice.

She followed him into the hallway to find Tahnir standing there rubbing the sleep from his eyes. The light had barely begun to trickle in through the windows. Normally they would not wake up for another few hours, at least. Her father grabbed both of their hands and dragged them both to the dining room, moving quicker than she had ever seen him move.

Once they were in the dining room, he released them. Only then did Tylanna realize how tightly he had been squeezing her hand, and she began to massage it with her other.

"What is going on?" she asked.

"No time to explain. I heard a commotion coming from village and the neighbor's place. Just do as I say, and pray that I am overreacting."

The village and the nearest home to theirs were so far that it must have been some commotion if their father had been able to hear it. As she rubbed her hand, Rynestian grabbed their table and lifted it, amazing both twins. The table was made of very sturdy wood, and the two of them had often struggled to move it together. Her father scuttled over to the other side of the room, set the table down, and then spun to face them, sweat teeming down his face.

"Now, I know you're going to have a lot of questions, but please, please be as quiet as you can. I am going to hide you away until this trouble passes."

Tylanna almost objected, but she caught Tahnir give their father a firm nod, keeping his mouth shut, and she decided against it. Her father bent down, grabbed the corner of the rug, and ripped it away. To Tylanna's astonishment, a rectangular door lay beneath the rug, a rug she had never seen moved once.

Rynestian dropped to his knees and ran his fingers along the edge of the doorframe until he was able to pry it open. The door rose from the bottom and revealed a narrow staircase leading down. In the low light, she could not make out the room well.

"Quickly, both of you get in, and do not make a sound. I will come for you when I can, but take care of each other until then. I will see you soon and explain everything."

Tylanna opened her mouth to speak, but Tahnir grabbed her by the hand and hurried her along behind him and down the stairs. Once they had reached the floor below, she found it just as hard to make out what was in this room. The faint glints of sunlight seemed to illuminate some sort of metal hanging on the walls, but that light was soon blocked by their father's frame as he stood with his hand on the raised door leading to the basement.

"I will see you soon, my children."

With that, he let the door drop with a loud thud, and what little light they had was completely obscured. Fumbling in the darkness, she reached for her brother's hand, squeezing it tightly when she found it. He gave her a reassuring squeeze back in the darkness. She heard the shuffling of the rug being swept back to its original position.

Not more than a moment after the rug settled into place, there was a loud crash above them, and she heard a group of people shouting. She could barely make out what they were saying, and they seemed to speak in an accent that she did not recognize. Over the chorus of confusing demands, she heard her father's voice cut through the racket.

“What do you want? You had better explain yourself and why you think you can barge into my home unannounced.”

She could just barely make out the reply, which came from a woman with a low and raspy voice.

“Gathering...stinking villagers...trouble...hiding... amongst good people... anyone else?”

“No,” her father replied. “It be just me here. My children are grown and moved away, and my wife is gone.”

“Fine...yewl come...or we can...right here...”

She heard a few scuffles, and then the sound of hurried footsteps running through the house. She felt her way through the small room they were in gingerly and felt what could only be cool steel along the wall. She tried to follow the noises above her, but just as soon as they had left, the footsteps returned to the dining room above them.

Her father’s voice rang out again.

“I no be wanting any trouble. No need to put your hands on me, I will come with you. I certainly have nothing to hide.”

More footsteps above them, and she could feel Tahnir grip her arm tightly as she tried to follow the noises again. She could feel his hand shaking, either with fear or rage, so she decided to stop where she was. After the footsteps had clearly gone through the front door, she waited a few moments before turning herself to face her brother.

"What in the world was that? Who were those people, and what are they doing with Father?" she asked in a barely-contained whisper.

"I don't know," he answered gruffly. She could tell now that it was in fact rage coursing through him, not fear. "But we have to do as he told us. He will be back to let us out. He has never gone back on his word to us, and he is not going to start now."

Despite his assurances that he would go along with them without struggle, four soldiers surrounded Rynestian with their hands resting on their sword hilts as they walked towards the village. The soldiers wore practical leather and metal armor, placed over bright white clothing. They each wore short white robes over their left shoulders, each stitched intricately with different designs. The rough-sounding woman with the dark metal mask seemed to be in charge of those who had burst into their home, but he wondered if she was running the entire operation.

His mind raced as he wondered who these people could possibly be. He had not seen armor like theirs in all of his years traveling, and he did not recognize any of the designs and patterns of being from a certain country. Certainly, they were not the Eodisian military, not with their accents and the way they were treating him, a well-respected citizen of Shae Glen. He was glad he had hidden the children away in time. He just hoped that they were not foolish enough to try and follow him, wherever he was being taken. The woman had said something about troubled ones hiding amongst good people. The people of Shae Glen were from all different parts of the world, most escaping from some sort of war in their homelands. Had one of those wars found its way to Shae Glen?

A gauntleted fist stuck him in the back, and he realized he had been moving slowly as he wracked his brain. He picked up the pace to match the woman leading him. Around him, he saw other groups of Shae Glen's people being escorted towards the village. Other groups included children, and again he offered another silent thanks that he had thought to hide Tylanna and Tahnir away in the basement. He knew he would now have to explain what he kept in the basement to them, but that was a problem for another time. Rynestian had known for a long time that the day for explaining everything to the children would one day come, but now he just hoped he would get the chance to tell them the truth. He cursed himself for not writing some sort of letter in case something such as this were to happen, but there was no point dwelling on it now.

"Pardon," he asked, doing his best to keep the rage bubbling within him from entering his voice, "might I ask who it is you people are?"

A low cackle rang from inside the woman's mask. "You will know soon enough anyway, so I may as well tell you," she replied curtly. "We are Those Who Serve."

Rynestian stopped dead in his tracks, and the two soldiers walking behind him crashed into him, both of them losing their balance and falling over in a clatter.

Those Who Serve, he thought, That fanatical religion out of Oromia. He now understood what these people were doing in Shae Glen, and who they were looking for.

They were looking for him.

Chapter 4

THE WARPED GLASS

The village center was nearly fully illuminated by the morning's light when Rynestian and his escort arrived. He was directed to stand in a large grouping of the people of Shae Glen, all of whom wore worried expressions on their faces. They were surrounded by more soldiers, all armed to the teeth, dressed similarly to those who had taken Rynestian from his home. He frantically searched through the crowd for the others that Those Who Serve might be looking for.

As he was searching, the woman in the dark metal mask stepped out from behind the line of soldiers. So, she *was* in charge of this gathering. Even though they were armed, Rynestian thought if he could just find the others and make a break for it, maybe they-

His train of thought was cut off when the woman began to shout at the gathered Shae Glenners.

"Quiet! People of Shae Glen, I do apologize for bringing you all here so early in the morning. Please excuse our behavior, and we would greatly appreciate your cooperation in our efforts here today. My name is Elder Prx, and we are a sect of Those Who Serve sent to find the heretics living amongst you."

A worried murmur and a few gasps rang out through the crowd of Shae Glenners. Those Who Serve were a religious organization devoted to the Preachings of the Eagle, an age-old legend of a mythological race of super beings that watched over the development of the world from a different realm. The Eagle was said to be the only one of these super-beings, known as the Watchers or Those Who Watch, to cross over to the mortal realm. Once they arrived, they spread advice and guiding wisdom that helped the early creatures of the realm develop into the world as they knew it today.

Over time, the Eagle's teachings were turned into a religion devoted to keeping the world as this figure had wished. In Rynestian's few encounters with followers of this organization, he had found them to be a mostly peaceful folk, though they were completely dedicated to their ideals. But the last he had heard of Those Who Serve, they were in Oromia, a nation settled in a mountain range near a large desert, a long way away from Eodisia. How had they come all the way to Shae Glen?

"I can tell from your whispering that some of you may know who we are and why we are here," Elder Prx went on, "so I will make this quick. We will be conducting a random screening of a few of your citizens, to see if any of you are heretics to the Eagle's teachings."

"You can't do this! You have no right here in Shae Glen, or Eodisia!" The Mayor, Brayn Dantes, had stepped forward from the crowd to voice his objections. "No right to drag these good people from their homes. I am in charge here, and I will not allow it."

Elder Prx leveled the mayor with what Rynestian could only assume was a glare; her mask obscured most of her face when she was not looking directly at you. Brayn was a good man who always had the villagers' interests at heart. Rynestian was certain that he would have not allowed this to happen had he known anything about it.

"I see we have our first volunteer! Wonderful," Elder Prx responded.

With that, a few of the armed soldiers left their line and roughly grabbed the mayor by his arms and shoved him to his knees on the hard cobblestone street. The woman in the mask then glided around the gathering of villagers, pointing every now and then to a Shae Glenner, who was grabbed by soldiers and shoved to their knees next to the mayor.

Anger boiled within Rynestian that he had not felt in years, not since his frustration at not being able to help his wife with her sickness, not since his years fighting in the duskward lands. Shae Glen was a peaceful place; its people had never hurt anyone. They did not deserve treatment such as this.

He clenched his fists as people he saw every day, people who had devoted their lives to peace, were thrown into the street with no regard for their well-being. His breath caught when he saw Nagashi Komoto selected from the crowd. Her daughter, who was about the twins' age, cried out and would not release her mother's hand. Nagashi calmly moved forward and gently pulled her daughter's hand – Akiye was her name – away. She gave Akiye and her partner, Ghanai'm, a reassuring nod as she was dragged forward and shoved to the ground. Ghanai'm, he noticed, had a wound on his forehead that was bleeding rather profusely. If Rynestian's suspicions about the invaders were correct, Those Who Serve would be looking for Nagashi as well.

He was so caught up in watching Nagashi being shoved to the ground that he hardly felt the soldiers grab his shoulders and try to drag him forward. After giving them a startled look, he solemnly nodded and allowed them to move him forward and push him to his knees. He was placed right next to Nagashi, with whom he shared a knowing glance. She nodded to him and gave him a sad smile.

Rain began to trickle down from the sky as a few more people were added to the lineup behind Rynestian. The soldiers surrounding the villagers tightened their positions to hold the remaining villagers in place, and a handful of soldiers came to stand behind the lineup.

Elder Prx stood before them, taking a long look at every one of them. She then walked over to Brayn Dantes and placed a firm hand on his shoulder.

"Now," she said, "this will all be over before you know it. You were asking what gave us the right before? Those Who Watch have guided us along from the very beginning of time, and they continue to watch over us, even now. All of this realm is their domain, and as their faithful servants, we will ensure that their will is being upheld."

She reached her hand behind the white cloak that draped across her back and procured a small piece of warped glass that had a strange prismatic sheen to it.

"This is Varnlass, or Sky Glass. Each of you will breathe directly on this glass, and as long as your breath makes an imprint on the glass, you are free to go about your lives. But if your breath does not register with the glass, we will be taking you along with us for further questioning."

She then pressed the glass just in front of Brayn's mouth. Brayn took a deep breath in and looked down the line of villagers all kneeling next to him. Deep sadness pervaded his eyes as he turned back to face the Those Who Serve elder. He let out his breath onto the glass, and it seemed to shimmer as if a light was passing through it. The light dissipated as quickly as it appeared.

"That wasn't so hard now, was it?"

Elder Prx moved on to the next villager and placed her hand on their shoulder again. She continued this process down the line, with each villager's breath creating the same shimmering effect.

Rynestian tensed as she worked her way closer to him and Nagashi. Both of them would not have their breath registered by that glass, no matter how long they had been away from home.

Rynestian leaned over to nudge Nagashi with his shoulder. She didn't turn to look at him, keeping her eyes trained on Elder Prx.

"We will be okay," she whispered.

And with that, Elder Prx was placing her gloved hand on Nagashi's shoulder. She raised the glass in front of her mouth, and Nagashi turned her head to look back at her family.

Rynestian wished he was able to do anything to help her, but his breath test would soon show the same result as hers. No matter. If they were taken, they could work together to escape and return to Shae Glen.

Nagashi turned back, curled her fists, and blew hard against the glass, but there was no reaction. Elder Prx pulled the glass away and leaned over to place her head next to Nagashi's, between Rynestian and the woman.

"Filthy sky rat," Elder Prx whispered.

Before he could react, Rynestian saw the elder pull a knife from her sleeve and stab Nagashi in the chest and stomach several times.

Even before Nagashi had fully fallen over into the street, Rynestian had jolted up and was holding Elder Prx by her metal mask, her feet dangling just above the ground. His fingers indented the metal in the mask, and Elder Prx let out a strangled yelp. A cry rose from the crowd behind them, and the village center of Shae Glen erupted in chaos.

The soldiers drew their weapons as quickly as they could, but most of them were being tackled to the ground by the enraged villagers before they could even tell what was going on. Screams and the sounds of metal clashing erupted throughout the village center.

Before he even knew what he was doing Rynestian had crushed the metal mask in his hand, and the zealot's blood was streaming down his outstretched arm. He threw the Elder's body to the ground in disgust and turned to check on Nagashi, only to see five soldiers standing behind him, all with swords drawn.

Just as he was about to make a desperate rush at the armed invaders, Ghanai'm came crashing through the line, hitting one of the soldiers over the head with a large rock he must have taken from the ground. The soldiers stared as their comrade fell limply to the bloodstained street, his eyes rolling to the back of his head.

Rynestian used this moment to lunge forward at another of the soldiers, striking swiftly at the man's wrist with his fist, causing him to drop his blade. As the blade fell, Rynestian brought his other fist crashing into the man's face, and the man crumpled to his knees with the sound of snapping bones. Rynestian kicked the blade over to Ghanai'm as he began to grapple with another of the soldiers.

All around them, the people of Shae Glen were fighting back against their invaders, and those who could not fight were running for their lives. Although the element of surprise as well as their numbers had aided the villagers at the start, the soldiers had regained their senses and were hacking with bloodthirsty abandon. Blood was spilled and splattered all around the village center, coming from the villagers and the remaining forces of Those Who Serve.

Rynestian had just finished overwhelming another soldier when he finally got a chance to take a look around the square. As he tried to process the carnage around him, his eyes settled on young Akiye, who stood fixed in the same position she had been standing in when her mother was taken away.

He turned to look to Ghanai'm just in time to see him run through with two spears from soldiers who had snuck up behind him in the frantic chaos.

Rynestian fought to hold back tears as he watched his friend fall before him. Pushing away his thoughts of desperation, he charged away towards where Akiye stood, knocking over a few soldiers on his way. When he reached her, he wordlessly lifted her from the ground and ran. He knew that it now fell to him to protect her.

It was only when they had run far enough from the sounds of battle that Rynestian realized how hard his heart was beating in his chest. He was not sure if it was from his advancing age, or the rage coursing through him. Ignoring his heart, for now, he pushed on, running as fast as he ever had to get back to his house, back to the twins. He had to keep them safe, no matter what.

Chapter 5

SECRETS

Just as Tylanna was about to insist that Tahnir help her open the strange door to the dining room, the sound of footsteps sounded above them. She braced herself and felt herself drawing in her breath, to make as little noise as possible. As far as she could make out, there was one loud set of footsteps that had entered their home, one soft thud, and then a rustling of the rug being removed from above them. As the rug was pulled away, small slivers of light leaked through the crevices in the wood, and she could still barely make out what was surrounding them on the walls of the tiny room.

The door swung open, and daylight poured in. There stood her father, panting and splattered with blood. Behind him was Akiye, her friend and fellow student at the sanitarium, staring blankly ahead at nothing, seemingly unfazed that the twins had been stuffed into a small room underneath the dining room.

The sight of her blood-soaked father had startled Tylanna so much that she forgot where she was. The glittering metal that she had noticed earlier was an array of weaponry and armor, finer than anything she had ever seen before. The shock occupied her mind for only a moment before her eyes snapped back to her father, and she dashed up the stairs to help him.

Tahnir was up the stairs just a moment after her, both of them raining questions down on the large man. Once Tahnir realized that Akiye was there, he dashed over to her, placing a hand on her shoulder, and asked if she was okay. Akiye recoiled at first, but she seemed to snap out of a trance at his touch, and she buried her head in his chest, releasing a few quiet sobs.

Tylanna inspected her father, looking for some wound that was a source for all the blood that covered his clothing. There seemed to be nothing in particular wrong with him, aside from some small cuts on his knuckles, but they were not serious. No, this blood had to have belonged to someone else.

"Enough, Tylanna, I'm fine," Rynestian snorted as he removed her hands from his, where they had lingered as she observed his wounds, however slight. "There's trouble in the village center."

He turned and slammed the door shut behind him, and bolted it. The bolt had been unfastened last night, as it usually was. He turned back to them, still sporting a wild look in his eyes.

"Now I have a lot I must tell you three, and not a lot of time to do it. So please, listen to what I must say, and try not to ask me any questions if you can help it."

Tylanna swallowed audibly. She had never seen her father act like this, and it was frightening her. She wanted to dive back into the small room beneath the house and hide there forever.

Akiye's head raised from Tahnir's chest as she wiped tears away from her eyes and focused on Rynestian. What had happened to her, and why had their father brought her here?

"The people who took me from the house earlier are from an organization known as Those Who Serve, devoted to the Preachings of the Eagle. How and why they have come all the way to Shae Glen is beyond me, but after this morning, I now know what they are after."

Tylanna stared at Akiye. She seemed to be trembling, overcome with emotion. The twins had been told of Those Who Serve before.

"They are seeking all those they believe go against their religion, and that is why they gathered all of us in the village center this morning. It seems they have become more radicalized as of late, and murderous."

Rynestian spared a sad glance directed toward Akiye before he continued. "In their eyes, those who go against their rules deserve to die, which is wrong. I fear this may lead to war not just in Eodisia, but all over the world. Those Who Serve coming to Shae Glen is a terrible sign of their wicked reach. The last I had heard of them, they were a small group in the land of Oromia, and certainly not violent. I've told you two the story of the Eagle and the Watchers before. The way I see it, there is nothing about doing violence to others involved. If I am not mistaken, I believe they are searching for Helanáians, or people from the Sky Islands. They take the part of the story about the Watchers only being able to walk the lands as they were originally formed literally, and see the Sky Islands and all who live on them as an affront to their religion and way of life."

Tylanna was taken aback. The Sky Islands of Helanái were a string of massive islands that had risen from the lands of Artani, a country that bordered Eodisia on the duskward side. The day the islands had flown into the sky had long since been lost to history, but the original occupants of the lands had developed slight differences from the humans that lived on land, but all in all, they were not that different. Certainly not enough to be sought out and killed.

"I am not sure if you two were aware of it, but many of the citizens of Shae Glen are in fact Helanáians that sought refuge here during the last war between Artani and Helanái, the Sky Succession War. And I know I have never told you this before, but I originally came from the Sky Islands myself."

Tylanna and Tahnir shared an audible gasp between them, and then they exchanged a glance. They had often played guessing games trying to figure out where their father had come from before coming to Shae Glen, but they had never thought it would be from the Sky Islands of Helanái. In the stories, they knew the people of the Sky Islands were near-superhuman adventurers who fought to bring peace to all the lands and gift those from the ground nations their advanced technology and weaponry. Yes, their father was a strong man, but nothing like the Helanáians they imagined from the stories.

"I know I kept this from you, and I do be sorry. I wanted to protect you from my past if I could, but that does not seem possible any longer. Through me, you two are both Helanáians, and so now that makes you the targets of Those Who Serve." Tylanna tried to calm the shock running through her as her father continued to speak, "Akiye, I suppose you may have known already, but your mother was also from the Sky Islands."

Akiye gave a small nod of confirmation before lowering her head. Was from the Sky Islands? Did that mean...

"So, what are we going to do now?" Tylanna asked. The revelation that they were all Helanáians had shocked her, but she could see from her father and Akiye's expression that there was no time to discuss their lineage, and they had to act fast.

"That is what I have been considering," Rynestian replied. Tylanna could tell that her father was still in some sort of shock as well; she could see that it was only with great effort that he could speak calmly to them. "What would be safest would be for all three of you to travel to the Sky Islands and seek refuge from the coming violence there. There you can seek my brother, Rheleus Altusborne. I changed my surname from Altusborne when I married your mother. If he still lives, he will be able to help you and keep you safe."

"Will you not come with us, Father?" Tahnir asked. He had remained relatively quiet throughout this conversation, Tylanna noticed. She figured he was just insistent on listening to what their father was saying. She could not believe that he was taking in all this new information so calmly though. Inside her emotions raged, and she was eager to learn more.

"I cannot. I have sworn to protect Shae Glen from any threat. We built this village together, and we as the people of Shae Glen will fight together to protect it. This was the oath we of the Village Watch took together, and as long as Shae Glen stands, we must remain to protect it. Besides, it will be safer for you to travel in a small group, so as to not attract the attention of any of Those Who Serve who may be scattered about the nations and any of their agents that were in the village center today would surely recognize me. Keep your identities secret, and do not put faith in anyone until you reach the islands. Who knows who can be trusted in this day and age?"

The next hour flew by. As quickly as they could, Tylanna and Tahnir packed everything they could fit into the few travel bags they had in their home, and as much food as they could carry with them. Akiye had eventually agreed to come with them on their journey. Their father told them that they could take Carrot if the old mare could be of any help. After they were all packed, Father walked into the room below the dining room and came up with an armful of weaponry and maps which, he let spill out onto the dining room table.

"I was waiting until you two moved out on your own before I gave you these, but I figure now is as good a time as any. I will give you two weapons that have been passed down through my family for generations now. I took both of them when I left home without telling my brother. I am sure he is still plenty upset about that, but he will be able to recognize them as soon as he sees them. It will support your claim that you are my children. First, I have this for you, Tahnir."

From the table, their father pulled a large hammer that was covered in a custom-made leash sheath that had detailed engravings etched into the thin leather. He pulled the sheath free and revealed that the hammer seemed to be made from a varnished gold material, inlaid with fine purple and green gems. The gold also had etched designs that seemed similar to the sheath. The hammer itself was large, but Rynestian seemed to hold it comfortably in one hand.

He placed it into Tahnir's hands and looked him deep in the eyes. "With such a tool, one may equally create or destroy. The power of creation is a wonderful thing, but the power of destruction is ever tempting. I hope with this hammer of my family you will be able to forge your own path."

Tahnir nodded and accepted the hammer. He ran his hand over the etchings, which seemed to depict scenes of early humans working with fire and building tall structures.

"For you, my daughter, I gift to you a blade that has been passed from the women in my family's line." While speaking, their father procured a long and slim blade from the table, sheathed in a long slender casing that was wrapped in red and gold cords, some of which stung the length of the casing to create a sort of sling for carrying. He placed the blade gently into her two outstretched hands. "Since I never had a sister, the blade was left as decoration at my family's estate. I took the blade in hopes that one day I would have a family of my own and would be able to pass this on to my own daughter. I have never used the blade myself, but I know it will serve you well on your journey to the islands."

She inspected the weapon with near shock on her face. A blade? Her? Why on earth would she be able to use a sword? She had never held a weapon a day in her life, and she was not sure she would have any idea how to use it.

Her father placed a reassuring hand on her shoulder and stared into her eyes. "I know this is all too much for you right now, but I know you will be able to handle it and reach the Sky Islands together, all of you. Let the blade guide you, and it will carve you a path to your destiny. The blade's name is Darkender, and apparently, it is older than the Sky Islands themselves, though still sharper than any blade I have ever made."

Their father then donned a pair of spiked gauntlets that seemed to be made of the same material as the hammer. He offered Akiye any of the weapons from the forge she wanted, to which she replied that she could take her father's knives from their home. Begrudgingly, Rynestian agreed to her going back to her own house, which was near the village center. Originally, he explained that the safest course of action would be to sneak away through the forest behind their home, but he seemed unable to say no to Akiye at the moment.

"You may go, but we will escort you there, and we will go quietly. There is no telling if Those Who Serve are still about, or if the others have driven them away. If you are all ready, I will take you as far as the village border before letting you go off on your own."

Tylanna heard a slight quiver in her father's voice and could tell that he was making an impossible decision. The last thing he wanted was to send his only remaining family away from him, for who knew how long, but he saw it as the only option. This was all happening so fast that Tylanna found it hard to keep track of the new information.

But she slung the blade over her shoulder and grabbed all the bags she could carry, and Tahnir did the same. As they passed through the threshold and out of the house, a strange sadness seeped into her body, and she stole one more glance back to their home and prayed that it would not be the last.

Chapter 6

AN OATH IN AN EMPTY HOME

Akiye's mind continued to simultaneously race and fog over, as it had since the village center. She wordlessly followed the Desqen family as they marched onwards. Tahnir led their family mare, Carrot, along with a tight grip on her lead. They did not know what they would find in the village, but Rynestian was standing in front of all of them protectively.

Before they had left, Rynestian had given them very specific instructions to follow his every command and stay behind him no matter what they encountered. He warned them that they might have to fight to protect themselves. Akiye had almost wished she took him up on his offer of a weapon from their forge, but the only weapons she knew how to use were waiting for her in her family study. She had to return home to retrieve them if only to see her home for one last time. She had a feeling that she would never be returning to Shae Glen.

They approached the village center, and Rynestian came to a stop behind a large building – the local weaver's shop, if Akiye wasn't mistaken. He held out a large arm to hold everyone behind him back, and carefully peered out from around the corning into the village center. When he turned to face them, he released a sigh, equal parts relief and grief.

"It appears that Those Who Serve have been driven out, at least for now. But Akiye...would you like me to come with you, to see your parents?"

Tears welled in Akiye's eyes. She had known that she would see them again if they passed through here. But now that the moment had arrived, she was not sure she was ready. She had seen them both receive mortal wounds, but she had been holding out hope that maybe they had been saved. Judging by Rynestian's tone, that was not the case.

She slowly shook her head before answering meekly, "No, I think I should go see them on my own."

Rynestian put a hand on her shoulder and nodded. As she walked away and rounded the corner, she heard Tylanna asking her father what he was talking about. She had not told the twins what had happened yet – she had not been able to. Surely Rynestian would tell them. She should not have to speak the words herself.

All thoughts washed away from her mind when she saw them. Together they lay, almost peacefully, side by side. Someone had moved them since they fell. There rested her entire family, her entire world, taken away from her before her very eyes. Just then she was filled with a profound emptiness that she feared would never allow her to feel whole again. She clutched a hand to her chest and fell to her knees when she reached them. Tears fell freely as she thought of all the conversations they had never gotten to have, and everything that would never be said between them.

She had known that her mother was Helanáian, who had come to Shae Glen after the Sky Succession War hoping to avoid getting caught up in any sort of politically-inspired violence. From what she had told Akiye, she was some sort of politician in the Sky Islands. Her father had come to Shae Glen around the same time from a nation across the sea known as Galedul. He had been the latest in the long line of a clan of assassins that were known as the elite forces of the Galedul military. When he rejected that life, he was disowned by his family, and he began to travel the world, eventually settling in Shae Glen.

There were so many questions she still needed to ask them, and at this moment she felt ashamed for how little she seemed to know about them. One thing she knew for certain was that they were both good people, and they did not deserve to die like this, alone in the street.

She took a moment to look at them and picture the time they did get to share. The village center around her had an eerie calm hanging over it now, a stark contrast to the raucous atmosphere earlier this morning. The quiet around her came to an abrupt halt when a voice sounded from behind her.

"I'm so sorry, Akiye. When I got to them to try and help, it was already too late. I did everything I could, but they were beyond any healing."

Xelina Marcs had approached from behind her. Her teacher's face seemed nearly gaunt, and her usually cheerful eyes hosted darkness that Akiye had never seen in them. Xelina's hands and robes were both covered in blood, and Akiye realized that she must have been trying to save everyone in the village alone.

"Thank you for trying, Master. I am sorry I was unable to do anything when it happened. Fear held me in place, but now vengeance will push me forward," Akiye said as she rose to her feet and turned to face her teacher. "I thank you for your teachings, but I am leaving Shae Glen. The Desqen twins and I will travel to Helanái to warn them of Those Who Serve's evil doings."

Xelina met her fierce stare with only sadness in her eyes. "This isn't the life we wanted for our children when we left the Sky Islands. We sought a life of peace here in the countryside. Be careful in Helanái. It is not all like the stories you have been told. Many there see themselves as a different breed of human, as being above all those that dwell on the ground. Do not think your heritage will grant you amnesty there. Trust in only those you hold close to your heart."

Akiye barely blinked at the revelation that Xelina had also come from Helanái. She was certain nearly half the village had come from the islands at this point.

"Thank you, Master. I have one last favor to ask of you before I go." She was surprised at how stable her own voice sounded, while within her a storm of rage and grief swelled against the calm outer shell.

"Anything, my dear." Lady Marcs now had tears rolling down her blood-stained cheeks, though she held an expression of determination.

"Please bury them somewhere nice. My father's people do not believe in honoring the body after someone has passed, but I believe they both would have wanted to be together."

"Of course, I will. Good luck on your journey, and I pray to see you again. Take this with you. It may prove useful to you." Xelina pulled the medical bag off her shoulder and handed it to Akiye.

She accepted the bag and turned away without another word.

A little later, Akiye arrived at her home. She had not waited for the Desqens before leaving the village center, but at one point as she stalked through the nearly empty streets, she had noticed them following her from a distance. The twins seemed equally distraught by the carnage, and Tylanna had tears coating her cheeks.

Akiye walked through the entryway of their home. The double-door entrance had been broken open by the invaders, and as she inspected the wood, she doubted that they would be able to be shut properly again with major repairs. As she entered the home, she was flooded with memories of her life here with her family, which she tried to stifle as much as she could.

There was no time to think of what she could have done. She had not done it, and that was that. She would have to be better, stronger, in case she ever encountered anything like that again. Pushing aside her feelings, she bounded up the stairs and dashed into her room.

She collected all items she deemed the most necessary for a long journey and packed them into a travel bag. Then she went into her family's study and found the small chest from below the desk. She lifted the lid and revealed her father's collection of knives that had been given to him at birth, as was a tradition in his culture. Seven small blades of various designs sat on a cloth wrap, each with their own deadly purpose. He had not given her any knives when she was born, as he had wished to break the cycle of violence that had plagued his family, but he had shown her the basics of how to protect herself with them.

Before she became too absorbed in memories, she gathered up the blades in their cloth wrap and looped them onto her belt. She would find out a better way to carry them later. She gave the room a final scan, and her eyes settled on a simple wooden mask that her father had hung on the wall. He had called it a relic of Galedul, but to her eyes, it always just seemed to be a wooden circle with two eye holes carved into it. Akiye regretted that she had made fun of something her father had cherished enough to bring along with him from his home country. She unhooked it from the wall and added it to her bag.

She exited the study and walked past her parents' room. The door was still closed, as both of her parents had been downstairs when the invaders entered. She placed her palm flat on the wood. In her heart, she wished she could push the door open to find both of her parents sleeping peacefully in their bed, however foolish she knew that to be.

"I promise," she whispered, "I swear to you that I will find whoever is responsible, and they will pay for your deaths. I swear it on my honor and the never-ending sky above us. I will have justice."

With that, she pulled her hand away and bounded down the stairs. She walked through the entryway without another look around and found the Desqens waiting for her in front of the house. In addition to

Carrot, they seem to have procured two more horses. One, she eventually recognized as Xelina's brown and white stallion that she called Yae'tal. The other was a very large black horse with flowing hair and a strange saddle that extended to the front of its body made of some sort of metal and leather combination she had not seen before. The horse must have been taken from the invaders.

Wordlessly, she approached them and grabbed the reins of the black horse. She would do whatever it took to get her vengeance on Those Who Serve, even using their horses or weapons against them. Whatever it took.

Akiye, Tylanna, and Tahnir were silent as they left the village of Shae Glen behind them. As they walked, Rynestian bombarded them with advice about traveling in the world, what paths they should take, what they should avoid, and who they could trust. Akiye hoped that the twins were listening intently because she could not bring herself to focus as thoughts of revenge clouded her mind.

When they reached the entrance to the forest, the twins shared a tearful goodbye with Rynestian, and Akiye felt a pang of jealousy. The three of them mounted their horses, Tylanna electing to ride Carrot, leaving Tahnir to ride Yae'tal, and Akiye on the black horse whose name she did not know. Rynestian walked over to her as she prepared to ride off.

"Dear Akiye, I know that the pain of this loss will never go away, but I promise you it will get better with time. Fill your heart with love and friendship, and do not succumb to the darkness that awaits us all in fear and anger."

Akiye offered him a slight smile and a nod before she pulled up her reins and spurred the large black horse to rush off towards the forest. She heard the twins follow behind her after a moment, the joint gallop of the three horses ringing through the quiet afternoon air.

She would have time for love and friendship once her revenge had been taken.

Tahnir and the others rode for nearly four hours before they all decided to stop and make camp for the night. The light had all but completely faded from the day, and what precious little remained struggled to make its way through the scattered treetops that towered above them. They had not yet made it out of the thick forest that surrounded Shae Glen, sometimes referred to as the Blooming Waste, but the terrain had rapidly gone from gently rolling hills to more severe cliffs.

The Blooming Waste had once engulfed the entire dawnward side of Eodisia. As more and more people settled the lands away from the sea that bordered the country to the duskward side, sections of the forest were cleared away to make way for civilization. The forest had earned its title in ancient times, apparently even before the founding of Eodisia. History described the area as a desolate wasteland, but when modernity had reached the land, it was filled with greenery, with trees towering throughout the entire realm. Tahnir could not help but feel slightly excited about traveling through this legendary forest, even with everything that they had all gone through.

Before leaving, his father had imparted to him the route he thought would be best for them to reach the Sky Islands of Helanái. Following his suggestion, they would avoid all of the main paths except when absolutely necessary and lie about their destination whenever they faced inquiries from strangers. They planned to journey through the Blooming Waste, hiding in the wilderness from any danger they might encounter, until they reached the city of Nicol's Wood.

Once they reached the city, they were to keep a low profile and somehow find a passage through the Jungles of Jiye, the wilderness that ran along the border between Eodisia and Artani. The two nations had their shared slew of geopolitical issues, but Rynestian had told them that no one should notice them entering the country through the jungle.

Then, once in Artani, they were to seek the city of Aynanu, which was a city that shared a domain between both Artani and Helanái. Trade flowed up and down between Helanái and all of the surface nations, so Aynanu had become a bustling city full of wonders from around the entire world. There, they should be able to find the sky bridge linking Aynanu with Helanái with relative ease and travel to the first Sky Island.

Tahnir hoped the journey would be as easy as that, but he doubted it.

The ride up until this point had been mostly silent, besides a few brief conversations between Tahnir and his sister. Akiye rode in front of them, silently, always keeping her gaze fixed forward. Tahnir had known the pain of losing a parent for some time now, but he could not imagine what Akiye had to be going through. Not only losing both parents to senseless violence but being completely uprooted from her home and sent off on some far-off journey immediately afterward.

When they stopped to break for the night, Tahnir leaped from Xelina's stallion and strode over to where Akiye was rearing her newly acquired horse to a stop. He offered her a stern hand to help her dismount. She accepted his help, and when she did, he noticed that her knuckles were all white from gripping the reins so tightly.

Once she was safely on the forest floor, he went about taking the saddlebags from the horses that they would need to set up camp for the night. Rynestian had instructed them to only make camp far from the riding path, and to use fire as scarcely as possible. He and

Tylanna went right about setting up camp. As they busied themselves around the area, Akiye stood awkwardly in the center of their work, clutching her travel bag tightly to her chest.

"Is there... Is there anything you would like me to do?" she asked meekly.

"No, Tyl and I have done this hundreds of times by now. We should have everything ready in no time at all," Tahnir replied. He continued to work on setting up their tents before she interjected again.

"I'd really rather help with something, if that is all right."

Tylanna rose from unpacking the food from one of the bags she had brought from their home and approached Akiye. "Well, I suppose you could go grab some wood to make the fire. We only need a bit to cook some of the meat I brought along, and we do not want to burn it late into the night anyway."

"Yes, that is fine. I'll be back as soon as I can."

With that, Akiye wandered away from the campsite, still clutching her bag to her chest. Tahnir looked at his sister and they shared a sympathetic look. What could they do for this poor woman to help ease her burden? Tahnir mulled that over while simultaneously trying to process the events of the day while he finished his preparations.

The twins finished their work in just under half an hour. The only difference to their usual setup was their desire for secrecy. Who knew what would happen if they were set upon by bandits in the night, or worse yet, Those Who Serve. Rynestian had not been certain whether or not their breath would register on the strange test he had told them about, the three of them only being half-Helanáian. It was best they took no chances.

They had made their camp beside the natural cover of a steep mountainside. They had set up each of their tents behind a few of the large trees that populated the forest. This should protect them from any casual passerby unless they were specifically seeking out those who camped here. He and Tylanna had agreed to sleep in shifts, just to be safe.

After some time, the light dwindled to only a faint glow in the far-off sky. Concerned that Akiye still had not returned, Tahnir rose to his feet. "I'm going to go find Akiye, be sure she did not get lost or run into any trouble."

Tylanna gave him a stern nod and handed him the hammer that their father had given him before they departed. He had left the hammer with his bag, not even thinking of using it to protect himself in the Blooming Waste. But he supposed if trouble could come all the way to Shae Glen, it could be anywhere.

He hefted the hammer in his right hand and set out into the thick of the wood to find where Akiye had gotten off to. The hammer somehow felt heavy in his hand yet did not strain him to lift. He gave the thing a few wild swings as he walked and confirmed that there was a good amount of weight to it. It was a sign of good craftsmanship, and he would have liked to meet the person who had forged it. He had never considered using a hammer as a weapon, but he supposed it would be the most comfortable thing for him. His father's words of creation and destruction ran through his head as he searched through the forest, raising his hammer about as he went.

Before long he came upon Akiye, crouched on her knees with a pile of sticks and broken branches in front of her. It appeared as if she had dropped them. As he got closer to her, he could hear the muffled sounds of crying. Wordlessly, he walked in front of her and began picking up the wood she had collected. When she noticed him, she stopped crying and began wiping her eyes.

"Oh, I am sorry, Tahnir," she muttered. "I was collecting the wood when I started thinking about all that had happened, and I could not hold it in anymore."

He did not stop picking up the wood as he replied, "Do not worry, Akiye. What you are going through is so painful, and I am so sorry for everything that has happened. But you needn't suffer alone. Tylanna and I are here for you. Our best chance is for all of us to stick together. The world will only get more troublesome from here as it unfolds before us. We will do everything we can to keep you safe, I swear it."

She gave him a weak smile as she finished wiping the tears from her eyes. He finished collecting the wood that had been scattered about on the ground and rose to his feet. Adjusting the wood and hammer so he gripped them both against his right hip, he offered Akiye a hand and helped her to her feet.

"And do not feel you have to hide your tears from us. We have had our fair share of pain in our lives, and we will do everything we can to help you get through this."

Chapter 7

TWO STRANGERS

Tahnir and Akiye had returned to their camp before too long and the group set up a fire together and ate. They talked of the events of the day, and what they might encounter on their journey to the Sky Islands. Before long, Tylanna and Akiye retired to their tents, and Tahnir stayed awake to keep watch.

As he watched the embers burn, he wondered what lay in store for their little group. The day before he had not even known that he and his sister were Helanáian, and now they sought refuge in the Sky Islands with an uncle they had never even met. Would he even believe they were related to him? Would he accept Akiye as well? The future held too many mysteries, and that made Tahnir uncomfortable. His life had been full of so much certainty for his entire adult life, and now it had all been thrown away.

He had long known that he was going to take over his father's forge and continue making the finest tools in the land and bringing pride to the Desqen name. One day he wanted to build his own home, as his father had done, and allow Tylanna to take their childhood home. She had never been any good at building things. He figured that he would eventually start a family to fill that new home with, though he considered that a long way away. It was even farther away than he had originally anticipated, now that he did not even know when he would return to Shae Glen again.

When his father had insisted that they travel to Helanái alone while he remained in Shae Glen, Tahnir had not known how to react. Surely at a time such as this, they should be sticking together, and doing whatever they must to protect their family and home. But he was not one to question his father's commands. If Those Who Serve had made it to Shae Glen, who was to say that they would not be roaming the countryside, testing each and every person they came across.

He had seen the chaos they had caused within the village center of Shae Glen. Bodies had been strewn about, and the cobblestone was splattered with blood. Tahnir had never before seen such carnage, and the scene still made him sick to his stomach. The bodies had not all belonged to the villagers though; he had counted a fair share of the Those Who Serve invaders amongst the dead. Even unarmed, the people of Shae Glen were a tough group, especially when fighting for that which they held dear. He wondered if he would have been of any help had he been there, not cowering away in a basement. Regret seized him as he thought of those he had not saved.

After a period of near-complete quiet, a soft chittering flew from high above Tahnir's head. He looked up and searched for the source of the noise, but it was beyond his vision, and he doubted if he lit his makeshift torch he would be able to see very high up the trees. He sat pondering when another sound interrupted him.

"Nightbeaks."

Tahnir had not even heard his sister rising from her tent, let alone walking to stand just behind him. He gawked at her as she stared up into the dark.

"Their call is very distinct. I have heard tales that humans used to follow their call to travel through the night. Apparently, they're lucky."

Tylanna plopped down next to Tahnir, using her elbow to nudge him to the side.

"Couldn't sleep?" he asked her.

"No, the dreams were too intense for me. I just had one last night too. They do not usually come this frequently. Maybe they are a sign of the dangers we face."

"What happened this time?"

He found his dreams mostly monotonous and boring, usually involving him working in the forge or walking through a never-ending forest path. He quite enjoyed hearing of her strange dreams, if only to live vicariously through her.

"I was not asleep for long, but from what I could tell, I was a figure with the strange skin, just as always. There was one other, and it was talking with me, but I could not understand the tongue. We walked together, and as we moved the land seemed to pass us by faster than any human could run, but we did not seem to be moving particularly fast, and I did not feel like I was running. Then the pair of us came upon a bright ball of light that shone in the center of a large tree, and the figure next to me approached it. That is all I remember before I awoke. Then I came to find you staring up at birds instead of keeping a lookout."

Before he could voice an objection, she threw her hand up, indicating to him not to interject. "Go get some rest. I doubt I will find any sleep tonight. I will wake the two of you at first light, and we can continue."

With only a few minor protests – he was tired, after all – he agreed and went off to the tent he had prepared for himself. They were nothing fancy, put together very practically and with no extra frills. On the floor of the tent laid a small bedroll, with a single pillow. It might not be as comfortable as the bed he had left behind in Shae Glen, but it would certainly do for now. He made himself comfortable and laid his head on the pillow. The sounds of the Nightbeaks were somewhat muffled by the canvas of the tent, and as he slipped into sleep, he wondered what it was they were singing of.

When the first light of morning began to dance through the forest, Tylanna rose to her feet. After waking from her dream, she had not slept a wink. Even now, her mind still raced from the events of the previous day, and the strange dream of the traveling figures had not made the situation better. She assumed that she might be feeling this way for quite some time, and just hoped that she could at least eventually find some sanctuary in a dreamless sleep.

She took down the campsite as best she could without Tahnir and Akiye's help. The cinders from the fire had long since burned themselves out, but she buried them with dirt just to be sure. It also could not hurt to try and hide the fact that someone had camped here, in case they were being pursued. Strange that in only one day she had begun thinking like prey running from the hunt. She supposed that as long as it kept them all alive, a little extra care was a small price to pay.

Once she had packed up all but the tents, she threw open the flap to Tahnir's tent and shook him awake. He woke with a start before realizing where he was. She saw a somberness settle into his eyes when the surprise faded.

When they were growing up, they each had bright green eyes, just like their mother. Their father had often jokingly called them shining emeralds. The fact that her left eye now shone gold did make her a bit sad – just another difference between her and her twin. She hoped they would not grow to be too dissimilar in what was sure to be a turbulent time to come.

As Tahnir stumbled out of his tent, Tylanna went over and woke up Akiye, albeit much more gently than she had woken her brother. The woman opened her eyes slowly but barely seemed rested at all. Tylanna was sure that she had also had a night of terrible dreams, and the life she woke to was surely just as grim.

The party broke down their tents and finished packing their horses with relative ease. Before they mounted, they discussed the path they would take as they rode, agreeing that Tylanna would lead the way today. This was only natural, as she had spent the most time outside of the village, though even she had not ever come as far as they had already ventured. From what she understood, either today or tomorrow, they should begin to see the terrain around them change. They would need to proceed with caution from there on out. She shook her head to herself, wishing that a steep mountain path was the only danger she needed to worry about.

Together they rode through the heavy greenery of the Blooming Waste. Sure enough, the terrain did become slightly rockier, and the vast expanse of trees gave way to steep hills. They slowed their pace and rode more carefully, guiding their steeds as well as they could.

Tylanna had always been the better rider between the Desqen siblings, but Tahnir seemed to be holding his own on Xelina's stallion. Akiye appeared to be dwarfed by the size of her black warhorse, but she seemed to spur it along with natural grace. Tylanna hoped that this long journey would not be too much for her old mare, Carrot. Its name was given by Tylanna when she discovered the horse's love of carrots, and from then on Tylanna had always snuck the mare a snack every time she rode.

Though this area was new for Tylanna, she did not feel out of place. They had hills around Shae Glen that got quite steep, and she supposed she simply looked at these mountains as larger versions of those hills she had played on many a time. The group rode past a small river. Her father had told her of this river, called the Elk's Blessing, as a landmark to indicate they were heading in the correct direction. The river was named after one of the figures from the Preachings of the Eagle, those known as Those Who Watch. The Elk was said to be a generous being who had a deep love of nature and those who cared for it. Each of the Those Who Watch had names that had long been lost to time and many translations of the original stories, but the modern interpretations used names of animals that were best believed to represent their personalities.

Once they reached the Elk's Blessing, they were meant to turn duskward to find a crossing that stretched from one mountaintop to another, with the bridge hanging hundreds of feet above the river. Rynestian had remarked that the view from the bridge was quite impressive, and one could see a large portion of the Blooming Waste from its middle. After a glance at the still-rising suns to figure out their direction, Tylanna led the others dawnward along the bank of the river.

Eventually, the river wrapped away from the travelers as they began to ascend the steep terrain. Once they reached a certain point on the mountain, they dismounted to lead the horses by the reins as the path narrowed. The path snaked its way up the side of the mountain. After about an hour of this careful trek, they had reached the summit.

Tylanna was the first to reach the top, with Carrot following just behind her. She was certain the horse had never faced terrain as rough as this, but she was proud of the old mare for staying strong. Tylanna set eyes on the bridge that spanned between the two peaks.

The bridge was made of wood and thick rope and seemed just wide enough for two humans standing side by side. Just before the bridge, a man sat on a remarkably high chair. The man was small in stature and wore a bright red cloak that he had wrapped around him tightly as if the weather was much colder than it was. The man eyed their group suspiciously as they clambered up to the summit.

Tylanna led Carrot over to the man and addressed him first in an attempt to dispel any suspicion. "Hello, stranger, we seek to cross the Elk's Blessing, and we have been told this is the only crossing."

The man bit at his lower lip and glared at the motley crew. "No horses," the man said bitingly. "Wood no can bear the weight." He spoke with an accent that was unfamiliar to Tylanna, which was odd so close to Shae Glen.

Tylanna looked down to the rushing river, which now sat hundreds of feet below them and had grown to a raging torrent of white water.

"Well, what are we meant to do with our horses then?" Tahnir asked.

"Well, either ye can march them back down the mountain and try to find another crossing, which there no be, or you can leave them with me, and I can keep them at me stable, for a small price. When you come back, you can pick them up, and I will only charge you for their lodging."

Tylanna stared at the river again. From what she understood, it stretched nearly to the Eodisian Sea. Going around it would put them far outside any of the directions Rynestian had given them. Why had he not warned them that the horses would not be able to cross the bridge? Had he really come all the way from Helanái on foot?

The group huddled together to discuss, while the small man sat atop his chair, glowering at them.

“We cannot go around the river,” Tylanna advised. “It would take us far too long. I do not like it, but I think we need to leave the horses behind.”

“But how will we pay for it?” Akiye asked. “We do not have any gold.”

To be fair, the group barely had any gold at all between the three of them. Rynestian had given the twins some of the advance payment for the large order he had received from the Eodisian military, but Akiye had not brought any with her. She had not searched her house for it, and the twins could not blame her.

“Well, if we pay when we return, we will just have to find a way to make some coin on our return journey,” Tahnir suggested. “I’m sure I could find some work in a forge, and you two each know enough to help out at any sanitarium we may pass.”

Tylanna wondered exactly how long it would be before they were even able to return, and when it would be safe again. She patted Carrot’s face gently and wished they could remain together, but it seemed like the horse would be yet another piece of home she would have to leave behind.

“All right, we will leave them with you at your stable.” Tylanna walked Carrot over to the man and reached up, standing on the points of her feet, to hand him the reins. “Please take good care of them. This one is called Carrot.”

The man snatched the reins from her hand and flashed her a curled smile. “Of course, me lady. The stable do be at the bottom of the mountain on the riverside. My name be Domar Truast. Ask for me when you return, and we will sort you out and collect our coin."

The others handed over their reins as well, each of them giving regretful pats to the horses' heads as they did. They began to strip the saddlebags from the horses and rearrange the bags so that they could shoulder the burden themselves. Tylanna would certainly miss Carrot, but the other horses she would miss mostly every time she had to pick up four extra bags whenever they set off. They each awkwardly gripped onto the bags, Tahnir clearly carrying too much but insisting it was fine. Tylanna shared one last sad look with Carrot before turning.

Just then, thundering across the bridge came the sound of hooves on wood. A lone rider galloped across on a large brown and white stallion. They were garbed in well-fitted green and black leather clothes, with a bow strapped across their back. The bridge seemed completely sound underneath the weight.

The group absorbed the sight and then spun around to Domar Truast, who now wore a wicked smile that seemed to stretch the corners of his mouth unnaturally wide and was brandishing a long, curved knife set in an ivory hilt. His eyes shone with a dark glint filled with malice. He yanked the reins closer to him and held the long blade to the neck of Akiye's horse before snarling at them.

"Bad timing, I guess. Empty yer pockets of any coin and valuables and hand them over, or I will spill each of these beasts dry and gut you lot next."

Tylanna stared at the man wide-eyed, Rynestian's warnings about trusting strangers now ringing through her mind just a moment too late. She noticed that Tahnir had dropped the bags and was brandishing his hammer uncertainly, and Akiye had somehow produced a pair of knives in her hands, one short and straight and another slightly longer with a rectangular shape. Tylanna had strapped the blade her father gave her onto the back of her belt, and she was not sure if she could draw it in time to save the large black horse.

Just as her fingers reached behind her, she jerked her head back and turned as an arrow flew past her.

The arrow landed with a wet thud in Domar Truast's hand that was gripping the knife, which he dropped as a strangled cry rose from his throat. The short man fell from atop the chair as it tumbled over and began writhing on the ground as he clutched his hand, which was bleeding profusely. He had released the horses as he fell, and all but Akiye's horse scampered around skittishly. The large black horse had clearly seen combat before, judging by its reaction.

Tylanna's eyes returned to the rider who had nearly crossed the entire bridge and reached them. She now saw the rider was a young woman with short-cropped hair, maybe a few years older than her. A string holding several dead animals, the results of a recent hunt, hung behind her on the horse's back. She pulled the horse to a stop at the end of the bridge and looked around at the scene before her. She observed her shot and gave a firm nod before turning to the young Shae Glenners.

Tylanna was nearly too impressed to speak at first but worked up the nerve once she had processed the situation. "Thank you. You saved us! He was trying to rob us of our horses and what little coin we have."

The woman stared intently at Tylanna's mouth as she spoke, enough to make Tylanna feel slightly embarrassed. When Tylanna was finished, the woman flashed them a small smile and nodded again.

With smooth grace, she hopped down from her horse and over to Domar Truast, who still rolled on the ground screaming. In a swift motion, she pinned his hand to the ground with the heel of her boot and ripped the arrow free his hand. She seemed unfazed by his piercing cries or the blood that splashed onto the front of her jacket. She flicked the arrow towards the ground, allowing the excess blood to slide off before pushing it back into the quiver that hung off her hip.

She turned to the three horses and held her hands up to quiet them and then gathered up their reins. Tylanna had never seen someone handle three horses they had just met with such ease before. The woman brought the horses over to the three of them and handed over the reins.

"What is your name?" Tylanna blurted out. Surely, they needed to know the name of the one who had rescued them.

The woman smiled sweetly, then held a finger up to her ear and shook her head. She closed her hand into a fist and placed it across her chest before bowing her head. With that, she grabbed her horse by the neck, swung herself up effortlessly, and rode away, without looking back at the confused trio.

Once the shock of the whole interaction had passed, the group re-saddled the horses and remounted to cross the bridge, all while Domar Truast screamed a slew of curses and threats after them.

As they galloped away, his vile words faded away with the rush of the surging river below them and the thunder of the horse hooves against wood.

The beauty of the Blooming Waste unfolded before them on either side of the bridge. Her father had not been exaggerating about how impressive the view was. As far as Tylanna could see in every direction, towering trees of green and grey mountain stretched out before her. The vastness of the nature around her struck a chord within her as she considered just how small they and their journey were in the grand scheme of the world.

Chapter 8

THE CAVE

Once Tylanna and the others had crossed the bridge, they proceeded to descend the second mountain with relative ease, not having to dismount from the horses. At the base of the mountain, they found the minor path that Rynestian had told them about and began riding along it for several hours without incident. Just before night fell, distant sounds of thunder rang from the sky as thick raindrops plopped down around them.

Tylanna shouted to the others as the rain increased, "We should stop soon and find some shelter!"

She saw Tahnir and Akiye nodding vigorously through the rain. Wiping the water from her eyes, she leaned over on Carrot, spurring the horse forward. The path they took carved its way through a mountain pass, with steep cliffs towering on either side. She heard the others pushing their horses to keep up with her as she searched frantically for a cave opening somewhere in the cliffs.

After some time in the rain, she saw a thin opening on the side of one of the towering cliffs, nearly obscured by the water falling down the sheer cliff face. She pulled Carrot's reins over sharply, and the horse followed her lead easily, surely also wanting to get out of the downpour. The opening was tall enough to ride through, so she and Carrot entered the cave, coming to a brisk stop once they had burst through the wall of water.

The others trailed behind her. After a few moments, Tylanna took a moment to look around. With the daylight almost completely faded, there was not much to see, but the room inside was nearly double the height of the opening they had entered through. The cave seemed to extend farther back than Tylanna could make out in the light, and the slightest noise sent an echo through the space.

"We need to make a fire first, to help us dry off. We will grow ill if we stay in this damp," Akiye said. She still seemed quiet and solemn to Tylanna, and she wondered how she was handling everything that had happened.

Tahnir volunteered to rush back into the rain to gather wood, while Tylanna and Akiye settled in the horses and began to make camp. Before long, Tahnir returned with an impressive pile of wood and began using a small axe he had brought along to peel off the outer layers.

Inside the cave, they should not have to worry about other travelers, nefarious or not, seeing the fire. Tahnir was able to get a small blaze going with the flint that he carefully nursed, using an excessive amount of kindling at first to make sure the slightly damp wood would catch properly. While Tahnir busied himself with the fire, the two girls changed out of their wet garments and into other outfits they had brought along, leaving the wet clothes out to dry.

When they returned, Tahnir had gotten a decent fire blazing, considering the circumstances. Once he was confident in the stability, he rose to his feet and gave a proud nod, clearly excited by his work. He went off to change himself and left Tylanna and Akiye to watch the flames. The girls hung their wet clothes near the fire and rubbed their hands together for warmth. The weather in the area leading to Nicol's Wood was generally warm, but it was the rainy season, and once you were wet, the cold could set in very quickly.

"Why do you think she helped us, the Soundless woman?" Akiye asked.

Tylanna sat for a moment before answering, looking at her old friend as the woman's dark eyes remained fixed on the fire. "Because it was the right thing to do, I suppose. Maybe she had seen that Domar fellow before and knew he was trouble."

Akiye shrugged, not convinced. Tahnir returned to the fire and joined them in warming themselves.

"I'm not so sure," Akiye went on. "Did she not expect payment of some kind from us? I half-thought she would run off with our horses herself after taking down Domar Truast."

"I don't know why," Tahnir answered, "but I trusted her. Who knows why people do what they do, really? I was more impressed by the accuracy of her shot, all while riding across a bridge hundreds of feet off the ground. And how she pulled her arrow out like it was nothing at all. Very impressive."

"I would have liked to get her name," Tylanna said. She wished she could have done more to thank the woman, but she had ridden off to who knew where. "I just know that we need to be more careful when dealing with strangers. We were ready to give away our horses to the first person we met on faith alone. I am sure they would have been sold off the first chance he had."

"I'm sure we will meet more of his ilk in Nicol's Wood," Akiye said with a tone of distrust, her expression souring. "My father always spoke of that city as a gathering of degenerates and thieves, as if Eodisia and Artani had agreed to ship off the worst of each of their lands to one city. We had best be on our guards, and not be afraid to use the weapons we were given."

The woman finally pulled her dark eyes from the fire to look at Tylanna. "I noticed how you did not draw your sword, but you dodged the arrow, though it was not going to hit you. I believe you might have good battle sense if you were to receive some training. I can show you what little I know of knife work, though I do not know how well it will translate to the blade you carry."

Tylanna's eyes darted over to Carrot, where she had strapped the sword to the horse's side. The thing was awkward to carry, and she was not yet used to bearing its weight.

She returned her gaze to meet Akiye's. "I would be happy to learn from you, Aki, but I think I am too tired for it tonight. Will you teach me when we make camp tomorrow night?"

The woman nodded. "I agree. I am still far too cold to teach you anyways." A small smirk pulled across her lips, and Tylanna thought it was the nearest she had seen to the woman smiling since Shae Glen.

"Did anyone else think it was strange when Domar called Tylanna 'my lady'?" Tahnir cut in.

Akiye and Tahnir both let out a burst of laughter as Tylanna reached across the fire and smacked Tahnir's arm. The trio talked into the night until sleep finally took them.

As she feared, Tylanna once again entered another strange dream when she fell asleep. This time, she stood atop a towering cliff. It could have been one of the cliffs in the Blooming Waste, except there was no vegetation around her.

Across from her a few miles away stood another of the ethereal figures. The two of them seemed to be communicating, as if they were standing right next to each other.

Again, Tylanna could not understand the words being spoken, but she could sense the general tone of the conversation. These words did not seem as filled with anger as in her previous dream. It almost felt as if she was pleading with the other figure. Pleading for what, she had no idea. The conversation went on for some time before the other figure opened a strange doorway behind it and stepped through. Tylanna then stood atop the cliff, alone, looking around at the sheer emptiness around her.

Her eyes fluttered open, and she released a deep sigh. She would have to get some real sleep sometime soon, or she was afraid she would go mad. She looked up at the ceiling of the cave above her, and the way the light of the fire danced, it appeared to be moving above her. No, at second glance, the ceiling of the cave *was* moving above her, sliding towards the cave's mouth.

She turned her head to the side and stifled a gasp. Tahnir and Akiye were both asleep in their bedrolls next to her, but they were being carried off the ground by several small creatures that scuttled their tiny feet over the floor. The creatures looked almost like the bats she had seen in the forest around her house at night, except their arms stretched out more than double the length of their body, and they did not seem to have wings.

The trio was being carried deeper into the cave. Tylanna was glad for her strange dreams waking her so quickly as the other two still seemed to be sound asleep. She turned her head in the other direction, and she saw hundreds of the creatures, scuttling along the walls and the ground behind them. She snapped her head back to her brother and friend.

"Wake up! We're being carried off!"

Just as she shouted, the creatures threw her forward, and she rolled across the ground. The ground gave way, and she fell until she crashed into another level of hard rock, hard. The creatures must have been about to climb down this ledge.

Tylanna scrambled to her feet. The light from the fire barely reached this far into the cave, but she could see enough to see what surrounded her. Bones, both human and animal, were scattered about in this pit. They had camped out in these creatures' hunting grounds, the fools. They would never make it to Helanái in one piece.

She heard the sound of tiny feet and claws crawling over the ledge before she could see them, but she knew the creatures were just about to attack. Looking around desperately for a way to defend herself, she cursed herself for not keeping her sword with her as she slept. The creatures that she could see encircled her and began swiping at her with their abnormally long arms and claws.

Just as she thought her situation helpless, the shapes of Tahnir and Akiye came leaping down into the pit. Akiye landed with a graceful roll and popped up to her feet brandishing two knives in her hands. Tahnir, much less gracefully but no less heroically, crashed to the ground near Tylanna. He pulled himself to his feet and backed himself in front of Tylanna, shaking his hammer menacingly at the creatures that surrounded them.

Akiye seemed to become a whirlwind of flashing blades, slashing at the approaching creatures as they lashed out with tooth and claw. Tahnir batted the encroaching horde with his hammer, swinging with all his strength and flattening multiple creatures with each stroke. Tylanna hid behind her brother, feeling defenseless without her sword.

Some of the creatures that had crawled down from the ledge began scratching at her back and head. She jumped closer to Tahnir to avoid their swipes and struck out at each of them with her bare hands.

When she had cleared the creatures from the ledge, she leaped up the wall and was just barely able to grip the top. With a little effort, she was able to pull herself up to the next level. Most of the creatures had descended into the pit, and the few that remained, she kicked at wildly. After the area was clear, she lay down while leaning over the ledge.

“Akiye, give me your hand!”

The tall woman had just finished slicing one of the creatures completely in half and had cleanly returned her blades into the bag on her waist while the sound of the creature’s shriek still echoed through the cave. She jumped to grab Tylanna’s outstretched hands and used her feet on the sheer rock wall to climb up the rest of the way.

Tahnir fell back to protect her as she climbed, but the creatures had retreated into the darkness of the cave, releasing tiny screeches that sounded through the whole cavern as they went. Tylanna could not tell if the noise just seemed to be getting louder because of the echoes or if they were summoning more of their comrades to help them fight.

Once Akiye was up onto the ledge, the pair of them reached down together to pull Tahnir up. His feet scrambled up the wall wildly, as a few remaining creatures nipped at his heels.

With one last tug, the two women were able to haul Tahnir’s considerable mass to safety. The trio sat on the hard stone of the cave for a moment, panting, before picking themselves up and running towards the entrance.

Tylanna reached their campsite first and packed whatever she could. The screeches boomed from deep within the cave as she threw what she could onto Carrot's back. The horses had been awake and prancing about nervously. Even Akiye's horse seemed alarmed by the strange noises.

Tylanna mounted Carrot and rode towards the entrance. When she spared a look back, she saw Tahnir and Akiye just getting to their horses. The only bleeding thing she seemed to be good at was running away, she thought to herself.

The rain still seemed to pour just as hard outside, but she spurred Carrot through the wall of water regardless. Lightning forked through the sky above as she rode away from the cave, pushing Carrot to run as gallop as she could, and she did not seem at all resistant to getting as far away from the cave as possible.

Tylanna glanced back to make sure that her brother and Akiye had made it out okay, and she saw them both burst forth from the entrance, one after the other. They eventually caught up to her, and the trio rode through the storm for nearly an hour before coming to a stop under a cluster of trees that could at least provide them a small slice of shelter from the onslaught of rain.

Fighting against the weather, they each set up their tents to help provide even a little bit more shelter from the rain. Inside, they stripped naked and slipped into new clothes, once again, and waited out the night.

Tylanna did not even try to sleep this time, choosing to just watch the rainfall, hoping the trees provided enough shelter for the horses. She thought of the strange creatures she had encountered in the cave. Never before had she heard of such vile creatures, but she was certain she would be avoiding spending time in any caves for the foreseeable future.

Chapter 9

NICOL'S WOOD

The rain let up sometime in the early morning, and light came to the forest a few hours afterward. Tylanna and the others packed up and rode away and prayed for no more rainy nights on their journey. For the next several days, they rode, stopped, camped, packed up, and rode again. Tylanna was glad for the lack of major incidents, but the days did begin to blend.

The terrain around them faded from bountiful forest to barren cliffs to nearly tropical vegetation. This was a sure sign they were approaching the Jungle of Jiye. As promised, Akiye had begun to instruct her on the basics of knife work, and they practiced with sticks each night when they made camp.

In about a week's time, Tylanna was riding at the front of their party when she caught sight of Nicol's Wood in the distance. The city was a welcomed spot of civilization in the middle of a bursting jungle. Using the main roadway to get into the city was the only option, as the only entrance was a large gate that stood nearly fifty feet high. Their father had told them that they would have to speak to guards to gain access to the city, but they should not have any problem as Eodisians. Though it was close to the border, Nicol's Wood did technically lie within Eodisia.

The light was just beginning to fade from the day as they approached. In the previous days, they had discussed their plan while in Nicol's Wood, to both avoid trouble and find a way to cross through the Jungle of Jiye. Their story would be that they were farmers from the country looking to sell their crops in the city to earn some money to bring home with them. The only "crops" that they carried with them was the food they had been able to scavenge during the journey, but they hoped that no one would go as far as to search through their bags.

Once they gained entrance to the city, they would head straight for the most reliable inn they could find. Seeking passage across the Jungle would be another issue, but they hoped they would encounter someone they could trust in the city. If not, they would simply find a way across the jungle themselves, no matter how long it took.

As they rode on the main road, Tylanna notices that no other people were traveling into the city. She supposed that it could have to do with the time of the day – the night was fast approaching, and the city did have quite the reputation. Still, the lack of people to blend in with did make her nervous as they approached the towering gate.

As they rode closer, they were accosted by a flurry of shouts sounding from atop the gate. Tylanna had to crane her neck to see who was making all the racket.

Two guards, at least that was what she assumed they must be, were perched about halfway up the gate leaning out of a window that had swung open. They wore dark patchy coats over some type of leather armor, and each was holding tall spears at their sides.

"You there! What business do you have in our fine city, entering so late?" one of the guards called down to them in a gruff voice.

Tylanna was confused by the way the guard had phrased the question, but Tahnir spoke up first.

"We are but simple farmers from the countryside, seeking to sell our stock in your city. We seek entry and an inn to stay in for the night, as we have traveled long to get here."

The guards snickered to themselves before replying.

"Well, we are sorry you came all this way then, what with the market in shambles as it is," the other guard interjected, his voice much smoother than his partner's. "Trouble from the country has spilled behind our walls, and a riot broke out in the market not but yesterday, and much of it is destroyed."

Tahnir glanced back to the two women, before turning back up to the guards. "We assure you that we bring no trouble with along with us. Just our humble crop. If the market is indeed destroyed, we will just seek shelter at an inn for the night and figure out what to do when the light blesses us again."

"All right, boy," the guard that was speaking to them replied. "No need to grovel. I do not be one of them Those Who Serve freaks. Just some fun for us guards. We have not had many through our gate today. Go with care though. This city can be a dangerous place for simple farm children such as yourself."

With that, the window slammed shut, and the gate creaked open. Tylanna wondered what large mechanism pulled those massive doors open before the view of the city was revealed to her, and all other thoughts were banished from her mind.

It was fair to say that Tylanna, who had never seen a large city, nor any village larger than Shae Glen, had expected much more from Nicol's Wood.

The city stretched before them as a series of winding streets, all cluttered with shabby buildings in disrepair and tired and hungry people littering the streets. The trio ventured into the downtrodden city while bringing the horses to walk as closely as possible to each other. Having all grown up in a quaint village such as Shae Glen, Nicol's Wood had made it clear to all of them that they were now a long way from home.

Various brawls seemed to be ongoing throughout the many streets they walked, and no one lifted a finger to stop any of them. Many of the buildings and streets appeared to be bars and taverns of some sort. The noise echoed out from each of these buildings, a wild mix of yelling, music, and breaking glass.

They tried to keep their small parade in the center of the road, though they once had to bring their horses to the rear when a drunken man spilled into the street and fell nearly directly in front of them. After they had reared their horses to a stop, the man's friends ran into the street, yelling at the young trio about them not watching where they were going. Tylanna led Carrot around them and picked up speed, and Tahnir and Akiye followed suit.

"What will we do, Tyl?" Tahnir asked. "None of these inns seem suitable to stay at if we do not wish to be stabbed and robbed in our sleep."

She mulled over their situation silently in her head before responding. "I say we venture a little deeper into the city and try to find a place on a quieter street. Hopefully, there are only so many people because we're close to the gate."

Sure enough, the violent scenes of drunken revelry seemed to fade away behind them as they ventured deeper and deeper into the city. Eventually, they came upon a quiet enough inn that seemed suited to their needs, far enough away from the hubbub of the city's entrance. It was called the High Chair's Seat, seemingly a reference to the High Chair of Eodisia. It appeared to be a cozy three-story building, with a stable on the right side of the building that would do nicely for the horses. Tylanna was glad that the horses would have a night out of the rain.

As they veered from the center of the road, a large block-shaped bald man and a thin woman in her middle years approached them.

"Weary travelers," the woman belted out in a tired voice. "Welcome to our inn! We offer lodgings for humans and steed alike, at a fair rate at that. Where are you joining us from?"

Tylanna looked back to Tahnir, who ushered his stallion forward and answered for her without hesitation.

"We come from a small village in the Eodisian countryside. We are farmers who have come to sell our crop, but we have heard of the trouble in the market yesterday, so we seeking lodging for the night so that we may decide what to do in the morning."

Perfect, Tylanna thought. He gave her the story without bending the truth completely out of whack.

"That'll be no trouble at all, young sir," the thin woman replied, and Tylanna could sense a kindness in her voice she thought would not be found in Nicol's Wood. "Go right on in, and my husband will get you all sorted for rooms, and Vymir and I will get the horses settled into the stable. Take whatever bags you would like to keep, and we can take care of the rest!"

With that, the woman stepped forward and began caressing each of the horses' heads gently. She seemed to have a natural way with the animals. The man, who must be known as Vymir, offered Tylanna and Akiye a head nod as they dismounted and even offered a hand with some of their bags to help ease their burden. The woman, whose name Tylanna had not gotten, walked the horses over to the stable once they had removed all the bags that they needed for the overnight stay. Tylanna was sure to keep Darkender strapped onto the back of her belt, and she noticed that Tahnir kept his hammer on his left hip. Akiye did not noticeably have any weapons on her, but Tylanna had a feeling she had several knives about her person.

They followed Vymir through the entryway to the High Chair's Seat and found a relatively quiet dining area and bar immediately inside the door. A large man with greying red hair and a large bushy beard stood behind the bar, deep in conversation with a group of three men in travel gear and a variety of weapons. The rest of the common room was filled with several other parties, most of whom sat brooding over mugs of ale or wine. A woman stood on a small stage that sat on the opposite end of the room, strumming a stringed instrument and singing. Tylanna assumed that must have been why the common room had seemed so quiet, and she was glad that they seemed to be showing the performer some respect. From what Tylanna could make out, she sang a sad song of a far-off land and a war long lost.

Vymir led them over to the bar and gestured the large man behind the bar over to them with a tilt of his bald head. The man lumbered over, moving his considerable girth with grace and unexpected speed. In no time at all, he was planted in front of the newcomers, eager to please.

"Well, well, well, what will it be? Are you three here for a drink, or will you be staying overnight with us?"

Tahnir and Akiye stepped up to the counter to discuss details with the man. Tylanna hung back, taking a moment to gaze around their lodgings. The patrons seemed to be from many different walks of life. She could not tell why, but a thrill coursed through her, making the fingers of her hands nearly shake with excitement. What was giving her such a feeling? Surely it was not just because this would be her first time staying at an inn. There was something more, something she could sense in her heart.

Tahnir placed a gentle hand on her shoulder, and she quivered the feeling free. "The rooms are a little expensive for us, so we'll all have to share one after we pay for the horses to be stabled and fed. You and Akiye can take the bed, and I will make do with my bedroll on the floor."

She felt a pang of guilt. Perhaps they could sleep in shifts again.

The man with the bushy beard, Taw Grint was his name, scooped the remainder of their bags from their arms and led them to a small stairway that wound its way up to the second floor. Taw, Vymir, and Tahnir barely squeezed their broad shoulders through the hallway as they worked their bags over their arms, while Tylanna and Akiye, now unencumbered, breezed through with no trouble.

The trio was led by the inn staff to the room on the far-right end of the hallway. Vymir swung the room open and place their bags near the foot of the bed with a gentleness that Tylanna would not have expected of the blocky man. The room was decently sized, with a large bed that would easily accommodate both of the girls. A small couch sat in the far corner beneath a bolted window, and a large basin of wastewater sat on a large dresser directly next to it.

"You were lucky to have gotten this room, but it had not been rented by this point in the night, and I reckon you do be the last we be having in tonight," Taw Grint puffed as he dropped their bags with a little less grace than Vymir had. "The corner room we usually reserve for any nobles that may grace our halls, but I suppose you all can fancy yourself royalty, if only for a night."

The pair from the inn left with a few brief farewells. Once alone in the room, the trio looked about at the furnishings. Tylanna might be a simple village girl, but she did not think that this room would be fit for royalty. They went about unpacking their bags, at least what they needed for the night. Tahnir decided to use his bedroll on the couch, which nearly fit his whole body. His legs dangled , but he insisted that it was plenty comfortable compared to the hard forest floor he had gotten used to. Once he had gotten the bedroll settled on the couch, he sprung up to his feet, resting his hand idly on the hammer that remained looped on his belt.

“Well,” he said, “who fancies a drink?” A wicked grin drew his lips wide across his face, pushing his cheeks into his eyes.

“Should we? I thought we meant to keep a low profile?” Akiye replied as she looked nervously between the siblings while running her right hand through her short dark hair. She had removed her over jacket, and her left hand tapped on the hilt of a dagger that rested in her belt.

“Well...” Tylanna bit the corner of her lip while she deliberated. “I suppose one drink could not hurt us. It is our first time in the city, after all, but we still need to remain aware of what is going on around us.”

Tahnir danced over to her, and when he reached her, he scooped her up in a large hug. He swung her towards the door with almost no effort at all, laughing as he did. “Come on, Aki, let’s have a bit of fun.”

Nearly an hour had passed since Tylanna and the others had meandered down to the common room. Taw

Grint had been glad to see them reemerge, and his wife, Faleyemi, had joined him behind the bar. The young trio had gotten a round of mugs filled with a stout ale and found a quiet spot in the corner of the common room. Akiye had found it the most suitable to view all the other patrons as well as the entrances and exits. The performer had finished her singing some time ago and had joined a table of other people that looked to be about her age. Tylanna imagined them to also be performers based on the way they were dressed. A few of the other patrons had filed out shortly after, and only a few tables remained crowded.

One drink had turned into two, and now the trio chattered eagerly over their third ale. Tylanna and her brother had had the odd ale or wine with dinner back in Shae Glen, but never three back-to-back as they drank now. Akiye appeared to have never had a taste of strong drink, but she seemed to be enjoying herself as her cheeks grew more and more flushed. It warmed Tylanna's heart to see her friend smiling again.

The light casting from the hearth and lamps seemed to grow shadowed as two looming shapes rose in front of their table. Tahnir halted the story he was telling, and the young trio gazed up at the two men. The men stood tall, nearly a head taller than Tahnir would be while standing. They each wore their arms bare, and a series of scars covered each of them. Each man wore his hair long and pulled back in a head wrap. The man on the right was clean-shaven, and the man on the left sported a scraggly mustache. They each had a mean glint in their eyes.

"Mighty fine weapons you have there, youngins. Where did you come across those?" the mustachioed man sneered.

Tylanna's hand reached behind her, and she found the hilt of Darkender slide into her hand smoothly. The jolt of excitement she had felt earlier shot through her again, tenfold. Beads of sweat formed on her forehead as her blood began to race. What was going on with her?

"They were gifts, actually," Tahnir answered confidently. "Where did you acquire those axes you keep on your backs?"

"We were asking you the questions, farm boy," the mustachioed man went on, leaning closer. Tylanna could smell his breath from where she sat, and it was not pleasant. "Our weapons be none of your concern, but the two of you brown-haired children carry the most finely crafted weapons my friend and I have ever seen, and we were curious. But if you wish to see my axe, I can surely give you a closer look."

With that, Tahnir jolted to his feet, pushing the table back and sending one of the mugs clattering to the floor. He stepped past Akiye and stood just before the man with the mustache, glaring at him directly in the eyes.

"Threaten my family again, and I'll have you before you have the chance to draw that simple axe of yours. It is none of your business where we get our steel from, but we are not looking for any trouble from you or anyone. Return to your seats, and we won't take issue with your rude comments."

Though he was much shorter than the duo, Tahnir did not look even the slightest bit intimidated. No weapons were drawn, but Tylanna's hands gripped Darkender's hilt fiercely, ready to throw steel through each of these men. What was she thinking? She had never even been in a fight with anyone – surely she could not attack a man with a sword. But deep down, she knew if they threatened her brother or Akiye again, it would be the end of them.

In a moment spanning only a breath, Tahnir and the troublesome duo were separated by one of the men who had been standing at the bar with Taw when the Shae Glenners had entered the inn. The man was a hair taller than Tahnir but seemed to hold all three of the men in place with ease.

The man wore simple travel clothes, but she could sense a formality about him somehow. His person was covered in weaponry, with a full sword on each hip, a bow across his back, and at least three knives running down a holster on his left leg. His hair was a dirty blond mess of shoulder-length tangles, and his beard matched, if only slightly darker in color. His gray eyes darted between the three men he held at bay, casual yet tactful.

"Easy, gentlemen. We will have no trouble in my friend Taw's inn tonight. Leave the village-folk be, Petra. Consider them under my protection. Any who come after them will have my claw to answer to, along with the Nox brothers', of course."

A jolt of recognition shot through the man with the mustache, who must be known as Petra. The two large men spun around, offering no rebuttal at all, but bumped into two short men who were standing behind them calmly, each sporting a dagger in each of their hands. The two men looked similar enough to be brothers, each with short but compactly muscular frames garbed in clothing made of leather and animal skin. Each had scraggly black hair, the slightly taller one with hair to his shoulders, the other with hair clipped short. Their dark eyes shone with a casual certainty that these two hulking men would be dead if they had the passing thought to make it so.

The large men shuffled around the two short men and dashed out of the inn, throwing a bag of coin at Taw Grint as they went.

When they had passed out the door, the two short men burst into a peal of violent laughter, sheathing their weapons as they tried to suppress their chuckles. The tall man that had initially stood between them and Tahnir also let out a small laugh, followed by a relieved sigh as he brushed the hair from his face. His gray eyes seemed much kinder than they had been a moment ago.

"Apologies for them," the man said, shifting his attention to the Shae Glenners after watching the vile duo depart from the High Chair's Seat. "They are wary of travelers after the trouble in the market the other day. I am Reynalor. May I have your names?"

Chapter 10

MONSTER HUNTERS

After making introductions, the three men offered to buy the young trio their next round of drinks and joined them at their table. The man who had interrupted the fight was Reynalor Astilyr, and the other two short men were Fayde and Laito Nox. The shorter men were in fact brothers. Fayde, the man with his hair clipped short, was slightly older than Laito by a few years. Each of them was somewhere nearing their middle years, a good fifteen to twenty years older than Tylanna and her friends.

"So," Reynalor asked as they all sat down, "what brings you all to Nicol's Wood?"

The young trio shared a glance around the table. Tylanna wanted to believe that they could trust these men that had rescued them from a messy fight, but her father's warnings of strangers continued to ring in her head.

"We are looking for passage through the Jungle of Jiye," Tahnir blurted out.

Tylanna shot him a shimmering look that she was sure everyone at the table picked up on.

"Is that so?" Reynalor replied. "It just so happens that we're also about to make the trek through the jungle in about a week's time. We have been hired to escort some researchers deep into the jungle and then take them out on the Artani side."

Tylanna snapped her head back to the bearded man. "So you know the jungle well? What can we expect?"

The man leaned forward over his mug and brought his voice to a dramatic, rasping whisper. "The Jungle of Jiye is no place for casual journeying. Ancient magic wraps its way through the roots of every tree, and strange creatures roam the jungle, day and night. If you do not know the path, it may be impossible to find your way out. We have traveled through it many times now, and still, each trip brings new challenges."

The young trio sat silently for a moment while digesting the weight of Reynalor's words. Magic, Tylanna thought, only existed in the old stories. Rynestian had told them stories of humans that could harness the energy of the world around them to do their bidding, but she had never seen it before, certainly not in Shae Glen.

"But don't let that put you off," Fayde interjected after taking a long swig of his mug. "There is plenty of fun to be had in the jungle. Lots of monsters to kill."

He and his brother laughed nearly in unison and clapped their mugs together and drank once more.

Reynalor also allowed himself a light chuckle before he sipped at his drink. "Yes, there certainly are plenty of strange beasts running through the jungle, and we have been hired to kill all sorts of them. We are bounty hunters, of a sort, usually hired to exterminate some sort of monster plaguing the Lands Below. The only reason we were hired for this escort job was apparently the researchers had heard of our work taking out a Krilrot, and they sought us out when we arrived in Nicol's Wood to offer us the job."

The trio of Shae Glenners shared a look of confusion.

"What's a Krilrot?" Akiye asked timidly.

Fayde and Laito let out another laugh before Laito replied, "A Krilrot, young lady, is a particularly nasty bastard that is known to lurk near the edge of a lake or river. They only hunt at night, and their prey is usually confined to small animals, but when they have over-hunted the area around their body of water, they have no issue going after larger animals, even humans."

Tylanna, Tahnir, and Akiye tightened their grips around their mugs as Laito went on.

"We received word of the beast when some farmer's daughter had been snatched by the Krilrot, may her light burn on forever. At the time we were in the countryside of Artani, having just come back from a visit to the Soulos Sea. We rushed to the lake as fast as we could and arrived in about a week's time. By the time we arrived, the beast had snatched two more people from near its waters. We had never done battle with such a creature. All we had to go off of was the stories we had heard of its description. It is said to have six long arms with several different joints all bending in different directions and stand as tall as two grown men. It can live on land as well as water, but it prefers the murky coolness of a lake.

"We approached the lake at night, with ropes and blades ready, and I stood on the shore myself as bait. When the beast came for me, Reynalor and Fayde were there to wrap the creature in two ropes, and together we dragged it out with great effort. Once the beast was writhing around on the shore, we went at it with knives and swords until it writhed no longer. Then we collected our gold and traveled back to Nicol's Wood."

The young Shae Glenners sat with their mouths ajar. Monsters such as this Krilrot had only been figures in stories to them while growing up, and here were three men who had battled and slain one themselves. The way they had discussed it seemed as casual to them, as if they were discussing the day's weather.

As the night continued, the three bounty hunters continued to wow the Shae Glenners with tales of their monstrous conquests and their travels around the world.

Them doing the majority of the talking allowed for the young trio to keep the details of their journey to themselves, though Tylanna got the sneaking suspicion that the three men were intentionally not asking them too many pressing questions.

After a few more hours, the three men rose from the table, mumbling about their early morning the next day. Before leaving, Reynalor went and paid the bar tab with Taw Grint. He then rushed back over to the table as Fayde and Laito stumbled up the stairs together, the two of them supporting each other and singing some raucous song as they swayed from stair to stair.

"One more thing," Reynalor said as the Shae Glenners were rising from the table, realizing how quickly the effects of all the ale could hit them since they had been sitting the entire night. "I heard from Taw that you three brought horses along with you. The Jungle of Jiye is no place for horses. The terrain is much too difficult and unpredictable for riding. I would find a trustworthy stable to keep them in, or sell them off before you go. Who knows when you will return, right?"

He gave the trio a wink and ran after the Nox brothers, joining in on their song as he got to the stairs. Only Taw Grint remained behind the bar, laughing and shaking his head as he cleaned a few glasses that had been left on the bar top.

It was only then that Tylanna realized that they were the last people left in the common room, and how late the hour had become. The first light of the first sun would be hitting the city soon, and they had much to do in the morning. They gathered up their mugs from the table and brought them over to Taw Grint, who thanked them graciously and gave them each a large cask of water, which he advised each of them to drink.

Tylanna led the way up the stairs, with Tahnir and Akiye giggling as they stumbled behind her. They all clattered into their room, and Tylanna fell straight onto the bed, not even bothering to change into her nightclothes. She barely felt Akiye crawl into the bed beside her with a huff, and she did not hear Tahnir collapse onto the small couch with a thud. The last thing she felt before losing consciousness was Darkender pulsing against her back.

The light seemed to tear through Tylanna's closed eyelids as she woke. The fact that she had not had any strange dreams was the least of her concerns. She felt as if she was nearly about to die of thirst.

She lifted her head, which weighed twice its normal weight, and she looked around the room. Akiye lay still, sprawled out next to her on the large bed. Tahnir had not made it all the way to the couch and lay on the wooden floor just before it. All of them still wore their clothes from the day before, and the room was hot and muggy with the day's heat.

Tylanna pulled herself up to sit and found that the cask of water Taw had given her the night before sat undisturbed on the end table on her side of the bed. She hefted the cask and took several long gulps, letting the water spill down the sides of her mouth. After she felt she had drunk her fill, she rose from the bed while keeping one hand on the bedpost to steady herself.

Too much damn ale, she thought. They had much to do today, and they were already off to a bad start. She shuffled over to the window and threw it open, allowing a blast of fresh air and the sounds of the city to come pouring in.

Akiye and Tahnir both rose with a start and looked around wildly when she opened the window. Tylanna looked at each of them, before pointing to the water casks nearest both of them. Once they had all finished reviving themselves from the previous night's revelry, they each took turns going about washing and changing their clothes to prepare for the day.

When each of them was ready, they packed up their possessions and left the room behind. They descended the stairs and saw Vymir, who stood behind the bar. At the moment, he was the only one in the common room.

"Bit of a late morning for you three, eh?" the block-shaped man said with a chuckle.

Tahnir let out an audible groan before responding, "Yes, we were quite tired from our journey, and the ale must have helped us realize it. Might we see about our horses?"

Vymir chuckled again. "Aye, Lady Faleyemi is out in the stable. She will sort you lot out, and you can be on your way. Thanks for staying with us, and please do return if you be in Nicol's Wood again."

The trio bid farewell to the large man and left the inn. They strolled over to the stable and found Faleyemi was putting out some feed for the horses. The thin woman moved from horse to horse with a grace that spoke of her years as a stable master. No two horses received the same treatment from her, yet they all seemed perfectly content. Tylanna watched the woman in awe, as she had had plenty of trouble with Carrot in the early years, and the mare was not quick to trust strangers. Faleyemi seemed so caught up in her work that she did not seem to notice them approaching. As they got near, Tylanna was possessed by an idea.

"Faleyemi," she blurted out as the woman turned with a small start, "would you possibly be able to look after our horses for a bit longer? We mean to travel through the Jungle of Jiye and have been warned against bringing them along with us."

Faleyemi was running a large brush through the mane of the large black horse that Akiye had ridden from Shae Glen. She looked at the young trio before eyeing each of the horses one by one. "I think I would be able to find some work for them about village, but how long will it be before you return?"

Tylanna shot a look to her brother, and he stepped forward to answer.

"We're not sure, exactly. Our journey could take quite a bit longer, but it's uncertain to us. We would happily sell the horses to you outright, and if we return soon enough, we would buy them back from you."

The offer saddened Tylanna, but she was glad her brother had understood her intentions without having to speak them aloud. Carrot had been a part of their family for so long, and she felt an obligation to her former master to return Xelina's horse to her when they returned to Shae Glen. *If* they returned to Shae Glen.

"Aye, we could buy the horses off you. Then we could rent them out with a clear conscience to our guests. The Jungle of Jiye do be no place for a horse. The path is too steep and overgrown. It is also a dangerous place for inexperienced travelers, so please take care of yourselves while crossing through." Faleyemi took a step closer to them, procuring a bag of coins from her pocket and organizing some of the coins into three neat piles. "I can do ten gold coins for the stallion and warhorse, and seven for the old mare. She may be old, but I can see she do be a good worker. Is this acceptable?"

The young trio stared at the gold. This was more than they had altogether when they entered Nicol's Wood the previous day.

"That will do fine. Thank you so much for taking care of them for us. We will return one day," Tahnir said as he accepted the coins from her, sliding them into the coin pouch he wore on his hip.

As he did, Faleyemi took another step closer and spoke in a harsh whisper. "Look out for Those Who Serve as you travel to Helanái. They seem to be crawling about everywhere, hunting for any with connections to the Sky People. Be careful, young ones."

As she stepped back, she flashed a quick sign with her right hand that Tylanna didn't recognize, where she intertwined her middle finger around her pointer finger and held her ring finger down against her palm with her thumb. She turned the hand to show both sides and then let both of her hands fall to her sides, and she straightened the front of her pants absentmindedly. Faleyemi pivoted back to the stable and busied herself with the horses, leaving the Shae Glenners to wonder how she had discovered that they were heading to Helanái, or that they were Helanáians themselves.

After leaving the stable and the High Chair's Seat behind, Tylanna and the others went about gathering supplies for their trek through the jungle. Nearby the inn, they were able to find shops with reasonable pricing and got what they needed without taking too long. Tylanna and Akiye found a small shop that had an impressive inventory of medicinal herbs and restocked the medical bag that Xelina had gifted Akiye back in Shae Glen.

Tahnir was in charge of food for the trip and returned from the open market with a wide variety of dried meats, fruits, and vegetables. While not the most appetizing choices, in Tylanna's opinion, he had purchased for longevity. They did not know how long they would be traveling, as Rynestian had only given them approximations on the travel length, based on his journeys some twenty-five years past.

Then, bags laden with supplies, they made way for the Jungle of Jiye.

Chapter 11

INTO THE JUNGLE

As soon as they left the village, the light from the suns was almost completely covered by a dense canopy of trees that towered above them, save for a few streaks of light. Tylanna had counted on them having at least a few more hours of light, but she had not taken into account just how dense the tree line would be. The path into the jungle was not so much a path as a thin line. Surrounding them were colorful flowers, plants, and trees that Tylanna had never seen before. She wanted to sit right there at the entrance and flip through her almanac of plant life, but she knew that they were pressed for time, and she would have to try and make mental notes of all that she saw.

After only a few minutes of walking, it was clear to Tylanna that none of the maps had been completely accurate. The path seemed to bend and twist wildly, turning them around so many times that Tylanna was not at all certain if they were indeed heading towards Artani at all. Her father and the others who had warned them not to underestimate the treachery of the jungle had certainly not been lying.

"Are you certain that this is the correct path, Tyl?" Tahnir asked, already huffing and puffing. Even though they were still on the path, the going was not easy.

Tylanna stopped for a moment to look around her. It was impossible to judge the direction of the suns from the few trickles of light she could see, and nothing on the plants around them gave her any indication of their direction. Moss seemed to grow from every direction on the trees. This contradicted much of what she had learned in her training. As her mind raced, she noticed how much she was sweating. Though it had been mildly warm in the city, the jungle seemed to be trapping what little heat it must get from the suns below the canopy. It was a thick heat, and Tylanna regretted that she had not packed more short clothes.

She rolled up the sleeves of her jacket to just below her elbows, as far as the fabric would allow. "I'm not sure. These turns do not line up with any of the maps I studied. But this little light we have will not last long. What do you think we should do?"

"Well, it's not as if I saw any other path," Tahnir said, folding his arms across his chest as he pondered. "But it makes more sense to me to cut straight through in one direction, even if the going gets to be a little rougher. At least that way we know we are heading in the same direction we set out in."

"I think we should stay on the path," Akiye countered. "We are all unfamiliar with this area, and at least this path seems to have been traveled recently, judging from the indents in the plants we tread over. If we follow the path for now, even if it turns us around a few times, I believe it will save us time in the long run, and we may even run into more travelers that can offer directions."

Tylanna mulled over both of their responses. It was just like Tahnir to suggest storming straight through the jungle that they had all been warned of the dangers of. She found Akiye's argument to be much more logical but did worry about upsetting her brother. But they were all out of their element here.

"I say we stay on the path for at least an hour, and then break to make camp early. I fear what little light remains will fade much faster than we expect. Hopefully, in the morning we will be able to get a better sense of our surroundings."

The next hour passed in relative silence, mostly just groans as the trio tried to navigate the gnarled roots that lay strewn across the jungle floor without losing their footing. They made camp with relative ease, after coming across a nice spot nestled under a large tree whose roots dangled from its outstretched branches. Since their dried meat was already prepared, they did not build a fire, which saved some time. The meat was tough and mostly flavorless, but after a tough hike, anything was appreciated.

After eating Akiye took first watch. As Tylanna stretched out in her bedroll, she wondered if all of the new places she went to on this journey would be as odd as the Jungle of Jiye.

When Tahnir woke in the morning, thankfully, the jungle was much brighter than when they had entered the previous afternoon. He crawled out of his tent and found Tylanna sitting on a root nearby, seemingly lost in thought as she stared up at the canopy. He approached her and cleared his throat, and she snapped to attention, spinning to face him.

"Some lookout you are, Tyl. I was right next to you before you noticed me."

She pursed her lips and leveled her gaze with his. "I knew you stopped sleeping when I couldn't hear your awful snoring anymore. I just assumed you would be coming out of your tent soon so I didn't bother to look is all."

Tahnir chuckled and stretched out his body. He was far too young for the amount of noise his joints made. He supposed all this camping out was starting to catch up with him. If only they had not wasted their one night in a bed for weeks in a drunken stupor.

"Well, I'll see if I can find us something to go with our breakfast," he said as he rubbed his hands together eagerly. "I'm sure there will be something exotic to add some flavor to this terrible meat."

Tylanna just grunted as he strolled away from the campsite. He made mental notes of each tree or plant he passed, knowing how easy it would be to get lost here. Even Tylanna and Akiye had gotten lost right away, and he relied on them for most of the navigating. He had always been directionally challenged, and that was in his hometown.

He thumbed the hilt of his hammer while thinking back to the two brutes who had assailed them in the inn's common room. Surely their weapons seemed fine, but was that any reason for them to demand to know where they had gotten them? Maybe they were Those Who Serve, and something about the weapon's crafting was distinctly Helanáian. Tahnir had certainly never seen the style of intricate crafting on a hammer, which he normally considered a simple tool.

Something about this weapon was anything but simple, however. In the cave with the strange creatures, he had sworn he had felt compelled by the weapon, somehow. It was as if it was pulling his arm along with it, not he who moved the hammer around. Each blow had landed true – he had not missed a single strike. He considered himself generally athletic, but he had never been in any sort of fight aside from a few scraps with other boys in his village. The thought of a weapon that could work on its own intrigued him, though he was sure it had been his imagination.

Before long he found himself in a sort of clearing, where large bushels of berries grew from the base of more gigantic trees. He could see that the bushes got a fair bit of sunlight, more than he had seen leaking through the canopy thus far. He plucked one and popped it in his mouth. When he bit into the berry, it burst into an explosion of juice and flavor. Satisfied with his findings, he began to gather as many berries as he could carry as he finished chewing.

As he walked along, he threw a few more berries into his mouth. If he made sure there were still enough for Tylanna and Akiye, he saw no issue with having a light snack as he returned. He was fairly certain of the path he had taken to get to the berry bushes, and he identified the plants along the way.

The light leaking through the canopy seemed to grow brighter, more vivid. Various plants swayed with the light breeze that must have been rolling by, though he could not feel it. In truth, he felt rather hot. He could already feel the sweat trickling down his back under his shirt. Each drop of sweat felt as cold as ice, though it offered little relief from the heat of the jungle.

It almost seemed as if the plants were swaying in response to his every stride, recoiling at first but then reaching for him as he ambled past. Their colors grew more and more vivid as mist clouded his vision. Wiping the sweat from his eyes, he pressed on back towards the others.

Akiye was helping Tylanna break down the tents at their campsite when she heard a loud crash behind her as something fell over the roots. She spun around and found Tahnir sprawled out over the jungle floor. He was drenched in sweat, with his face shoved directly into the dirt, and he did not appear to be moving.

She and Tylanna dashed over to him and turned him on his back. His face was pale, and a strange red and white foam was bubbling out of his open mouth. His breath came in harsh gasps.

Tylanna clapped her hands over her mouth, and Akiye saw that her hands were shaking. *It must be poison*, she thought. *He must have eaten something in the jungle, the fool.*

Without taking an extra moment to collect her thoughts, Akiye turned Tahnir's unconscious head to the side and stuck her fingers down his throat, hard. Once she had gotten him to purge his stomach, she searched him for any trace of what he had eaten. His entire body was sweating profusely and had started to shake. His hands seemed to be locked together around something, so she pried them loose, and a clump of crushed red berries spilled out. The veins in his hands around the berries were bulging, and the skin was agitated.

So it was not just what he ate. Even holding the berries could be dangerous.

She looked up to Tylanna, who still seemed to be in shock. “Tylanna! Go get some water for him. We need to flush his system and wash his hands.”

Realization settled into Tylanna’s eyes, and she bolted up, rushing for one of their water casks. While she ran, Akiye pressed her hand to Tahnir’s forehead. He was still far too hot; they would need to cool him down somehow. She wished Xelina Marcs was here. The woman always knew what to do in moments like these. Akiye’s mind raced for solutions, and she remembered that Xelina had gifted her an assortment of remedies.

“Tylanna, grab Xelina’s bag from right in front of my tent! I’m sure we have something for poison in there.”

Tylanna was already most of the way back with the water, but she pivoted and dashed towards Akiye’s half-disassembled tent. She snatched up the bag and bounded over awkwardly, nearly spilling the contents of the water cask. After crashing to her knees next to Akiye, she handed the water over and began rifling through the bag.

“Direroot... Rotbrew... Willowseed...” Tylanna muttered hurriedly as Akiye poured water into Tahnir’s open mouth.

After, she pushed his head to the side again to fully rinse his mouth. Once he regained consciousness, she would get him to drink as much as he could. She then went about rinsing his hands and arms before tearing a piece of fabric from her undershirt to make a cool compress for his forehead.

"Here!" Tylanna shouted. She held aloft a piece of folded parchment paper. Akiye recognized it as one of Xelina's pre-ground powders. Akiye grabbed the folded paper and inspected its contents. It was a white powder with flecks of green and black. *It must be salt, atropine, and charcoal*, she thought. *This should do the trick for now, but we'll have to find something to bring down his fever soon.*

She poured the contents of the folded paper into his open mouth, along with a small amount of water, and began to gently rub his throat to get him to swallow. Before long, he let out a loud gulping sound, and the antidote dissolved.

Akiye fell back onto her haunches and released a loud breath. With any luck, Tahnir should be able to make a full recovery soon.

"That fool," Tylanna said shakily. "He should have known better than to just eat whatever he found. He should have let me check it in my almanac first."

Tears streamed down Tylanna's cheeks as she gripped her brother's hands. His breathing already seemed to be growing steadier. Akiye decided to give them some time alone and rose to her feet.

"Keep watch over him, and give him anything we have for a fever. When he wakes, just have him focus on drinking as much water as he can. We still need to flush his system. I will go explore the path ahead for a while and then return."

Akiye returned to her tent and grabbed her travel bag, just in case she got lost in the treacherous path.

"Thank you, Aki," she heard Tylanna whisper as she left the camp.

Chapter 12

LONE WANDERER

Akiye walked along the winding path for nearly three hours, lost in her thoughts. She was certain that this would not be their group's last close brush with death, and she wondered if she would be able to react as quickly next time. Tylanna was just as accomplished as her in medical training, but she had been nearly useless at first. Would Tylanna react in the same way if it had been Akiya who ate the berries? Not that she ever would have, but that was another story.

Tahnir had always been a lovable man, who always knew how to turn any situation into a fun time. Unfortunately, to Akiye, he did not seem to possess much intelligence outside of the forge. Though she had heard he was nearly as gifted as the Desqens' father when it came to metalwork, so it was clear that he was not stupid. She supposed he just prioritized certain things above others.

In her childhood, she had possessed romantic feelings for the Desqen boy, but she outgrew those feelings the closer she grew to Tylanna during their studies. She considered Tylanna to be one of her closest friends, and she was unwilling to risk that friendship over some fleeting feelings for a boy.

The path before her had grown even more difficult than what they had traversed on their first day in the Jungle of Jiye. It was easier for her to move alone, and she was not worried about protecting the others. She was more than confident that she would be able to handle herself in any kind of encounter, but she worried about the twins in a fight.

She could not help but feel slightly jealous of the twins as they traveled together. Their bond was unshakable, though they argued plenty. All the family that she had in the world had been taken from her on that fateful day in Shae Glen, and they still had each other for comfort. She wondered if they were as driven by revenge as she was.

She heard a leaf crunch beneath a footstep somewhere behind her. Without hesitation, she leaped into the plants on the right side of the path, covering herself. When she landed, the wooden mask she had taken from their family home slipped from her bag. As the sounds grew closer, she reached out for the mask, which she was just barely able to brush with her fingertips. Knowing it would give away her location, she leaned forward and grabbed the mask. Instead of bothering with her bag, she threw the mask over her face and tried to sit as still as she possibly could.

She waited to see what the source of the noise had been. Before long, she saw it.

A small and exceedingly beautiful woman with eerily pale skin and garbed in a flowing white dress moved through the thick vegetation opposite where Akiye hid. She seemed to glide through or around the roots and plants with little to no effort. Akiye could barely even see when she took each step. Her dress was cut with a high neckline and a pinched waist, but the trail of the gown seemed to flow behind her without snagging on a single branch or root. She wore bracers made of gold on both of her wrists, both of which were inlaid with large white gems.

Her hair was as white as her gown and flowed well beyond her waistline behind her. Binders of gold arranged her hair so that it elegantly flowed down her back. The light that trickled through the canopy of trees caused her dress and ornamentations to shine, nearly glowing. Her face wore a calm expression, unconcerned with the difficult terrain she crossed.

Akiye felt strangely at ease. She lifted her mask to get a better look at the woman. Just as she did, the woman stopped her movement and raised her head into the air.

Akiye's breath caught in her throat. Now that the woman had stopped, she felt a sickly mix of menace and fear. All of the confidence she had had about protecting herself drained away, as she was now somehow certain that this otherworldly woman was extremely dangerous.

She had to get away. She must. Back to the twins. She had to warn them.

A hand gripped her shoulder, and she spun around, grabbing the wrist and twisting with all her might. When she finished her turn, she saw that she held Tylanna in an exposed grip, with Tylanna's arm twisted behind her back.

Once she realized who it was, she let go of Tylanna and turned back to face the beautiful woman in white.

There was no one there. Had she imagined it? Or had she fled at the commotion that Akiye and Tylanna had caused? Akiye had a hard time imagining the woman running, but she supposed it was possible. The fear that had been coursing through her very being had melted away.

When she finally released her breath, she demanded, "What are you doing, sneaking up on me like that?"

Tylanna, still rubbing her wrist where Akiye had nearly wrenched it out of its socket, replied curtly, "You seemed to be looking at something, so I didn't want to make a noise to disturb you. What was it you were looking at?"

Akiye glanced once more to where she had seen the woman, and then fully rose to her feet to have a full look around. "There was this strange woman, dressed in a majestic white gown moving through the jungle as smoothly as if she walked down a village street. Did you not see her?"

Tylanna just shook her head. "I only noticed you when I saw part of that mask sticking out from this bush. I came back here off the path at first to avoid you, but then I could tell that it was you, so I approached. I'm sorry for startling you."

It was only then that Akiye realized that she still wore the mask, and she pulled it off and stuffed it back into her bag, slightly embarrassed. "It's something my father left behind for me, something from his home country." She couldn't seem to make eye contact with Tylanna.

"That's great that you brought it with you. You should treasure it and keep it safe. I think it looks rather interesting."

Akiye glanced back up into Tylanna's eyes and allowed herself a small smile. While they had been unusual to look at, at first, Akiye had grown used to Tylanna's strange eyes, one bright green and the other a deep gold.

"Why did you come all the way out here after me? What of Tahnir?"

"He's fine. He awoke not long after you left, and once I got some water in him, he was back to his usual self, though I told him that he should not travel more today. Again, I can't thank you enough for saving him." Tylanna looked so deeply into her eyes that Akiye became slightly embarrassed and looked past Tylanna as she continued. "I came to find you to bring you back to the camp since we'll have to spend another night there. I'm glad I told him not to come with me. The path did seem to get quite a bit rougher than it was yesterday."

Akiye nodded in agreement, and the pair of young women turned around and returned to the path, back the way they had come. As they walked, Akiye could not get the strange woman in white out of her mind.

Tylanna and Akiye returned to the campsite in about three hours. The little light that could penetrate the thick canopy above was just beginning to fade from the jungle, and Tylanna silently cursed to herself that they had wasted another day of travel because of her brother's foolishness. Thankfully Tahnir had reset most of the camp for them while they were gone, and he was now able to walk around on his own again. He greeted them as they entered the camp while he made the final preparations to get a fire started.

"Hello, my lovely savior! Tyl told me all about what you did, Akiye. I owe you my life. Thank you."

Akiye's pale cheeks flushed nearly scarlet, and she averted his gaze. Tylanna smiled to herself to see that Aki's childhood crush on her brother had not really dimmed as she had previously claimed to her in confidence, swearing on all the stars in the sky.

"It was nothing, really," Akiye muttered, bringing her hands up to clasp over her face. "I just did what my training told me."

"Yes, but I really do appreciate it., Tahnir said earnestly, his cheeky smile sliding from his face. "Tyl gave me a proper talking to when I woke up, and I'll be sure not to put you both through anything like that again."

With that, he struck the flint, and the kindling in the fire was set ablaze. He had created a small circle of stone around the fire, cautious of the many flammable plants that grew around them. They would not want to be the ones responsible for burning down the Jungle of Jiye.

Tylanna dumped her bag onto the ground and sat down with a loud thump. Even the short trek to bring Akiye back to the camp had tired her out. She was not sure how she would be able to walk all day through this thick jungle. She was mostly exhausted from the emotional trauma of the morning. She regretted how slow she had been to react and was ever so thankful for Akiye's cool composure under pressure.

"Akiye, would you mind showing more of your blade steps tonight? We do not have to practice for long, but I would very much like to use the light we have left to accomplish something today."

Their training had been interrupted by their stay in Nicol's Wood and skipped over after the confusion as they entered the Jungle of Jiye, but Tylanna did not wish to fall behind. Akiye had years more experience than her, but Tyl felt as if she was beginning to catch up to her. She supposed that she might have a natural gift for this sort of thing.

Akiye had just sat down next to Tylanna, but she stood up again, dusting off the legs of her pants. "Of course, though I am still feeling a bit jittery about that woman I saw crossing the path. But a little blade work may help me take my mind off it."

Tahnir stared at her with obvious confusion, but Akiye did not bother to elaborate. Tylanna gave him a look that meant she would explain to him later. Akiye ignored them both as she unsheathed two knives from the straps running down her long legs and spun them in both hands absentmindedly.

"Now, I will show you the steps with my knives, and then we will practice together with sticks. Ideally, we would use blunt blades, but this will have to do for now."

Without another word, she leaped backward from the fire pit and landed with a cat's grace. As smooth as a winding river, her body stretched and twisted, her blades stabbing and slashing some unseen foe before her. With each thrust she released a soft but sharp breath. She had explained to Tylanna before that controlling one's breath during combat would allow for longevity if the battle were to last longer than expected.

Tahnir sat watching her, mouth ajar. Tylanna rose to her feet and studied the way the woman's body moved. She could follow her every movement, but the trouble was recreating it when it came time for her to join in. After a few minutes, Akiye ended her routine with a jumping slash forward with both blades and threw them into a large root that protruded from the ground before her. She released a long, controlled breath and then straightened herself out.

"Right," she said calmly as she turned back to face Tylanna. "Now it's your turn."

Tylanna stepped forward and tossed a stick she had procured from Tahnir's pile of firewood to the tall woman. Akiye had the advantage in height, but she was built much leaner than Tylanna. Tyl supposed the little time she had spent in the forge had helped her pack on some muscle, at least a minor bit.

Akiye snatched the stick out of the air nimbly and gave an approving nod. With two quick movements of her free hand, she released the buckles of her straps, and her knives and their sheathes came free and dropped to the ground.

Tylanna, much less graceful, tucked the stick she had brought for herself into the nook of her arm while unstrapping her pant belt to let her father's blade, Darkender, free from its place on the back of her waist. For a moment she felt regretful about leaving the blade on the jungle floor, but before she had time to collect her thoughts, Akiye was dashing forward, stick held low with both hands grasping where the hilt would be as she ran.

Tylanna barely had time to roll her body out of the way as Akiye stabbed forward with a fearsome strike. Before she had even returned to her feet, the short-haired girl was swinging her stick downward across Tylanna's body. Just in time, Tylanna brought her stick up to parry, up and away just as Akiye had taught her. She used this opening to return to her feet and take a large bound backward, putting some distance between her and her instructor.

For a moment, they stalked each other in a tight circle, Tylanna desperately searching for any opening in Akiye's defenses. The only problem with practicing against your teacher was they knew everything you were thinking, and if you ever wished to beat them, you would have to come up with something they had not taught you.

Another slash came from above, followed by a flip of the stick and a stab that nearly took all the air from Tylanna's chest. She stumbled back, clutching her ribs with her free hand. Not letting up, Akiye used her moment of weakness to dash forward and stab again, at almost the exact spot she had just hit.

Tylanna saw the woman lurch towards her and let her instincts take over. Akiye's words to release herself into the stream of battle flashed through her mind.

Nearly adeptly, Tylanna spun out of the way of the woman's strike and used the momentum of the spin to crack her stick clean across Akiye's back. The stick splintered into hundreds of pieces in an explosion of wood and dust, and Akiye was tossed to the ground with a loud thud.

After staring bewilderedly at her hand, she dashed over to Akiye's side to help the woman back to her feet. Akiye waved that she was okay and propped herself back to her feet using her stick. She rubbed at her back with her free hand and let out a small chuckle.

"Damn, Tylanna, that was some blow. You caught me by surprise, and the force behind it was something else. I think we stop for tonight, what with you breaking a stick off my back and all."

Tylanna also released a laugh, and Tahnir shot up from his seat and began applauding.

"Incredible, Tyl, you finally got her! And what a swing it was! Now both of you, come sit down. I have some dinner ready for us over here. Take a break from bashing each other's heads in a moment and let us eat."

Tylanna helped Akiye over to the fire, and they all sat together and ate in peace. After a few silent moments scored only by the ripping of bread and soft chewing noises, Akiye spoke up.

"After all my years of practice with my father's blade steps, you are able to best me after only weeks of training. You really must have a gift, Tylanna." She looked at Tylanna seriously and then at the blade she had discarded from her waist. “I am certain once you are ready to draw that blade, you will be hard-pressed to find your equal.”

What Akiye said struck a strange chord with Tylanna. Why had she not drawn Darkender yet? She almost had in the inn with the ruffians, and surely she would have if she hadn’t left it on Carrot’s back in the cave with the strange creatures. But even when her father had given her the family heirloom, she had taken one look at the ornate sheath and strapped it to her belt as if it was the most natural thing in the world. Now she feared she would never have the courage to draw the blade, after building the thought of it so much in her head. She made a quiet vow that she would only draw Darkender for something truly important.

“I still think I could beat both of you with my hammer,” Tahnir goaded.

Akiye laughed, and Tylanna ripped off a bit of crust from her loaf of bread and threw it at her brother’s head. The trio ate and laughed together well into the night, almost forgetting that they were as far from home as they had ever been with no return in sight.

Chapter 13

NOT LOST, JUST LOOKING

The next morning, Tylanna and the others packed up their campsite without incident and continued their trek into the Jungle of Jiye. If their progress into the jungle thus far was to be any indication of how long they would take to cross, Artani and Helanái were certainly still a far way away. Tylanna and Akiye led Tahnir down the trail they had followed the previous day. He had insisted that he felt much better after a night's rest, but Tylanna could tell how much her brother still struggled. She had insisted they take more frequent breaks for rest and water, slowing their journey further.

When they reached the point where Akiye had seen the strange woman garbed in white, they stopped for a moment to look around. Tylanna could see no trace of a person having cut through the path on either side, but

Akiye had said that the woman had moved incredibly lightly.

For a short moment, Tylanna did feel a strange tingling sensation run through her person, as if she had been seized by a sudden cold. The moment passed as quickly as it had set upon her, and she noticed no further sign of anyone. She believed that Akiye had seen someone, and the fact that they could not find a single trace was deeply troubling. Perhaps it had been one of the magical beings that Reynalor and the other bounty hunters had told of roaming about the jungle.

Tylanna felt a strange mix of both fear and excitement at the idea of encountering magic. The stories her father had told her and Tahnir when they were younger spoke of massive creatures roaming the land, soldiers with inhuman strength and speed, and even the islands of Helanái being raised from the ground with ancient magic. The Sky Islands of Helanái had been flying above the Lands Below below for as long as written history recorded, so Tylanna had never attributed them to magic – it was simply the way of the world.

Soon the path seemed to fade away to nothing before them. Tylanna ripped at the roots of the plants that seemed to grow over where the path should lead but found no sign of anything. The trio deliberated amongst each other before deciding to just continue in the direction they were already heading.

Almost instantly, their pace was reduced to a crawl, each of them constantly having to stop to rip their feet free of the roots below. After nearly half an hour of struggling, Tylanna called for them to take a break, and Tahnir nearly collapsed to the ground in sheer exhaustion.

He guzzled the water from his cask loudly and then leaned his head against the tree behind him before exclaiming, “We’re already lost again, aren’t we?”

Tylanna scanned their surroundings while catching her breath. “*Lost* is not the right word. We are simply searching for the path to present itself to us. It will appear sooner or later.”

For a few hours, they continued blindly wandering and resting, never seeming to find the path they searched for. With any luck, if they only continued in this direction, they would at least reach a section of the jungle that was not as thick with greenery. Tylanna felt guilty that her survival training was not in the least bit helpful in this strange terrain. Before long, frustration began to bubble forth in their conversation.

“Once we reach the Sky Islands,” Tahnir asked, “what sort of welcome are we even expecting?”

Tylanna mulled over the question as she struggled with her jacket being caught in the prick of a thorn. “Well, I’m sure they will at least take us in once we tell them that we are Helanáian.”

"I, personally, do not feel very Helanáian," he said, the venom of frustration coating every word. "All we know of Helanái is the precious little Father included in his stories, and we only just discovered that he was originally from there! Will we even be able to convince them of our own heritage with what little we know?"

"You have your hammer," Akiye pointed out, "and the blade that your father gave you. He said that they were precious artifacts, did he not? Maybe they will be enough to prove what we are, at least prove that we are not their enemy."

"That's right, Aki," Tylanna chimed in. "I'm sure these will be enough to prove who we are."

Tahnir muttered about anyone being able to steal a weapon, but the girls ignored his sour remarks. The conversation did lead Tylanna to think about Those Who Serve, and that as a religious organization they really could be any person of any heritage. That fact was what made them so menacing. Just as they had encountered people such as Faleyemi and Xelina, who had secretly been Helanáians, the same could be equally as true for Those Who Serve.

When she was growing up, she had always found the stories of the Eagle and the other members of Those Who Watch to be wildly entertaining and interesting, but she had never taken them as fact. Her father had often remarked about the original meaning being twisted wildly out of context to suit whoever chose to enforce their interpretations of ancient stories. Tylanna assumed that Those Who Serve were just the latest in a long line of zealots who wished to impose their agenda on others, whether they were willing or not. She supposed that if she were to draw her blade for anything, it would be for justice against those who had invaded her home. It would be for Shae Glen.

"Akiye, what do you think of us being sent off to the Sky Islands?" Tylanna asked. Thinking back on the past few weeks, she realized that Akiye had been swept up in their father's plan for the twins, and they had never really stopped to ask her opinion. She, like the twins, was only half-Helanáian. Surely wherever her father was from was just as much home to her as Helanái.

"Well, at first I was just following along with you two out of some combination of shock and wanting to belong somewhere. But I do believe that the best place for all of us is in the Sky Islands of Helanái," she said, frowning grimly. "If there is to be a war, I think the safest place for us would be as deep into the islands as we can get. My father comes from Galedul, which I am certain would not offer us near as much protection. It is a rough land, and it is right on the border of Oromia."

Oromia was an expanse of desert and mountains, rough land for farming, or any sort of growth. The entire nation had only come into existence some five hundred years ago, far more recently than most of the others that made up the realm.

Tylanna knew very little about Galedul, but from what little Akiye had shared about her father's training, she believe every word about the harshness of the land and its people. She knew that it lay somewhere to the north of Eodisia and Artani but was not certain about where it began and Eyendor ended.

"Well, if Akiye thinks the plan is right, I will believe in it." Tahnir readjusted his pack on his back and pressed on, somehow revitalized by their conversation. His pace increased to nearly a jog, at least as much of a jog that was allowed by the rough terrain.

The women ran after him, Tylanna catching up to her brother and laughing. She supposed there was no harm in increasing their pace, as long as Tahnir could handle it. Both she and Akiye could handle themselves at this pace, and they might save a lot of precious time getting to Artani if they could run through the entire jungle.

She stared at her brother's back bobbing up and down before her as they ran. They had not run together like this since they were children.

Tahnir vanished from sight. He had seemed to trip forward, and then he was gone. She came to a halt as her mind raced, but just as she stopped, Akiye's body crashed into her back, propelling them both over the edge of the cliff. In the freefall, Tylanna saw her brother spinning through the air below her, and Akiye reaching her hand out just out of reach.

Together, they fell.

Chapter 14
DEEP WATER

From immense heights they fell, and into deep water they plunged. Tylanna forced her eyes to open. She frantically searched around her as she floated through the dark, deep water.

They seemed to have fallen from a sharp cliff face into a pond, or even a lake judging by the depth. She could barely make out the bottom of the water in the darkness, but she could tell that it was littered with jagged rocks from which grew all sorts of strange plants that swayed with the strong currents. That same mighty current seemed to pull at Tylanna, dragging her deeper and deeper into the darkness.

At last, her eyes fixed on Akiye, who was floating just below her, but she did not seem to be swimming at all. Tylanna let the current pull her and kicked along with it until she came up right beside her friend, who was unconscious from the fall and had blood seeping from a wound in her head. The wound did not look particularly serious.

Tylanna pulled Akiye's arms around her shoulders, turned both of their bodies around towards the surface, and began kicking desperately. Once she turned, she saw her brother swimming towards them from above, seemingly uninjured. When he reached them, he grabbed hold of both and swam alongside Tylanna as they fought their way against the current that pulled at all of them.

The little light that could barely be seen from the depths they swam in seemed so far away. *How far have we sunk*? she thought. With their combined might, they seemed to be making progress towards the surface, but she could feel that she would soon run out of air. She felt her muscles crying out against the strain, desperate for a breathe to rejuvenate them.

Their progress to the surface halted as Tylanna felt something coarse and sinewy wrap around her leg. She looked down to see one of the strange plants from the water's shallows squeezing tighter and tighter as the moments passed. Each split second seemed to last an eternity as the corners of her vision blurred.

The vine wrenched her towards the bottom, and she lost what little breath she had still been holding in an explosion of air bubbles ascending towards the surface. She was pulled free of Akiye and Tahnir, and she plummeted.

She looked up as her brother stared back down at her, his eyes wide with bewilderment. Her vision was a lot darker now, and she did not know if it was from the darkness of the water or if she was just losing consciousness.

Drowning never seemed a likely way for her to die a second time; she had avoided water ever since her accident at the waterfall in the forest of Shae Glen. There was no kind old hermit to save her this time. As she was dragged lower and lower, she thanked the stars that Tahnir and Akiye had not been caught in the vine's grasp.

There was an explosion of bubbles around Tahnir as something else crashed into the water next to him. Before he could tell what was going on, a strong arm wrapped around his chest, and he was being pulled toward the surface. He, Akiye, and the mysterious person who had grabbed him all shot above the surface, and air rushed into his lungs. He gasped as he spun to see who had rescued him.

It was none other than Reynalor Astilyr, the bounty hunter they had met in Nicol's Wood. Tahnir could see the shore from where they emerged, and he could just barely make out Fayde and Laito Nox standing there alongside a man and woman in patchy grey travel robes, each sporting shaved heads. Without another thought, he shoved Akiye's still unconscious body into Reynalor's arms and ripped one of her knives from its sheath.

"Tylanna is caught on something!" he yelled just before he placed the knife between his teeth and drew a deep breath. He dove beneath the surface without waiting for the man's response.

Once the current caught him, he moved with such speed that he struggled to keep his eyes open. Even as he moved, he could not see his sister anywhere. Deeper and deeper, he swam until he finally spotted the bottom of the pond. Though he could barely see, he could tell that he was surrounded by sharp rocks and other plants that looked similar to the ones he had seen grab Tylanna. The vines of the plants reached for him, but he slashed through the water with Akiye's blade, and they seemed to recoil whenever he got close to them. Yet no matter how many he swung the blade, more and more emerged towards him.

There. Tylanna — and where the current was taking him. The bottom of the pond boasted a massive hole, much like an oversized drain. It was covered in the thrashing vines that had grabbed Tylanna, and she was now wrapped up in several different ones that pulled her farther and farther inside.

After stomaching his fear, he swam into the current once more and plunged into the hole. He could only use his left arm to paddle, as his right arm was busy cutting at the plants. Few succeeded at intertwining themselves around him, but he was able to extricate himself.

Before long, he came upon Tylanna and ripped at the vines with his free hand while working the knife with his right. She floated unconscious, her mouth ajar. *She's drowning*, he thought. *I have to hurry.*

As he ripped the last vine free, he grabbed ahold of his sister and kicked against the current. It was so powerful here, but he did not want to find out where this water drained. Surely there would be no escape.

He thought of his mother and father as he fought. They had made him promise to protect his sister when he was very young. Before her accident, she had always been the more adventurous of the two, always getting herself into trouble of some kind, or landing herself in some precarious situation with no way out. Though she had hated to admit it, he was the older twin. To Tahnir, that made him responsible for Tylanna and her safety. He was not about to let her die on him a second time.

With all his might, he was able to pull them from the current, and together they began to ascend. The air seemed to be seeping out of his body. He did not have to survive as long as he got Tylanna to the surface. Akiye could get her the rest of the way to Helanái. If anything, he had been a hindrance to their journey through the Jungle of Jiye. He was sure they would do just fine without him.

Just as his vision began to fade to complete blackness, he saw another explosion in the water, and Reynalor dove toward them. The man grabbed both of them and helped Tahnir swim the rest of the way, and they surfaced. Tahnir was filled with energy as soon as he could breathe again, and he rushed towards shore with Tylanna. Akiye was awake and standing waiting for them, a fresh bandage already on her head.

Reynalor followed just behind them, and Fayde and Laito rushed into the water to help Tahnir carry Tylanna. It was only then that Tahnir noticed that the Nox brothers wore strange contraptions on their faces that seemed to cover their eyes with a thin, dark layer of amber glass. The man and woman in robes stood a few yards behind Akiye, seeming almost disinterested.

Together, they rested Tylanna's unconscious body on the shore, and Akiye rushed over to her and began pumping her chest with her hands. Tahnir stood back and watched with desperation, once again unable to do anything to help. She pressed rhythmically for nearly a minute until Tylanna spurted water from her mouth and gasped for air.

Tahnir fell to his knees, tears streaming down his face, not that it was not already soaking wet. He grasped Tylanna's hand fiercely as he smiled, so unbelievably happy to have them all together and alive again. The three young Shae Glenners sat on the shore , all drawing ragged breaths in between hearty laughs and comments of thanks.

"Well, now that you have pulled these soaked children from the water, might we be on our way again?" the woman snapped over the Shae Glenners' jubilation. Her voice was harsh and acidic, and much lower than Tahnir would have expected. "Need I remind you of the urgency of our quest?"

Now that he got a better look at the pair of travelers, Tahnir saw that each of their earlobes hung lower than normal under the weight of what looked to be two small white gems that dangled from small chains. They each wore an impatient expression on their faces. From her tone, it was clear that she would not have cared if all three of them had drowned.

Reynalor finished wading out of the water and walked over to the robed duo. "Give them just a moment. These are actually our friends from Nicol's Wood. If you would allow it, let us just make sure they are all right before we continue."

The robed woman turned with a dismissive snort, and the man followed suit. This was some sort of confirmation, as all the bounty hunters rushed over to the young Shae Glenners and helped them to their feet while checking to make sure they were all right. Once it was clear that they were uninjured, besides Akiye's cut and a few scrapes and bruises on Tylanna, Reynalor leaned in towards them and whispered.

"What happened to you three? How did you fall from that cliff? Were you being chased?"

"We were running through the jungle, quite lost actually," Tylanna answered as she hugged her arms to her chest. "And before we knew it, the ground beneath us gave way, and we were falling. We are lucky the water was below to break our fall or else..."

Stress wrinkled Reynalor's brow, as he seemed genuinely concerned for the Shae Glenners he had only just met, while Fayde and Laito cracked wide smiles.

"You are bloody lucky for that." Fayde laughed as he brushed his long black hair back away from his face, the corner of his mouth twitching in the strange, animalistic fashion that Tahnir recognized in both of the Nox brothers. "Something...off...seems to lurk in those waters. Don't like the smell of it one bit. But we did warn you about this place, full of unexpected creepy beasts."

"I heard you all hit the water and came running from the path we were taking. We had no idea it was you three, but I am glad we decided to rescue you all the same." Laito joined his brother's laughing, clapping Tahnir on the back.

"We are rather glad as well," Tahnir said, chuckling along with them.

"Now, will you all be able to find your way from here?" Reynalor asked. "You should dry your clothes out before traveling. All sorts of sickness can spread if you travel in damp clothing in this muggy heat." He looked up to the sky beyond the canopy. “The light is not long for the sky. I will try to convince the researchers to make camp here for the night, and we can help get you back on the correct path.”

With this, the researchers both spun around. Tahnir noticed their earlobes swinging a little more than they should as they spun.

“Make camp, already? We have hours left of the day! I will not have our business delayed for the sake of some vagabonds we have picked up along the way!” the robed woman shouted.

The man beside her rested a hand on her shoulder, attempting to calm her. “We can spare a few hours, Vistari. We have made much progress today thanks to them. Making camp now will allow us to make an early start tomorrow, and these children do appear to be in a bad state.”

While Tahnir did not appreciate being referred to as children, he was glad to see that the robed man at least seemed to be more reasonable than the woman, this Vistari. Both of them appeared to be around sixty years old. The man had coppery skin that seemed to be wrinkled from age and prolonged time in the sun. The woman was eerily pale, but still quite beautiful despite her apparent distaste for the Shae Glenners. Their robes and their shaved heads matched, but their personalities seemed very different.

"Fine," Vistari conceded, "but we will be packed and leaving at first light."

"Wonderful. Thank you, my lady," Reynalor said. His tone was extremely formal, just like he had used when he first met the young trio in the High Chair's Seat. Though that night, he had descended into a much cruder dialect the more ale and wine he had drunk.

The three bounty hunters set about arranging the researchers' tents first, then helped Tahnir, Tylanna, and Akiye with their equipment. Most of it had been completely drenched in their fall, so they hung all of their clothes on a thin line of rope borrowed from Fayde. They stripped down to just their small clothes and wore some spare cloaks of Reynalors. They were very oversized for Akiye and Tylanna, but Tahnir's fit nicely. Much of the food they had brought along was ruined, but Tahnir offered whatever was usable to the bounty hunters as payment for allowing them to make camp alongside them. The two researchers retired to their large tent as soon as it was finished being prepared for them.

As the light nearly completely faded away, Tahnir noticed that they had not made any arrangements for a fire. Hoping to seem useful, he began assembling any large rocks he could find in a circle pit at the center of the campsite. When he reached for the final rock to complete the circle, Fayde caught his hand.

"No fire," he said plainly. "Not this deep into her belly."

With that, he walked away and went about his business as if that was a completely natural thing to say.

Whose belly? Tahnir thought. Not wanting to upset their rescuers, he abandoned his fire pit and instead helped Tylanna and Akiye finish setting up their tents, realizing without daylight or fire they would almost be completely blind in the jungle.

Once they were finished, they returned to the center of the campsite and found the three bounty hunters stretched out around Tahnir's would-be fire pit, relaxing from a long day of trekking through the Jungle of Jiye. Fayde and Laito had both taken off the strange contraptions from their faces.

"Come, young ones," Reynalor barked out. He was holding a metal flask in his free hand, and the cork had already been undone. "Join us. We wish to hear of your time thus far in the jungle."

The three sat down to form a complete circle with the bounty hunters, and Reynalor passed Tahnir the flask as soon as they were settled. Now that they had dried off, the cool breeze of the night was quite a relaxing reprieve from the heat of day. The flask was full of a strong spirit that Tahnir had not tasted before, and just one sip had him coughing and gasping for air, which got a raucous laugh from the three older men.

The Shae Glenners took turns telling of their first few days traversing the jungle. Tahnir's ears grew hot when they told of his misadventures with the berries on their second day. The others just waved the story off as a rookie mistake, with several chortled remarks about watching what you ate in the wilds. Akiye's tale of the small woman in white drew some interest from the bounty hunters, and the three of them deliberated on who or what she could have possibly been. They eventually settled on the idea of a ghost of a dead woman haunting the jungle, which they claimed happened all the time before Laito flashed Akiye a reassuring wink that they were just joking.

The bounty hunters had set out the day after the young trio but took several shortcuts they had learned on their previous excursions to progress as far as they had, including scaling down the cliff that the Shae Glenners had fallen from.

The Jungle of Jiye was split nearly directly down the middle by a large chasm known as the Fracture. The Fracture was the beginning of the natural border between Eodisia and Artani. Reynalor told the young trio that their current expedition was also taking them up around the Fracture, though after passing around it, they would once again go into the deep jungle on the duskward side. If the researchers would allow it, Reynalor suggested that they all travel together so that the young ones did not go falling off any mountains again.

As the light faded, Laito began to play the kalalin he carried on his person. It was a soft and solemn sound, very different from the light and jovial tone their conversation. Tahnir was amazed he could even see the strings to operate the machine in this darkness but took it as a sign of Laito's mastery. The calming music rang through the campsite up to the canopy.

Before long, Akiye and Tylanna retired to their tents. Tahnir elected to stay up a bit longer, eager to hear more of the bounty hunter's tales. He learned much about them. Reynalor had come from Eyendor, the son of two prominent knights of the realm. He had struck out on his own at a young age to forge his way in the world and used his practical combat training to earn money as a mercenary and a bounty hunter just to get by.

On his journeys, he met the Nox brothers, and he took them both on as his apprentices. They had traveled together for nearly thirty years, defeating monsters and evil men. Some years ago, they had battled a large panther that was attacking citizens of a village, but instead of killing the beast, Reynalor had tamed it and made it his pet. He named her Amelie, and he often brought her along on their journeys, though for this particular mission he had left her in Artani at one of their many safe houses.

Their battle instincts had been forged over time in hundreds of tough fights with impossible opponents, but their time as bounty hunters had also led them all to prefer life in the wilds of the world. Their time in cities and villages was always brief; they usually found the complicated lives of the general public to be more of an annoyance than the simplicity of nature.

The Nox brothers, though they had been traveling their entire lives, told Tahnir that they sought to settle down in a permanent home one day. They joked that when the old man was ready to hang up his sword that they too would retire to live a long, peaceful life. Laito dreamed of writing his own music, and Fayde wanted to uncover the ancient truths of the world through research and study.

Tahnir envied their untethered lifestyle and found their sense of pride and justice admirable. He fancied that he could be a bounty hunter as well if he did not have to take over his father's forge. No, his adventures would come to an end as soon as this business of Helanái and Those Who Serve was sorted, and he would return to Shae Glen and take over the forge for his aged father.

Laito's playing came to an abrupt stop. Tahnir realized he could barely see any of them at all anymore. The darkness truly had settled.

"Those fools are striking a fire," Laito said. "We must stop them."

Tahnir heard the sounds of the three of them jumping to their feet, their equipment rattling against their belts as they stood.

"You two go. You know I can't see a bloody thing in this pitch black," Reynalor grumbled, and Tahnir just barely heard the smooth movements of the Nox brothers as they slipped away into the night. Tahnir strained his eyes in the dark to look after them, but he could not see their shapes at all.

A bright light erupted from in front of the researcher's tent. Tahnir could see the male researcher, whose name he had learned was Sumantoro, rubbing sleep from his eyes as he waddled away from his tent, holding a torch aloft in his right hand. In mere moments, the Nox brothers were next to him, grabbing the torch from his hands and extinguishing it on the ground. The last thing Tahnir could see of Sumantoro was a look of startled confusion on his face.

There were a few moments of tense silence. Tahnir rose to his feet, unsure of what exactly was going on. His right hand drifted towards his hammer. The bounty hunters had seemed deadly serious about extinguishing the fire, almost as if their lives depended on it.

After only a breath, the Jungle of Jiye came to life around them.

Chapter 15

ANGER OF THE JUNGLE

A loud screech echoed from all around them, as if all of the trees in the jungle were crying out in agony and fury. Tylanna rushed out of her tent to find the source of the noise and found nothing but darkness. The loud screech pinched off and faded away as suddenly as it had started, and the campsite was silent. She frantically searched the pitch black night for any sign of her friends, or whatever had made the strange noise.

She felt a strong compulsion emanating from her lower back. The blade resting on her belt seemed to be screaming out to her, encouraging her to draw it. While she had hoped to actually see Darkender the first time she drew it, she indulged the compulsion and pulled the long sword from its sheath. As she held the blade in her hands, she felt a strange blend of emotions rush through her. Excitement, longing, and hunger.

She gripped the hilt of the blade as if holding on for her very life and fought back the bubbling emotions until her mind was clear.

A loud yelp ripped through the cold silence that had settled over the campsite. Tylanna turned to face the sound but still could not see anything. She decided to progress towards the noise, taking sure footsteps, each toe searching the ground before it. Her arms trembled as they gripped the sword, but she felt more excitement than fear. She somehow knew that the blade would taste flesh tonight.

Shoving aside the strangely morbid thoughts running through her head, she inched forward as quietly as she could, trying to feel out the area around her as best she could without any light.

She could just barely make out the shape of Tahnir's tent when she heard another yelp, followed by what could only be described as a horrific, screaming roar.

She finally saw the beast that had set upon them. The creature itself seemed to emanate glowing white dust that constantly fell from its form, especially as it moved. Standing nearly twice the height of Tylanna, the beast was comprised almost entirely of thorned vines that formed a nearly humanoid cloaked figure. Where its head should be was a massive ivory skull of some large horned creature, some sort of gigantic deer as far as Tylanna could tell. While the vines seemed to wrap around the skull, they also seemed to be emerging from inside it at the same time. The glow surrounding the beast illuminated the area around it, and she saw a vine wrapped around the male researcher, swinging him about in the air.

Tylanna ran at the beast at full speed, surprising even herself at her lack of hesitation. She raised her blade above her head as the others around her exploded into action. She saw Akiye dashing out from her tent behind her, knives held outstretched in both hands. Laito and Fayde stood just below where the creature had grabbed the male researcher, and the woman – Vistari – stood at her tent with a look of pure horror plastered on her face. Reynalor and Tahnir were rushing towards the creature while the former began barking orders.

"Cut Sumantoro free! Mind the vines. They will be sharp! Young ones, stay back. This thing is dangerous."

Despite his warning, none of the Shae Glenners even slowed their pace as they sprinted towards the beast, though the Vistari woman came running past them, barely suppressing a scream with her hands clasped over her mouth.

Fayde moved first, pulling a white dagger made of bone from his belt and slashing at the thick vine that held the researcher. With a few slashes, the vine was torn asunder, and the bald man crashed to the ground. He scampered away from the monstrosity behind him, running on all fours before setting himself right on his legs and running away as fast as he could.

Coward, Tylanna thought.

Why she had had that thought was peculiar to her. How could she blame someone for running from a beast such as this? Surely, she too would flee had she not brandished Darkender in her hands. She did not feel that defeat was possible for her on this night.

As she approached the beast, the light exuded from the strange dust finally allowed her to see Darkender for the first time. The blade was as black as the night that surrounded them, and the metal was inscribed with strange symbols that she did not recognize, nor did she have the time at the moment to analyze them. She would have to get a better look in daylight – that was, if they survived this attack.

Fayde hacked at all of the outstretched vines of the creature, who had now turned its focus onto its attacker. The beast lashed out in a flurry of strikes, only half of which Fayde was able to block or dodge. The lashing vines left the short man bloody, with several large gashes littering his person.

Arrows pierced the vines of the beast from afar, and Tylanna glanced back to find Laito calmly releasing a volley at the creature, even as his brother was being ripped to shreds before them.

By this point, Reynalor and Tahnir had jumped in front of Laito, Tahnir brandishing his hammer and Reynalor holding a longsword in his right hand and a long dagger in his left, with the blade of the dagger facing the ground. Their position shielded Laito from the thrashing vines as they readied to charge to assist Fayde. For a brief moment, Tylanna was interested in studying the stance he was using herself. But the moment only lasted until the action exploded around them.

Tahnir and Reynalor rushed forward and swung their weapons to hold the beast back. They reached Fayde's position quickly and were able to pull some of the beast's attacks towards them. Tylanna soon joined them and cleaved through the beast's outstretched vines with ease, as if she was cutting through butter to smear on her bread.

The blade had always seemed heavy as she carried it, but it moved through the night air just as if she had been swinging a thin stick. The more she used the blade, the more her speed increased, the precision of her strikes more and more accurate. Though it was her first time wielding the blade, she already felt as if she was one with the weapon.

Akiye crashed past her and stabbed at the creature's vines wildly. The tall woman danced through the swinging vines with ease, though the concentration in her eyes was apparent. Tylanna noticed the bandage on her head was bleeding once more.

Just as Tylanna began to edge her way towards Akiye, the beast swung a thick vine towards Tahnir, Reynalor, and Fayde. Tahnir was just able to roll below the vine, but Reynalor leaped to protect Fayde from the strike and was thrown from the force of the blow out into the tree line somewhere beyond the light. Tylanna heard them land with a loud crash.

Laito rushed forward, firing arrows all the while, with a trained efficiency only years of practice could produce. "Brother! Reynalor! Get behind it!"

Tylanna had assumed that the two who had been thrown into the jungle were at least knocked unconscious, but Laito seemed to believe that they were fine. She supposed this must be just another day for them, not the deathly battle with a terrifying creature it was for her. She was fairly certain she did not ever want to pursue a career as a bounty hunter.

The monster lashed out at Laito, and he dove out of the way of the onslaught of thorn-covered vines, not without taking a few strikes to his legs as he leaped, each point of contact blossoming red with fresh blood. Tylanna stole a glance away to where Reynalor and Fayde had been thrown but could make out no movement or sound coming from that direction.

Just as she looked away, she heard Akiye cry out beside her, a vine wrapped around her wrist, causing her to drop one of her knives. The beast easily lifted the woman into the air as she slashed desperately at the vine hanging hung just out of her reach. Tylanna could see the blood pouring down her friend's arm, and rage ripped through her.

Before she could react, Tahnir brought his hammer down through the vine that held Akiye aloft. Though it did not tear it, the force of the blow brought the vine low enough for Tylanna to carve through it with Darkender.

The beast released another howl, and more vines sprung forth from the floating skull. They wrapped around Tahnir's hammer and began to lift it, and him, into the air. Vines flew at Tylanna from every direction, but she was able to slice through each of them as they appeared.

Laito's shout rang through the night. "Now!"

Without warning, Reynalor and Fayde leaped up behind the beast and grabbed hold of the horns jutting from the skull. As they fell, they dragged the skull with them, causing the creature's figure to bend inhumanly backward. Laito crouched and pulled various items from his pouches. He struck a flint against a clump of leaves and twigs.

Tylanna saw this and realized his plan. She pulled her blade back as she desperately tried to think of a way to free her brother from the vines.

Throw me.

The thought rang through her entire being as surely as she had had the thought herself. Without stopping to question the strange compulsion, she held the blade with both hands above her head and swung with all her might.

Darkender sailed into the night, turning over on itself over and over again, each rotation ripping through several vines at once. She heard the blade come to rest in the bark of a tree, and she spun around to look at Laito as her brother fell to the ground, now free of the vines.

Laito was just blowing on the sparks he had created to form a flame. Tylanna bound to where Laito crouched and grabbed a nearby thick branch and snapped it into two. The two of them lit their branches while the other two bounty hunters struggled to hold onto the beast's skull, and Tahnir and Akiye were scrambling back to their feet to fend off the next onslaught of thorns.

Once the flame had fully caught her branch, she turned to face the writhing creature. She ran forward with her burning branch and plunged it as deeply as she could into what she thought was the center of the beast.

Instantly, the flames caught and spread to the vines. Laito followed behind her and stabbed his burning branch straight up into the underside of the creature's skull.

The white glow burnt away with a burst as each and every one of the vines withered to ash. As it faded, the skull clattered to the jungle floor.

They had done it. They'd defeated the beast.

As she stared down at what remained of the creature, a hand clapped down on her shoulder from behind.

"Not bad, young one," Laito said. He patted her shoulder before rushing into the darkness, presumably over to his brother and Reynalor.

“Tylanna! Are you okay?” she heard her brother’s voice call out.

Cautiously, she felt her way towards the sound as she called back, “I’m fine. Is Aki with you?”

“Yes, she’s hurt but says that it isn’t serious.”

Tylanna made the rest of her way over to them without much trouble, only stumbling over a few roots and branches. When she got close enough to see her brother and friend, she saw that they were both drenched in a fair amount of blood, but Akiye looked worse off than Tahnir. He was supporting her with an arm around her slender frame. Tylanna put her arm around Akiye from the other side.

“Let’s get back to the tents,” Tylanna said. Before she could take a step, she felt a strong compulsion drawing her to the area behind them. *The sword.*

“Wait here for a moment, Tahnir. I need to grab Father’s blade. I think I threw it into a tree just behind us.”

With an affirming grunt, Tahnir shouldered all of Akiye’s weight, and Tylanna left the pair standing alone in the dark of the jungle.

She found her way to the sword without missing a step. The sword sat in the tree with half of its blade buried in the thick, splintered bark. The strange feeling drawing her towards the blade seemed to grow more intense the closer she got, almost as if she could feel all the blood in her body flowing towards it. As she reached her hand out, the feeling intensified until it subsided as her fingers curled around the leather of the grip.

She yanked the blade free from the tree with far less effort than she expected, almost sending her toppling over. Faint whispers danced in the corners of her mind now that she held Darkender again, but she pushed those thoughts away as she rushed back over to Tahnir and Akiye, sheathing the blade as she did so.

The pair had been joined by the bounty hunters. Reynalor and Fayde were each torn and slashed from head to toe, blood running freely from nearly every inch of their bodies. Yet they stood unperturbed, seeming only worried about the condition of the young Shae Glenners.

"We told you to stay behind," Reynalor stated sternly as Tylanna approached. "You handled yourself well, but a Hollowpod is a dangerous foe to even the most serious warrior. You all could have been killed."

"You're one to talk." Laito laughed. "You both look as if you've fallen through a thousand thorn bushes."

Reynalor grunted dismissively and put a hand around Akiye to help Tahnir carry her back to camp. She had grown paler in the few moments that Tylanna had been gone to retrieve Darkender, and Tylanna knew she must do everything she could to save her friend.

Laito shouldered his bow and moved to support his brother, but Fayde waved him away and walked by himself. Together, the bloodied lot marched back to the camp, some limping, some supporting the others, but all alive.

Chapter 16

IN THE DARK

When they returned to the campsite, Tylanna saw that Vistari and Sumantoro were standing next to their large tent. The pair wore stern expressions, but Tylanna could see a sheen of sweat on their foreheads. They clearly did not have much belief in the men they had hired to protect them, let alone the Tylanna and the others.

"Is it finished?" Vistari asked, her tone as biting as ever.

"The creature is vanquished," Laito responded. "But it only attacked because of the fire you lit. No more flames this deep into the jungle."

Sumantoro looked at his feet with a bashfulness that Tylanna found strange for a man of his advanced age.

"I am...sorry," he muttered. He returned his gaze to the injured group. "I thank you for your protection."

Laito met the man's gaze with a severe stare before releasing a large breath from his nose. "We have injured to attend to. Did you not tell us before that you are able to heal wounds?"

Tylanna saw a slight smile almost form on Sumantoro's face before he regained his composure. It seemed he was grateful for a way to redeem himself. "Well, it is not so much healing wounds as it is –"

"Enough, Sumantoro!" Vistari called out, placing a hand on Sumantoro's chest to hold him back. "We will not waste our blessings on the likes of them. They will survive. The cuts do not appear to be too deep."

In an instant, Reynalor had left Akiye's side and was towering over the woman, his bloody face glowering at hers. Tylanna was sure that the blood from one of the gashes on his face could have dripped right onto the woman, but she did not budge an inch.

"The 'likes of them' just risked their lives to protect you, even the young ones who had no reason to do so," Reynalor said with a quiet but harsh voice. "If you have it within your power to help them, I expect you will do everything you can. After all, the expedition will go much slower if we are injured."

Vistari bit her lower lip as she glared daggers at the hulking, blood-soaked man. "Fine, we will do what we can. Bring that girl into my tent first. She looks to have gotten the worst of it."

For the next hour, each of the injured took turns filing into the researchers' tent one by one. Reynalor ensured that everyone was looked after before him, even as he had to wipe the blood from his eyes to look over everyone else.

When Akiye had left the tent, she had still seemed to be fairly injured, but her bleeding had stopped. She said Sumantoro had just moved his hands about around her wounds, and they had ceased their bleeding. He had informed her that what he had done was extremely temporary and that they should still treat the wounds as if he had done nothing at all.

So, Tylanna ran to Akiye's tent to grab Xelina's medical bag. She began to clean and wrap each of Akiye's wounds. In truth they were not as deep as they had seemed in the moment. Tylanna felt that she might have just overestimated their severity because of the heat of battle and the darkness. Treating her friend was difficult without any light, but she made do. A few times, Akiye had to hold her wounds directly in front of Tylanna's eyes so that she could be treated.

Once she was bandaged, Akiye helped Tylanna with Tahnir's wounds when he left the researchers' tent and did the same for Fayde and Reynalor. Once everyone had been treated, Vistari came out to inform everyone that they would be retiring for the rest of the night, as Sumantoro was exhausted from whatever he had done.

Reynalor insisted that everyone should try and get some rest, saying it was good for their recovery. He volunteered to keep watch in case they were set upon again in the night. Tylanna volunteered to join him. She was certain she would not be able to sleep, and frankly, she did not want to be alone with the strange thoughts that had been echoing through her head. Everyone else trudged their way through the dark back to their tents.

Tylanna and Reynalor sat together at Tahnir's would-be fire-pit. Bandages littered his body, but he bore the brunt of the attack on his back.

"Had you seen one of those creatures before, the Hollowpod?" she asked.

"Not personally, no," he answered, "but I had heard tell of them roaming about in areas of deep nature. Ancient beings said to be manifestations of nature itself, far more common in the olden days when nature dominated the world. They are known to hate fire for what it can do to a forest. I have heard more stories of their appearances as of late. I suppose something may be awakening the old magic of the land."

"Is magic real?" she asked innocently.

He stared at her as if she had asked if water was wet. "Of course it is. Magic is just the energy of the world we all live in. You and I both are filled with unexplainable mysteries. There is great magic even within us. That beast we slew tonight had magic within it just the same as we, only arranged slightly differently. We are more similar to the animals and creatures of the wild than you might expect. What Sumantoro did to our wounds tonight could be called magic. Old tales tell of a land far more magical than the one we live in today. When I was young like you,

I supposed that the stories were just fables, fun tales for children's imaginations. But the more I travel, the more I see the remnants of great magic throughout this land, both that which is gone and that still weaves the world as we know it together."

She sat silently for a moment, processing what he had said. If what Reynalor said was true, she supposed she had encountered magic her entire life. She had always assumed there was something strange about what had happened to her as a child at the waterfall outside of Shae Glen, but she found an issue with attributing all of the mysteries of the world to magic.

"I suppose you are right. Though I think that Hollowpod was the most magical thing I have ever encountered, save for some weird little bat creatures we met in a cave."

"It was no more magical than you or I, though perhaps a bit more unique in today's age." Reynalor had a faraway look in his eyes as he spoke. "In my opinion, the humans of the world are spreading the magic too thin, and that is why we see less and less of monsters such as the Hollowpod."

"You are more right than you know, bounty hunter."

Vistari's cold voice startled Tylanna. She silently swore that she would stop being snuck up on so easily.

The woman gathered up her robes and sat down next to them. She straightened the fabric covering her legs and then moved her gaze to the two of them. "I came back out because I feel I spoke too harshly earlier." Her voice still had a chill, but Tylanna could hear the sincerity behind her words. "I wanted to offer my thanks for your protection. It is true that it indeed was our fault the creature attacked, so I should have been willing to do whatever I could to help, especially since you were hurt protecting the two of us." She looked to Tylanna before continuing, "Especially you three, who are not even being paid to protect us. Stars, you have wonderful eyes, girl. I hadn't noticed the color difference before."

In Tylanna's mind, she had just been fighting to protect her and her friends, but she was not about to tell Vistari that, especially not now that the woman seemed to finally be showing them a sliver of warmth.

"It was nothing, just doing what you hired us for," Reynalor replied. "I was more impressed with the young ones jumping in to help us. The fight may not have had the same outcome without them."

"Yes, you all did splendidly. That foul spawn of the Elk's hatred certainly seemed powerful. I doubt Sumantoro and I would have survived alone."

Tylanna's ears perked at the mention of the Elk. The Preachings of the Eagle describe the Elk as one of the Watchers who had a love for all things having to do with nature and growth.

"I would not call it foul. We simply brought what would destroy it into its home, and it reacted out of self-preservation. Surely any of us would do the same," Reynalor said in a level tone.

"While that may be true, an unholy creature such as that has no right to attack us, who enact the Watchers' will," Vistari muttered while folding her arms to herself. "We who serve the Watchers vow to always walk in their sight and avoid all things unholy. Beasts such as that have long left their sight."

Tylanna could hear her heartbeat in her ears. She clenched her teeth so she would not make a sound and strained her entire body not to run away right then. This woman – no, both of these "researchers" were Those Who Serve. Did Reynalor know this, and did he support them? Did he know that the Shae Glenners were on the way to Helanái?

"I thought everything under the light of the sun was watched over in the Preachings of the Eagle?" Reynalor asked coolly. "Though I cannot say that I am as familiar as you."

"There are many in this world that walk outside of their watch, which is why we complete our mission as quickly as possible and bring what we have found to the Maiden Rhiannon." With that, she rose to her feet. "Be sure you get plenty of rest. We will have a long day trekking through this accursed jungle come morning."

She turned and returned towards her tent, her form fading into the darkness once more. Tylanna released a long breath, slowly so as to not arouse suspicion from Reynalor.

"Are you all right, Tylanna?" Reynalor asked, seemingly not fooled.

"Yes...yes, sorry." Tylanna struggled to put the words together as she spoke. "I think the weight of the day is just finally resting on me."

He looked deeply into her eyes and nodded. Something in the way he stared at her told her that he knew everything, but somehow, she did not feel worried.

"Do not let what she says upset you," he spoke calmly, with a comforting tone. "If Those Who Watch are in fact real, they do not play favorites, no matter what people like her say. They watch everything equally. Humans will twist anything to fit their own need. Some will do whatever they can to gain even a scrap of power."

"Did you know what she was? When you accepted the job?" she asked in a hushed tone.

"I had my suspicions, but we take whatever work we can get." Tylanna felt her nails digging into the palm of her hand he spoke. "One of the few downsides to our line of work – jobs are not as easy to come by as they always were. Not many are willing to spend their precious coin on anything but themselves."

"Those Who Serve mean to start a war with Helanái, and any others that oppose their views. Will you support them in this?"

Reynalor pulled his eyes from her and stared away into the pitch black of the night. "I take no side in the conflicts of humans. War comes and goes and evil lives on every side. There will always be a new cause to rally for, and there will always be those with power who are willing to send people like you and me to their deaths all for their idea of right and wrong. To live in this world we live in, I believe that everyone needs to have their own moral code. Make sure that you do not lose yours along the way."

"And when was it when you lost yours? They are killing people in the streets all over Eodisia!" She jolted up to her feet, heat blazing through her veins. "I know war is complicated, but right and wrong seems to be quite plain to me."

"Sit down, girl, and I will tell you," he said flatly. "I will tell you of a time when I was around your age and thought I knew the way of the world."

Begrudgingly, Tylanna returned to a seated position. She would hear him out, at least. He was owed that for saving them so many times.

"As I said," he began, "I was very young when this story takes place. I left home to make my way in the world. My parents were both well-esteemed knights in my home country, but I knew from a young age that I did not want to follow in their footsteps. They lived their lives constricted by rules and the laws of the land. To me, they seemed no better than leashed animals, living at the beck and call of their master, willing to do anything in their name. I loved them both but knew that I had to leave.

"The first few years were the hardest. All I knew was the blade, from training I had been made to endure from both my mother and father. I found work as a mercenary at first but did not like doing violence in the name of the highest bidder."

Tylanna failed to see how that was much different from what he was doing now, but she let him continue.

"I was staying in this hovel of a place on an island to the north of Eyendor and Galedul, known as Drayalmor. I am sure you have never heard of it. All those years ago, the place was barely developed at all, just a few small villages here and there. I had gotten word of a village that had been losing children, and many rumored that a monster had been taking them. I arrived on the island and began searching for the village, asking around wherever I stayed. When I finally found it, I learned what I thought was the truth. The villagers were not losing children – they were willingly sacrificing them to the monster that lived in a nearby cave to satiate the beast."

Tylanna let out a small gasp, and she silently cursed herself for letting her emotions get the best of her.

"The people of the village did not wish to lose their children, but they saw no other way to keep the creature from attacking the village. When the first humans had settled the area, the monster had come nearly every night, killing indiscriminately. It was an incredibly poor village. They had no real weapons, nor defensive walls to protect themselves. So when I arrived, I fancied myself to be their savior, here to slay the monster and avenge the children the beast had already eaten, as well as save any children from facing the same fate.

"Some of the villagers pointed me in the direction of the cave where the beast had made its lair, and I was off to be a hero. I waited outside the cave for an entire day and the creature never came out. But when night fell, the monster crawled from his cave and set upon me. I had never seen its like before, nor have I ever seen anything like it since. It had a long body that was lean and tough, with two sets of arms and small hind legs. It moved about with the hind legs and the middle set of arms on the ground, with the top set of arms reaching out in front of it with long, clawed fingers. The beast was covered in black hair, yet its bones grew over the top of the fur and jutted out at sharp angles.

"But what scared me, what I can still remember to this day, were the eyes. Even in the dark, they glowed bright white, like two orbs of moonlight bouncing about. I saw the eyes leaving the cave first, then the rest of the beast came slithering out. It had a elongated head, almost like a horse's, but with a gnarly set of jagged teeth and a strange skeleton that grew from the outside of its body.

"Right away it lunged at me, slashing with both of its claws. I was barely able to dodge the strike by rolling away and spent nearly half an hour trying to make any kind of mark on the beast. Its skeleton served as impressive armor, and the thing knew how to fight. In a moment of pure luck, I was able to slide under the thing and stab wildly at its underbelly, which was not protected. Its blood poured over me in waves, and the beast collapsed, dead. The monster was slain. I struggled to pull myself from under the creature for a while.

"Just as I stood next to the body, still trying to recover from the fight, children rushed out and fell at the beast's side, weeping. Devastated that I had killed their protector. It turns out that the 'monster' was in fact caring for all of the children that the villagers had abandoned. This arrangement had been going on for years, and the oldest of these children were at least five years old. They could not speak, but I did what I could to gather them with me and take them back to the village.

"The villagers did not know what to do with the children they had thought were dead for years, so they decided to ship them to the mainland to be sold off as workers. Anything for a bit of extra coin. I begged them to care for the children. Many of them had developmental issues from growing up in the cave, but they refused and told me it was not the place of a bounty hunter to make such decisions.

"The next day, I returned to the cave. I searched the inside to find any other children. Sure enough, in the dark of the cave, I found two young boys, holding each other for comfort. They had not left the cave with the other children, and I assume they never had. The darkness of the cave was the only life they had ever known. I tried to get them to come with me outside, but they would not step into the light. So I shared my food with them. They were reluctant at first. The older one stopped the younger one from taking anything at first, actually. But after they saw me eating the same food, they took a few bites before retreating into the deep dark of the cave.

"I went outside and waited by the cave entrance for the rest of the day. Once the light had faded, the two children came and sat at the cave's entrance. After some convincing, they slowly crawled out to me, using their hands as much as their legs to walk. Like the other children, they couldn't speak, but I decided then that I would not return them to the villagers just to be sold off as laborers. I chose right then that I would take care of these two myself.

"Together we left the island of Drayalmor and came back to the mainland. Because of their time in the cave, their eyes could not handle the light of the day, so I fashioned them eye-covers that filtered most of the light and allowed them to see. I taught them how to speak, read, and write. Once they could understand what I was saying, I named them. Fayde and Laito, the dark and the light, I thought their names should reflect at least part of their stories."

Sudden realization seized Tylanna. Those two? They were so full of humor and joy. How could they have had such a dark beginning to their lives? She had sensed the deep bond between the bounty hunters, but she had not known that Reynalor was basically a father to the Nox brothers.

Reynalor stared out in front of him, into the darkness of the night. She supposed she understood them a bit better now and understood his general distrust of humans as well. She prayed that she would not have to experience something so traumatic to find her way.

A burst of laughter sounded from the other side of the campsite. Tylanna strained her eyes to see them, but she could tell from their voices that it was Fayde and Laito. They walked over to where Tylanna and Reynalor sat, caught up in a conversation about some inn they had stayed at in southern Artani.

"Good morning, you two! We thought you might want some sleep, and figured we would probably be better lookouts in this dark anyways," Laito said cheerily. "Unless... Tylanna, does that shiny eye of yours see in the dark?"

Instinctively, her hand shot up to cover her eye, and she blushed. "No, no, unfortunately, nothing such as that. Just a rare defect that happens to women in my bloodline."

Laito, either not detecting her embarrassment or choosing to ignore it, crouched in front of her and pulled her hand away from her face. “No matter. It is still beautiful,” he said as he flashed her a smile. “Do not hide what makes you different. Embrace it, for what kind of world would we live in if we were all the same?”

Chapter 17

THE LAST OF THE JIYE

Tylanna lay in her bedroll for only half a heartbeat before she was racing to her brother's tent. She shook him awake, keeping a hand over his mouth so he wouldn't cry out. Once his eyes were open, she hurried to explain that the researchers were the very same people they had been traveling across the world to escape and that they were going to meet up with someone known as the Maiden Rhiannon.

He ran his fingers over his healing scratches and cuts and grimaced. "What should we do then?"

Tylanna did not wish to seem cowardly, but she only saw one option. "We need to run. Leave the camp tonight and make our own way through the jungle. It will be difficult, but we cannot risk them finding out who we are."

Tahnir nodded, still shaking the sleep from his head. "I think you're right, but one more thing before we do anything."

"What is it?"

"I don't think we should tell Akiye that they are Those Who Serve until we are well gone from the campsite."

"Why not?" she asked incredulously. Lying to her friend was not an option, no matter what purpose it served.

"Have you not noticed the hate she carries? If we tell her who they are, I'm certain her first instinct will be to stalk over and knife them in their sleep!"

Akiye? Akiye kill someone in their sleep? It was impossible. What she had experienced was tragic, and she had to blame Those Who Serve, but it was not Vistari and Sumantoro who had come to Shae Glen and killed her family. Could she be pushed to kill these two just for being members of the same organization?

Tylanna ended up agreeing with her brother. When they woke Akiye, they told her that Reynalor and the others had suggested they leave before daylight because the researchers were still upset about them making camp with them and slowing their journey. Working together in silence, the young trio broke down their tents and packed their bags as quickly as possible. They were ready to move in only ten minutes.

They left the campsite while remaining as tight-knit as they possibly could. The morning's light was still a few hours away, and visibility was incredibly low. Not knowing which way they were going, Tylanna just picked the direction leading away from the pond they had plummeted into the day before.

Before they had made it very far, Laito and Fayde sprung up in front of them. The trio leaped back in surprise, but the Nox brothers gestured for them to be quiet.

"I think," Fayde whispered, "that if someone were to be sneaking off in the middle of the night, it would best for them to head in this direction, right, Laito?"

Laito nodded vigorously as Fayde pointed his left hand firmly in a direction the trio was not at all heading.

"Certainly, Fadye. Much easier footing and a more direct path around the Fracture, I think. Though I do think we will be taking a different path tomorrow."

The two brothers flashed the three Shae Glenners toothy grins and nodded a silent farewell. Tylanna looked to Akiye and Tahnir, who nodded in agreement, and they adjusted their course to follow the brothers' advice. Tylanna spared one last look back at them as they faded into the darkness of the jungle. She so hoped she would see the three bounty hunters again. Maybe they would be on the same side next time.

After several minutes of blind stumbling, they found the path the Nox brothers had described. It was indeed much surer footing, though the plants and roots still overlapped wildly under their every step.

After traveling along the path for nearly an hour, the path once again gave way to the fierce growth of the jungle. They slowed their pace to a crawl and climbed their way forward. Another hour of this, and then they stopped in a small clearing.

"Aki, I want to tell you the truth," Tylanna said after a moment of regaining her breath.

Tahnir shot her a look when she spoke.

"What do you mean?" Akiye questioned. It hurt Tylanna to look into her friend's eyes, knowing she trusted her completely.

"Reynalor never asked us to leave during the night. The truth is we found out that the two people they were escorting were actually members of Those Who Serve."

Akiye's eyes grew wide, and she rose to her feet. "You are sure about this?"

"Yes," Tylanna replied, again feeling the shame of lying to her friend, though she knew it was the only way to get them away safely. "She all but admitted it to Reynalor and me during the night. I kept calm when she said it but rushed to wake you both up as soon as I thought she was asleep."

Akiye nodded. Wordlessly, she pulled two knives from their sheaths on her right leg and turned back towards the campsite.

"Akiye, wait! You can't go back there!" Tylanna shouted.

Tylanna bounded after her, Tahnir following close behind. When she caught up to Akiye, she put a hand on her shoulder and spun her around. Tears were streaming down the tall woman's face, but her face was set in anger, not sorrow.

"They have to *pay*, Tylanna! They don't get to live! And we fought to *protect* them!"

She threw Tylanna's hand from her shoulder and dashed through the overgrown jungle floor before her. Just as the twins had almost caught up with her again, Akiye tripped on an outstretched root.

Tylanna's face was buried in the dirt before she even knew what happened. Groaning from the strain her body had gone through the past few days, she lifted her head from the ground to look up at where they had fallen.

Light pierced through the canopy above, brighter than it ever had in the previous days in the jungle. The three Shae Glenners had fallen into a large clearing, one that Tylanna distinctly did not remember passing. Even more surprising than all of that was what sat before them in the clearing.

A massive being sat at the base of a knot of gargantuan trees. In appearance, it was not dissimilar to a human, but was nearly five or six times the size and overgrown with plant life. The figure was positioned in a stance that did not budge, with one knee on the ground and the other raised close to the being's face. Its facial features were slightly different than a human's, much wider and stouter. Where the mouth should have been on the face was completely obscured by leaves and branches. The legs could barely be seen; they seemed to be buried beneath a mass of intersecting vines and roots.

Though its form barely moved, Tylanna could feel its eyes shift to regard them as she lifted herself to her feet. Akiye and Tahnir also rose next to her, the former brandishing the knives she held in a defensive stance.

There is no need for those, child. I will do you no harm.

It was as if nature itself was speaking to them. Akiye hesitantly dropped her knives and then returned them to their sheaths.

You have my thanks, human. Now, what is it that brings you to my home? Are you lost?

The trio stood silently. After a moment of contemplation, Tylanna was the first to speak.

"We wish to cross the rest of the Jungle of Jiye, into Artani, if we can." She added the last bit after a moment of hesitation.

Akiye shot her a sharp glare at the suggestion of leaving the jungle.

Very well. But the jungle does not belong to the Jiye. It belongs to all who still walk it. The seven of you enter, and the seven of you shall leave. As the last of the Jiye, I will provide you with safe passage.

As the being spoke, the vines and plant life seemed to ebb and swell towards them. When the tendrils reached them, they were shown a vision of the giant creature's previous life.

The morning had come once again to the Growing Fields. Grornot rose from his brief slumber and pulled himself to his feet. He stretched his body free of the aches of the day before, and then set out to walk the forest. Though they were all quite new, the trees around him already towered well over his head. They would dwarf a human or most of the other creatures that inhabited this part of the realm.

He walked alone like this every day, seeking any that might require his assistance. That was the role he played, the role all the Jiye played in this world. Using the power gifted to them through their blessing of the Leyline, he and the others had brought much life to this once-barren land. Now the Jiye patrolled the land, helping any and all that might pass through. As a people, the Jiye did not believe in countries or lines on a map. But they were known to take care of what they had helped create.

The Jiye craved all things natural in the world. The workings of humans were of little interest to them – how could something wrought from stone or metal possibly compare to the beauty of nature? Grornot had been born in a Growing Field much like this, though that field had been around for nearly four hundred years before that. When he came of age, which for the Jiye was around ninety years old, he and a group of similarly-aged Jiye and a few elders were sent to a land far away that had suffered from generations of drought and death. They were tasked by the other Elders of the Field to bring growth to the land and given the ancient secrets of creating a Leyline that the Jiye had passed down for thousands of years.

The travel had taken nearly a year. Once the Jiye had reached the center of the barren land, they joined hands and performed the ancient ritual that the Elders had instructed them about. Thus, the Revery was born. The Revery appeared like one large golden tree, but it was much more than that. It was the Living Leyline that connected their world to another, a world whose energy could be harnessed to make this world a better place.

Once the Revery was created, the Jiye that were responsible were blessed with several abilities, all of which they used in service of the land. From the Revery sprung a immense forest, covering the land in all sorts of greenery that had long since died out. The Jiye mainly helped facilitate the spread and growth of the forest, but also helped any that crossed their path. In ancient times, there had been war between Jiye and humans, but they now lived in peace. Grornot had never known war, only peace.

After they had created the Revery, all of the Jiye went their separate ways. About once a year, they returned to the Revery to once again receive its blessing. Grornot was on the way back to the Revery now. Though Jiye usually led solitary lives, he could not help but feel some excitement to see the others again. He had found much in his year away and wished to discuss his findings with the others. Humans had begun to inhabit areas of the forest, even clearing down sections of wooded areas and using the wood for building. They tore down the Jiye's hard work with no regard for the pain they caused. This would need to be brought to the attention of the Elders.

Just as the light had begun to fade from the day's sky, Grornot reached the Revery. The mighty golden tree stood as strong as ever, basking in the soft pink glow of the sky as the suns set. Each step he took seemed to fill him with new energy. He found it odd that the other Jiye were not already here. Their compulsion to return to the Leyline was so strong that they had all arrived at precisely the same time in the many years since they had created it. This beacon of unlimited potential was the most beautiful sight he had ever seen.

He placed the flat of his palm against the Revery, and pure power flowed through his body. Rivers raged in his veins, his bones. He pulled his hand away before he drew too much; even Jiye could only handle a sliver of the Revery's power. Any human would perish as soon as they touched the golden tree's surface.

Grornot curled the thick fingers of his hand together, forming a tight fist. He could do much with this power, much good, and much growing. Something pricked the back of his leg, and he turned his attention to see what he had come into contact with.

A human's spear stuck out from his leg, drawing a fair bit of blood for a wound so small. He raised his gaze to the thick barrier of trees surrounding him to find where the thing had come from but could not see anything. He pulled the tiny spear free and tossed it to the side.

Just as he did, he heard a loud cacophony of whistling air followed by the sound of metal meeting wood. Hundreds of flaming arrows had plunged themselves into his arms, legs, and torso. The fires had mostly gone out when the arrows punctured his skin, but he had to pat a few small flames away.

What was happening? The arrows had hurt, but they were no more than a minor annoyance to one of his size. Why were humans doing this, especially in such a holy place?

Pain ripped through his chest as if a sliver of his very soul had been torn free. He dropped to one knee, gripping his chest. Heat rose behind him, and realization dawned.

He spun around to see that the Revery was ablaze. He had been a fool to think that he was the target of the arrows.

But why would anyone seek to destroy the Leyline? He rushed to the golden tree to try and pat out the mighty flames that sprung up. He saw a group of humans crossing the barrier of trees with spears pointed up at him and the Revery. How small they were constantly amazed Grornot. As they got closer, they stabbed wildly at both him and the golden tree.

Each moment when his hands connected with the Revery to extinguish the flames, its power coursed through him. If he could just get all of these flames out, he would be able to turn his attention to the humans and try to convince them to leave the Revery be.

Where were the other Jiye at such an important time? All of them could quell these flames in no time.

Another rain of the arrows fell on him and the golden tree, and the flames were multiplied tenfold. Desperation wracked his mind. What could he possibly do? The Revery must be saved at all costs.

Humans stabbing. Flames spreading. Power threatening to burn him away. Jiye missing. Dying. He was dying. The Leyline was dying.

He took a deep breath and plunged both of his hands into the wood of the golden tree. Power and heat flowed into him as it never had before. He was overwhelmed almost instantly, and he collapsed to his knees, his arms still deeply embedded in the Revery.

Grornot released a scream as the Leyline exploded around him, releasing a wave of force that decimated all of the humans nearby. Growth exploded all around him. Trees and plants seemed to have hundreds of years flow through them all at once, and the humans that had survived the initial blast were instantly skewered or ground to death by the shifting plants. The ground itself split and shifted around him. Surely no one deserved this, not even those that would bring harm to the Revery.

When the violent growth finally settled, he found himself deeply buried in roots and branches. The Revery had lost its golden glow and appeared to be made only of rotting, burnt wood. It crumbled away from his hands, and tears streamed down his face.

He felt empty, completely devoid of energy. The Leyline had been destroyed, and it had been his fault. His body slumped, and he found that he could not move no matter how hard he tried. So there he sat, covered in the final growth of the Revery he had so dearly loved.

Tylanna gasped and collapsed to her knees. She saw that Tahnir and Akiye had done the same. Thousands of years had unfolded before their eyes. How long had that taken? The years felt every bit as real as all that she had lived before she had entered the jungle. Her mind struggled to separate her thoughts and memories from Grornot the Jiye's.

Fear not, humans. Once you leave this place you will have no memory of me of my life. It is one of the many burdens I must bear for my crime. Now go and remain noble in your journey.

Behind the giant, nature itself bent and twisted to form a clear path shrouded in golden light. Tylanna saw the darkness of night melt away as the path extended through the jungle. It seemed to generate its own sunlight, just like the clearing around Grornot.

The blessing of the Leyline, Tylanna thought.

Farewell, and may you find peace in your days.

Tylanna spared one last look to the Jiye. It saddened her to see him trapped there, forever alone besides the trees and plants that grew around him. Why he thought they numbered seven, she did not know, but he very well might be the very last of his kind alive today. She had never heard of the Jiye, or giant creatures that had roamed the land all those years ago. Regret pierced through her that she would forget all about him.

Reluctantly, she rose to her feet and led the others down the golden path, which continued to open before them even as they walked. She glanced back one more time just as the trees began to close in around the Jiye. As he was obscured from her vision, she offered a silent goodbye to the peaceful guardian of the forest.

Chapter 18

THE MAIDEN RHIANNON

Reynalor used the flat edge of his sword to move a large clumping of vines from their path, allowing Fayde, Laito, and their two clients to pass before slipping through himself. They had been traveling for four days since the young ones had left during the night. Their departure had caused a commotion the following morning, with Vistari demanding that they must be Helanáian spies stealing their secrets and insisting that they must be hunted down and killed.

Fayde and Laito had claimed not to see them leave, though Reynalor knew this could not be true. The brothers had near-perfect vision in the dark. Reynalor had insisted that he had argued with Tylanna in the night over something trivial, which much have caused them to run off under the cover of darkness. While this did not completely soothe the vicious woman, it did convince her to cease demanding the bounty hunters go “rip their tongues from their throat so that they may never spill another secret.”

Their journey around the Fracture had not been as eventful as their first few days in the Jungle of Jiye. They were now heading south, back into the depths of the deep jungle, just on the Artanian side. The researchers, who Reynalor was now all but positive were members of the cult he had heard many rumblings about as of late, were to be delivered to meet with someone they referred to as the Maiden Rhiannon in an area to the north of the Artanian city known as Fas Drüeth. Reynalor had been told they would only be paid if the two researchers arrived completely unharmed, which would be more than difficult if they encountered another creature such as a Hollowpod.

He had visited Fas Drüeth many times in his travels. It was one of the most prominent cities in Artani, second only to the capital of Fas Eith or the joint territory city of Aynanu. A busy place, overrun with aristocrats and beggars alike. Too much noise for Reynalor’s tastes. Though, most populated places were not suited to his tastes.

This job could not be completed soon enough. What that young woman had said to him in the night of the jungle still haunted him. If these Those Who Serve were really killing innocents in the streets, was helping these two cross the treacherous Jungle of Jiye in some way helping their cause? Though he did not believe in taking part in the wars of humans, he did not want to directly contribute to a force that had caused so much pain to so many.

Though the young woman had not said it, he believed that Tylanna and the others must be Helanáian, at least to some degree. He had seen her shock when Vistari had let slip her beliefs, and that would explain the pain he could see in the girl Akiye's eyes, as much as she tried to mask them. He truly hoped they made it the rest of the way out of the jungle unharmed, and that they then found safe passage the rest of the way to the Sky Islands of Helanái. Despite himself, he liked those scrappy young adventurers. Perhaps they reminded him of more hopeful days.

Fayde and Laito had seemed sullen to him since the young trio had departed as well. He was certain they had picked up on their secret heritage, so they could not possibly be angry with them for fleeing in the night. Perhaps they had just enjoyed fighting with someone else for a change. They were not quick to trust, given their complicated upbringing, but when they did find someone they both trusted, it was for life. Reynalor was certain they would encounter the three of them again.

As his mind wandered, their party had reached the tunnel they were heading to. Reynalor had discovered the tunnel some years ago when traveling through the jungle with Amelie, his panther friend. The tunnel burrowed underneath the denser parts of the duskward side of the jungle, which would shave days off their trip.

"Are we still not permitted to use fire?" Sumantoro asked nervously.

Reynalor did not like this man's personality, but he had helped him and the brothers with the strange healing process. Their wounds had never started bleeding again after and seemed to be recovering nicely.

"No fire," Reynalor answered gruffly, "lest we draw the attention of another beast like the Hollowpod. We move silently and without fire. The tunnel is not long. We will only be in the dark for about an hour."

To be fair, without Laito and Fayde, they probably would not be able to make it through the tunnel at all. The first time he had found the tunnel, he was only able to make his way through by keeping a hand on Amelie's back.

"I will trust you, bounty hunter," Vistari said as she turned to face the entrance of the tunnel. Her voice always had a bitter edge to it, but Reynalor did not sense any actual malice coming from her.

The party assembled with Fayde leading the way and Laito bringing up the rear. Reynalor positioned himself just behind the two researchers. Together they entered the tunnel and were almost immediately in the darkness of the earth.

The going was slow, but the surface of the tunnel was mostly smooth, with only a few roots or rocks here and there to trip them up. Reynalor heard Vistari mutter a few curses ahead of him, but he took it as reassurance that she was still moving forward. He nearly tripped once or twice, even though his footing was overly cautious. The tunnel seemed to be fairly more overgrown than the last time he had used it.

After about twenty minutes, they heard the sound of water trickling from above. That certainly had not been there last time.

As they approached , water dripped on them. The louder the sound, the more frequent the drops. When they finally came upon the source of the noise, they were all sufficiently soaked.

“Hold here,” Fayde spoke quietly, though his voice carried easily to the back of their group. “There is a small hole draining water steadily into the tunnel. The ground before us has turned into thick mud. Should we press on, Reynalor?”

Reynalor drew within himself to think. This water certainly had not been present on his last trip through the tunnel. There were not many large bodies of water in the Jungle of Jiye that he remembered, besides the deep pond that Tylanna and the others had fallen into. But he could not risk the ceiling giving way.

"If it looks to be serious, we should turn back. We can traverse the land above. It will only add a few days to our journey."

"A few *days*?" Vistari shrieked. "We cannot afford to lose another few days. We have wasted so much time already, and the Maiden waits for nothing. We carry with us information that could change the very course of history. If we do not reach her before she leaves Fas Drüeth, we may never get another chance to see her."

"Who is this Rhiannon woman?" Laito asked bluntly.

Reynalor sighed internally. It was not part of their job to dig into the particulars of their employer's plans. But Reynalor figured that Laito had the same suspicions as he and was possibly souring on the mission.

"The *Maiden* Rhiannon is a high-ranking official in our organization, one of the chosen elite. A very powerful ally for you all to make if you deliver the two of us safely. That is all you need to know for now," Vistari rattled off, the pride evident in her low voice. "I say we press on through the water and the mud, and out the other side of the tunnel as we originally intended."

The silence was palpable, save the steady trickle of water coming from above.

"What shall we do, Reynalor?" Fayde spoke first. He must have been thinking of the politest way to ignore Vistari, the young fool.

"If they wish it, we will continue to move forward. Move with caution, and allow Vistari and Sumantoro to place a hand on your shoulders. Avoid the water as much as possible." Reynalor dropped back until he could feel Laito directly behind him. "Let me hold you as well, boy. I can't see anything at all in this dark."

Together the group advanced. Water poured over each of them as they passed under it. Once they were drenched once again, they found the mud to be much harder to maneuver, each step requiring them to rip their feet free.

Just as Reynalor and Laito joined the others beyond the trickle, a deep rumble sounded above them. Reynalor looked up just as the crack widened, and a wave of water spilled forth.

Reynalor and Laito were knocked to their feet as the water crashed against their backs. Though the current was powerful, Reynalor did not lose his grasp on Laito's shoulder. He knew that without the other man's sight, he might never make it out of this tunnel alive. The shouts and screams of the others echoed in front of them. He trusted Fayde to be able to take care of the researchers.

Digging his fingers into the wall beside him, Reynalor was able to drag himself and Laito both forward, out of the direct path of the water being drained into the tunnel. Once they were free, they were able to pull themselves back up to their feet.

The entire tunnel was filling up, water reaching Reynalor's knees. He pulled Laito forward along with him and ran as the water crashed behind them.

“The others are running ahead of us,” Laito said seriously, which was very unlike him. “They were not knocked down by the impact. But the water is rising quickly.”

“I can bloody feel the water rising,” Reynalor barked to Laito. He then projected his voice to try and reach the others. “Run for your life, or we will be swimming to the other side of the tunnel! Run as fast as you can!”

As the water pooled below them, each step became a battle. Reynalor could not yet see the light illuminating the other side. He dragged Laito along behind him, hoping that Fayde was doing the same with the researchers. The water had risen to his waist.

“Reynalor, we should swim now,” Laito told him. “You don’t have to hold me. Just keep swimming forward. I’ll stay right behind you.”

After releasing Latio’s shoulder, Reynalor dove forward, tearing through the water stroke after stroke. Once he was swimming, he realized that the current was actually pushing him along towards the other side of the tunnel.

“Use the current! Swim!” he yelled as he forced his head above water. The current was flowing faster now. A few times, he felt Laito’s arms brush against his legs behind him, surely the boy’s way of showing him that he still followed.

He crashed into someone who was standing. He came to a halt, and Laito stopped swimming behind him. The surface of the water touched his shoulders.

"Bounty hunter? Is that you? Please help me. I cannot swim, and I lost my grip on the other one!"

The voice in the dark belonged to Sumantoro. *Of course, this fool can't swim*, Reynalor thought to himself.

"It is Reynalor. Grab hold of my neck and hold on tight. Laito is just behind us if you slip again."

He grabbed the man and positioned him behind him. Once he felt the man link his hands over his neck, he dove back into the water. While carrying Sumantoro's weight, the swimming was noticeably slower, but the current intensified. He struggled to bring his head up for air. When he did, he noticed that the water was now nearly to the ceiling. Sumantoro was pressed against the roof of the tunnel.

"Sumantoro! Hold...your breath!" Reynalor gasped out. Once he heard the man draw in a deep breath, he sunk below the surface of the water.

Panicked splashes faded to quiet.

At last, he could see the light at the end of the tunnel. With all of his remaining might, he thrashed wildly towards daylight. Just as he felt he could go no further, he and Sumantoro emerged out the other side of the tunnel and crashed into the ground.

A moment later, Laito followed behind them, sputtering water from his mouth. Once Reynalor had recovered his senses, he raised his head and saw that Fayde and Vistari had also made it out unharmed, just soaked and panting for air.

"I'm glad we are all unharmed," Reynalor said with a twinge of frustration in his voice. "Next time, I say we take the long way around."

As they dried themselves and their clothes, the rush of water that exploded from the mouth of the tunnel dissipated until it stopped completely. He supposed that he and Amelie had just been lucky when they traveled through the tunnel previously, which was for the best because she abhorred water.

Vistari appeared uncharacteristically bashful. "Yes, I think that would be for the best. I am sorry that I did not trust your judgment in the tunnel, bounty hunter. I will follow your every order from now on until we arrive in Fas Drüeth."

In about three days, they had traversed the rest of the Jungle of Jiye and exited into Artani. The terrain beyond was mostly rolling countryside with the odd village popping up here or there. They traveled through Artani for nearly two days before they reached the area north of Fas Drüeth. Reynalor noticed that the roads leading to the city were oddly empty for this time of year. Trade should be flowing freely from the surrounding farms.

Vistari and Sumantoro spent much of the days following a few paces behind the three bounty hunters, whispering intently. Reynalor could not tell what it was they discussed, but he assumed it was preparation for their meeting with this “Maiden Rhiannon.”

Fas Drüeth sat positioned between two massive cliffs that formed an easily defendable position for the city. They were instructed to meet this Rhiannon woman at the plateau that crested the top of the northern cliff. Both had easily accessible pathways, so the climb was not difficult.

While the two researchers lagged, still caught up in their whisperings, Reynalor pulled Fayde and Laito closer to him.

“Listen, boys, I don’t like the feel of this,” he whispered. “Keep your eyes open here, and once we get our coin, we are leaving as quickly as possible. Time to put all this Those Who Serve business behind us.”

“I agree.” Fayde nodded. “While these two do not seem particularly villainous, I have heard much about Those Who Serve recently. They are not a people I wish to support.”

Laito merely assented his head, and the three split apart to avoid suspicion from the researchers. Climbing up the cliff took about two hours. At the end of the pathway sat the plateau, and standing in the middle of the clearing was the Maiden Rhiannon.

She was a relatively small woman, garbed in all white with a few gold ornaments on her wrists and interweaved in her hair. She stood with her back facing them, seemingly overlooking the city below from the edge of the cliff. As their group approached, Vistari and Sumantoro rushed in front of the bounty hunters, as if they had been leading the way the entire time. Once they were close enough, they fell to their knees and pressed their hands and foreheads to the ground before them.

Reynalor and the Nox brothers remained standing, unfazed by their bowing. Vistari shot them a venomous glare before returning her head to the ground and addressing the woman.

"Oh, great lady of the Promised Dawn, the Maiden Rhiannon. It is we, your loyal pawns, Vistari Demaltrael, Elder of the Ninth Circle, and Sumantoro Yerl, Elder of the Twelfth Circle. We have come back to you as we swore we would."

Without turning around, the woman responded, "Have you brought what you were sent away for?"

The woman's voice was light and calm, but for some reason, the sound of it sent ice shooting through Reynalor.

Vistari raised her head from the ground and said proudly, "We have, my lady. The ancient secrets are secret no longer."

Rhiannon turned around, and Reynalor was taken aback by her beauty. Her skin was eerily pale, but perfect in every way. No scar or scratch marred her form, and her face took the very air from his body. Never in his days had he seen beauty such as this. As she turned, her cascading white hair flowed behind her with unnatural grace. He thought, judging from her appearance, that this was possibly the woman Akiye had described seeing gliding through the jungle.

She looked down on the two researchers, her gaze full of caring and compassion. "Splendid. Well done, my children. You have done the Promised Dawn proud."

The Promised Dawn, Reynalor thought. *Who are the Promised Dawn, and do they have anything to do with Those Who Serve? Have we been completely wrong about these two?*

The Maiden Rhiannon gracefully slid forward, as if her feet barely touched the ground, and placed her hands gently beneath Vistari and Sumantoro's chins, raising both of their heads until they met her gaze. It was only then that Reynalor truly noticed her eyes. They glowed with the vibrance of rubies. The two researchers seemed to shrivel in on themselves as they gazed into her eyes, overcome by the weight of her greatness.

After smiling down at the pair of them, she brought her stare up to look at Reynalor and the others. "These must be your escorts?"

"Y-yes, my lady," Sumantoro stuttered as he tried to compose himself. "It was only with their help we were able to cross through the Jungle of Jiye so quickly. They saved our lives many times."

"I see," Rhiannon said as she cocked her head to one side, allowing her expanse of shimmering white hair to fall over her shoulder. "Then it is a pity we must imprison them for what they surely know."

Without warning, Fayde collapsed forward as if he was struck by some massive force. Reynalor saw his unconscious body fall right next to the two bowing researchers just before he turned to see what had caused Fayde to fall.

A massive human in full ebony plate armor had snuck up behind them without making a single noise. The figure stood nearly three heads taller than Reynalor and was twice as wide. Their hands clutched a massive longsword that seemed to be coated in rust.

At the moment Reynalor turned, the massive figure had brought its blade back from striking Fayde and was already swinging it at Laito. The thing moved at an inhuman speed, especially for its gargantuan size. Before Reynalor could even draw his blade, Laito, too, had crumbled at the force of the assault and was lying in the dirt.

Reynalor readied himself as the figure reared its blade back again. Just before it could strike, Reynalor thrust forward and stabbed into its armor directly below the breastplate with all of his might.

Seemingly unfazed, the giant figure swung its blade once more, this time bringing the flat side of the longsword straight down towards Reynalor's head.

At the last moment, he was able to pull his head out of the sword's path, and the blow landed on his right shoulder. He dropped his sword, and judging from the shooting pain and the sounds of bones shattering, he would not be using that arm for some time. Leaping backward while clutching his right arm with his left, his eyes darted around, looking for any opening.

Blood poured freely down his left hand. Though the figure in black had only used the flat of his blade, his bones must have punctured the skin.

Vistari and Sumantoro were on their feet, looking from Rhiannon to Reynalor in confusion. He took little comfort knowing that they had not known that trapping the bounty hunters was part of the plan.

The massive figure dashed at him.

Reynalor only had time to pull his second sword free from its sheath with his left hand and hold it in a defensive position before the figure's blade reached him. When the flat side of the being's blade connected with Reynalor's second sword, he saw his own blade begin to rust, as if the mere touch of this creature's sword decayed the very metal. In a moment, Reynalor's sword shattered, and the figure in the ebony armor's sword came crashing into his ribcage.

He felt more bones break as all the air was expelled from his body. Black blurred the edges of his vision as he crumpled to the ground, gasping for air.

He cursed the Promised Dawn and Those Who Serve, and any others that might be responsible for this. As his vision faded, he saw the being in black armor stride towards Vistari and Sumantoro while they cowered in fear.

His last thoughts were of Tylanna, Tahnir, and Akiye. They had been right not to trust the researchers. He had led his boys into a trap, one which they might not escape alive.

Chapter 19
STRIFE IN SHAE GLEN

As Rynestian strode through the streets of Shae Glen, he barely recognized the village he had loved for so long. Since the attack from members of Those Who Serve, the once-quiet village had been in full disarray. Many were killed in the riot in the village center, including the Mayor Brayn Dantes.

After a few weeks of panic, the Village Watch met and decided to form a sort of committee to organize the rebuilding and protection of Shae Glen. Besides Rynestian, there was Darayk Yolu, Wills Emit, Saralh Rhys, Emili Rhys, Xelina Marcs, and Norantho Nartil that had survived the attack. The rest of the Watch had been killed in the fighting but had protected many of those who could not. Together, they had decided that they should send Emili Rhys to the Eodisian High Chair directly to request aid in defending the village.

She was the youngest member of the watch, only twenty-six years old. She and her partner Saralh had fought together valiantly to defend a group of children that had been cornered by members of Those Who Watch. During the fighting, she had received a nasty wound that left her right arm completely useless, and despite Xelina's best efforts, it had not recovered. Thus, it was decided that she should be the messenger to the Eodisian governing body, along with a few of the young men from the village to guard her.

There was no telling if Those Who Serve would return, now that the village had struck back against them. The villagers had killed most of the cultists that had attacked them, but few escaped with their lives and would surely be reporting to their leaders about the village in Eodisia that had inflicted such damage to their forces. But if they were to return, Shae Glen would be ready.

Rynestian was placed in charge of arming the citizens of the village, as well as teaching those without any battle experience. He spent each of his mornings instructing on anything he could about battle, from weapon combat to more large-scale tactics. Though it soured his soul to speak of it, he did have quite a bit of knowledge on the subject from his days as a general in the Helanáian army.

His evenings were spent in the forge, crafting as many weapons as he could as quickly as possible. He had accepted a few volunteers to help, though they were no replacement for Tahnir, or even Tylanna for that matter.

But he had managed to finish most of the order for the Eodisian Master General before Emili left for the capital, so arrangements were made to send whatever excess weaponry they did not need along with her, in hopes to serve as reason enough for the main Eodisian force's assistance.

With the new batch of weaponry, he focused primarily on quantity over quality. He meant to put a blade or a bow into every willing hand in the village. All in all, there were only about three hundred people that populated Shae Glen. Not counting the children and those who couldn't fight, they were left with just under two hundred fighters, or at least those who were willing to try. In truth, most of them had never even seen an actual sword before the invasion of Those Who Serve. But a foreign force coming into their village and killing their own was enough for even the weakest among them to want to raise a blade in defense and defiance.

Norantho Nartil was a hunter by trade, and extremely talented with a bow. He was given charge of training some archers. Before long, they had erected targets in the field next to the village center and were practicing every evening after Rynestian's lessons. Rynestian would often watch the archery practice while stroking his thick mustache for a moment of rest before entering the forge.

The rest of the duties of running the village were left to Darayk, Wills, and Saralh. Darayk had worked in Brayn Dantes' Mayoral Palace as his assistant, so he was very knowledgeable in the workings of the mayor's station. Wills was a stable master. Besides helping Darayk with the more tedious work of running the village, he also sent riders to neighboring villages, spreading word of their stand against Those Who Serve.

Over the weeks following the attack, many people from the surrounding villages began to pour into Shae Glen seeking refuge, or just as often a chance to strike back at the ones who had brought terror and death to their homes.

Saralh helped Darayk and Wills with the basic duties of running the village, along with helping Xelina Marcs run the sanitarium. Before she got married, she had been one of Xelina's apprentices, so now she was able to use her training to help. After all, Xelina had lost two of her most prominent apprentices in Tylanna and Akiye, and the injured continued to flow in from the other villages.

Each night when Rynestian finally doused the fires of the forge and dragged his tired body to the empty home, he pondered his decision to send his children and Akiye on a secret journey to Helanái. Surely, they would be safer deep within the Sky Islands, but the journey to get there would be perilous. It was an entirely different realm when he had made the trek from Helanái to Eodisia all those years ago, and with each person from a far-off village arriving with stories of Those Who Serve's attacks, his worry grew deeper.

But the twins were Tritelle's children, after all. They were more powerful than they would ever know.

Sleep became more and more elusive each night. They had positioned lookouts with horses along every conceivable path leading to Shae Glen, but he still feared that their enemies would be able to slip by unnoticed. During those sleepless nights, he thought of many things: his past life in Helanái, the many battles he fought as a part of their military, but mostly, he thought of his wife, Tritelle.

What would she have done in this horrible situation? Would she have sent the children away, or kept them close to try and protect them herself? Certainly, she would not have understood his vow to protect Shae Glen as a member of the Watch. She had always found such things trivial and constantly remarked that above all worldly bonds were the bonds of family. He so hoped that their bond would transcend this life and keep them together as their energy became one with the world.

After one of his many sleepless nights, he began his walk towards the village center before the sun had even risen. When he approached the square, he noticed something strange propped up on a tall wooden beam. As he neared it, he let out a gasp before a series of disappointed grumblings.

In the night, someone had taken Elder Prx's body and hung it from a tall pole at the head of the village. The body, now weeks devoid of life, had already begun to rot away, and her white robes barely hung on to her thinning frame in the morning wind. The black metal mask that Rynestian had crushed with his bare hands still clung to her head. No doubt it would be holding her shattered skull in place. He could not believe that anyone from Shae Glen would do this.

He went to work taking down the pole. It was a thick slab of wood that had been wedged into the earth beyond the cobblestone of the village center. He threw his body against the pole, and it only budged a little. He did it again and again until it finally came crashing to the ground.

As he walked to Elder Prx's sprawled body, he rubbed his shoulder, which would definitely be forming a hearty bruise already. When he saw her there, splayed out from its collision with the ground, tears flowed freely.

He had not wanted to hurt this woman. He did not want to hurt anyone. But seeing her kill Nagashi right in front of him had been too much. He had left his life of violence behind him, and he truly feared what would happen to him if he allowed himself to be overtaken by his rage once more.

Gently, he lifted Elder Prx's body into his arms and carried her away from the village center, each step sending pain and regret through his entire body. He placed her in the mass grave the Shae Glenners had dug for all the members of Those Who Serve who had died in the attack.

Wordlessly, he searched for a shovel to begin filling in the grave himself. Before too long, he had found one and went right to work. The sun had long risen, and many from the village had come into the village center to start their day. When they found him, at first no one assisted him, only stared as he worked. It was the mind of many in the village that the Those Who Serve who attacked the village did not deserve a burial, even in a mass grave.

After nearly an hour of filling in the grave alone, the other members of the Watch joined him, then many to do their part. Together, the people of Shae Glen shoveled dirt. He would have to figure out who had moved Elder Prx's body later.

After, Rynestian went about his day working with any who wished to learn the ways of battle. It seemed many of those he taught looked at him with a newfound respect for the way he had treated the corpses of the enemy, though a select few seemed to watch him with contempt in their eyes. He certainly still had much to teach them before they ever saw war.

Chapter 20

THE LAND OF SHADOWS

Tahnir and the others had spent the past few weeks traveling through Artani. They had made it out of the Jungle of Jiye without much incident. During their time in Artani, they kept a low profile, electing to camp rather than rent a room at an inn or find a place to stay in the many villages they passed.

The most shocking thing about entering Artani had been seeing the Sky Islands of Helanái for the first time. Though they had been told of the islands that floated in the sky their whole lives, finally seeing them defied all imagination.

Each of the islands was massive, large enough to house multiple cities. They cast gigantic shadows on the ground below, depending on the positioning of the suns. Much of the Artanian lands were often covered in shadow. Apparently, *Artani* was the word in an ancient language for the Land of Shadow. How high the islands floated varied from island to island, with the lowest being the one directly next to Aynanu.

They would have no choice but to take the main road into Aynanu now that they had gotten so close. There was only one path into the trade city. The three of them all agreed to wear the cloaks that Reynalor had given them in the jungle.

Whenever he thought of Reynalor, and the others, pangs of regret ran through Tahnir. He had trusted them and still could not believe that no matter in how minor a way, they were helping Those Who Serve. His dreams of traveling the land as a bounty hunter for hire were dashed, and he was left disappointed.

Most of that disappointment left him when they traveled down the main road toward Aynanu. This was what he had imagined when he thought of the great cities of the world during his childhood in Shae Glen. Even just on the road, there must be hundreds, if not thousands, of people milling about. Most of them wore clothing from different regions and spoke with accents he had never heard before. Even though the area was crowded, the mood was incredibly joyful and fun. It seemed most of the travelers were just as excited as he was about entering the great city. He imagined that the three of them could not possibly stand out, which helped his general paranoia about being hunted down by Those Who Serve.

Behind the gate towered the city itself, with buildings reaching higher than any he had ever seen before illuminated by the morning light. Aynanu was a joint territory split between Artani and Helanái, and the combination of the two civilizations' technology and craftsmanship came together in a glorious chorus of wonder and intrigue. The craftsman inside of Tahnir was itching to get a better look at all of the immense buildings to see how they were put together, both at a macro and micro scale.

Something brushed against his hip. He turned just as Tylanna yelled, "Your hammer, Tahnir! That thief just took your hammer!"

She pointed toward a man in strange green clothes sprinting away with Tahnir's hammer clutched to his chest.

Tahnir was already running as he called over his shoulder, "Don't worry, I'll get it back! You two stay together!"

Tylanna's objections faded into the sound of the crowd coming into the city.

The man deftly carved his way through the people in front of him, putting a lot of distance between himself and Tahnir. Not as smoothly, Tahnir had to utter nearly twenty apologies as he pushed his way along before he resorted to just shouting, "Thief!"

This cleared the way nicely.

Before he had even realized it, he had entered the city's open gate, and he was in Aynanu. He cursed this mysterious thief who had taken away his chance to really bask in the entryway of the city, but he would have time to do that later.

Once the line of people cleared before him, he was able to close the distance between himself and the thief. He speared the man to the ground with a diving tackle that would have made any on the Derby-Ball field back in Shae Glen proud. With the man pinned, he was able to wrestle the hammer free without much effort.

Master.

Ignoring the strange, whispering thought in his head, Tahnir turned his attention to the man who had robbed him. The man thin as a tree sapling, and the green cloth wrapped around him appeared to be some sort of gauze. The poor fellow must have not eaten in days.

Rather than punishing the man, Tahnir simply stood up and let the thief free. He checked the hammer before he pivoted. After a moment of searching, he spotted his sister and Akiye looking around worriedly. He raised the hammer into the air in victory.

Tylanna could just barely make out Tahnir's figure as he brandished the hammer in the air. He stood there like a fool in a pose as crowds of people washed around him. She was happy he had gotten the hammer back though; she did not think she could stand to lose one more piece of home.

A low rumbling rocked the earth beneath their feet.

Tylanna stopped walking to catch her balance and reached out to hold onto Akiye for support. She sought the cause of the rumbling, and as she turned her vision to the sky above the city, she found it.

For as long as modern history had been recorded, the Sky Islands had flown in the skies. But she saw with her own eyes that the island before her was plummeting toward the city below.

Screams sounded from the crowd and the city alike. The people changed course and sprinted away.

Panicking, Tylanna turned back to where Tahnir was and saw him gaping at the island above. He faced them, fear etched into his face, and ran, hammer in hand. Tahnir gestured wildly with his free hand for her to flee, but she was not about to leave her brother behind as one of the Sky Islands came crashing down onto him.

Without another thought, she fought against the flow of the crowd.

Akiye tugged on her cloak. "Tylanna! We have to run away! Tahnir will be right behind us!"

Tylanna ignored Akiye's cry. She could see her brother, trying to run along with the crowd, still so far away. The island seemed to be falling faster and faster the closer it got to the city. The impact would be devastating.

Before she knew it, she was off of her feet and being carried by Akiye. The slender woman was hauling Tylanna away from the city against her will. Tylanna cast a glance over her shoulder and saw Tahnir a moment before the Sky Island collided with the ground.

A huge shockwave rippled from the initial impact that crumbled buildings and destroyed everything in its path. She searched desperately through the chaos, trying to find Tahnir.

At last, she locked eyes with him. He gazed back at her, smiling oddly.

And then the building next to him collapsed, burying him and all within the vicinity.

A scream rose in her throat as the wave of rubble reached her and Akiye, and the world went dark.

Tylanna's eyes fluttered open. Dust hung heavy in the air, and light was already beginning to fade from the sky. Ringing filled her ears as she sat up. She looked around her and saw mostly debris, with large groups of people scattered around her. Some were moving, searching through the chaos. Others, however, were not moving. Realization dawned on her as she saw the carnage surrounding her.

Tahnir.

She leaped to her feet. When she did, she became lightheaded, and the ringing intensified. She stood with her eyes closed until it faded away.

I have to find Akiye too, she thought. *She was near me during the explosion.*

She opened her eyes and scanned the area around her. Her eyes stopped when she saw Akiye not too far from where she was. She was unconscious, and her left leg seemed to be pinned beneath a large rock. Her face was caked with dried blood, but Tylanna could not see any major wounds. The ringing returned as she jolted into a sprint. Slowing her pace to nearly a crawl, she made her way over to her friend.

My friend who had kept me from reaching my brother.

When she finally got to Akiye, she was able to lift the rock to free her leg without much difficulty. The only issue was the strain intensified the ringing. Beneath the rock, Akiye's leg was bloodied, and Tylanna could tell that several bones were broken. She searched until she spotted Xelina's medical bag that Akiye had dropped during the impact.

Tylanna went about doing everything she could for Akiye's leg, cleaning the wounds without water or alcohol and then bandaging each one. Then she fashioned a wrap out of the cloak she wore. The bone would have to be set, and it would be extremely painful. She was glad that Akiye was unconscious for what was about to happen.

She placed a small chunk of wood into Akiye's mouth between her teeth, but she still did not wake. Without hesitating, Tylanna placed her hands on the mangled leg. She would only get one chance to do this, and it had to be perfect.

With a swift, twisting motion, she reset the bone with a loud crunch.

Akiye shot up and released a strangled cry from behind the wood gripped in her teeth, which she had nearly snapped in two. Her eyes darted around wildly before focusing on Tylanna.

After removing the piece of wood from her mouth, she spoke in a raspy voice. "What happened? I was knocked out during the impact."

"I only woke a few moments ago," Tylanna replied, her voice emerging as a croak. "The city looks to be destroyed. I just set the bone in your leg. I am going to look for Tahnir. Just wait here ,and we'll be back for you."

At the mention of Tahnir's name, the little color she had drained from Akiye's face. "Tahnir..." Without a moment's hesitation, she began to pull herself up using the rubble around her as support. “You will not look for him alone. I am coming with you. Just help me find a stick to support my weight.”

Tylanna put her arm around Akiye and helped her the rest of the way to her feet.

Akiye kept her broken leg lifted from the ground, hopping in place. “You should bandage that gash on your head too, Tylanna. It looks rather serious.”

Tylanna had not even noticed that she had been wounded. She lifted her free hand to her face and brought it away when she felt the stickiness of half-dried blood.

“Later,” she dismissed, “after we find Tahnir.”

Together they hobbled away from where Tylanna had found Akiye. The city gate had been blown apart. Echoing all around them were the cries of the injured and cries of those in mourning. Tylanna tried not to focus on the noise or look at the dead bodies that surrounded her. She just had to focus on finding her brother.

Akiye was able to find a suitable walking stick without much difficulty, and once she was able to support herself, she told Tylanna to go on without her, and that she would catch up as soon as she could. Tylanna regretted leaving her injured friend behind, but she had to get to Tahnir.

She ran toward where she had last seen him jumping over heaps of destroyed stone and metal. On multiple occasions, she accidentally stepped into a pool blood. She tried to push the thoughts of all of the suffering out of her mind. When she did, she heard the strange whispering that she had heard when fighting the Hollowpod in the Jungle of Jiye.

You are still alive. Good.

Tylanna's head spun to look for the source of the whispering but saw no one. She did not have time to lose her mind now. Before long, she identified the building she had seen collapse next to Tahnir.

She saw no sign of him. There were bodies of those that had been crushed by the falling building, but luckily none appeared to be her brother. *Maybe he already got away*, she thought, *He might be searching for me just as I am searching for him.*

She took a moment to collect herself and allow the ringing to fade from her ears. Then she went about digging through the rubble. He must not be here any longer, but if he was buried and needed help, she had to try and free him. She felt a rush of energy as she pulled away rocks that would normally be much too big for her to lift. Her hands grew bloody as they scraped on metal and stone, but she ignored the pain.

Before long, Akiye arrived and wordlessly helped her. As they dug, the thunder of hundreds of boots running sounded from behind them.

Akiye turned, but Tylanna ignored the noise.

"Tylanna, soldiers are coming," Akiye said, her voice hollow and raspy. "They wear armor of black."

Tylanna took a break to face the soldiers rushing into the city. They were a mass of dark black armor and robes marching in sync. Now and then one or two would splinter off from the group to rush to the assistance of a survivor that they passed.

"They must be Artani's military," Tylanna said as she resumed digging. "When they reach us, we can ask for their help searching for Tahnir."

Akiye helped Tylanna with a particularly large rock. When they removed it, they revealed the remains of a woman who had been completely crushed in the collapse. Akiye blanched, and the sight and smell threatened to do the same to Tylanna. She fought the urge and moved to a new section of the collapsed building.

Once Akiye had finished retching, she crawled over to where Tylanna had moved and joined her.

"Excuse me, are you both all right?" a smooth and gentle voice asked from behind them.

Tylanna ceased her work to face the voice that addressed them. Before them stood a tall and gaunt man who appeared to be only a few years older than her wearing black robes with green gilding sewn into the seams. He was dark-skinned and had braided dreadlocks running down his back. The irises of his eyes were a milky white, but he appeared to see them just fine.

"My brother..." Tylanna said. "We are looking for my brother. He was right around here when the island fell and destroyed the city."

The man strode over to them, robes billowing. Without another word he knelt and started to dig along with them. After some time, he spoke.

"So you were here when the island fell? Did you see how it happened?"

"We were just outside the city gate," Akiye answered. "We just felt the ground around us shudder and then we saw the island fall. It only took a few minutes for it to hit the ground."

"I see," he replied. "What an absolute tragedy."

Tylanna noticed that the other soldiers had run into the ruined city. *They must be looking for survivors,* she thought. *Maybe Tahnir is deeper in the city somehow.*

Together, the three of them dug through the rubble until the light faded from the sky. Throughout the evening ,soldiers returned with any survivors they could find. Some just carried the bodies of the fallen. Tylanna did not slow her digging, even when she could barely see the rocks in front of her. The soldier that was helping them had demanded they be brought torches for light, but even that did not help much.

"I hate to suggest this," the soldier said hesitantly, "but we should probably take a break for the night. It is dangerous to continue this digging in the dark. If we pull the wrong rock away, it is possible we could collapse parts of the building that are being held up. We have put together a camp for the victims alongside our tents. You two would be more than welcome to stay there for the night, then I and a few of my comrades in the Night Legion can come back at first light to help you search again."

"I am not leaving him," Tylanna said flatly.

"Tylanna..."Akiye sighed. "He's right. We might do more harm than good at this point."

Akiye placed her free hand on Tylanna's shoulder. Tylanna had not even noticed her get to her feet, but she and the soldier were both standing behind her with sympathetic looks on their faces.

"We can come back in the morning and start again. If Tahnir is still here, he will be fine until morning," Akiye continued. "He may already be at the victim's camp looking for us."

After a little more convincing, Tylanna agreed to come along with them. The soldier, who introduced himself as Nuwitzwe of the Banéhûl, led them away from the wreckage of the city and towards the camps. He was a member of the Night Blades, a faction of Artani's standing military known collectively as the Night Legion. They came rushing to Aynanu whenever news of the island falling had reached them, but for many, they were too late.

The Sky Bridge connecting Artani and Helanái was also destroyed. Many in the victim's camp were Helanáians that had been stranded on the surface when the bridge collapsed. The Sky Bridges were translucent bridges made of a strange glass that never chipped or broke. One of the bridges breaking had never been heard of before, but neither had one of the islands of Helanái falling back to the surface.

As they crossed over where the city gate once stood, Tylanna's gaze lingered on the devastated city. She knew her brother was still alive – she could feel it. Tomorrow, she would find him, and together they would figure out what they were to do next.

Chapter 21

THE NIGHT BLADES

Before long Tylanna, Akiye, and Nuwitzwe arrived in the victim's camp that had been erected just outside the wreckage of the city. The air hung heavily on the shoulders of the people, and Tylanna did not see a single smiling face among those gathered. Most ate or sat in silence. Tylanna hugged her arms tight to her chest, feeling the emotions she had been pushing away while she dug through the rubble.

She fought back tears as the two of them were led to a medical outpost that had been set up. There the healers complimented her work with Akiye's leg and gave the girl another wrapping and a proper crutch. They then treated Tylanna's head wound, informing her that she was lucky to be alive after such a blow.

Once they were treated, Nuwitzwe escorted them from the medical outpost. As they left, they ran into a tall and muscular young man in fine black armor.

"Ah, Nuwitzwe, there you are," the man said. "I was worried when you did not return once the light had faded."

The man was just slightly shorter than Nuwitzwe, and still at least a full head taller than Akiye and Tylanna. He had a broad frame and smooth olive skin. His short hair was a bright pink color that Tylanna had never seen before. Two sheathed curved blades hung from his left hip. He wore a serious expression, but she could tell that he was normally a cheerful man.

"My apologies, Captain," Nuwitzwe replied. "I was escorting these two women I came across in the city to the healer center, then to their tents. I did not realize how late it had grown."

"I have told you not to be so formal, especially now that you are my vice," the man said, the sternness fading from his voice. "Call me by my name from now on, please."

"Yes...Pahlio."

Being informal with this man seemed to pain Nuwitzwe emotionally, but the man flashed him a smile that seemed to ease his tension.

"Thank you, brother," the man called Pahlio replied. "All of the others have returned, and I have dismissed them for the night. Allow me to walk with you, and tell me what you have learned. I mean to send a report to the other captains tonight."

Pahlio leaned to look around Nuwitzwe and seemed to finally notice Tylanna and Akiye. "Excuse me, in all the chaos, I have forgotten my manners. I am Pahlio Leor, Captain of the Night Blades, a sworn member of Artani's Night Legion, and I am at your service. I am so very sorry you were swept up in this mess, but we will do everything in our power to help."

"Thank you, Captain Leor," Akiye said graciously. "I am Akiye Komoto, and this is my friend Tylanna Desqen. We come from Shae Glen, a small village in Eodisia. We meant to flee from Those Who Serve's culling by escaping to the Helanáian Islands."

Pahlio nodded grimly as she spoke, while Tylanna shot an incredulous stare at Akiye. They had not told anyone of their intentions since they had left Shae Glen. Sure, these *Night Blades* were helping them, but Tylanna still found it far too early to trust them. She had trusted Reynalor, Fayde, and Laito, and look where that had gotten them.

"Many I have spoken with here have a similar story," Pahlio replied. "The tales of Those Who Serve's attacks are disturbing, and I will include them in my report to the other captains. We in Artani will not allow such injustices to take place, no matter what land they happen in. Did you two see what made the island fall?"

Akiye shook her head. "We just felt the ground shake, and then the island was plummeting towards us. We lost our traveling partner, Tylanna's brother Tahnir, in the explosion from the impact. We searched the rubble where we last saw him but did not find him. We wish to continue looking in the morning."

"Of course, I will send a few of our warriors with you to help with the searching. Any and all survivors will find shelter with us."

"Have you heard of anyone named Tahnir in the camps already?" Tylanna asked, her voice faltering. She found she had been holding back tears for the entire conversation and was glad that Akiye had been doing most of the talking. "He looks just like me, only a little taller and wider, and both of his eyes are green. His hair is cut short, but the color is the same as mine. He carries a large hammer on his person."

Pahlio thought for a moment before shaking his head sadly. "I have not heard of or seen anyone with that description. I am sorry, my lady. Feel free to search through the camps if you wish, either tonight or in the light of the morning. Our resources are for you to use, and we will do everything we can to help find your brother."

The four of them resumed walking, at a slow pace to allow for Akiye to hobble along with them, and Nuwitzwe explained all he had learned from the survivors he had encountered. He and Pahlio discussed plans for the coming days and what should be done for any survivors they found, and also what to do with the dead.

Tylanna did not hear much of their conversation as she was busy searching the campsite for any sign of Tahnir. She did not find her brother, just more sad and broken people. The other members of the Night Blades were rushing around, doing anything they could for the victims. She could see how tired they all seemed, and all of their armor and robes were covered in dust from a day of digging through rubble.

Eventually, they came upon a stretch of tents that had been allocated for the victims. There were only a few tents left, so Akiye and Tylanna volunteered to share a tent. They said goodnight to Nuwitzwe and Pahlio and retired for the night.

Most of their equipment and gear had been lost during the impact. The tent had blankets and a few pillows already inside, and that would have to do for now. Akiye all but collapsed to the ground, dropping her crutch to the floor. She slid herself over to the blankets and spread two of them out on the ground.

"Tylanna, are you all right?" Tylanna could tell that Akiye knew her pain. Though Akiye didn't meet her eyes, she could tell from the quiver in her voice that she was holding back tears herself.

Tylanna took a moment before answering, dropping to her knees and arranging the pillows. "I will be fine. We will find Tahnir tomorrow, and once we are all reunited, we can decide what we should do."

"Tylanna...you saw that building just the same as me. And that woman..." Her voice trailed off as she bit back a whimper.

Tylanna turned to face her, and she saw that the woman was lying down staring at the ceiling with tears welling in her eyes. "We will find him," Tylanna answered. "Even if he's hurt, we can heal him together."

"But he might be more than hurt, Tylanna!" Akiye yelled.

Tylanna was taken aback by Akiye's outburst. The woman had never yelled at her before in their whole friendship.

"People die," Akiye went on, "even family. You have to accept that he might be gone. We need to figure out what we're going to do, even if it's just the two of us."

"He is not dead," Tylanna asserted, her tone no longer gentle and hopeful. "I am telling you that he still lives. We will be together again."

Tylanna stormed out, leaving behind a litany of objections from Akiye. Before she knew it, she was walking through the rows of tents. Most of the people had returned to their tents, but she came across Nuwitzwe sitting alone in the dirt, stoking a fire pit with a stick. He did not turn his head when she stalked over and sat beside him.

"You could not sleep either?" he asked.

Tylanna looked into the fire for a moment before responding, "No, not while my brother may still be out there."

"I figured as much. You will see him again. I can feel it within me." His voice was calm and reassuring. The smoke from the fire billowed out around them into the night sky, and Tylanna did not find the smell off-putting.

"How can you tell?" she asked, looking for any reassurance of what she already believed.

"It is just a feeling. I can do much, but even I cannot tell the future for certain. But I feel very strongly that the two of you will be reunited once more."

"Thank you, Nuwitzwe." She did feel comforted by his words, and it was precisely what she needed to hear after Akiye's harshness. "So, what brought you to fight with the Night Legion?"

"Well, I am one of the Banéhûl, as I said before," Nuwitzwe replied after a short pause. It seemed he had not expected her to ask about his past. "I am one of the few in the modern generation who was born on the island. I left the island when I was thirteen years old and came to Artani. My time on the island imparted me with certain gifts that made me a powerful warrior, and in one of my first weeks in Artani, I was attacked by a group of thieves. I had very little to steal, save the clothes I wore, a bag of soil from my homeland, and this ring I am wearing here."

Tylanna looked at his hand. He was rubbing a ring with a large emerald set in a silver band. From what she had heard of Banéhûl, it was an unlivable island to the south of Eodisia. She had no idea that people still lived there, but she had heard of the descendants of those born there referred to as a "wandering nation" or a "people without a land."

"While I fought the thieves off," Nuwitzwe went on, "some soldiers saw what was happening and rushed over to help me. By the time they had reached me, I had already knocked all of the thieves unconscious. The soldiers were so impressed that they offered me a place in their training academy. One of those soldiers was Captain Pahlio's father, Nero Leor, who is now one of the most prominent captains in the entire Night Legion. From then on, he was like a father to me, and I met Pahlio at the training academy. We have been friends ever since, and it was only recently that he was raised to captain and I was made his vice. This is one of our first assignments as the Night Blades."

"What of your real parents?" Tylanna asked. His story was amazing – alone without a real family at thirteen. Tylanna wondered how she would have fared in the same situation.

"The true Banéhûl never know their parents. Those born on the island are made to fend for themselves until they are able to leave of their own volition. I was lucky that some older children cared for me through infancy, but as soon as I could walk, I learned to collect food and protect myself. The island of Banéhûl is a brutal place, and it is extremely difficult to survive. But my time there made me powerful, so I do not regret it at all. You too, know of power. I saw you when you were digging through the rubble, and you are much stronger than you appear. I see you carry a blade on your person. Have you ever thought of drawing to defend the less fortunate? Those without the strength to defend themselves?"

Tylanna's hand drifted to Darkender's hilt, and she fingered the pommel. "I have not, to be honest. For the most part, I have been too worried about protecting myself, my family, and my friends."

"Well, think on it, Tylanna Desqen," he said as he rose to his feet. "There is a whole world out there that needs protecting, and we could use the help of someone as strong as you. I must be going if I am to have any sleep tonight, but I will see you in the morning. Meet me here at first light, and we will look for your brother together."

He threw his stick into the fire, and it burnt away in the flames that he had fully resurrected while he spoke. Tylanna sat for a while longer before returning to the tent.

Akiye was already asleep. Tylanna was thankful, as she did not feel like talking to the woman again. She lay down, trying to make herself comfortable. Once she was staring at the ceiling of the tent, she realized just how tired she was. As she faded to sleep, her last thoughts were of her brother, smiling.

She stood on a beach of black sand. The suns were rising over the vast ocean, and she could see the waves crashing on the shore. It had been a while since she had dreamt, and one look at her hand confirmed that she had once again taken the form of the strange being made of what appeared to be pure, burning energy.

She strode towards the water, moving as if she and the ground below her were both soaring at insane speeds. As she approached the water, she felt her form shift. She dove into the waves, and her body elongated, growing as she worked her way through the current of the sea. Her body slid through the water easily, her skin smooth, and her form worked its way forward in a way that felt unnatural to her. She crossed an entire ocean in almost no time at all. She came to the beach on the opposite side, and she felt herself return to her former form, one of a humanoid shape.

As she ran up the beach, she saw another of her kind. This form was humanoid, but from its back sprouted several arms that appeared to reach forward until they met with nothingness, disappearing as if cut from a certain point. She moved until she stood right behind the other form, but it did not turn to face her.

A loud cry of anger emanated from her, and the other shape spun around to face her.

As it did, the extra arms appeared to slide out from their invisible pockets of air and become whole again. The form spread its arms wide and released a vicious scream back at her, and she fell backward into the sand. The being stepped until it crouched directly on top of her form. Its many arms lashed at her while it screamed once more.

Chapter 22

BLOOD IN THE STREETS

Rynestian pressed his back against the hard wooden wall behind him. He had climbed over a fence and hid behind the firm planks of wood, silently cursing his luck.

They were not supposed to return this early.

The people of Shae Glen were not yet ready to fight off the invaders, especially not the insanely large force they had brought with them this time. Emili Rhys had not yet returned from her trip to the Eodisian capital, and they had not the men nor the equipment to take on the enemy that faced them.

Rynestian slid his bladed gauntlets onto his hands as quietly as possible. He was wearing the fine armor he used to wear as a general of the Helanáian forces, which covered the majority of his chest and his torso but left openings on both sides to allow for unrestricted movement. His shoulders and upper arms were also left bare so he might swing the gauntlets freely. The gauntlets and armor had served him well in his past, and he would make sure he drew blood once more before he fell.

Those Who Serve had been seen marching with a massive force down one of the main roads leading to Shae Glen in the early morning, and if they continued to pass the village, the road they traveled went on to lead straight to the Eodisian capital. This was not a group of soldiers to put down a small-time rebellion in a village. This was an army ready to lay siege to an entire country. Shae Glen must be a stop along the way for them. At the head of the marching troop was a huge carriage being pulled by a team of eight horses.

As soon as the messenger that they had positioned to watch the road arrived in the village, what was left of the Village Watch did everything to organize the chaos of people. Saralh Rhys and Xelina Marcs led the elderly and the children into the forest, hoping that the invaders would not bother to chase after those who could not fight.

Rynestian, Darayk Yolu, Wills Emit, and Norantho Nartil were left behind to defend the village, as they had sworn to do those many years ago. There had been so many more of the Village Watch back then, but the four of them were all that remained. Darayk and Wills had not had time to get much training from Rynestian or Norantho, so he hoped they would be all right. When they had sworn their oaths of protection, he was certain that they all envisioned something much different than what they were about to encounter.

The plan had been to let Those Who Serve pour into the streets of Shae Glen, and then once their forces were stretched as thin as possible, those who were left to defend would leap out of their hiding spots and launch an attack from the rear. He hoped that they would stand a chance, but after hearing the size of the force that was coming for them, Rynestian did not believe that any of them would live to see morning.

The sound of boots and hooves on the cobblestone had begun to echo through the village. Every precaution had been taken to make it appear as if the village was abandoned.

Before the sound of the approaching army had reached his position, Rynestian smelled smoke. It grew stronger and acrider as the moments passed.

Anger surged through him. He could not believe they would resort to burning the homes and shops that made up Shae Glen, many of which he had helped build himself. He did not hear the sound of combat yet, so no one's position had been compromised. His hands gripped tightly inside the gauntlets as he let rage fill him.

The thundering of steps and hooves finally sounded from beyond the fence Rynestian was hiding behind. He felt his breath catch in his throat as they passed. The sound did not seem to fade, only continue. Their force must truly be massive. Fear trickled past the rage that consumed him, but he pushed it away. There was no time for fear, only justice.

A large bottle filled with some sort of thick oil crashed into the house next to him and released a foul explosion of dark orange flames. As the house was set alight, he wondered how long he would be able to hide behind the fence. If nothing was done, the fence too would burn. A lone glance upward revealed that the sky above Shae Glen was black with smoke.

Crouching, he sent out a silent prayer. He was not a religious man, but if anyone would listen to his prayer, he would have them. He wished for the safety of his children and Akiye on their journey, and he wished that if he were to die today that he be rejoined with Tritelle.

Just as the flames licked at the fence next to him, he heard a cry go up from somewhere in the village.

"SHAE GLEN! TO WAR!"

Battle exploded all across the village. A hail of arrows cut through the blackened sky and rained death on the members of Those Who Serve. Shae Glenners leaped free of their hiding spots and began slashing into the surprised troops before they had a chance to react.

Rynestian barreled through the burning fence, which itself crashed into nearly four soldiers, knocking them to the ground. Their fellows nearby turned and looked wildly at the big man just in time for his bladed fist to meet with each of their unguarded faces.

One went down, then two, then three. They fell before him in waves.

He saw the other warriors of Shae Glen crashing into the enemy line all around him. These first few moments were crucial to the plan. The Shae Glenners must inflict as much damage as they possibly could in these first moments of the battle, or else all would be for naught.

As the soldiers turned to defend themselves, Rynestian still found those before him to be no more than easy targets. It was all coming back to him now, all those years of training, all those years living in his brother's shadow until he was finally able to prove himself on the battlefield. The battlefield was where he ruled, where he was king.

As he tore through the enemies that were unlucky enough to be set before him, he let up a cry.

"Shae Glenners, to me!"

He figured that he would have a better chance of protecting the young ones he had trained if they stuck as close to him as possible. Before long, the far-off sounds of combat echoing around him shifted towards him, and the young Shae Glenners, along with Wills Emit, came rushing towards him.

Just behind them followed another troop of Those Who Serve. Not wanting them to get pinned by two different groups of soldiers, Rynestian led the Shae Glenners down a narrow side street. If Those Who Serve followed, it would force them to funnel their people, and they would lose the advantage of numbers.

Once he saw that all the Shae Glenners had followed, he positioned himself at the head of the group, ready to face the waves of soldiers that were to come. Wills Emit bravely stood next to him, swinging his bloodstained sword through the air wildly, shouting a string of profanity at the invaders that Rynestian had certainly never heard from the kindhearted man.

Sure enough, the soldiers of Those Who Serve began to pour down the side street. Rynestian made short work of the first few, but the soldiers behind them realized that they would meet the same fate and allowed a few others past them that held long spears.

They did not have many shields in their arsenal in Shae Glen, but there were a few behind Rynestian that dashed forward to block the spearpoints.

Not wanting to be shown up by the young ones he had trained himself, Rynestian turned his body to the side and allowed a spear to pass by him. He then looped his arm around the spear and shattered the wooden shaft with a hard thrust downward. The man holding the spear stumbled forward, and Rynestian caught his exposed chin with a clean upward swing that sent the soldier's body flying backward into his comrades.

Though the battle seemed to move in slower-than-real-time for Rynestian, they held their position for nearly an hour. A few of the young ones fell, and Wills took a nasty slash across his face that seemed to be pouring blood as if from a faucet. Rynestian had taken a few glancing strikes in order to gain a more advantageous position to work his gauntlets closer to his target, but none of them were serious. He could barely feel them at all in the heat of battle.

Eventually, they advanced from their position on the narrow street when the soldiers of Those Who Serve refused to give chase. The Shae Glenners crashed into the main road and met with another group of villagers who were attacking from the other side. Rynestian saw Norantho Nartil and his young hunters on the rooftops above them, still loosing arrows deftly into the enemy even while flames danced around them.

When he followed Norantho's trajectory, he saw that the man was aiming just for the enemy archers, leaving the martial combat to those on the ground. Rynestian had been wondering why no arrows were coming at them in the air, but his old friend seemed to be taking care of that issue. Before long, they would eventually run out of arrows to shoot, and then they would have to join the others fighting in the streets.

Rynestian turned his attention back to those that were before him. He, Wills, and the young ones they had trained were hacking into the intruders, leaving them dead or dying in the street, and then moving to the next wave.

We're making remarkable progress, Rynestian thought. He had not expected them to make such a dent in Those Who Serve's forces.

Just as he thought this, the forces before them withdrew from their location. As he looked around, he saw that all of the Those Who Serve's forces were retreating.

Have we done it? Have we forced them to retreat? He let up a cheer that was soon chorused by all those around him. Those who had blades were banging them against the ground in celebration. His inner forge master wanted to admonish them, but he was overcome with such elation that he could not bring himself to do it.

The flames dancing on the homes and shops wavered in the wind and grew to double their size before they all were pulled inward. The flames were ripped from the buildings, and it seemed as if they were all extinguished simultaneously. Rynestian had never seen anything like it and believed it must be some sort of blessing.

But it was not.

Shortly after the flames disappeared, a wall of fire ripped its way through all of the streets of Shae Glen, burning and scorching all that came into contact with it. At the last moment, before the fire reached him, Rynestian leaped into an open door of a home. The flames rocketed into the home along with him, and the structure crumbled from the force of the explosion.

Rynestian was momentarily buried, but he was able to rise from the cinders and bring himself back to his feet with some effort. He was badly burned in multiple places, but he still had to help the others.

The village was in flames. People lay dead or dying, or dragging themselves to their feet with muscle showing beneath blackened skin. Rynestian stumbled back outside, realizing the burn on his leg was much worse than he thought. He desperately scanned for the source of the explosion.

A bit further down the main road, the flames in the street parted, and walking towards Rynestian in the calmest manner was a tall, thin man in a flowing white cloak wrapped over a simple ivory robe. He had shaggy white hair and incredibly pale skin. The man carried a single sword on his waist, its hilt embedded with gold ornamentation, but his arms swung casually next to his body.

As the man approached, Rynestian drew himself up as best he could. His burns were bad, but he was no longer bleeding. He still held his gauntlets, and his armor was still intact. As long as the man did not use unspeakable magic again, he stood a chance.

"Who are you?" Rynestian called out. "Why are you doing this to our village?"

The man took a few more steps before coming to a stop. He casually placed his left hand on the hilt of his blade. His head cocked to the side as he looked at

Rynestian. "You must be the Helanáian who killed my precious underling, Elder Prx of the First Circle." The man's tone was almost joyous, even though what he discussed was deadly serious.

The name caused Rynestian's breath to catch in his throat. "I did not mean to kill her. She killed a dear friend of mine right before me, and I reacted in rage. I will ask again, who are you?"

"Me? Oh, it is of little matter to you who I am, for you will not be leaving here alive," the man said with a sickly smile spreading across his face. "I am Agrimal of the Promised Dawn, and you will pay for hurting one of my children."

"Why do you seek to harm the Helanáians? We have no quarrel with your religion."

The man's head fell backward, and his cruel smile grew even wider as if he was hearing the best joke he had ever heard. "You sky filth do not even know the ancient wrongs of your people, your infractions against those who have worked so hard to watch us grow and flourish on this plane. But no matter. Soon the world will know what happens to those who go against our word."

In a flash, the man had drawn his sword and closed the distance between Rynestian and himself. He brought the sword slashing upward and across Rynestian's body, aiming to cut across the exposed section of armor on his side.

Not a moment too late, Rynestian was able to raise his gauntlet to block the strike, but the impact of the sword striking his hand was bone-crushing. For a thin man, this Agrimal was hiding some inhuman strength behind those flowing white robes.

As soon as Rynestian blocked the first strike, the pale man pulled his blade away and brought it down, this time slashing at Rynestian's face. Another block, more broken bones, but he was able to use the momentum of the blow to roll away from the reach of the man's curved blade.

Rynestian knew he would have to close the distance to use his gauntlets against this man, but the insane reach of the blade kept him edging backward. Flames licked at his feet as he crept away, and he stole a look behind him to see that the rest of the street still burned wildly. All those who were still alive were dragging bodies away, and in a moment, he saw Wills Emit's burnt corpse being dragged by two others.

"You had better pay attention, or this will be no fun at all." Agrimal's cheerful voice tore through his consciousness and snapped his attention back to the man. "Forget about the others. They will all burn just like this village. Just like the rest of Eodisia if your High Seat does not submit to us."

Agrimal smiled and the flames around them shot up to nearly ten feet high, creating a barrier around the two of them. The sweltering heat singed the tips of Rynestian's mustache. He knew he would not be able to last long in this inferno. Agrimal, on the other hand, appeared completely unbothered by the fire surrounding them, as if this was completely normal to him.

Rynestian would have to finish this quickly.

He rushed toward the man as he released a mighty roar. This man meant to destroy him, his friends, his family, and his very way of life. He must take a stand, do everything he could right here to stop him.

As he entered Agrimal's range, the man slashed across his charging form. Rynestian allowed the blade to slide into his side, and he felt the cool steel easily tear into him. He used the opening to lunge forward with his right gauntlet. His hand came swinging forward with all his might, but Agrimal simply spun his body away. The momentum of his spin also pulled his blade free of Rynestian's side, and a spray of hot blood shot from the wound.

Rynestian made to turn and face the man once more, but the pain from his side caused him to stagger and fall to one knee. Panting and clutching the wound in his side, he sprung back to his feet. Blood poured freely over his hand, despite the pressure he was applying to the wound.

Agrimal had his head cocked to the side, his face plastered with morbid curiosity.

Rynestian gritted his teeth. He would not let this man win.

Chapter 23

THE FIFTH DAY

For the past several days, Tylanna had gone to search the ruined city of Aynanu for her missing brother. Akiye had joined her at first, but today, on the fifth day, she had elected to stay behind and rest her broken leg. Nuwitzwe had joined Tylanna each day, bringing a small group of the Night Blades along as well. Every day they found someone, but never Tahnir, and not always someone alive.

Each survivor they found thanked them profusely, but Tylanna never had anything for them but a feigned smile before she went right back to digging. They had nearly excavated the ruins of the building that she had seen collapse next to her brother but found no sign of him. So they had begun to search farther into the surrounding area.

He must have escaped, she thought. *He had to have gotten away somehow*. How he might have gotten away, she did not know.

Whenever they found someone, a member of the Night Blades would escort the survivor back to the campsite, and two would go if the person needed carrying. The other members of the Night Blades she had met during their digging were barely older than Tylanna at all. Nuwitzwe had informed her that the troop was new, but she had expected at least some of their soldiers to be a bit more advanced in years. But they used their youth to their advantage and scoured the ruined city tirelessly from dawn till dusk.

Another day had passed, and Nuwitzwe suggested they return for the night. After they returned to the camp, he pulled her to the side and whispered to her, "Meet me right here in the morning, and I will search with you one last time. I think I have figured out something that could help us."

With that, he strode away, and she did not see him for the rest of the night. She ate with the other members of the Night Blades that had helped her that day. The rations were stretched thin amongst all of the survivors and soldiers. The Night Blades offered most of their food to the victims, and Tylanna always elected to take the same portion as them. There were plenty who needed it more than her.

After eating and talking, Tylanna returned to the tent. She was dreading seeing Akiye. As each day passed, the woman grew more and more impatient with Tylanna and her search for Tahnir. Tylanna hoped that a day of rest would have improved her mood. Akiye was one of her oldest friends, but it was as if she did not know how to talk to her anymore.

When she pushed the flap of the tent to the side, she saw that Akiye was lying in her bedroll, facing away from her. Tylanna tried to enter as quietly as she could, in case the woman was awake.

"Nothing again?"

Akiye's voice was cold and dismissive.

"Not today, but Nuwitzwe told me –"

"Enough!" Akiye rolled over and threw her blanket to the side in a flourish. Her face was nearly red with anger, and it was clear from her eyes that she had been crying. "He. Is. Gone. Tylanna, you have to see it by now. He is dead, and not coming back. We are alone!"

She had pulled herself up to stand on her two feet. Her broken leg was heavily wrapped, but she still should not be standing on it.

"You're wrong, Aki," Tylanna said certainly, a bit of anger leaking into her voice. "I know he is all right."

"You are a fool, Tylanna! You live in your own world if you think he still lives. I saw that building fall on top of him same as you. He was crushed in an instant. Look what happened to us all the way outside the city!"

She gestured to her leg and Tylanna's still-healing gash on her forehead.

Tylanna ran her hand over the scar absentmindedly before folding her arms across her chest defensively. "I would know if he was dead," she offered meekly.

"You would not! I can tell you, there is no feeling that tells you your family is gone! It is something you have to remember all over again every time you think of it, and the pain blooms anew. But we cannot spend the rest of our lives in Aynanu searching for him! What are we going to do?"

"We can figure that out when we find Tahnir."

Akiye leaped across the tent and pushed Tylanna to the ground. "Wake up, woman! He is dead!"

Tylanna stared up at her friend incredulously.

Kill her.

Akiye had never seemed taller to Tylanna as she towered over her, shouting. "You need to move on before the grief destroys you! Let revenge fill your heart, as it has mine, and let us do whatever we can to take down Those Who Serve."

"I do not want revenge," Tylanna retorted, trying to keep her voice level while her friend shouted at her. "I just want to find my brother."

Akiye shrieked as she dove forward and tackled Tylanna, her hands going straight for the older woman's neck. After a moment of shock, Tylanna rolled the two of them over so she sat on top of her friend and pinned her hands to the ground easily. Tears rolled from Akiye's wide eyes, but she was smiling a toothy grin.

"You are lost, Tylanna, hopeless. Nothing I say can get through to you. I will drag you away from here if I have to."

Akiye flung Tylanna from her waist with her legs then flipped herself back to her feet nimbly. She swung her bandaged leg at Tylanna's head.

Not wanting to hurt her leg, Tylanna leaned back and was able to avoid the strike completely. Before she knew it, she was right in front of Akiye, pinning both of her arms again.

You could do it easily. Why wait?

Tylanna ignored the strange whispering as she struggled to hold Akiye in place.

"What is the matter with you, Akiye? Are we not friends?"

The woman stared back at her with a wild mix of fear, rage, and sadness in her eyes. "I cannot be friends with someone so lost. I need to live on. I need my revenge. I cannot be stuck here with you forever."

She threw her arms down, and Tylanna lost her grip. Akiye turned away to face the other side of the tent.

Perfect. Allow me to do the rest.

Before she knew what was happening, Tylanna was drawing Darkender free from its sheath. She looked at her hand in horror as she raised the black sword into the air, ready to strike. With all of her might, she seized control of herself again, and the blade came clattering to the ground.

Akiye spun around, and she looked from the sword to Tylanna. "What...were you... You were going to?"

Without another moment, Akiye drew two long daggers from the belt on her free leg.

"Akiye, no, I only –"

Before Tylanna could finish her sentence Akiye lashed forward with the blades, and Tylanna only just dodged their steel, using the chance to roll out of the tent.

"Akiye, stop! It wasn't what it seemed!"

The flap of the tent was slashed free, and Akiye came storming out, still holding her knives ready.

"First, you will not listen to me. Now you try and kill me?" Akiye screamed. "I thought you were my *family*, Tylanna!"

Akiye sliced forward again, again only meeting the air around Tylanna. Tylanna danced from side to side, doing everything she could to not be cut by Akiye's blades.

"It wasn't me! I dropped the sword!"

Just as she finished shouting, Akiye thrust forward with her knife. Tylanna knocked her arm up and away with her open palm, driving the blade away from her torso. The force of the block shot Akiye's arm up and across her body, causing her to spin through the air before she collapsed to the ground, dropping both of her knives. Tylanna gaped at her hand, wondering how she had thrown Akiye through the air with just a simple block.

Akiye scrambled back to her feet, picking up her knives as she did. She threw them back into the sheath and limped her way back into the tent, fuming. Tylanna merely stared after her in confusion.

When she came back through the opened tent flap, Akiye had all of her belongings bundled up in her arms, and she was wearing the wooden mask she had taken from her family's home in Shae Glen.

"I am leaving, Tylanna." Her voice was muffled behind the mask, but her tone was serious. "Go to the Sky Islands alone, if there is still a way. Hide away as the world around you is thrown into chaos. I am going to do something about it, even if I have to do it all alone."

With that, Akiye turned and hobbled away from the tent into the night. Tylanna started to run after her but held herself back. Maybe Akiye would be better off without her.

She was not sure what had happened with Darkender in the tent, but surely Tylanna was a danger to those around her. Everything they had encountered on their short journey from Shae Glen had been dangerous. She could not ask her old friend to wait with her any longer. Not for her, and not for Tahnir.

Chapter 24

AFTER THE FALL

After a long slumber, finally, a noise reached him. It was the chirping of a blue sparrow, a sound he remembered fondly from his childhood. The bird chirped somewhere nearby, then he heard it flutter away.

He pried his eyes open with some great effort, and the light filling the room nearly blinded him at first. As his eyes adjusted to the daylight, he looked around to see where he was. It was a small room, and he lay in a strange round bed with metal frames encircling him.

A strong breeze blew through an open window, the cool wind felt refreshing on his skin. Both of his legs were wrapped in some strange form of green bandages, and he could not move them. A glance at the rest of his body revealed more bandages, and several other cuts and gashes.

Without wasting another moment, Tahnir sat up. When he did, his head swam, and he had to grab hold of the strange metal bar to steady himself. When he did, pain shot through his bandaged arm, and he let out a low yell in reaction. Where was he, and how did he get here?

Not long after, a man in sweeping blue robes came rushing into the room. He was a man of medium height and had a stocky frame. The robes were fashioned in a cut that Tahnir was unfamiliar with, but the man had a gentle face.

"Ahh, good, you are awake! Do you mind telling me what happened to you?"

"I was..." Tahnir's voice was harsh and quiet. He cleared his throat and then continued, though still quietly, "I was about to ask you the same question. Where am I?"

"You were brought to us after the island of Lahawi fell from the sky. You were severely injured, so we treated you. It was very serious, but it seems you will make a full recovery with some rest. You have been sleeping here for five days and five nights, but we have no idea who you are."

It all came flooding back to him: the thief stealing the hammer, searching for Tylanna and Akiye, the island falling, the building next to him collapsing from the impact. How he had made it out alive, he did not know.

"My name – my name is Tahnir Desqen," he said, regaining some of the usual volume to his voice the more he spoke. "Who brought me here?"

"All right, Tahnir Desqen it is then. As for your rescuers, we do not know," the man with the gentle face answered, his voice very level and calm. "You and several survivors of the impact were dropped off here, but whoever carried you disappeared before we arrived outside."

"My legs – can I walk?"

The man looked down at his legs before answering, "Not right now, unfortunately. The feeling should return to them after a week or so, but we have done everything we can for now."

Tahnir stared down at his heavily bandaged legs. He had never been one to ask for help, but he needed answers. "Could you take me over to the window? I would like to see where I am."

"Of course, Tahnir. I will roll you over."

The man gripped the metal railing on the bed and pushed it towards the open window. To Tahnir's surprise, the bed rolled smoothly across the room. Once he was positioned correctly, the man helped him sit up with a gentle hand.

They were positioned on top of a hill. Before him stretched a massive city, full of towering buildings of metal and clear glass that seemed to shine as the wind passed through it, smooth roads intersecting pathways of smaller buildings, and people milled about on the roads, as well as gliding through the air on strange contraptions that looked like mechanical wings to Tahnir. The city stretched for nearly as far as he could see, but then ended. The area around the city was not filled with rolling grasslands or farms, but the sky itself. Somehow, he was in the Sky Islands of Helanái.

After he had processed the shock, he looked back to the man in the blue robes. “But how?” he asked breathlessly. “I was in Aynanu when the island fell. I figured the Sky Bridge would have been destroyed. How was I brought all the way here?”

“Relax, Tahnir, you are safe. You are right to think that the Sky Bridge was destroyed, but we Helanáians have ways of traversing the realm without using it.”

While that did not explain much to Tahnir, the man’s soothing tone did calm him a little. “Yes, I’m sorry. Thank you for all you have done for me. What is your name, healer?”

“I am Healer Kalahana, and we are happy to help. Now that you are awake, I must ask, once you are completely healed, do you wish to remain here in the Helanáian Islands, or return to the surface? I can make arrangements for whatever you wish.”

Tahnir thought hard about the decision before answering. Tylanna and Akiye must still be down there unless they too were brought up to the Sky Islands. But he was sent here by his father to tell of Those Who Serve’s attacks and find his uncle.

"Tell me, would you happen to know the man known as Rheleus Altusborne?" Tahnir asked, deciding to seek out his uncle himself.

Surprise sparked in the man's eyes. "I am aware of him, yes. Why do you ask?"

"He is my uncle. My father is Rynestian Desqen, formerly Rynestian Altusborne. I was only in Aynanu to travel through the islands to find my uncle, so I will stay. But tell me, were two women around my age brought here with me? One is my twin sister Tylanna. She is shorter than me, but we have similar faces and hair color, and the other is a woman named Akiye. She is about my height and slender, with short black hair."

Kalahana thought for a moment before answering, "No, there was no one matching that description brought before me. Besides you, there were three people of middle age and one child. I am sorry, but I do not know where they are."

"It's all right," Tahnir reassured. "They were outside the city when the island fell, so I'm sure they're all right. They're tough women, tougher than me anyways. They'll be fine."

Healer Kalahana smiled. "I'm sure they will be. Now, you just try to rest as much as you can, and I will send word for someone to contact your uncle. Everything that was brought in with you will be in the drawer on the side of the bed. Though your clothes were mostly destroyed, we saved them just in case they had any sentimental value."

"Thank you, Healer Kalahana. You have surely saved my life."

"Think nothing of it, Tahnir. May your stay in Helanái be filled with peace."

With that, the man slipped from the room, and Tahnir was alone with his thoughts. He was in Helanái. Finally, after all their traveling, he had made it to the Sky Islands.

But he was the only one to make it, and Tylanna and Akiye must be wondering what to do without the Sky Bridge. He believed in them. If anyone could find a way, it was his sister and Akiye together. They each had always been far smarter than he, even though he hated to admit it to them.

Sleep addled him once again, and the aches in his body cried out to accept it. He leaned back into the strange round bed and felt his eyes pull shut. He let the cool wind of Helanái soothe him as he drifted off to sleep.

Tahnir woke the next morning when the light of day heated his bed through the open window. The suns were much more intense here, and he could see that his normally fair skin had burned slightly. His head still felt as groggy as it had the previous day, but the various aches and pains that scoured his body seemed to have lessened. With a deep breath, he gripped the metal railing and pulled himself up to a seated position.

He looked around the room he was being kept in. The walls were all painted a plain white, and small paintings adorned the bare walls. They depicted different Helanáian Islands, all covered in the beautiful scenery of unfamiliar terrain. He wondered how many of the islands he would get to see during his stay in Helanái.

The door leading into his room swung open, admitting Healer Kalahana and a woman Tahnir had never seen before. She was short, about Tylanna's height, who wore neatly wrapped white and blue robes that silhouetted her figure. She seemed to be about the same age as Tahnir, if not a year or two older. Her head was turned down, staring towards the floor before her as she shuffled awkwardly behind the healer. Medium-length dark blue hair fell from her head in waves, which she kept swept behind her ears. When Healer Kalahana came to a stop, she almost crashed into the man before straightening herself and turning to face Tahnir.

"Hello!" she belted at him, her voice light yet commanding. "You must be the boy claiming to be Lord Altusborne's nephew. Tahnir Desqen, is it? Well, you do look a bit like him. I could see it being true. Who did you say your parents are again?"

"Uhm, hello," Tahnir offered. "My father is Rynestian Desqen, formerly Altusborne, and my late mother is Tritelle Desqen."

The woman ran her hand through her hair, her face construed in deep thought. When she did, the strands she had just tucked behind her ear came loose. She had a round face, but her features were sharp. Tahnir supposed that she was quite beautiful if he could ignore her fidgeting and intrusive questions.

"I do remember him speaking of his brother," she muttered, seeming to speak to the room more than to Tahnir directly. "He left the islands some time ago, yes?"

"Yes, around twenty-five years ago. Before my sister and I were born."

"Hmm..." she pondered while fixing her hair. "Well, I do not see why I can't take you to see him, and we will see if you are who you say you are, not that I don't believe you, mind. So where have you traveled from?"

Tahnir took a moment to process the question. Her speech was erratic, yet bubbling with energy and charisma. He found it oddly intriguing. "I am from Shae Glen, a small village within Eodisia. My father settled there after he left Helanái, looking for a life of peace."

"I see, yes, that would be the place for it," the blue-haired woman replied. "Well, what brought you to the Islands then?"

Tahnir met her gaze. "We were attacked."

The woman leaned forward, her eyes bulging wide. Healer Kalahana looked concerned, if not the slightest bit uncomfortable.

"In Shae Glen? Really?" the woman said as she strode closer to Tahnir. "What of your family? Is that what happened to your mother? Who attacked you?"

"Uh –" Tahnir stumbled on his words. Something about this woman was making his tongue feel as if it weighed triple its normal weight. "Yes, really. My father hid my sister and I away during the invasion, so I did not see most of it, only the bloody aftermath. The invaders claimed to be members of Those Who Serve, and according to my father, they were seeking to kill Helanáians or those that were descended from them. But my mother passed from sickness many years ago, not during the attack. Several villagers were killed, though, including the parents of the woman my sister and I traveled here with, Akiye Komoto. Her mother was Helanáian. Nagashi Komoto was her name."

"I have heard of her, actually!" The woman's excitement at recognizing the name seemed to outweigh her grief at the tragic news. "Yes, she served the Governor's Council for many years before she left the islands altogether. She quit after she was the victim of a failed assassination. That is quite horrible to hear that she was killed."

"It was horrible. My father sent myself, my sister, and her daughter on a journey to tell the Helanáians of what happened as well as hide away in the islands while whatever trouble on the surface is brewing."

The woman strode across the room, gracefully now, and placed a hand on the metal railing. Tahnir could not help but notice how close to his own hand hers was.

"And now that you have reported the attack, what do you mean to do?"

Tahnir thought long before answering. His father had told them to hide away in the islands to avoid trouble. "First, I mean to find my sister and Akiye. Then, I will do whatever I can to end the flagrant violence against Helanáians. I am not much of a fighter, but I will help any way that I can."

The woman smiled, as warm as the morning sun, and patted his hand gently. Tahnir felt his skin prickle where she had touched it, and he had to push down a swell of embarrassment.

"Well, if I were a betting woman, I would put all my money on you being Rheleus's blood. You sound just like him. I am Iridia Neversky, personal aide to Rheleus Altusborne. I work as a researcher and assistant to the Governor."

"My uncle, he is a Governor? Is that some sort of leader?"

"Why, yes," she exclaimed, her voice bouncing all around. "Your father must have not told you much of his family. I suppose I will leave most of that tale to Rheleus or your father. However, the Sky Islands of Helanái are ruled over by seven Governors who represent different factions that are scattered about the islands. Your uncle, Rheleus, represents the United Kingdom of Helanái, the largest political representation in the Islands. He lives on Mete'olu, or we sometimes call it the Central Island. We are currently residing on Talakoko, which, now that Lahawi has fallen, is the lowest flying of the islands. Though the Sky Bridges that connected with Lahawi have all collapsed, the Sky Bridges connection to the other islands still remain intact. Getting to Mete'olu will only take a few hours from here if we hurry. Then it will only be a matter of finding your uncle and telling him of the violence that has befallen your village, and how Those Who Serve are targeting Helanáians."

Tahnir's head raced as he tried to process all of the information she was spouting at him. The way she spoke of everything made it seem as if it were all so natural, but he was struggling to keep up with her.

"Wait a minute," Healer Kalahana interjected, "Tahnir is to rest for several more days. The injuries he sustained in the impact of Lahawi falling were quite serious."

Iridia spun to face the Healer, her robes twirling far more gracefully than she moved, Tahnir realized. "I will be escorting him personally, and I happen to have quite a knack for healing myself. Do you have a transport chair that I could take along? Our office will send you another one as soon as possible."

"Well, I suppose we could allow it..."

The healer's voice trailed off as he stood in deep contemplation. He strode over to Tahnir's bedside. "All right, Tahnir, you may go. But you *may not walk*, or be able to walk, for that matter, for at least a few more days. Remain in the transport chair at all times, unless you are sleeping, then have someone help you into a bed. The healing we performed will hold for a while, but eventually, the pain from your injuries will increase – that is only natural. If you have any questions, I am sure the Mistress Neversky will be able to assist you."

He gave Tahnir and Iridia a nod, and then strode out of the room in a rush. Iridia helped Tahnir sit the rest of the way up in his bed and collapsed the metal railings from the side of the bed with deft precision, at least to Tahnir's eyes. He had not even known that the railings could be removed.

"Is there anything you need to bring with you, Tahnir?" Iridia asked him hurriedly.

In the rush to leave and finally meet his uncle, he had almost forgotten what Healer Kalahana had told him. "Yes, apparently they stored everything they found me with inside the drawer on the other side of the bed. Would you mind getting them for me, Iridia?"

She scuttled over to the other side of the bed and pulled the drawer out. There was no outward handle, and Tahnir did not see how she had opened it. There were many new things about the tools in Helanái he would have to puzzle out.

She placed a neatly packed bundle on his lap, and the weight surprised him as it settled on his legs. Surely enough, his hammer had made it to the Sky Islands along with him. He was glad he had not lost the only family heirloom his father had given him. All that was not ruined of his belongings were the hammer and the belt he kept it attached to, so he strapped them both to his waist with a bit of odd maneuvering.

Healer Kalahana reentered the room, pushing a wide chair that had four wheels affixed to the base. It glided over the floor easily, and the healer brought it to a stop just before Tahnir's position in the bed.

Wordlessly, Healer Kalahana and Iridia each wrapped an arm around Tahnir's back and lifted him into the wide chair. Pain ripped through him as they moved, but it settled once he was positioned well. He dreaded the healer's words about the pain of his injuries returning. If what he was feeling now was not the full brunt of it, he was certain he would be in complete agony once the healing wore off.

Iridia jumped behind him and grabbed the handles to steer him out of the room. "Thank you, Healer Kalahana. I'll be sure to be careful with him."

"Yes, please do," the healer said. "Be strong, Tahnir. The coming weeks may be rough, but you will find yourself as good as new when you are fully recovered."

"I will be. I cannot thank you enough for your help, Healer Kalahana. I surely would be dead were it not for you. Thank you," Tahnir said as earnestly as he could.

"It was the least I could do, Tahnir. Good luck with your uncle, and may all of us find peace."

With that, Iridia pushed him through the open door of his room. As she rushed behind him, Tahnir was able to glance into the other rooms that passed them by. Many patients looked much like him, nearly covered head to toe in bandages.

Then, they blasted through the main door into the city.

Before him was the second Sky Island, or Talakoko, as Iridia had called it. Iridia pushed him through the winding streets of the city, never seeming to cease telling him everything she knew about everything they passed. She was a nearly limitless source of information, not that Tahnir could absorb nearly any of it. He found himself far too occupied with the buildings that surrounded them. It amazed him how they dwarfed even the buildings that had astonished him in Aynanu. They were made with such intricate craftsmanship, that Tahnir would have loved to stop and get a better look. But he supposed that finding his uncle and warning the Helanáians of Those Who Serve was more important, at least for the time being. Iridia continued, unaware that he was not listening.

It took them about an hour to find their way to the other side of the island. Along the way, they passed towering buildings made of the glowing glass and metal. He saw inns much fancier then the High Chair's Seat, as well as nature parks, education centers, and so much more. There was a lot to the city that Tahnir had never encountered before. He wasn't even sure where to begin with his questions to Iridia. As they approached the Sky Bridge leading to Mete'olu, all other questions that were bubbling in his mind fell away.

The Sky Bridge was as clear as the finest glass Tahnir had ever seen. Despite this, people were milling over the bridge as if it were made of solid rock. Tahnir was certain that it could not possibly bear all the weight that it held, but it did not even seem to waver. The Sky Bridge spanned about two miles at an upward slant. He could see the bottom of the other island beyond the clouds that obscured the top of the bridge. Tahnir had not yet grown used to being amongst the clouds as opposed to staring up at them.

Iridia leaned over to whisper in his ear, "Do not worry about crossing the Sky Bridge. Many surface-dwellers are scared at first, but they have never cracked or broken. Well, that is, until the bridges connected to Lahawi fell, but that was a once-in-a-lifetime occurrence."

Not at all reassured by her two-pronged statement, Tahnir gripped the handle of the transport chair as tightly as he could as Iridia pushed him towards the entry gate. The gate was guarded by a lone woman who wore armor that seemed similar to the armor he had seen in his father's secret room in their house. Twin blades hung from her right hip, both sheathed in black leather. She addressed Iridia with a nod, and the two women both flashed the strange hand salute that Tahnir vaguely remembered the innkeeper Faleyemi showing them in Nicol's Wood.

"Mistress Neversky. Returning to the Center Island?"

"Why, yes," Iridia replied, "and I am bringing Rheleus Altusborne's nephew Tahnir along with me."

The guardswoman looked over him with a stern eye, seemingly noticing him for the first time.

Not a great trait for a guard to have, he thought.

"What has happened to you, then?" she asked bluntly, eyeing his bandages and wrappings.

"I... Well, I was in Aynanu when the island fell. I was swept up in the explosion of the impact, and when I awoke, I was in a Healing Center here on this island."

The guard's mouth fell open, and she stared at him wide-eyed.

Iridia pushed him forward through the gate, laughing. "Oh, he certainly has his uncle's sense of humor! He was just in an accident recently, and his head is a little confused from the healing."

The guard offered a polite chuckle before shaking her head and turning to address the next group that was about to gain passage onto the Sky Bridge.

Iridia leaned forward to whisper into Tahnir's ear frantically. "Not everyone knows of the ways to travel to the surface without the bridge. The surface-dwellers that were brought to the islands to receive Healing are a secret held only between the top healers of the islands, the Governor's Council, and the troop of warriors that were sent to rescue any survivors they could find in the wreckage of Lahawi and Aynanu."

Tahnir had not even noticed them roll their way onto the bridge as she whispered. The wheels of his chair were smooth on the strange glass-like substance that comprised the Sky Bridge, and as he looked below him, he could see straight through the bridge to the cloud-filled sky that sat below them. He wrenched his head back up and tightened his grip on the handles of his chair, his head swirling.

"I am sorry, Iridia," he said through clenched teeth. "I did not know my being here was a big secret. How did I get to the islands, anyways?"

"There is a Transport, beneath what used to be Aynanu, that connects to Talakoko, that Helanáians have used for centuries. Think of Transports like tunnels, except the two ends of the tunnel are not connected physically. We were afraid that the connection would not work with Lahawi collapsing, but after we tested the Transport a few times, we sent a small group of seasoned warriors to search the wreckage. Many were lost in the impact, but we saved as many as we could. When the Artanian forces arrived on the surface, our warriors stopped searching the wreckage, fearing that they would be discovered. If your sister and your friend survived the impact, I am sure they were rescued by the Artanian forces that arrived shortly after the Helanáian warriors."

Tahnir sat back in the chair. He had not even considered that Tylanna and Akiye had not survived the impact. For some reason, he was positive they had. He knew it to be true.

As the Sky Bridge passed beneath him, he wondered how long it would take for the three young Shae Glenners who had set out together into the world to be reunited.

Chapter 25

ONCE MORE INTO THE RUINS

Tylanna had not slept for a moment throughout the entire night. Multiple times she debated running after Akiye to apologize and bring her back. But her mind kept drifting to the moment that she had not been able to control herself, and she had raised Darkender to strike at her oldest friend. The blade lay where she had dropped it the night before, and many times, she had felt drawn to it. What was it about this sword that compelled her so?

When the light of the morning had brought the heat of her tent to a nearly unbearable level, Tylanna finally drew herself up from her bedroll and readied herself for the day. Once she had slipped into her traveling clothes and strapped on the belt for her sheath, she eyed Darkender once more. She supposed she could not leave it in the tent. There was no telling if anyone would take it, and she would lose the precious heirloom her father had gifted her. Setting her jaw, she grabbed the sheath and slid the blade into it before strapping it to the back of her waist. She did not like the feeling that the blade resting against her body gave her. It was as if she was whole again.

Memories of the previous night came back to her as she passed through the torn entrance flap of the tent. Akiye had slashed at it in anger, anger that Tylanna thought was completely justified. Would the woman ever be able to forgive her?

As her eyes adjusted to the light, she saw that most of the usual noise from the camp was gone. By this time of the morning, there would normally be victims milling about, helping prepare food, or heading to the tent for help with their injuries. But there was an eerie quiet that danced on the air.

She walked along through the rows of tents, and from what she could see, many of the tents were empty of people or their belongings. She snaked her way until she came upon Nuwitzwe, who was crouching in the same location he had been in the night before.

The man had been tremendously supportive of Tylanna and her mission to find her brother. She could tell that he truly wished to help everyone he could, and she was just lucky that she had been the first survivor he had encountered. His words from the night before had also plagued her in the night, that this would be the last time he helped her look for Tahnir.

Nuwitzwe rose to his feet when she approached. "Just you again today?" he asked as he rose.

"Yes." She was not proud of how her voice wavered slightly when she answered. "Akiye left the camp last night. We had a fight, and she told me she would find her own way from now on. I do not know where she is going."

"I am sorry, Tylanna. That must have been difficult for you. Many of the victims departed from the camp this morning as well, now that they have mostly recovered. They go to make new lives for themselves elsewhere."

Nuwitzwe placed a comforting hand on her shoulder for a moment and then turned away. He strode towards the city, his robes billowing in the wind, and Tylanna followed close behind.

"What I am going to attempt today should put me in contact with those who were lost when the island fell," Nuwitzwe said, his tone shifting from comforting to matter-of-fact. "I have not attempted this before, but I have heard tell of the Banéhûl of old convening with the dead. My gifts allow me to harness the energy of the recently deceased for combat, and instead of dreaming, I am able to speak with those in my bloodline who have perished. But I have never been able to contact those I am not related to. If this does not work, I am afraid I can do nothing more to help you find your brother."

Tylanna took a moment to process what the man was saying.

"You can speak to the dead?" she asked incredulously.

"It is a blessing of Banéhûl, as well as a curse. The price we pay for the gifts of our homeland," he answered, looking ahead to the ruined city, his head held high. "There is no rest for a true Banéhûl. When we sleep, we are confronted with all those who have come before us in our bloodline. Only the strongest of the Banéhûl are able to sort through the noise and speak with their ancestors."

Tylanna knew a few things about strange dreams, but this was something beyond her comprehension. "So, how will you be looking for my brother with this power?"

"Well, if the worst has happened, I will be able to draw out his energy as I do for battle, but instead of transferring his energy to fuel my magic, I will try and hold it in place so I may speak to him. But if I cannot find him with my ritual, we will know he got away, and somewhere he still lives."

Tylanna stopped asking questions for the remainder of their walk, as she seemed to become more confused every time Nuwitzwe answered her. She had never heard of this Banéhûl magic before, but if he really could speak to the dead, it was worth trying. She was certain that Tahnir still lived, but it would be nice to have proof. If only Akiye had just stayed one more day.

After several minutes, they passed what was once the gate to the city of Aynanu. With every day of searching, fewer and fewer survivors had been found. They reached the spot where Tylanna had begun her search so many days ago, where she had seen her brother standing before the debris of the impact had reached him.

"Right here will do," Nuwitzwe said as he held an arm out to indicate to her. "Please stand back while I attempt this, and whatever you do, do not break the circle I am about to create."

She took a few steps back as Nuwitzwe crouched where he stood. From somewhere on his person, he brought out a small cloth bag that appeared to be filled with dirt.

"Corrupted soil, from Banéhûl. In order to use my gifts, I must bring the land of Banéhûl with me," he said as he began to sprinkle the earth to create a small circle around him, making sure it was completely solid and every part was spread just right. Once he seemed satisfied, he rose back to his feet and looked to Tylanna. "I will not be able to hear you or speak to you while I am completing the ritual, but do not be afraid of whatever you may see."

His hands, which rested at his side, lifted into the air. He pressed his eyes closed, and breathed deeply in through his nose.

The soil he had spread ascended from the ground. The soil floated and encircled him, spinning faster and faster as he continued to raise his hands higher into the air. He appeared to be buffeted by a windstorm that was only taking place within the circle he had created, his long hair and robes flying around.

Just as she began to lose sight of him, she saw two bright lights emanating from his hands. The lights formed into tendrils that reached out into the air above him. He spun his hands upside down, and the tendrils of light snaked their way towards the earth below him. When the lights reached the ground, all around Nuwitzwe, rubble and rock hovered, joining the swirling circle of soil and light.

Tylanna had to take several more steps backward to avoid being caught up in the hurricane of a ritual. In the few glimpses of Nuwitzwe she got through the torrent that surrounded him, she could see that he was straining. The tendrils of light reached out, beyond the circle, and began to grow brighter the further they reached. They grew so bright that it was difficult for Tylanna to even look, though she was curious to see how the ritual worked.

Nuwitzwe let out a loud yell, and his eyes shot open. His white eyes glowed with the same brightness as the tendrils of light. His body shook violently as he yelled. Tylanna fought down every impulse to rush to his aid, remembering his warnings about breaking the circle.

The radiant tendrils that reached out around the storm drew themselves back towards the circle. Nuwitzwe cried out in pain as the light snaked around his body, wrapping around him over and over again, until he seemed to be comprised completely of brilliant light. His form lifted into the air, floating in the middle of the ritual circle. She could hear his screams heighten.

Then, the soil, the rubble, and Nuwitzwe all fell back to the ground, and the light winked out. Tylanna rushed to his side. When she got close, she saw that the soil had fallen back perfectly into the circle, so she pulled herself to a stop just before crossing the border.

Nuwitzwe pulled himself up to sit on his haunches, his eyes squeezed shut. He opened his eyes, and for a moment, they glowed. Slowly, the light faded, until the normal whites of his eyes showed once more. He sat there, panting before his hand lashed out and broke the circle before falling face down.

Still minding the border, Tylanna grabbed Nuwitzwe's outstretched arm and lifted him from the ground. Though the man was much larger than her, she did not have any difficulty lifting him to his feet again.

"Thank you," he whispered meekly. His voice was hoarse and filled with deep sadness. "He is not here, Tylanna. Your brother is not here, neither dead nor alive. I... I could feel it all. All who died in the crash. I saw each of them. So much pain..."

His voice trailed off, agony etched into his face.

"Thank you, Nuwitzwe," she said. "Thank you for going through that to help me. I know it mustn't have been easy to feel all of that pain. I will help you get back to camp, and you can rest."

"No one is left that lives," he muttered as she helped him hobble. "They have all fallen now."

Within the grief for those who lost their lives during the impact was a glimmer of hope. Her brother was alive, wherever he was.

When they found their way back to camp, Tylanna was all but carrying Nuwitzwe. The strain of the ritual had sapped him of nearly all of his energy, and he was unconscious. He muttered constantly, but it was so low that Tylanna could not make out what he was saying.

Captain Pahlio Leor stood outside Nuwitzwe's tent. When he saw her carrying Nuwitzwe, he rushed over to help her.

"What happened to him?" he asked as he grabbed Nuwitzwe's other arm.

"He performed a Banéhûl ritual to search for my brother in the wreckage. He said that Tahnir had gotten away, somehow, but he saw that none still live within the city. He... He said he saw all who died in the crash."

Pahlio stared at her, wide-eyed. "I did not know he could do that. I have only ever seen him use his gifts for fighting."

When they entered Nuwitzwe's tent, they laid the tall man down in his bedroll as gently as possible. Tylanna looked around and saw that it was as barren as hers was, with no extra decoration or equipment, even for the vice captain of the entire force. Almost the same instant as his head was laid flat, Nuwitzwe's eyes shut, and he seemed to be sleeping. Both Pahlio and Tylanna stood over the man, watching him rest.

"The power of the Banéhûl continues to baffle me," Pahlio said with a chuckle. "He will be fine after some rest. I have seen him like this a few times before after overusing his gifts. It does me proud that he would go so far for you, Tylanna."

Tylanna felt a twinge of guilt that she was responsible for the state Nuwitzwe was in. "Well," she said sheepishly, "I suppose I should let him rest then."

Without another word, she slipped out of the tent and back into the nearly empty campsite. She only saw a few soldiers milling about. What Nuwitzwe had said about most of the victims had been true. She supposed she was one of the last victims that still remained.

"Wait, Tylanna!" Pahlio called out from inside the tent.

He swooped through the entryway of the tent and stood before her, bringing her to a halt by placing his hands on her shoulders. His deep brown eyes stared intensely into hers.

"I have a proposition for you. I know you still wish to travel to Helanái to tell them of Those Who Serve's attacks here on the surface. But how would you feel about staying and fighting with us, the Night Blades, until we find a way to reach Helanái once more? I, too, want to fight back against Those Who Serve if they are targeting people for their heritage. I am sure half of Artani is Helanáian, at least by descent. Even I might be, as far as I know. But I have heard tell of your strength from my soldiers, and I know we could use the help of one such as yourself in the coming battles."

Her, a soldier? For Artani, no less. She had only been in the country for a few weeks and knew so little about the land. The idea of helping people as Nuwitzwe had interested her, but could she commit to fighting in an army? She had only left Shae Glen to hide from the conflict in the Sky Islands of Helanái, but now that the Sky Bridge connecting the islands to the surface was gone, should she not just return to Shae Glen?

"I am not sure, Captain," she said. "Can you even have someone from Eodisia fight in your forces?"

"Of course," he replied quickly. "Nuwitzwe is not from Artani originally, and several more of our band have come from foreign lands. Still, I would fight and die for every one of them."

"But I have never even been in a battle before. I have only ever fought to protect myself or my friends."

"Are we not friends, Tylanna?" he asked with a grin. "Would I not fight to protect you, and you me? I can train you myself. I see that you have a sword already." He gestured to the swords that dangled from his hip. "I am a swordsman myself, though I have dabbled in all manner of weaponry as part of my training. If you will join us, I will be sure that you become a master swordswoman in no time at all."

Learning to make better use of Darkender did interest her, though she had felt confident when she had brandished the blade against the Hollowpod in the Jungle of Jiye. Even when she raised it against Akiye, fear and surprise were overtaken by confidence.

"I suppose I could help you, at least until the Sky Bridge is reconnected," Tylanna said, though still not completely convinced. "Nuwitzwe told me that my brother is no longer in Aynanu, alive or dead, but I haven't the faintest idea where to look for him. Maybe if I travel with you, I will run into him again. He always did have a knack for finding trouble wherever he went."

"That is excellent news, Tylanna Desqen. Welcome to the Night Blades, and by extension the Artanian Night Legion." He clapped his hand on her shoulder as he went on, "As your captain, I swear I will do everything in my power to protect you if you would swear to follow my every order in the heat of battle."

Tylanna looked into Pahlio's deep brown eyes. "I swear it, my Captain."

Later that very night, Tylanna stood in the middle of a ring made up of all of the Night Blade soldiers, brandishing torches and whooping wildly. Captain Pahlio and Nuwitzwe stood calmly behind the ring on a nearby hilltop, watching Tylanna intently. Nuwitzwe was leaning on Pahlio for support, as he still was not back to his full strength. The man looked thinner than the last time she had seen him, as if the strain of the ritual had taken the very meat from his bones.

She had been brought here to take part in an initiation ritual that the Night Blades had created for all new members. It was inspired by an ancient ritual from the Artani of old, in which any wishing to join the Night Legion would fight to the death with another who wished to join, and only the winner would be accepted. Now the ritual used practice swords, and the new member fought the most recent addition to the Night Blades. The outcome of the battle did not affect your candidacy. She had been told it was just a way to gauge her skill level in combat.

The man she was going to fight stood in front of her, egging on the ring of soldiers around them to make more noise. The soldiers were meant to provide as many distractions as possible, to try and simulate real battle.

The man she would fight was named Milon Taran. He was several years older than her, nearly a head taller, and had a wide-shouldered frame. They had only been briefly introduced before the match, but Tylanna had gotten the impression that he did not feel threatened by her at all.

As he goaded the crowd, Tylanna watched his movements. He was light on his feet for his size, but not as light as her. She would have to use her speed to her advantage with the man. She was certain he would probably overpower her in strength and prowess with a blade. As she gripped the leather handle of the practice blade, she was acutely aware of Darkender hanging from the sheath on the back of her belt. She knew that if she were to use her real blade, she would win.

The noise of the crowd came to an abrupt halt when Pahlio raised a closed fist into the air. He yelled into the still night air in a gruff voice Tylanna had not heard him use before. “Night Blades, stand ready! We welcome the newest Blade, Tylanna Desqen of Shae Glen, the Girl with the Golden Eye!”

He dropped his fist, and the crowd erupted in noise once more. She turned back to focus on Milon Taran just in time, as the large man was already barreling towards her with his blade poised to strike.

She hefted her practice sword up before her. The grip was not as comfortable in her hand as Darkender’s, but it would have to do. In an effort to use the man's momentum against him, she stepped out of his path while she smacked his swinging blade back at him. Her parry sent the man's arm flying backward, leaving him wide open. She brought her sword slashing across his exposed chest in a strike that would have killed him had the blade been sharp.

He staggered backward, rubbing his chest where she had struck him. His eyes stared up at her, the jovial confidence now replaced with something much more sinister.

He raised himself up to his full height, holding his blade horizontally above his head. He lashed forward, and Tylanna stepped out of his path with ease. His speed and ferocity increased with each strike, and she matched it without strain.

She waited for his flurry to stagger, and when he overextended himself on the final stab, she slipped underneath his arm and grabbed hold. With all her might, she heaved the large man over her shoulder, and he came crashing down onto the ground.

As he lay on the ground gasping for air, she casually placed her foot on his chest and pointed the practice sword at Milon's neck.

Use me, and you would have killed him.

The noise halted into a strangled silence. All at once, all of the torches fell to the ground and were extinguished. Tylanna looked around wildly, barely able to make out anyone in the darkness of the campsite. She felt Milon Taran squirming below her foot.

Then, a unified chorus of voices rang out.

"WE ARE THE NIGHT, AND THE NIGHT IS WE!"

A cheer rang out after the chant, and she felt herself being lifted into the air. Torches were relit, and soldiers had heaved her up on their shoulders. Even Milon was cheering from the crowd, though he still was rubbing his chest.

Captain Pahlio and Nuwitzwe smiled and laughed as Tylanna was thrown into the air in celebration. Chants of "Golden Eyes" and "Tylanna" rang forth from the mass.

As she flew into the air and then back into the outstretched hands of her new comrades, she felt more at home than she had since leaving Shae Glen.

Chapter 26

THE GOVERNORS' COUNCIL

Tahnir and Iridia were through racing through the wide streets of Mete'olu. They had arrived on the island about two hours previous, but it proved much larger but it proved much larger than Talakoko.

Iridia's information-laden monologue never ended, with Tahnir only half-listening. He was more and more distracted by each structure they rushed past. He had never seen a palace before, but he imagined they would look something like this. Had Helanái ever been ruled over by kings and queens? There was so much he did not know about this place that was meant to be his motherland. He decided that he had better listen to something that Iridia was telling him, so he did not look like a complete fool when he met his uncle.

"Anyways, that is why there is now a Governor's Council. This all only happened some fifty years back, so the elders still talk about all of it as if it just happened. For my whole life, this has been the way of the islands, so it feels natural for me. But now that the Sky Bridge has fallen, Helanái will once again have to become self-sufficient and not rely on trade with the surface. We cannot be expected to use the Transports to trade, especially since they are largely kept secret."

"Iridia," Tahnir interrupted, "you said you work with my uncle. What is he like?"

Iridia slowed the pace of Tahnir's chair just for a moment, presumably thinking of the best way to answer. "Rheleus is a straightforward man. His one and only goal is the preservation of Helanái and taking care of everyone who resides within the islands. He cares deeply, and honestly. In my few years of working with him, I have never once seen him falter in his vision for a better Helanái."

Tahnir smiled to himself. That sounded a lot like his father and Shae Glen. It seemed his uncle could be just as stubborn.

Before long, they came upon a rounded building with towering columns of white supporting the rooftop. The entryway was wide and led to stairs that descended downwards. Iridia exchanged some quick words with the guards inside before they allowed her and Tahnir to pass. They went through a looming door leading into a circular amphitheater that had a stage at the center. The seating and stairs ran at a sharp angle downward towards the stage, but there was no one there.

"Listen, Tahnir," Iridia whispered over his shoulder. "It is probably best if I do most of the talking while we are in here. I know how these council meetings go, and the Governors may not appreciate me bringing an outsider, let alone a surface-dweller."

She drew herself up again as they continued to descend. Tahnir was glad for the smooth pathway, as bouncing down all these flights of stairs surely would reignite the pain of his injuries. As they drew closer to the stage at the bottom of the arena, Tahnir could more clearly make out the seven people that stood in a broad circle. Some were men and some were women, but they all stood on the stage as equals. Tahnir could hear their conversation clearly as they approached.

"We must return to how Helanái used to be before we relied on the trade of the surface," a man with a booming voice was saying. "With the Sky Bridge destroyed, we must use our stockpiles to make sure our people are fed and safe, while we figure out how to provide for everyone once again."

"Of course," a woman with a sharp voice replied, "but our first move must be to discover why Lahawi fell at all, else who is to say that it will not happen again with all of the islands? We must protect the islands no matter what."

“The ancient magics must be failing,” a calm woman’s voice said. “The Golden Forge has not been lit for more than centuries. If the legends are to be believed, unless we can relight the Forge, the islands will continue to fall, causing devastation for us and Artani below.”

“What you say of the Golden Forge is true,” the booming man’s voice said. “But the Forge not being lit has never led to an island falling before – why would it start now? Also, there are islands that are much farther away from the Golden Forge than Lahawi. If this were the cause, would they not be the first to fall?”

“But what else could cause an island to fall from the sky?”

Before Tahnir knew it, Iridia was pushing him up onto the stage, cutting off the conversation the Governors were having. Tahnir felt a surge of embarrassment at Iridia’s shamelessness, especially since he was a stranger to all of these people. Even in Shae Glen, he would never interrupt a meeting of the mayor and the Watch, not if the whole village was burning down.

All of the Governors wore regal robes in different colors. Tension decorated their faces. When he saw him, Tahnir’s eyes fixed on the man who must be his uncle.

He looked just like his father, though a bit older, and he wore a neatly cut beard instead of a mustache. His hair was a little longer but swept back, and was completely white, not the peppered gray and red his father sported. Their faces were remarkably similar, and he had the same wide frame as his father and stood maybe a few inches taller.

The Governors cried out in protest, but Tahnir did not pull his eyes away from the man.

"My apologies, honored Governors," Iridia said. "This matter was far too pressing to wait until the end of the Emergency Council Meeting. Please forgive me, Mother and Governor Altusborne."

Iridia looked at the woman dressed in blue and white robes when she said *Mother*, Tahnir noticed. So she was related to a Governor as well. He found it odd that she chose to work alongside his uncle when she had a parent that worked in the same capacity. Tahnir sat himself up as much as he could in his chair, pain echoing throughout his body.

"Uncle Rheleus?"

The man who he had thought was his uncle snapped his eyes from Iridia to Tahnir. His cold stare washed over him, taking in every inch of him in moments. Then, his stare softened.

"Stars in the sky..." the man muttered. Tahnir could tell even now that he had been the man with the booming voice. Rheleus strode forward until he was standing just before Tahnir. He fell to one knee to look deeply into Tahnir's eyes. "You... Are you Rynestian's boy?"

Tahnir nodded before being swept up in a mighty embrace by the large man. Memories flashed of all the times that his father had grabbed him in the same way, and he was certain that this man was Rheleus Altusborne, his father's brother.

Rheleus pulled back from the hug and held Tahnir by the shoulders. "I am sorry. You seem to be injured. What happened to you? What of my brother? Where has he been all these years? I have not heard from him since he left Helanái all those many years ago. What became of his life?"

Tahnir smiled as he tried to think of how to describe his father's entire life to his brother. He thought of his father playing together with himself, his sister, and mother in the fields of Shae Glen. "He traveled the Lands Below after leaving. When he finally settled in one place, he came to rest in Eodisia, in a small village created by refugees of war called Shae Glen. As the forge-master, he helped turn the village into what it is today: a haven for peace and growth. There he met my mother, Tritelle Desqen, and together they had twins. I am Tahnir, and my sister is named Tylanna."

The man gripped his shoulders tight as tears welled in his eyes. A broad smile stretched across his face, reminding Tahnir once again of his father.

Iridia drove an elbow into Tahnir's ribs, hard. Once the pain receded, he looked up to her incredulously. He saw that his uncle also was looking at Iridia with confusion clouding his happy face.

"Tell them why you've really come, Tahnir," Iridia said with an insistent tone. "You two will have time to catch up later."

Rheleus returned his gaze to Tahnir. "What is it, boy?"

Tahnir nodded and gently removed his uncle's hands from his shoulders. He tried to get himself up to his feet. He struggled at first, but Iridia swept herself under his arm to support him. When she did, the hammer he had strapped back to his belt on his waist pressed against her leg.

As he stood, Rheleus took a few steps backward to rejoin his place in the circle of Governors. Tahnir looked around at each of them before he began to speak.

"I departed Shae Glen when our village was attacked by Those Who Serve. They came into our houses, rounded us up, and began testing the citizens with a special glass to see if they were Helanáian. When the first person was revealed to be from the Sky Islands of Helanái, they killed her on the spot without another thought. Her name was Nagashi Komoto."

Akiye's mother's name drew some gasps and worried whispers from the Governors.

"When she was killed, the village struck back and tried as hard as they could, fighting with everything they had, but we are a peaceful people, and Those Who Serve carried weapons. Many were lost in the riot, but the invaders were eventually driven away. My father, Rynestian Desqen, formerly Rynestian Altusborne, survived the attack and kept the village safe. He then sent me, my sister Tylanna, and Nagashi's daughter Akiye Komoto on a journey to go to the Sky Islands of Helanái and warn you of Those Who Serve's transgressions against our people in the Lands Below.

"During our travels, we heard of many other places that had encountered Those Who Serve in the same way. We made it all the way to Aynanu on our trek, and I had just entered the city when the first island, or Lahawi, fell into Aynanu. We felt a rumbling all around us, and before we knew it, the island was falling on top of us.

"I...don't remember much after that, but apparently, I was rescued by a group of your warriors using the Transports. I am not quite sure how they work, but when I woke, I was in a Healing Center in Talakoko. I have come to your islands to request Helanái's help in putting a stop to the violent actions of Those Who Serve, as well as ask for shelter for all of the Helanáians on the surface who are unable to fight. I know that the Sky Bridge being destroyed complicates this request, but I must ask it all the same."

The circle of Governors all stared at him, their faces lost in deep thought. He glanced to Iridia for her reaction but saw that her gaze was fixed on the hammer that hung from his belt, and her brow was furrowed. The silence went on for so long that Tahnir grew antsy, but just as he was about to speak, he was cut off.

“That is terrible news, my nephew.” Rheleus was the first to interrupt the stunned silence. “This is the first the Council has heard of Those Who Serve attacking our people in the Lands Below, though we have heard the rumors that our very islands somehow go against their religion. Governor Neversky, is there any way they could bring down an island?”

“I have not heard of an ability to do so,” one of the Governors answered. “But the histories do tell of Leylines being destroyed or closed in certain cases.”

The word *Leyline* seemed oddly familiar to him, though he could not remember where he had heard it before.

“I suppose it is possible that somehow,” she went on, “someone is destroying the connections to whatever Leyline gives energy to the Islands of Helanái. It is possible, but I do not know how it could be done, or if Those Who Serve would be able to do it.”

“I believe that, if this Eodisian boy is finished, we should discuss this further in private,” said a tall, thin man garbed in green and yellow robes. He had a serious face, and long black hair worked in intricate braids. “There are preparations to be made if we are to go to war.”

Tahnir thought he should maybe be offended at being referred to as the “Eodisian boy,” but he was honestly relieved to be taken out of the center of attention. He had never enjoyed public speaking, though after Tylanna’s accident he often had to do most of the talking for the two of them. He eased himself back into his chair, and Iridia helped him after a moment's delay.

"I will escort them out," Rheleus boomed. "I have a few more words for my assistant, as well as my nephew."

Rheleus strode over towards them and wheeled Tahnir back up the pathway, giving Iridia a break. As they walked, he whispered to Iridia, "Take Tahnir around the island as we discuss this. I am sure there is much he needs to learn about his motherland, and I could not think of anyone better to teach him."

"Of course," Iridia answered.

Tahnir had never heard her say such a short sentence. It was clear her mind was elsewhere.

"And you, Tahnir, I swear I will do all I can to protect the Helanáians in the Lands Below," Rheleus said seriously. "We will talk at length when I am finished with this Council."

Tahnir glanced back at his uncle as he was being pushed up through the amphitheater. "Another thing, Uncle," Tahnir said. "My sister Tylanna and dear friend Akiye were just outside of the city when the island fell. If you have it within your power, could you find them and make sure they are safe, even bring them here, if you can?"

"Anything for my brother's child," the massive Governor replied. "I swear it to you, Tahnir. On the Sky Crown of Old, I will return your sister and friend to you."

With that, they had reached the door. Rheleus handed the handles of Tahnir's chair back over to Iridia, and she accepted with a stiff bow. "Take good care of my nephew, Iridia. Thank you for all your help."

Iridia nodded and pushed open the doors before rolling Tahnir forward, out of the amphitheater. As soon as the door had closed behind them, she broke into a full run, and before he knew it, Tahnir was being propelled from the building and into the courtyard outside.

"Iridia, what are you doing?" he cried out. He was growing tired of not being able to move about for himself. Even the moment he stood with her help in the amphitheater had left pain shooting through all of his joints.

"The hammer on your waist, where did you first get it?" she replied in a breathless voice.

The courtyard led into an open-air pathway of paved stone that was lined with immense pillars. Moving at this speed would certainly be painful if the ground below him were even slightly uneven.

He decided to answer honestly. "My father gave it to me before I left Shae Glen. He said it had been in his family for a long time, and he took it along with a sword he gave to Tylanna when he left Helanái. He wasn't proud of taking them, but he thought we should bring them back with us if we were returning to the Sky Islands. Why do you ask?"

"Some of the symbols look similar to something I have been researching with my father. He is an archeologist and historian, who focuses on the ancient histories of the Helanáian Islands," Iridia said, excitement bubbling in her voice. "I believe those symbols are from an old language of an extinct race of humans known as the Forgers. Have you used the hammer for anything?"

"Only to defend myself on the trek to Aynanu," he answered truthfully.

"Did anything feel strange when you held it?" she asked without missing a beat. Still, she ran, pushing him as fast as ever.

"Well," he said thoughtfully, his head still a bit jumbled from the impact and the healing, "there were moments when it felt as if the hammer was compelling me to swing in a certain direction. I had never been in any sort of battle before leaving Shae Glen, but I felt as if I had been using the hammer as a weapon my entire life. Also, there was one moment where... No, it must have been my imagination."

"A moment where the hammer spoke to you?" she inquired seriously.

"Yes...at least it seemed like it." Tahnir strained to remember the incident, as it was right before his accident. They flew past several groups of people that had to dive out of their way as Iridia kept up her ridiculous pace. "It was just before Lahawi fell into Aynanu. A thief had snatched the hammer from my belt without my noticing. Tylanna pointed it out, and I chased the thief through the Aynanu city gates. When I pried the hammer from his hands, I heard someone whisper to me, but it seemed to be coming from inside my head."

"What did it say?"

"'Master,'" he replied simply.

She came to an abrupt halt, and Tahnir had to latch onto the arm of the chair to not spill forward onto the smooth stone. He spun around to look at her but held back his angry words when he saw the shock on her face. Her eyes were flicking from side to side wildly as if she was puzzling something together in her mind. Beneath her ornate robes, her chest heaved, and Tahnir could not blame her after running all this way while pushing him along. When her puzzling seemed to come to an end, her eyes stabilized, and she looked into his eyes.

"I think that hammer may be more important than you know, or your father ever knew. I will take you there, to the Golden Forge. I will explain as we go."

With that, she pushed him again, at a brisk pace but not the full-on sprint she had been doing before. "I believe that hammer is one of the Spirit Blades, ancient weapons created by the Forgers to fight in the Ancient Wars of Old. According to the legends, the Forgers used some lost form of magic and were able to imbue souls created from pure energy wrought from the world into the weapons they crafted. The weapons had souls and minds of their own and were able to speak to those they chose to be their partners in combat. They were even able to possess those who wielded them in the heat of battle.

"If the old stories are to be believed, Spirit Blades gave the Forgers an advantage in the Wars of Old. However, their enemies began to steal the weapons somehow, and the battles grew more evenly matched. Using their own weapons against them, their enemies were able to drive the Forgers back to their homeland, which was in modern-day Artani. There, it is said that in a last-ditch effort, the Forgers used the last of their power to somehow rip the very land apart to flee from their enemies. This was the day the islands flew, and they have been floating in the sky since that day all those ages ago. Until Lahawi fell last week."

"In the stories, what happened to them, the Forgers?" Tahnir asked. It was the most interested he had been in any of Iridia's ramblings.

"Slowly, after the islands flew, they all died out," Iridia continued in her exited voice, even though the subject matter she discussed was somber. "Several had children with the other humans that were brought along with the islands, and their descendants became what are now known as native Helanáians. All those with Helanáian blood are descended from the great Forgers, but ever since the last true Forger died, the Golden Forge will not reignite, and no Spirit Blades have been created since then.

"Over time, the Spirit Blades were scattered across the world. Most were lost to the turning of time. The Golden Forge is kept as a memorial to them, and a symbol of Helanáian pride. But it is a dusty shell of its former glory."

Tahnir's hand drifted to his hammer and rested on the grip.

We are home.

He heard the whisper as clear as day in his head but decided to keep the message to himself. This meant whatever Iridia had said was true, and he had unbeknownst to him been carrying one of the most powerful relics that existed in modernity.

Chapter 27

CAGES

Another day began as many of the last had. He was woken by a splash of cold water on his face and greeted by the same ugly face that had stood before him all the other days since he had been imprisoned. He was in a small room made of uneven stone, blocked off by a large door of hard iron bars.

The man was put in charge of extracting any information Reynalor might have gleaned from his time with the two researchers, Vistari and Sumantoro. The ugly man, who had never given his name, was quite good at his job, but as Reynalor must have told him nearly a hundred times, he did not know anything about why the researchers had been delivered to that bloody Rhiannon woman.

His denial of knowledge was not satisfactory to the ugly man, and when he was not satisfied, he struck at Reynalor with a barb that he always kept on his person.

Reynalor thrashed at his shackles every time he was struck, desperate for a chance to wring this man's neck.

As the days passed, he wondered if he would ever leave this damned cage. Would he ever get to see Fayde and Laito, ever get to apologize for leading them down the road that led them here? He had demanded that the ugly man tell him if they lived, but the man had given him not a word.

"Today will be your last chance, boy."

Reynalor did not remember the last time he had been called *boy* by anyone. After all, he was nearly fifty years old. This man did not seem to be older than him, but he felt the disrespect dripping from every word he spoke.

"If you do not tell me what I need to know, I'm afraid there is nothing more I can do for you."

Reynalor did not know what this man had thought he had done for him, but all Reynalor knew was that he came to beat him senseless every day and left disappointed.

"I have told you everything I know," Reynalor growled. "Vistari and Sumantoro did not tell us anything, only that they were to be escorted to meet with someone known as the Maiden Rhiannon, and that their mission was very important. We were to be paid when we delivered them unharmed, but when we arrived, we were attacked by some huge person in black armor, and then I woke up here. There is nothing more to tell you, so do what you will."

“What of the young ones you encountered in the jungle?” the man shouted as he struck at Reynalor again with the barb. “What of the girl with the golden eye?”

Reynalor paused at the mention of Tylanna. Why did they single her out amongst the three? “They were nobody of importance. Young travelers that I met a few days previous in Nicol’s Wood, and we rescued them from drowning in a lake. That night they helped my boys and I protect the researchers from a Hollowpod, an ancient beast of the jungle. They left during the night. I am assuming that they did not want to be a burden on our quest.”

“Where did they come from?” the ugly man demanded, sprinkling Reynalor’s haggard face with flecks of saliva.

“They did not say. They only told us that they were crossing through the Jungle of Jiye to get to Artani.”

“Lies,” the ugly man snapped.

The barbed switch cracked across Reynalor’s stomach, ripping open a wound from the previous day. Blood poured freely, and Reynalor felt a fit of wooziness nearly overtake him. He had lost a lot of blood since he had been imprisoned, and he was unsure how much longer he could survive. Of all the monsters and beasts he had done battle with, to meet his end at the hand of this vile man before him was unacceptable.

"It is not a lie," Reynalor panted out, hating how weak his voice sounded. "I have told you nothing but the truth. Whether you choose to believe it or not is up to you."

The man released a horrid chortle, laughing in Reynalor's face. "You proud fool. If you will not cooperate, you bring death on yourself. The Maiden Rhiannon does not tolerate those who are impure."

The ugly man raised the switch in his hand and lashed repeatedly across Reynalor's chest and stomach. Each slash ripped at his taut skin and created a new spring of blood flowing down his front, his legs, and pooling beneath his feet. Reynalor had never seen the man this frenzied. He really meant to kill him this time.

Then, the man froze in place. He seemed to shrivel and fold in on himself, his eyes growing bright blue before shutting in pain. A hissing sound emanated from his body as his skin drew itself tighter and tighter, and the muscle and fat that sat below seemed to melt away until the man collapsed in a heap of shriveled skin and bone.

Behind him stood Vistari, who held her two hands outstretched before her, her fingertips stretching towards the ceiling. Her eyes were pressed shut, and she seemed to be muttering under her breath, so quiet that Reynalor could not hear her.

"You!" he shouted, though his voice could barely manage anything louder than a whisper. "You damn witch. You led us into a trap."

"Quiet, bounty hunter," she said. The softness of her reply alarmed him.

Slowly, she rotated her hands so her palms were laid flat before him. Briefly, he saw a light blue glow coming from her palms, then he felt the icy feeling he had felt when Sumantoro had healed him in the jungle. His bleeding stopped, and he felt some alleviation of the pain in his shoulder and ribs.

Her arms slumped to her side, and she opened her eyes. It was only then he noticed how rough she looked. Her once-ornate robes were torn. He could see she had been switched as well. Her eyes were dark, and the skin beneath them hung heavy with lack of sleep. Her hair had begun to grow back slightly, and she was covered in nearly as much blood and grime as he.

"I am getting you out of here," Vistari said, an extra rasp to her already low voice. "The other hunters are alive. They wait in the hallway beyond your cage. I will free the shackles from your wrists. Do you think you can walk?"

"I will manage," he said gruffly, "but why are you helping us? You dare go against the wishes of your precious *Maiden?*"

"This is not the organization I thought I was a part of. We are meant to spread the Preachings of the Eagle, not inflict violence. The Promised Dawn have corrupted the very core of Those Who Serve, and they must be stopped. I assure you I knew nothing of their plans. We were sent to learn more about the Leylines that draw together the powers of the world. We were told that we were trying to create a pathway to the Realm of the Watchers, but their plans were much more nefarious.

"They plan to use the information we found concerning the Leyline that connects the Sky Islands of Helanái to the surface to bring the islands down. They wish to make the world as it once was, as the Preachings of the Eagle state that the Watchers may only walk the world as it was at the beginning. Thus they wanted to return the flying islands to the surface to make the world whole again."

"Unlock my shackles," Reynalor said seriously. "We must go warn the Helanáians. Is there any way to stop them?"

Vistari knelt next to the body of the ugly man and rustled about his person. When she drew herself upright again, she held a large set of iron keys and went about unbolting Reynalor's shackles. "The ritual to corrupt the connection to the Leyline below the islands is a long, complicated thing. The process takes two weeks and involves twelve people with an advanced mastery of Leyline energy manipulation working in perfect synchronization. There are only a few of those amongst Those Who Serve powerful enough to complete the ritual, including Rhiannon."

When both of his arms were free, he fell forward, and Vistari tried to catch him, but they both crumbled. Both of his legs had been completely asleep, and he struggled to get them working properly. Once he was able to, he got to his feet, leaning on Vistari a bit more than he would have liked.

"So if we can find wherever the ritual is taking place and kill one of the casters, we can stop it?" Reynalor asked through clenched teeth. Each step sent a jolt of fresh pain through his body as his body struggled to wake up.

She nodded as she strained to support his remarkable mass. "And I know where the ritual will be taking place. First, they will target Lahawi, the first island, to sever the Helanáian's connection to the surface. Then, the Helanáians will be unable to stop as the ritualists move to the land beneath each island, bringing each of them crashing back into Artani. The death toll will be enormous. We must not let them succeed."

"We won't," Reynalor stated, as assuredly as he could muster in their current predicament. "As soon as we're out of here, we must find horses, and ride as fast as we can to reach the first island. Let's go."

His injured arm hung limply at his side. No feeling had returned yet. Together they limped out of the open metal door, and he was free of his cage.

There in the hallway, he saw Fayde and Laito, both standing guard facing opposite directions.

"Boys! You're all right," he cried out.

They turned to face him, both wearing wide smiles. They appeared to be as bloodied as he and Vistari, but their spirits were still strong, and that made him proud.

"We're glad you survived, old man. Wasn't sure you could still take a licking like that." Laito laughed.

Reynalor wanted to smack the man for being so casual about their situation, but Fayde spoke up.

"It is great to see you alive, Reynalor. We must be free of this prison, quickly. Did she tell you of their plans?"

"Aye," Reynalor grunted. "We must be swift. Thousands of lives depend on us."

Fayde held out a shortsword, hilt facing Reynalor. "You will need this. The guards carry them. There is no clean way free. We will have to fight our way out."

Reynalor nodded and accepted the blade with his good hand. He was able to pull himself up to his full height and stand free from Vistari's support.

"I will come with you," Vistari declared. "There are complications to the ritual only I will understand. Also, I owe it to you for leading you all into this."

Reynalor grunted in approval. "What of Sumantoro? Did he also have a change of heart?"

Vistari's face darkened. "He is dead. They Drained him, as I did to the torturer. Stole his very life force from his body, leaving him an empty shell, only driven by hunger and the will of the one who Drained him. I pretended to go along with their plan to save myself and earn my freedom, but he refused to go against his beliefs. He died thinking me a traitor and a coward."

A thrashing noise sounded from the cell Reynalor had been kept in. Vistari slammed the door shut just in time as the strange creature that had once been the ugly man slammed against the iron bars. Its strange, gaunt arms reached through the cracks, clawing wildly at the air in front of Vistari's face, which did not flinch at all. A deep sadness stretched across her whole face.

"He will remain like this, growing less and less human with each passing day. I gave Sumantoro's shell a quick death before I came to free you."

Reynalor limped over to the bars of the iron cage, still recovering the feeling in his legs. He looked the gnarled creature in the eyes, already barely recognizing the man whose face he had come to loath so. Without another moment of hesitation, he slipped his sword through the bars and through the beast's head, and it collapsed to the floor, dead.

He turned back toward the Nox brothers. "Let us be off. Stay together, and move as quietly as you can."

Allowing the boys to lead the way, Reynalor followed closely behind them. He could barely see in the dim light of the dungeon, but he trusted Fayde and Laito's vision. He felt Vistari trailing closely behind him.

After a few moments, they came across two dead guards sprawled across the rock floor. After quick confirmation from Laito that they had killed these two when Vistari had freed them, they advanced. The more he moved, the more feeling Reynalor could feel returning to his body. He even felt a few pricks of sensation in his injured arm. With proper healing, he might yet be able to save it.

They walked for several more minutes before Fayde gestured for them to come to a stop. He and Laito dashed forward, and there was the brief sound of a struggle. The two brothers returned, each holding a new sword in one of their hands. They walked by the guards they killed without stopping, and before long, they came to a locked door at the end of the hallway. Vistari stepped forward with the keys she had taken from the torturer's body and after a few attempts was able to swing the door open.

It was the middle of the night, and the door led to an alley. They all crept cautiously outside, not seeing any more guards stationed beyond.

"We are in Fas Drüeth," Vistari whispered. "Avoid anyone you see, Those Who Serve or not. We look a suspicious lot, covered in blood, wearing rags, and brandishing weapons. First, we should find clothes to change into, then horses to ride to Aynanu."

Laito grunted as if he did not see any problem with the way they looked, but Reynalor nodded in agreement. They dashed from alley to alley, doing everything to avoid catching the eye of any who were still walking about the city at this hour. The city was eerily empty. Not even a drunkard coming home from an inn crossed their path.

After nearly an hour, Fayde spotted a clothing shop that was closed up for the night. In no time at all, he had jimmied the lock open, and they snuck into the shop. Wordlessly, each of them went about grabbing whatever they could to replace the shredded and bloody garbs they were currently wearing. Fayde and Laito shamelessly stripped naked in the middle of the room, as they always did, and threw whatever fit them together, completely disregarding color or cut.

Reynalor saw Vistari spin away with embarrassment, then slip into a back room to change. While she was gone, Reynalor slipped into a decently made cotton shirt and riding pants. He grabbed a long coat that he slipped over the shirt, knowing that regions of Artani grew rather cold beneath the shadows of the sky.

Vistari reentered the room as he finished buttoning the front of the coat. Her head was wrapped in a yellow scarf, hiding nearly everything except for her eyes, and she had found a practical purple and yellow riding dress, with a slit in the skirt to allow her to spread her legs over a horse. He saw that she also wore short pants beneath.

Once they were ready, they departed from the clothing shop. Reynalor wished that they could pay the owner for the clothes, but these were desperate times. They discarded their shredded rags into the next alley they dipped into and slipped into the night. He prayed they would be able to steal decent horses to make the rest of the trip. Speed was of the utmost importance if they were to reach the ritual in time to stop it.

As they crept through Fas Drüeth under the cover of night, he hoped that the three young Eodisians had not made it to Aynanu yet.

Once they had found enough horses for each of them around the city, they rode for nearly a week, stopping only to rest the steeds and themselves, but only for a few hours at a time. But when they approached Aynanu, they knew that they were too late.

The city had already been destroyed, and the remains of the Sky Island of Lahawi lay strewn across the land below.

Reynalor cursed himself for not being able to reach Aynanu in time. They entered the wreckage of the city from the south side and had to bring the horses to a steady trot to navigate the debris. Homes, trade buildings, and towers – all had been destroyed, and none were left alive as far as they could tell.

Fayde and Laito gave the reins of their horses to Reynalor and ran off on foot, scouring the ruins for any that might still live. When they could not find anyone, they returned to the horses.

"We were much too late, I think," Vistari said in a tired whisper. "The dust has settled over the ruins. The crash must have happened some days ago."

Reynalor shook his head. How quickly had the island fallen once the Leyline connection was corrupted?

He trotted along with the others in silence, taking in the sight of the ruined city. So much death, so much pain.

Chapter 28

A WARNING

The morning after her induction into the Night Blades, Tylanna was gifted Night Legion armor by Captain Pahlio and Nuwitzwe. The armor was bulky and black, and the back of her chest piece was decorated with a bright red design of a sword springing forth from a snake's mouth. Captain Pahlio explained that their faction of the Night Legion was once known as the Night Snakes before he was given charge. He wished to pay homage to the previous faction with the design, hence the snake.

Wearing the armor took her several hours to get used to, as she felt that it constricted her movements. Along with the various plates and guards, she had also been given a new sword belt to hold Darkender. The sword now hung from her left hip, a position that Pahlio had told her would allow her to draw the blade much faster.

In the next few days, she had begun swordsmanship lessons with Pahlio every morning, before general training with the rest of the troop. Nuwitzwe would come to watch them, offering advice and words of encouragement when he could. He still was not fully recovered from the ritual he had performed beyond the gates of Aynanu.

Tylanna and Pahlio used practice blades when they fought. She did not find Pahlio to be the simple opponent she had found nearly everyone else to be. The man was an incredible blade master, and what he lacked in speed he made up for with advanced technique and the ability to predict her movements based on the way she held herself. He taught her the signs to watch for, the turning of a foot, the twisting of the torso, the twirling of the wrist. He told her once she could read all of these signs of the body, she would be able to perfect her technique and match even the most talented sword users.

Pahlio and Nuwitzwe had both described her skill with a blade as a once-in-a-generation talent, to her embarrassment. She did not have the heart to tell them that she had only recently picked up a sword for the first time in her life.

This was their fourth day training together. The night before, Captain Pahlio had addressed the entire troop and informed them that they would be returning the next day to the Artanian capital, Fas Eith, to await further orders. Tylanna still felt a touch guilty for leaving the ruined city of Aynanu before finding her brother, but Nuwitzwe had told her that he was no longer here. How that was possible, she was not sure, but she had no reason not to trust the man who had been nothing but kind to her.

Now that he had instructed her on the basics of swordplay, Pahlio was training her on how to use swords to combat different forms of weaponry. They were in the middle of a heated bout, with Tylanna barely able to deflect his short spear thrusts in time, when the sound of horses galloping sounded from within the wreckage of Aynanu. Tylanna dropped her stance to investigate the noise, and Pahlio used the opportunity to smack her breastplate with the dull end of his spear.

"Never be distracted in the middle of battle," he barked. "When it is life or death, your opponents will use whatever means they have to make sure it is you who falls, not they. With your natural skill, I anticipate a great many of your opponents resorting to trickery in order to defeat you."

She grunted and nodded in understanding, and he flashed her a friendly smile. Did he really have to smack her with the spear to teach her that point?

The chorus of galloping hooves drew nearer, and Tylanna looked to see who could be riding out of the city. Had Tahnir found his way back already? Tylanna strained her eyes to make out the figures as they turned a corner, and she saw four riders. One was a large man in a billowing coat, and two were shorter men wearing mismatched clothes. The last rider was a female in a purple dress, with her head completely covered in a wrap of some kind. It was only when they crossed the threshold of what had once been the great city gate of Aynanu that she recognized them.

"Reynalor! Fayde! Laito!" she shouted, throwing her practice sword to the ground. "It's me, Tylanna!"

The riders came to a stop in front of her, and Fayde and Laito nearly leaped from their horses clear over to her and swept her up in a hug.

Captain Pahlio was tossing his practice spear from hand to hand, eying the strangers. Nuwitzwe stepped towards them, looking serious.

From the embrace, she saw Reynalor struggle to dismount his horse, his left arm hanging limp at his side when he planted his feet on the ground. She flashed him a smile, and she noticed that the woman stayed put.

"It is so good to see you three," Tylanna said joyously. "I am sorry we left you in the jungle. We just could not trust that woman from Those Who Serve."

Reynalor staggered forward and joined their embrace, only using his right arm. "It is good to see you alive and well, Tylanna," he said in a rough whisper. His voice seemed much emptier than it had the last time she had spoken with him. "What of Tahnir and Akiye?"

Tylanna felt all the elation from the reunion seep out of her. She fell away from the bounty hunter's embrace and cast her gaze down toward the metal boots of her armor.

A hand rested on her shoulder from behind, and she saw that Nuwitzwe had approached noiselessly. He gave her a comforting nod.

"My brother was in the city when the island fell," Tylanna answered, frowning. "We searched for days but could not find him. My friend here, Nuwitzwe, used a Banéhûl ritual to detect if he was anywhere in the city, alive or dead, and he was not. Somehow, Tahnir escaped. Akiye and I each were injured, though we were outside of the city. We were rescued by the Night Blades, a faction of the Night Legion, and taken care of by their healers. Akiye became bitter with my need to find Tahnir and decided to leave, and I do not know where she went."

She felt a pang of guilt for leaving out the part where she had nearly killed Akiye when she lost control, but she did not have to burden them with everything, at least not right away.

"I have decided to join the Night Blades," she went on, trying to suppress her emotions. "I want to do anything I can to stop the violence that is engulfing the world. Since we know that Those Who Serve were targeting Helanáians, I am going to do everything we can to protect the Helanáians that were trapped on the surface when the island fell, as well as any that already lived here. I cannot shake the feeling that they are also responsible for the island falling from the sky, though I do not know how they did it."

"You are right about that, girl," the woman on the horse said coldly.

Something about the comment made the skin on the back of Tylanna's neck prickle, though she could not quite place why it seemed so familiar.

The woman began to unwrap the scarf from her head as she went on, "The island was brought down by twelve members of Those Who Serve, including one of their elite leaders, who are known as the Promised Dawn. She is known as the Maiden Rhiannon, and she possesses immense power."

The woman revealed her extremely short white hair. Looking at her eyes and pale skin, the woman did seem oddly familiar to Tylanna. It was only when she dropped the scarf away from the rest of her face that Tylanna saw it. The dangling earrings, the sharp nose, and the cruel mouth that had barked so many insults at them in the Jungle of Jiye.

Before she knew what she was doing, Tylanna had Darkender out of its sheath and was racing towards the woman. She gritted her teeth into a fierce snarl and leaped into the air. With little effort, she tackled the woman off of the horse and into the dirt.

As the dust settled around her, Tylanna found herself holding Darkender pressed against the woman's neck, breathing hard. Rage coursed through every part of her very being.

Vistari, the member of Those Who Serve she had met in the jungle. Had she been responsible for the island falling? She seemed to know enough about it.

"Tylanna, wait!" Reynalor barked. "She is with us now. We were all imprisoned by Those Who Serve, and she set us free. It was only through her we learned of their plan to bring down the island, and we raced here as fast as we could to try and stop it, but we were too late. Do not kill her – only she knows how to stop them!"

Tylanna glared down at the woman who lay defenseless underneath her. She looked up at Tylanna, almost expressionless, definitely not scared. It was as if she did not care if she lived or died.

"Tylanna," Captain Pahlio said. "We do not kill outside of battle. If this woman has wronged you, we will talk about it. If she has broken the laws of the land, she will be punished, but only when she has been proven guilty. Killing her now would make you no better than a roving bandit, dispensing justice as you see fit."

Do it.

When she heard the whisper, she sat upright, dropping Darkender into the dirt next to Vistari's head. She pulled herself back up to her feet but offered the woman no hand. Tylanna spun to face Reynalor.

"I told you that you should not trust them," Tylanna snapped at him.

He met her gaze with a frown before answering. He looked much thinner than she remembered. They all did.

"And you were right, woman," Reynalor said, "but she did not know that she led us into a trap, nor of Those Who Serve and the Promised Dawn's larger schemes. They were captured, same as us, and Sumantoro was killed for standing up to them. We all would have died in their prison if she did not free us. Now she may be our only chance to stop them from bringing the next island down."

Captain Pahlio took a step forward to address the bounty hunter. "They plan to bring down another island? When? Can we stop it?"

Vistari had pulled herself up to a seated position, and she brushed the dust from her skirts. "The ritual itself takes two weeks of constant Leyline energy manipulation by twelve casters arranged just so beneath the island. They are destroying the island's connection to the surface, which causes it to fall free from the forces of the world that hold it aloft. How long ago did this island fall?"

"Ten days past," Nuwitzwe said, brows furrowed.

"Including time for them to travel, they could already be underneath the second island as we speak," Vistari said urgently, all the while giving Tylanna a dirty look. "We must reach them and kill any of the casters of the ritual to halt it. Who is the leader of your troop?"

"I am," Pahlio said confidently, all the casual joviality gone from his face. "And Nuwitzwe here is my vice. I will send word to the other factions of the Night Legion, and we can make way to the land beneath Talakoko immediately."

The next hour passed in a flurry of chaos. Tylanna had raced ahead of the others to inform the other soldiers to prepare to depart immediately and prepare for battle. The camp erupted at the news, and her fellow members of the Night Blades rushed about making all preparations necessary.

Captain Pahlio returned to the site on Vistari's horse, with her clutching onto him as he rode like a man possessed. Nuwitzwe and the bounty hunters arrived moments later, and Nuwitzwe and Pahlio each went about organizing the troops.

First Pahlio went about securing enough horses and riders to send off to the other factions of the Night Legion that were scattered about Artani. They each carried a short message: "Those Who Serve are trying to bring down a second Island, Talakoko. The Night Blades ride now to stop the ritual below the island, requesting any reinforcements that are available to dispatch immediately."

When he was organizing the messengers, Tylanna saw Reynalor pull Captain Pahlio to the side and talk with him. After they spoke, Pahlio barked an order to one of the riders, and he heeled his horse over to where the soldiers were amassing.

Tylanna strode over to Reynalor. She was ready to leave at any moment, as she did not have many belongings. Once she had retrieved Darkender, she had been packed. As she approached, Reynalor regarded her with a dim look in his eyes.

"You will ride with them then, Tylanna?" he asked.

"Of course. It is my duty, after all. I am now one of the Night Blades, same as any of them," she said, sounding much more confident than she actually felt. "What was it you were saying to the captain?"

"I ride for Fas Eith. I told him that I could deliver the message to the legionnaires there."

"You will not come with us? Reynalor, you could be all the difference we need to defeat Those Who Serve today. I have seen how you can fight!" she burst out, confused on how he could not assist in the coming conflict.

Several of her comrades looked to her as they ran about with their preparations.

"The lad that was going to ride as a messenger will surely do just as well as I could," Reynalor said gruffly, looking off at the scrambling members of the Night Blades. He took a deep sigh and turned to face Tylanna directly before continuing. "I was injured, you see. We were surprised when we met with that Rhiannon woman by a mysterious figure in black armor with a blade made of rust. They crushed my left shoulder, and I have not been able to use my arm since. If you encounter them on a battlefield, do everything you can to get away from them. You are strong, but this mad beast is stronger. I would be no good in a fight. I need healing, and then I will return to the safe house I have in Artani. Maybe see Amelie again."

"You with one arm is still twice the fighter as most who are here," she snapped. "How can you *still* not stand against Those Who Serve?"

"Believe me, woman," he grumbled, "I do stand against them. No matter the outcome, this battle will not be the end of the conflict. I must recover so that I can stand another day. When word gets out that it was Those Who Serve that brought down the island, it will spark an explosion of violence across the entire world."

"And what of Fayde and Laito?" she asked curtly. "Will they ride to Fas Eith as well?"

"They are free men," he replied. "They will do as they wish. But they are not soldiers, Tylanna, and neither were you until a few days ago. You must be careful and know that the greatest victory is to live on and fight another day. We each only get but one life. We must be sure to do as much good as we possibly can. There is no sense in dying namelessly in a pile of bodies on a battlefield."

"Worry not, Reynalor," she said still frustrated that the old man was being so stubborn, "I will not die. I will strike back against Those Who Serve, and continue fighting until all can live without fear of being killed for who they are."

"Are you not going to kill the members of Those Who Serve for who they are?" he asked quietly. He turned away, leaving her in stunned silence. He mounted a horse with some notable effort and departed camp. She saw Fayde and Laito follow behind on the horses they had ridden in on. Disappointment flooded through her as she watched them go.

"You cannot change him, Tylanna," a voice said from behind her. "He is a stubborn old man who is set in his own ideals."

Tylanna spun around to see Vistari clutching the reins of her horse in her hands. "Those Who Serve must be stopped before another island is brought down. In doing so, you will save thousands of lives. It is the right thing to do."

"Pardon me if I do not trust your judgment," Tylanna scoffed. "It seems only moments ago that you were a member of Those Who Serve yourself."

"I follow the Preachings of the Eagle," Vistari snapped back, regaining some of the harshnesses she once had. "I thought we all did. But what they are doing is clearly wrong, so I will do everything I can to stop them. Then, if I succeed, I will try to bring the organization back to its roots and burn away any corruption that lies within."

"I still do not trust you, Vistari," Tylanna growled, stepping in so she was nose to nose with the woman. "And the last people whose trust you had just left camp. I would tread carefully, were I you."

Tylanna whirled away and tried to busy herself helping her comrades prepare. In less than an hour, they were ready to depart, and Tylanna sat atop a horse that had been provided for her. She had been positioned as a member of the advance guard. There were only enough horses remaining in camp for a little less than half of the Night Blades, so all that were riding would rush to below Talakoko. The rest of the faction would follow on foot, running the entire way. Captain Pahlio would ride with the advance guard, and Nuwitzwe would take command of the foot soldiers. Vistari was also to ride with the advance guard next to Pahlio to guide him to the ritual when they arrived.

The area beneath Talakoko was said to be a barren stretch of valley in the center of a mountain range. It was about a day's ride away. The suns had just begun to set in the sky as the advance guard tore away from the campsite, riding as hard as their horses would allow.

The wind whipped through Tylanna's hair as she rode, doing everything she could to remain calm. She was riding into battle, where it was kill or be killed. It might fall to her to kill one of the ritual casters. Could she justify killing someone in order to save the thousands of Helanáians that lived on the island? Logically, it made sense to her. But could she bear to live with herself knowing that she had ended someone else's life?

Once the suns had fully set, still the Night Blades rode on. If they did not reach the land beneath Talakoko in time, thousands would die, and once more, they would be left to do nothing but sift through rubble, searching for survivors.

Chapter 29

BATTLE IN THE SHADOW

Tylanna and the other members of the Night Blades' advance guard crested the mountain that guarded the valley below the Sky Island of Talakoko. They had ridden without breaking, and Tylanna could tell that her horse was nearing the limit of its ability. The horse had begun to lag behind the other riders, no matter how she urged it to press on. She did not want to ride the animal to death, but the other members of the advance guard of the Night Blades showed no sign of slowing.

It was only when the first riders arrived at the summit that they came to a crashing halt. When Tylanna's horse caught up with the rest of the pack, she saw what had caused them to stop.

The mountain they sat upon was part of a large chain that wrapped around the deep valley meant to be a barren stretch of wilderness, but it was anything but barren.

From where she sat upon her tired horse, Tylanna could see a force of nearly two thousand soldiers milling about in a well-defended perimeter. They all wore the stark white armor that she recognized from the carnage in Shae Glen. Surely, these were members of Those Who Serve.

For a moment, her vision flickered. Her sight was drawn to the center of the valley, where it seemed the soldiers were focused. She could not quite make out any of the people that stood beyond the line, but for a moment, as her vision blurred, she could see a series of gigantic ethereal green chains that stretched from the ground all the way into the clouds above.

Twelve chains. Tendrils of white energy wrapped around the base, clear as the light of morning that had begun to spill over the peaks. The chains seemed to be darkening from the bottom as if they were growing old before her very eyes.

Just as quickly as they had appeared, her vision blurred once more, and she could no longer see them.

"They have already begun."

Tylanna had not realized that she had crested the mountain directly next to Vistari, who had muttered the comment almost to herself, fear etched into each word.

Just beyond her sat Captain Pahlio, his eyes wide as he took in the force before him.

"So many..." he whispered. "I did not expect so many of them."

Tylanna did not think that anyone but him was meant to hear that.

"Those Who Serve are numerous and everywhere, Captain Leor, but we... They are meant to be peaceful worshippers," Vistari said. "All those in the valley have forsaken the Preachings of the Eagle. They carry weapons and are committing atrocities in the name of the Watchers. If we do not stop the ritual, all of those Helanáians on the island will die."

"What are we to do, Pahlio...erm, Captain?" Tylanna asked, trying to keep fear out of her voice.

"Vistari is right. We have no choice but to fight," he said matter-of-factly. "Where will the casters be?"

"At the center of the valley, where the chains are reaching from," Vistari replied quickly.

"What chains – what do you mean?" he stammered.

Tylanna wondered how he could have missed those gargantuan green chains of glowing metal, but he seemed genuinely confused.

"You may not be able to see them," Vistari added apologetically. "But the twelve casters will be positioned behind the perimeter, arranged at different points in a complex pattern necessary for the ritual. Each of them will be locked in a trance-like state, unaware of what goes on around them, which should make them easy targets. If we can kill but one, we can end this before the island ever begins to fall. But we must hurry."

Pahlio scanned the mounted soldiers that surrounded him, desperation in his eyes. Not including the troop that Nuwitzwe was leading behind them on foot, the Night Blades numbered a mere two hundred. Tylanna wondered what chance they could have against such a massive force, even if they were mounted. She had not seen any horses among the enemy forces.

"Night Blades!" Pahlio shouted. "Our objective is to locate the casters of this dark ritual and kill them! We must save those who are on the Sky Island above at any cost. Break through the line, any way you can, no matter the price. We will not have the tragedy of Aynanu repeat before our very eyes, not when we may stop it."

He pulled at his reins and trotted forward down the broad path that stretched before them, cascading down the mountain range into the valley. Once he had gotten several yards in front of the rest of the riders, he heeled his horse to turn and face his followers. His face held a dark seriousness that she had never seen on the young captain before. When he next spoke, his voice boomed and echoed all around Tylanna and her new comrades.

"We ride this day, and we will ride again this night. If we fall, we ride forever in the hearts of those who would stand up against the forces of evil that plague this realm, Artani, and beyond. We will never ride alone. We will be together, as one force, forever. Night Blades, ride with me! We are the night, and the night is we!"

The other Night Blades erupted in a cry. Tylanna even found herself yelling along with them, and Pahlio turned his horse back around and thundered down the mountainside. As Tylanna spurred her horse after him, she saw him draw the two curved blades he wore at his waist and release a loud yell, using only his knees to grip onto the horse that raced down the steep path at full speed.

The yell was echoed by the other riders, who Tylanna saw were all swarming down the mountainside along with her. There was a song of steel ringing through the air as the other riders drew their weapons. With only a moment's hesitation, Tylanna gripped the hilt of her black blade and drew forth Darkender.

To Death!

To her surprise, the whispering voice that had invaded her head for the past several weeks had grown to a roar, impossible to ignore. Now that she brandished the blade above her head as she rode, a sickly mixture of fear, rage, and glee raced through her as the Night Blades descended the mountain path. She noticed the white-clad soldiers scattering, rearranging their formations.

So they see us coming. It matters not.

As their storm of hooves drew nearer, the enemy became more clear to Tylanna's vision. True, they numbered more than the Night Blades, but their formations were much less tightly knit than she had thought. Her mind raced as she traced several paths she could take to skirt around their forces and rush straight towards the ritual. If she could see the chains that Vistari had talked about one more time, she knew she could find the ritual casters. As the woman had said, once they killed the caster, the ritual would end. Then it did not matter what happened afterward, as far as she was concerned.

"Arrows!" she heard Pahlio call out, and before she knew it, the air around her was filled with the twanging of bowstrings and the whistle of feathered arrows screeching forward from their notches.

Soon, a downpour of death rained down onto the front lines of Those Who Serve. Many of them fell, but even more rose to replace them. The closer the Night Blades got to the line of the perimeter, the tighter the line seemed to grow.

They must be diverting all of their forces to stopping us, she thought. *If we could just get around them, we could make a clean break to the casters.*

In the moments before the two forces collided, all thoughts of strategy and aggression fell from her mind, and she thought of home. She thought of her brother, her father, and her mother, all happy and smiling around the large wooden table that their father had built with his own two hands. Before the secrets, before the tragedies, before it all, they were just a simple happy family who wished for nothing more in the world than to be with each other. Her attention returned to the valley once more, and she was calm.

There was an explosion of breaking wood and clashing steel as the knot of riders bashed into the front line of the perimeter Those Who Serve had managed to erect before them. Tylanna's horse seemed to stamp its way over three or four of the white-clad soldiers before she even had a chance to see their faces.

Then, a large bolt weaved its way through the crowd and struck her steed in its head, and the horse fell, dead.

Tylanna was thrown forward, hard, and crashed into a large man's long shield. He was dressed in white plated armor that nearly covered every inch of him, and he shoved Tylanna to the ground.

The current of horses parted around her as she fell, and she was thankful that her fellow Night Blades had even seen her at all in this chaos. She supposed that they had more experience in battle than she did.

The man before her drew a long steel blade from behind his shield and looked at her with hate in his eyes.

Luckily, she had not dropped Darkender in the fall, and she brought the blade to a ready position.

Too much metal. Will be slow. You will dance on him with ease.

She knew the thought to be true when the man clumsily swung the longsword towards her. She was able to duck from the path of the blade and drive Darkender below the man's arm. The metal of his armor crumpled inward as the blade ripped through the thin layer, and he collapse into a heap of flesh and metal.

Without stopping to think of what she had done, Tylanna continued into the thick of the battle.

For a moment, she had lost all semblance of her location. Around her were merely bodies, living, dead, and dying. Several more of Those Who Serve lashed out at her, probably seeing her as a small woman and an easy target. Once she had proved each of them wrong with a quick strike of Darkender, she took a moment to try and discern where the defensive line began and ended.

Many of her fellow Night Blades had been thrown from their horses around her, and they were doing their best to hack their way through the perimeter. She searched for Captain Pahlio, but he was nowhere to be found.

Her searching was interrupted by a swinging axe that she was just barely able to pull one of her arms away from. It was swung by a woman in chainmail with a white helmet covering her face. Tylanna parried the swings of the axe a few times before driving Darkender's tip into the woman's stomach. She twisted the blade before pulling it free, and her opponent fell to their knees, collapsing to the trampled dirt.

Still, the Captain was not in her sightline, but she did find Vistari struggling to fend off an attacker that had set upon her with a long, curved blade.

The woman carried no weapon, but she seemed to be able to dodge the swings of the blade with little effort. Several times, the fabric of her purple riding dress was torn by the tip of the blade.

On one particular step backward, she tripped over a body of a Night Blade rider that had fallen behind her. She sprawled onto the ground, and her attacker strode forward, raising their blade.

For a moment, Tylanna debated if the woman was worth saving. She had been a member of Those Who Serve, the organization that had brought death and suffering to Shae Glen. But if what Reynalor had said was to be believed, she had not been aware of their more villainous transgressions. She had told them of the ritual, and how to stop it, as well as ridden with them into the heat of battle to do everything she could to stop her former comrades.

Tylanna was pulling her blade out of Vistari's attacker's back before she even realized that she had made up her mind. She lent Vistari a hand to help the short-haired woman back to her feet.

"Thank you, Tylanna."

Vistari laid two hands on Tylanna's back.

Tylanna felt a surge of warmth snake its way through her body. She felt fully rested and powerful, even after the night of riding.

"I have given you a part of my blessing," Vistari said in her low voice, straining to be heard over the noise of the battle. “These heretics deserve to have their own abilities used against them. Use it to cut as many down as you can.”

“I will!” Tylanna shouted over the rage of battle around them. “Can you still see the chains?”

“Yes, twelve of them for each of the casters. We are still hundreds of feet from any of them. It will be nigh impossible to reach them through this line. But I think there were still some riders that managed to stay on their horses. May Those Who Watch guide them to the casters in time.”

One of the soldiers of Those Who Serve came crashing towards them from close combat with one of Tylanna’s comrades who had just fallen while clutching at a hemorrhaging wound in his neck. She knew that he was lost, but still wished she could do something for him. His face had been one of the many that had watched her initiation ritual and cheered for her.

Tylanna made quick work of the soldier that had wounded him and dashed over to her injured comrade, supporting his head as his already-fogging eyes gazed up at her.

“Golden Eyes,” he murmured, his voice wet with blood. “You must stop them. My family is... My family is Helanáian. They must be stopped.”

Tylanna looked down at the dying man, and all fear and sadness fell away. She would stop them. She would save this man’s family.

Vistari dove towards them, just barely avoiding a spear that flew through the air from nearby combat, from who knew which side.

As she scuttled across the bloodstained ground, she laid hands on the man. “I can try and stop the bleeding, but I do not think he will fight again. Protect us for a moment, Tylanna.”

Tylanna gently set the man back onto the ground and drew herself up to her feet. She inhaled deeply as she brandished Darkender. The battle raged in every direction around them, but oddly she felt at peace. She could see the flow of battle before her. The next step each enemy would take, where their weapons would fall – it was all so clear to her. She drew the black blade up even higher and stepped forward into the chaos.

Allow me, Master.

Before she knew what was happening, she was seeing her body move through her own eyes, but doing nothing to control it. Her arms swung Darkender with a deadly efficiency that she had never achieved before in any of her training. In seconds, she carved a circle free of Those Who Serve around Vistari and her dying comrade.

Enemies dashed toward her as they saw their compatriots fall. But they too met the black steel of Darkender and fell in a bloody heap. The bodies of her victims piled around her until she saw herself leap over them to drive Darkender through the face guard of an encroaching soldier.

Her body used the momentum of the jump to roll forward, all the while slashing wildly at the ankles of the enemies she passed. She saw herself spring out of the roll and lunge forward at her next victim, who was a man in black armor whose face held only shock.

With all of her might, she forced herself to take control of her own body once more and stopped Darkender before it cleaved through her fellow Night Blade.

Once she had regained her composure, she nodded an apology at her comrade before turning back to where Vistari sat with the dying man. Vistari had risen to her feet and was rushing toward Tylanna.

"He is gone. I was too late!" she yelled as she approached. "But I did not know you could fight like that. We may yet have a chance of reaching the casters from here. I will follow behind, helping when I can."

Tylanna turned back to the battle before her, her fingers gripping Darkender's hilt apprehensively. She could not lose control again. She could not lose control again. A breath, and then she plunged into the frenzy once more.

The fighting continued for many hours. Tylanna and Vistari had managed to inch their way a few hundred feet closer to the ritual, but Vistari had informed her that they still had a ways to go. With each duel Tylanna entered, she felt her body growing more and more tired. Her enemies' movements had also become more sluggish, and most fights were finished after one sloppy swing of her blade.

She had seen many Night Blades fall to Those Who Serve. For every comrade she stopped to help, another two fell on the other side of her. Still, she had not seen Captain Pahlio the entire battle, and she worried for his safety. Several times she had been wounded by a blade she just could not dodge, and Vistari had done what she could to stop the bleeding each time. Tylanna could tell the aged woman was approaching her limit, no matter how she protested that she could go on. Though, Tylanna supposed that neither of them had the choice to stop fighting this deep into the battle. If they stopped now, they would be killed.

A cry rang out over the din of the battlefield that drew Tylanna's gaze. She saw a member of the Night Blades fly through the air and land in a crumpled mass of black armor, broken limbs, and blood. As she stared, she saw the armor on his body rust and crumble away, as if years were passing before her very eyes.

"Tylanna!" Vistari yelped. "That is the magic of Rhiannon's Madness. We must do everything we can to avoid it."

"What evil is this?" Tylanna asked.

"It manifests as a large fighter garbed in ebony armor wielding a rusted blade. It is an extension of her mighty power. When we were to meet with Rhiannon, it appeared from nothing and defeated Reynalor and the others, and then captured Sumantoro and I. We cannot win against such an opponent."

Tylanna looked in the direction from which the body had flown and thought she could just barely make out a horned helmet that stood well above any of the other fighters around it. The helmet weaved at a speed that should be impossible for one so immense, and Tylanna could see the blade of rust raised into the air for a moment before it swung down into the crowd.

Vistari placed a firm hand on her back. "Now is not the time to prove your worth, girl. We must reach the ritual in time."

Tylanna shook her head and turned her gaze back to the path they were hacking. Vistari was right, as much as she hated to admit it. She did everything she could to ignore the cries of her comrades as the blade of rust crashed through the crowd and sprinted forward with all of her might.

The enemies before her gave no indication of running out of fighters to replace each she felled. Though the fighters seemed far slower than they had a few hours before, more appeared. Tylanna thought that the fighting would never end, that surely she would collapse from exhaustion far before the battle could be won.

Just before she gave up hope, she noticed something trailing down one of the mountainsides in the distance. She peered closer and saw a stream of black-garbed people racing down the steep mountain face on foot. The group was on the opposite side of the valley from where she had ridden in the morning. If she squinted, she could see Nuwitzwe at their head.

Had the captain and Nuwitzwe planned this the entire time? she thought. *Had Pahlio wanted to draw their forces towards the advance guard to create an opening for the foot soldiers?*

A cry of elation rang out from the members of the advance guard that still fought on. She could see several of the Those Who Serve fighters with confused expressions peeking out from below their white helmets.

Tylanna used this opportunity to push forward, further into their tight perimeter, all the while cutting down any she could.

Even with Nuwitzwe and the others, they would still be wildly outnumbered in the valley. But stretching the forces of Those Who Serve to defend both sides of the ritual might allow for an opportunity for the Night Blades to slip through and kill one of the casters.

As she dashed through the fighters in white armor, she kept a hand on Vistari to ensure that the woman would stay close to her in the chaos of battle.

She came to an abrupt stop when Vistari called out, "Tylanna, there! One of the chains leads directly over here. The caster bringing it down must be close."

The woman was pointing to where there was a clump of heavily armored fighters standing in a knot, not engaging in the battle besides cutting down the odd Night Blade that ventured too close.

Tylanna took a deep breath to prepare herself. "Stay behind me," she shouted back to Vistari. "We will cut our way through and kill the caster, no matter what may become of us."

She readjusted her grip on Darkender as she saw Vistari's face fall into an expression of grim determination, though she did her best to ignore the voice ringing inside her head asking her to let it take over once more.

Dashing forward with Vistari right behind her, Tylanna dove towards the line of heavily armored members of Those Who Serve. As soon as she got close, a downpour of blades came falling through the air above her.

It was all she could do to swing Darkender at the falling steel to attempt to parry. She blocked most of the swords, axes, and spears, but a few evaded her block, and she received several gashes and cuts in just a moment.

Leaping back, she reassumed her stance, hoping to draw them out toward her, to take away from their advantage in numbers.

But they did not take her bait, standing in the same position they had been in, glaring at her with venom.

Warm blood poured from her newly acquired wounds. She had been nicked by the point of a sword on her forehead, and she struggled to wipe the blood free from her eyes. A warm feeling coursed through her as she felt Vistari's hands rest on her back, though each time she healed Tylanna, it was proving less and less effective.

When Vistari had finished, Tylanna looked over her wounds. While they still bled, they did not seem as deep as they had a moment ago. Once more, she wiped the blood away from her face and drew Darkender to prepare for a frontal assault.

A whistling sound rang from beside her, and a spear rocketed past her towards the wall of guardians. She watched the weapon sail through the air in a neat line. It struck true, and one of the heavily armored soldiers was felled in an instant.

She turned back to see who had thrown the spear, only to reveal Captain Pahlio rushing past her, pulling one of his curved blades free from his waist while brandishing his other in his opposite hand.

Without sparing a look in her direction, he let out a cry as he crashed into the clump of Those Who Serve soldiers that stood before him. She regarded him, shock and relief flooding her as she realized that Pahlio was still alive. He was covered in blood, and Tylanna could not tell if any of it was his.

As he leaped, he plunged both of his blades into one of the armored fighters, easily maneuvering the swords through the small gaps that the armor left unprotected. He wrenched the two swords free and parried the onslaught of weaponry, his steel flashing through the air at a speed that even Tylanna could barely keep up with.

Realizing that she was only standing there, watching her captain locked in deadly combat, she rushed in after him, holding Darkender poised to strike.

Side by side with Pahlio, Tylanna slashed furiously at the line of enemies before them. They worked together wonderfully, supporting each other with each step closer to the line of enemies.

One by one, each of the defensive perimeter fell to their steel. Slowly but surely, Tylanna and Pahlio advanced.

Once they had cleared a gap in the line of defenders, what they had been defending was revealed. At the center of the knot of soldiers was a thin man clad in white robes and the same white gem earrings that Vistari wore who hung suspended several feet above the ground with nothing supporting him. His eyes were stretched open, and his face held a look of horror as he looked up at the sky above him. His arms hung limply at his side, motionless.

For a moment after she saw him, Tylanna's vision blurred again, and she saw that one of the gargantuan chains she had seen earlier stretched from the ground directly in front of where the man was floating. Where before they had been a vibrant green, the chains were now a molten copper, as though rust had overtaken them.

"That is the caster!" Vistari cried from behind her. "Kill him, and the ritual should end! Hurry, the chains are weakening!"

Tylanna lifted Darkender to strike, only to see one of Pahlio's swords fly through the air and strike the man in the chest. He fell to the ground in a heap, blood pooling on his white robes.

Her vision flickered once more, and the chain disappeared. The remaining soldiers around them let up a cry and attacked them with full force.

Just as Tylanna felt her back press against Pahlio's, she heard Those Who Serve's cry answered by another, and a wave of Night Blades on foot came rushing to their support. A wave of brilliant white light erupted from around Tylanna and Pahlio, and the soldiers from Those Who Serve were all blown back from their positions.

As they fell, the approaching Night Blades dove forward and finished them off, one by one. Behind them strode Nuwitzwe, his eyes glowing white, and the same brilliant light that had just erupted around her wrapped around his arms and hands. Tylanna could see plumes of light floating from all around them on the battlefield toward Nuwitzwe, becoming one with the light he controlled with his hands.

He is using the energy from the death all around us as a weapon, she thought. Banéhûl magic was amazing to her.

Nuwitzwe walked the rest of the way over to them and dropped his hands to his sides, and the glow faded from his eyes. Vistari hobbled over to their cluster. The fighting raged on around them.

"I'm glad you're all okay. How goes the mission?" Nuwitzwe asked.

"My brother, I am glad you are well," Pahlio answered. "I have just slain one of those casting the ritual, so it should all be ending soon. Now our priority is to assemble the Night Blades and defend our retreat."

Tylanna could not believe they had accomplished their mission. With the caster killed, the ritual could not be completed, and the Sky Island would not fall.

Dread settled over her. She could feel a menacing presence rise behind her. Turning as quickly as she could, she saw a towering figure garbed in deep ebony armor who was at least twice her height. The figure wore a horned helmet, and she could not see their face through the gaps. A large, rusted blade was held before its chest with the tip of the blade plunged into the ground before it.

She noticed Vistari, Pahlio, and Nuwitzwe all turn a moment later than her.

Before any of them had a chance to react, the figure lashed out with its giant hand and grabbed Vistari, lifting her from the ground by her head as if she weighed nothing at all. Vistari grabbed at the creature's hand, crying out.

Without wasting another moment, Tylanna struck at the being's arm with Darkender, but before she could make contact, the massive creature had already slipped away from their grouping, seeming to disappear and reappear as it moved, racing over to where the ritual caster lay, bleeding on the dirt of the valley.

Tylanna and Pahlio dashed after it, with Nuwitzwe following close behind, the tendrils of light encircling his arms once more. Rhiannon's Madness reached the the caster and forcibly thrust Vistari into the same position. Golden light emanated from the earrings.

Before Tylanna and the others could even reach her, Vistari's eyes rolled back in her head, and her body grew limp. She seemed to shrivel, as if drying in the sun for years, and from the golden light spawned thin chains that appeared to be made of golden metal. They wormed their way around Vistari's throat before maneuvering their way around the rest of her body and tightening dramatically.

Tylanna's vision flickered, and she could see the massive green chains. It seemed that the being, what Vistari had called Rhiannon's Madness, had forcibly used her body to fill the space of the ritual caster Pahlio had just killed. The chain appeared to be corroding away.

All of their work had been for nothing. The ritual was continuing, and they had delivered Vistari to be used as a replacement.

Rhiannon's Madness released Vistari, and she hung suspended in the air, her body limp. It turned to face Tylanna and the others and lifted the giant, rusted blade from where it had dragged it through the ground and held it aloft.

Fear raced through Tylanna. *How can we fight a supernatural monstrosity such as this*? she thought. *What can we possibly do?*

Allow me, Master.

As the thought rang through her head and she lifted Darkender to defend herself, a loud rumbling sounded from above them.

The Sky Island of Talakoko was falling.

Chapter 30

THE GOLDEN FORGE

Tahnir couldn't count the minutes he'd been holding onto his chair for dear life today. As Iridia wheeled him down the streets of Mete'olu at full speed, her lecture on the Forgers and the Spirit Blades sent needles through his body. Had his father known the importance of the hammer he had gifted him? Was Tylanna's sword one of these Spirit Blades? So many questions raced through his head that he found it hard to focus on what Iridia was trying to tell him.

Before long, they came upon a long staircase made of white marble. From what he could see, there seemed to be two others leading up to the building, which was a large rectangular hall with ceilings supported by interlacing columns that allowed fresh air to flow through.

Iridia brought his chair to a halt at the base of the stairs before them. "We have arrived at the memorial to the Forgers. I will have to help you up the stairs from here. There is no ramp."

Begrudgingly, Tahnir allowed Iridia to help him out of his chair. He grit his teeth to try and muffle the sharp gasp that he released as he rose. His injuries had not yet healed, and his body ached. While trying to put as little of his weight as he could on the short woman, he took the first step up the marble stairwell.

"The memorial has been preserved as it was the day the forge went dark," Iridia continued to lecture Tahnir as they trudged up each step. "Helanáians visit the forge to reflect on our history. I am hoping that the hammer will serve as some clue to our ancient past, but no matter what happens, I think it is important that you see it. You have much to learn about your homeland, Tahnir."

"A forge may be the one thing about these islands that is familiar to me," he replied as they struggled up the steps. "My father was the best forge master in Shae Glen, maybe all of Eodisia, and I was his apprentice until I left the village. I hope to return to my work after all of this is sorted out."

"Is that so?" she asked inquisitively. "Then you may have some more insight into the forge than I expected."

As they reached the top, Tahnir gripped onto a ledge beside him and doubled over to catch his breath. He was embarrassed at how tired ascending a simple flight of stairs had made him, but he felt as if he had absolutely no energy at all.

Iridia kept her hand underneath his shoulder, waiting patiently, though he could feel the urgency emanating from her. Once he had caught his breath, he pulled himself up straight. When he did, the Golden Forge lay bare to his hungry gaze..

It was by far the largest forge he had ever seen and could easily fit ten or twenty of the Desqens' forge inside with room to spare. The floor and walls were composed of the same white marble as the staircases. The high vaulted ceiling had several openings that he assumed were crafted to allow the smoke of the forge to escape. Lining the back wall were several rounded metal tanks that he assumed would hold the fires, but he could tell that they had not been used in ages. In front of each tank was a large anvil, at least he assumed that was what the large block of metal was. They were shaped differently than what he was used to. Quenching stations sat empty. He would be curious to see what mixture the Forgers had used.

The forge had anything he had ever dreamed of, and at first glance, he thought not of the ancient history of this hallowed place, but of all he could accomplish if he had access to a forge such as this.

All the entrances were roped off by thick violet barricades. Tahnir now saw that four staircases led to the forge, one from each side of the rectangular room. Even standing where he was, he felt a tremendous flow of air which drew his eyes to the intricacy of the marble walls. It seemed that they channeled the air through the room and up towards the ceiling.

The entire space was coated in thick layers of dust and the rust of aged metal. It seemed to have been at least a year since its last good cleaning. Still, he marveled at the varnished gold and wondered if the entire room was filled with it. From what he knew of the little gold he had worked during his apprenticeship, forging on gold made little sense, apart from being aesthetically pleasing. He would love to get a closer look to see if he could tell what the strange metal was.

Before he could speak, Iridia was lifting the violet rope and glancing around. “Hurry, before anyone sees us!”

Tahnir raised his eyebrows. “Are we allowed in? I thought you said this was some sort of a memorial.”

“If we were to follow all the rules and wait for every permission, nothing would ever get done. Hurry up, you big lump.”

Tahnir stole a look behind him. There was no one to be seen, and he really did wish to get a closer look at the forge. Before giving it too much thought, he ducked under the rope she held aloft and steadied himself on the ledge as Iridia entered just behind him.

As he went inside the chamber of the forge, the breeze grew stronger. The intricate marble of the walls did work the wind through the room nicely. He took a moment to take it in.

Everything was set up precisely as he would have done himself, save one large anvil that was set in the center of the room. It was near no furnace or quenching bath and was shaped differently from the others, more angular and jagged.

"According to the legends, the Forgers never let the fires dim for a moment, forging day and night, crafting all sorts of wonders that still exist to this day," Iridia said with wonder hanging from her every word. "They never tired or required sleep and were said to possess immense strength, beyond that of other humans. But when the last true-born Forger passed on, it is said that all of the fires died out at the same time, and the Golden Forge went dark. The runes and markings of your hammer are from the Forgers' language, so in all likelihood, it was crafted right where we now stand."

As Tahnir reached the strange anvil in the center of the room, he used his hand to brush away the dust that had settled on the surface. Beneath lay the same tarnished golden metal that he had seen around the forge. As his hand lay pressed against the metal, a tingling sensation danced across his skin.

"What is this anvil, Iridia?" he asked.

"While we are not entirely positive about any part of the Forgers' history, it is upheld that the anvil you are touching was either too misshaped to be used, or it was bent out of shape in the forging of the Spirit Blades."

Tahnir's fingers traced along the edges and contours of the anvil. Small shivers shot into his fingers. *This metal is not misshapen*, he thought. *Each line was done purposefully.*

He was so caught up in examining the anvil that he did not hear Iridia approach to stand just behind him. In truth, he did not seem to notice anything around him. For this moment, it was only he and the odd-shaped anvil at the center of the Golden Forge.

He pressed both of his hands firmly against the sides of the anvil and found a groove that allowed his hands to rest comfortably. Each prick or thrill could be felt so clearly, as if he could feel the metal between his hands just as clearly as his own body. The way the matter of the metal was stitched together, the way the metal had been shaped and bent, the fires that had forged it.

Master, use me.

Tahnir released his hands from the anvil and stumbled backward as the voice rang through his head. He had heard this voice before, and he now believed, if what Iridia had been saying about Spirit Blades was true, that this voice was his hammer communicating with him.

Iridia rushed to help him back to his feet, but he held a hand aloft, indicating for her to wait. Slowly, he slid his hand down towards the handle of the hammer and undid the clasp that held it in place on his belt. His hands found the perfect groove for his hand, as they always had since his father had given him the hammer.

He gathered all his focus towards the hammer and pressed his free hand on the cool metal of the anvil. This time the inner workings of the hammer itself were laid bare before him.

In his mind's eye, he could see the hammer being forged on the very anvil grasped in his hand. He could see the hammer striking other weapons against the anvil. What he had thought was a weapon had been a tool for crafting, he realized. He now knew why the hammer had felt so natural in his hands.

Before he knew what was happening, he was standing on his feet over the anvil. He was unaware if Iridia had helped him up or not. The hammer almost seemed to be vibrating with energy.

Strike the anvil and relight the Forge. Let the fires of the creator burn once more.

Tahnir raised the hammer above his head and brought it down on the misshapen anvil.

His ears rang as metal struck metal, and blinding light erupted from the anvil. Tahnir was blown backward into Iridia, and the pair of them fell to the marble floor in a heap.

"What have you done?" Iridia asked, a mix of fear and excitement in her voice.

The light from the anvil faded, and Tahnir could finally see what was happening. All dust and signs of the ages that had passed since the anvil was last used seemed to be burning away with a flare of golden light originating from the point where Tahnir had struck the anvil. When the pulse of golden light reached the metal tanks, each of them roared to life, blaring with fires. They shone with a golden light, and the fires they housed burned blue and yellow. The flames seemed to swirl about in the tanks freely, without ever passing the precipice of the exposed front.

Once the entirety of the forge had been returned to its former splendor, Tahnir saw the pulse of golden energy pass through the walls that surrounded them and towards the rest of the island.

Iridia scrambled to her feet to watch the light go through the open gaps in the wall, and Tahnir lifted himself to his feet and looked around in awe at the forge that surrounded him, gripping the hammer in his right hand.

Before him was the Golden Forge in all of its glory. The fires burned, the wind sang through the walls, and once more he could see the echoes of the hammer's history. Tools, weapons, and complex machinery had been forged here, many beyond Tahnir's understanding.

It was around this moment that Tahnir noticed he was standing freely, without holding onto anything but the hammer for support. He looked over his body and could no longer feel the pain of his injuries. His leg supported his weight without trouble, and his other injuries were healed.

In fact, he felt better than he ever had before, as if the light of the forge had done to him what it had done to the metal tanks. Those blue and yellow fires that swirled about in the tanks seemingly now burned within him, filling him with an energy he had never possessed. He strode over to where Iridia was peering through the gaps in the marble walls.

“Do you feel it, Tahnir?” she asked in a breathy whisper. She seemed to not notice that he had walked all the way over to her without assistance, but he did not blame her after all they had just witnessed. “You have relit the Golden Forge, and its blessings are returning to the islands. I feel it within myself as surely as I feel it coursing all around us. Whatever you did, you have given Helanái a great gift today. I am positive that history will tell of the day that Tahnir Desqen brought the fires back to the Golden Forge and changed the Sky Islands forever.”

She turned and looked him in the eyes, and he could see the wonder and amazement etched into her face. Frankly, it made him slightly embarrassed, as he had not really known what he was doing.

Iridia reached out and held onto his right arm, where he still held the hammer. Together, they watched the pulse of golden light race across the surface of the island around them and deliver its blessing to all it touched.

Chapter 31

FOR HELANÁI

Panic raced through Tylanna as she saw the bottom of the Sky Island emerge from the clouds above them. The sounds of battle around her faded as everyone's attention was drawn to the falling island. Surely they would all be crushed if they remained where they were.

Tylanna's vision blurred, and the rotting chains that somehow held the island aloft became visible to her again. With Vistari being forced into the casting by Rhiannon's Madness, the ritual seemed to be progressing even faster than it had been before. Large pieces of the ethereal metal fell from the chains and came hurtling to the ground. Tylanna feared they would crush those they fell on, but they did not seem to make any physical contact with the people below or the ground they fell on.

She turned her head back to face Rhiannon's Madness, raising Darkender to strike.

Her vision did not return to normal, but instead, she could still see the skyward chains crumbling behind the monstrosity. The very air around the being burned with rot and acrid black smoke, obscuring its form. It was difficult for her to not let terror seize her heart.

The creature held its rusted blade above its dark black helmet and strode towards Tylanna, Pahlio, and Nuwitzwe.

"Nuwitzwe, take everyone and run," Pahlio said through gritted teeth as he readjusted his stance to better utilize his one remaining sword. "The Sky Island is falling. The battle is lost. Help as many as you can escape, and I will deal with this beast."

Nuwitzwe's eyes glowed, and tendrils of pure white energy wrapped around his arms as he looked at his captain. "Brother, you have learned little about me if you expect me to leave you at a time such as this. I will stand and fight, as is the way of the Night Blades."

"No one is leaving you behind, Captain," Tylanna said.

Pahlio looked to both of them with exasperation creasing his already tense face, but when he returned his gaze to Rhiannon's Madness, he let out a short laugh. "Then let us share in a glorious death, and ride together on the winds of the forevermore."

Just as the beast brought its rusted blade back to swing in an arc that could cleave the three of them in half at once, an explosion of golden light erupted from the base of the Sky Island above.

Light rained down from the island in a cascade of sparkling flecks. The twelve chains that had been rotting from the ritual burned away all signs of decay and shone a brilliant golden. A myriad of additional golden chains sprung forth from the base of the island, anchoring it in place.

The Sky Island ceased its descent, and from the shimmer, a large pathway appeared from the north-facing side.

Tylanna felt an amazing surge of energy from somewhere unknown within herself as if she had just unlocked a door containing power she never knew she possessed. Just as she saw the pathway begin to stretch and coil towards the surface, Rhiannon's Madness released an inhuman roar of anguish.

The creature had reared its head as it released the terrifying cry before turning its attention to the three of them. It brought the rusted blade towards them.

Tylanna and Nuwitzwe dove out of the way to either side of the strike. Pahlio, who was positioned right where the blade was swinging, was just barely able to bat the blade slightly to the side, just enough for him to avoid being carved in half. He stumbled backward and dropped his sword. As it fell, it began to crumble away, just as she had seen the armor of her fellow Night Blade soldier do. The sword disintegrated to nothing as Pahlio pulled a pair of knives from the belt on his waist, though Tylanna could not imagine how small knives such as these would stand any chance at parrying such a huge weapon.

Rhiannon's Madness turned its attention to Tylanna with a lightning-fast strike of the rusted blade.

Without time to do anything but block, Tylanna threw up Darkender to prevent the strike from making contact with her. She had seen what the rusted blade could do to a person, and that was a fate she did not wish to meet.

The two swords clashed with a loud ringing of metal on metal, and the monstrosity staggered backward.

Tylanna dropped to her knee to block. She had not felt the force behind the strike, but Darkender seemed to vibrate in her hand from the contact.

Very powerful. Let me, girl, and I will end it quickly. You cannot hold out against a foe such as this.

Tylanna tried to suppress the voice in her head. She could not lose control again, not with Pahlio and Nuwitzwe so close. Endangering them was the last thing she wanted to do. She would beat this beast with her own strength, and she would protect her friends no matter the cost.

At the moment Rhiannon's Madness was shoved backward, the white tendrils that wrapped around Nuwitzwe's arms exploded outward from him. They draped themselves around the ebony armor of the monstrosity and tightened, binding it in place. The creature thrashed against the luminous shackles.

“Pahlio, Tylanna!” Nuwitzwe yelled, his voice straining. “I cannot hold it for long. You must finish this!”

Tylanna’s vision was once again drawn to the Sky Island above them. From the north side, alongside the pathway that was still coiling and stretching towards the surface in an explosion of golden light fell thousands of small shadows. Together they descended, shadow and light, falling in beautiful symmetry.

Tylanna could see that the shadows were in fact people, diving from the edge of the Sky Island towards the surface. Just before they came crashing into the battlefield at full speed, she saw them stretch their arms and legs wide open. Strange fabrics flew backward from their bodies, catching the air, reducing their speed dramatically and allowing them to land as if they had leaped from a distance of ten feet, not several miles.

As they rose to their feet, they produced poles about their person. They held weapons in front of their bodies as the rest of the shadows landed and repeated the process. Once gathered, all of those standing in formation released a unified cry.

“*FOR HELANÁI!*”

Twin short blades erupted from each end of the poles wielded by these sky warriors, and together they rushed forward, diving headfirst into combat with the remaining members of Those Who Serve.

Catching their opponents off guard, for the most part, the Helanáians carved through the enemy lines with ease.

Wonder and relief filled Tylanna's eyes before she returned her attention to the fight at hand. Now that the Helanáians had joined them, this was not a desperate fight for survival for the Night Blades. This was now a battle they could win.

Tylanna let out a cry as she charged Rhiannon's Madness. The beast swung the rusted blade toward her, but Nuwitzwe's power slowed the creature greatly.

Tylanna rolled beneath the blade and sprung back to her feet just in front of the creature. So close, she saw that her head barely reached its waist.

Pahlio appeared next to her and stabbed wildly at the being's armored legs. Each strike of his knives bounced back from the armor, not appearing to make any mark at all.

Gathering all of her strength, she brought back Darkender to stab it forward into the beast's right leg. Her black blade cut through the armor without resistance.

She ripped the sword free as violently as she could, slashing outward from her initial point of penetration.

A plume of black smoke shot into the air from the wound.

The beast released another horrid noise before bringing the blade down toward them. Tylanna dove to Pahlio to shove him out of the way of the strike, and together they tumbled into the dust.

"Tylanna," Pahlio barked, "it has to be you! Your sword seems to be the only weapon that affects that monster. I will protect Nuwitzwe, but it must be you who fells the beast."

He helped her back to her feet, and she stood ready, Darkender hanging freely from her right hand.

Surrender to me all your power, blade, she thought. *I am your master, and you will do my bidding. Together we will destroy this enemy.*

As you wish, Creator-daughter. I will give you as much of my power as you can handle.

Starting from the hand that gripped Darkender's hilt, stark heat erupted throughout Tylanna's entire body. A fire burned below her very skin, filling her with strength and speed not yet known to her in this life. It mixed with the strange feeling she had felt after seeing the explosion of golden light and coursed through her body until she felt as if she could nearly burst. Her muscles tensed and flexed as she dropped into a swordplay stance Pahlio had taught her.

Nuwitzwe released a scream and collapsed, the light fading away from him. Pahlio caught the man as he fell and looked to Rhiannon's Madness with fear and anger etched onto his face. Tylanna stalked toward the creature in ebony armor, and it turned its attention to her.

Now unhindered by Nuwitzwe's Banéhûl magic, Rhiannon's Madness dashed toward Tylanna and brought the rusted blade down with a speed that a normal human would never have been able to stop.

But Tylanna was more than a normal human.

As the giant blade swung toward her, she sidestepped and brought Darkender down on the rusted blade as hard as she could.

The huge weapon was plunged deep into the ground. As she pulled Darkender back from the blow, she pressed her boot against the flat of the rusted blade and leaped. She soared through the air of the battlefield toward Rhiannon's Madness and swung Darkender at the beast's black metal helmet in one clean strike.

The helmet clattered to the ground as Tylanna landed gracefully behind the monster. She turned back, readying for another strike, but black smoke erupted from the hole she had ripped in the beast's neck until nothing held the armor aloft anymore, and it came clattering to the ground. The cloud of black smoke gathered together before flying away across the battlefield, leaving Tylanna's vision.

Tylanna heard Darkender cry out in sickly delight at the slaying of the beast, and the heat faded from within her. She should be exhausted, but she still felt she had energy to spare.

Turning towards Nuwitzwe and Pahlio, she noticed that her metal boot had disintegrated after touching the rusted blade, which still remained stuck in the dirt beside her. Taking extra care with her one bare foot, she ran back over to Pahlio and Nuwitzwe, who she saw was unconscious.

"Is he all right?" she asked.

Pahlio took an extra moment to respond as he seemed to be distracted by something. "He... He will be fine. This happens when he draws too much from the dead. Banéhûl magic takes a toll on the user, a toll I could not even imagine. But Tylanna, you were incredible. I knew you possessed great strength, but nothing such as what you just did."

Tylanna looked down at Darkender, the black blade that she still gripped tightly in her right hand. She wondered if she would ever be able to release its lure. "I... I do not know how to explain it, but this weapon is more than a sword. I was able to borrow its power during the fight somehow."

Pahlio stared at her, and then at Darkender. "I have heard of weapons that held their own power in the songs of the old wars. It would explain why the beast's blade did not rot and decay the metal, as it did mine. Maybe that sword you carry is more important than we realized. If you would continue to fight with us, it could be the key to defeating our enemies and bringing peace back to Artani and the lands beyond."

Tylanna contemplated for a moment as she stared at valley. The battle continued to rage around them, but the Helanáians and the surviving fighters of the Night Blades had driven back the members of Those Who Serve, and it seemed that they had begun a full retreat towards the southern side of the mountain range. If the Helanáians had come to support them, that meant that they had somehow learned of the threat Those Who Serve posed to them, as well as knowing that Talakoko would be the next target after the first island fell. She saw that the large pathway had finished its spiraling journey to the surface, and more Helanáian warriors were pouring down the newly formed Sky Bridge.

The way was open for her to travel to Helanái, to the safety of the extended family she had never met. She could complete the journey her father had sent her on and hide from this horrible conflict on the surface. While waiting in the Sky Islands, hopefully, her brother would find his way there, and they could finally be reunited. Together, in the safety of the Sky Islands.

But the conflict would continue, whether she was there or not. If she truly possessed the power to shift the scales in the coming war, then she owed it to her fellow members of the Night Blades to fight alongside them. She would find her brother, and Akiye, and bring each of them to safety.

"I will fight with you, Captain."

Pahlio clapped his hand on her back, a wide smile of approval stretching across his face. The sounds of battle faded from Tylanna's ears as she looked forward to the day she could finally be together with her friends and family in a world ruled only by peace.

Chapter 32

FIRES OF REBIRTH

Rynestian mustered all of his strength to block the incoming attack from Agrimal. He held his gauntlets with the metal facing the swinging sword, hoping it would be enough, but knowing it would not.

A strange heat began to burn from within him. But it was not like the heat he felt from the fires scorching Shae Glen to the ground around him – this heat seemed to fuel him, empower him.

As Agrimal's blade met his gauntlets, he felt nowhere near the force behind the blow he had been expecting, or rather, he was able to resist the strength of the blow much easier. This seemed to shock Agrimal as much as it shocked Rynestian, but he did not give the pale man a chance to react.

Lunging forward, he struck the man. Before Agrimal had a chance to figure out how he was moving so much faster, Rynestian scored two shots to his body. Serious wounds, but not fatal.

Agrimal threw himself backwards, away from Rynestian, clutching his free hand over the reddening robes that now dangled from his chest.

"How? You were beaten, sky rat!" Agrimal hissed, his voice much more serious than it had ever been before, though he still wore his eerie smile.

Not willing to answer the cretin, and honestly not knowing how, Rynestian barreled forward. Using his newfound speed, it was a simple matter of evading Agrimal's wild slashing, scoring a few hits, dodging, and repeating the process. Before long, Agrimal was staggering from side to side, robes torn asunder and blood pouring freely from many wounds.

Now that he saw the fight was won, Rynestian took a moment to compose himself. "I want you and your kind to leave Shae Glen and never come back."

"Shae Glen?" Agrimal wheezed irritably, both his sword arm and his free hand swinging about wildly. "This nothing little village in the middle of more nothing? Trust me, sky rat, I will *never* be coming back here. That is, there will be nothing to come back to when *I burn it all to ash!*"

The flames around them exploded with newfound ferocity. Without thinking, Rynestian closed the gap between them and held Agrimal by the throat. With his free hand, he bashed the man in the face with his open palm again and again, until Agrimal's head hung limply from his neck, and he smiled no more.

He dropped Agrimal to the ground. Shaking the extra blood free from his gauntlets, Rynestian let out a sigh of relief. He drew himself up to his full height as he tried to fill his lungs. The air all around him was filled with smoke and the stench of burning wood and flesh. Pain from the wound on his side and the many burns he had sustained in the explosion set in, and he knew that he would have to receive some form of treatment very soon, or else he would not survive much longer.

He prayed Xelina and the others were okay as he looked around him, through the diminishing flames that had surrounded him until moments ago, and saw the ruin that was once the peaceful village of Shae Glen. All of the work they had put into creating a perfect haven outside of the conflicts of the world was all for naught. He could not decide what emotion he felt more strongly – rage or despair.

He heard a gurgling noise from below him and returned his attention to the pale man who lay beaten and bloodied below his feet.

Just as Rynestian had thought he stood no chance of defeating the man, he had felt a surge of power unlike anything he had ever experienced before. He had found himself able to easily keep up with the thin man's swiftness, and even dodge the slashing of his narrow steel blade.

Presently, Rynestian gave the man a hard kick to the ribs, and after a bloody cough, the man grew silent once more. Agrimal's once-pristine white robes were torn and stained red. The urge to kill the man had been strong for Rynestian, but he had decided it would be better to keep him alive if they were ever to get answers about why Those Who Serve had begun to seek out Helanáians as far as Eodisia.

A thundering of horse hooves sounded through the cobblestone streets of Shae Glen as Emili Rhys and a force from the Eodisian army arrived at the battle, helping what Shae Glenners remained to defeat the soldiers of Those Who Serve who had retreated to the outskirts of the village before the explosion, which Rynestian was certain had somehow been Agrimal's doing. Judging just by the number of fighters that had arrived from the Eodisian capital, the remaining soldiers from Those Who Serve would not stand a chance. Especially now that their commander was defeated.

Rynestian rolled the man's body over with ease and pinned his arms behind his back. His sword lay shattered several feet away from him, but Rynestian still did not want to take any chances leaving him unbound. If his forge still stood, he had chains that would do the trick.

Grabbing the man's two arms in one hand and a bundle of his robe's waist in the other, Rynestian hoisted the man into the air and marched towards the outskirts of the village, where the battle would still be raging, and hopefully where his home still stood intact.

Though he could feel the many pains all along his body, the burst of strength had not left him. He wondered what could have caused such a thing to happen, but he did not think too long on the matter. There was plenty else to worry about, and he was not about to second guess whatever blessing he had received.

As he drew nearer to the sounds of battle, he heaved the man's unconscious body above his head. Maybe whatever soldiers of Those Who Serve would see their commander defeated and turn tail and run. That, or they would charge him to find vengeance, but Rynestian was confident that with his newfound speed and strength, all they would find was a swift death.

When he finally reached the site of the battle, he found that the combined forces of the surviving Shae Glenners and the Eodisian army had nearly routed all of the remaining force of Those Who Serve. The few who still lived were all corralled in a circle, surrounded by mounted Eodisian soldiers, who pointed long spears in their direction.

When Rynestian got close enough to hear them, the remaining fighters for Those Who Serve all threw down their weapons.

"Good. Now, you will be taken alive to our capital for questioning," said a man who appeared to be leading the Eodisian soldiers. His armor was a bit more ornate than the others, with fine etchings of orange and blue adorning the silver plate armor. He was the only one of the Eodisian riders that was not wearing a helmet, allowing his shoulder-length red hair to flow freely as he moved about on his horse.

Seeing that the battle was won, Rynestian paid the Eodisian no mind and trudged along with Agrimal's body draped across his shoulder. He still had a bit farther to walk. This area had not received as much fire damage as the village square, but still, homes burned all around. As he passed them, the man who appeared to be leading the Eodisians shouted after him.

"You there! Might you be Rynestian Desqen, the forge-master?"

Rynestian came to a stop and turned to face the man. "I am," he said. His voice was harsh from the smoke's effects on his throat, and he was sure he sounded gruffer than he had wished to a man who had helped save them from certain death.

The man dismounted smoothly from his steed and strode over to Rynestian. He seemed to be about ten years Rynestian's junior, but he had found it more and more difficult to guess someone's age the older he got.

"I have heard of your bravery, forge-master," the red-haired man said as he approached. "They are calling you the hero of Shae Glen."

Rynestian scoffed.

The man had a square head, and now that he was closer Rynestian could see that the sides of his head were shaved nearly bald, as was the traditional Eodisian fashion for soldiers. A thin scar stretched across his face, spanning from below his left eye to the right side of his square chin.

"So many were lost," Rynestian grunted, "and the village is burned. I am no hero."

Rynestian's eyes drifted to the ground with despair, but the man placed a comforting hand on his shoulder and met his gaze.

"Surely without your aid, they all would have been lost. Madam Emili Rhys told me of your efforts to train the village folk that lived here, and Norantho Nartil explained the fighters you led in the streets and your battle with the commander, who I presume is this poor bastard you carry about like a sack of flour?"

Rynestian grunted in agreement. "He lives – Norantho?"

The man nodded. "He and most of the young archers survived and helped us take on the remaining forces. In truth, they gave us an advantage, probably saving a number of my soldiers by raining death down upon the enemy. Though, Those Who Serve certainly did us a favor by gathering all of their fighters in one place. I am Twann Lastel-Reaver, and I currently hold the rank of General-Master of Eodisia. I believe I placed an order with you not so long ago, before all of this trouble with Those Who Serve."

Rynestian's eyes widened. "General-Master Lastel-Reaver, thank you for your order. I am afraid many of the weapons that I had prepared for your order were used to help us defend our home. It will take me some time to complete the order."

The General-Master shook his head with a smile. "Do not fret. I can think of no better use for the weapons than to defend Eodisia from invaders." The man's expression grew grim as he looked to the man draped across Rynestian's shoulder. "What do you intend to do with him? Did you get his name?"

"I am taking him to my forge if it still stands," Rynestian said plainly. "There are some heavy chains there I wish to bind him with before trying to get some answers from him when he wakes. He gave his name as Agrimal of the Promised Dawn."

"I have not heard of this Promised Dawn, but maybe they are behind Those Who Serve's sudden turn to violence. I shall accompany you to your forge, if you will allow it, forge-master. I fear his answers may have massive implications for all of Eodisia."

Rynestian nodded and hiked the man's body higher onto his shoulder before leading the General-Master to his forge. As they departed, Twann shouted back to his soldiers to imprison the remaining members of Those

Who Serve and await his return. Together, they meandered further into the outskirts, and Rynestian answered any questions he could for the General-Master, while all the while silently praying that his home stood untouched.

Thankfully, when they reached the Desqen home, it seemed that the fires of Those Who Serve had not reached it at all. After taking a moment to let the elation of the sight wash over him, Rynestian rushed into the forge, with the General-Master following right behind.

Rynestian dumped Agrimal's body on the dirt floor, and the man let out a pained grunt. Quickly, Rynestian grabbed one of the metal chains he had hanging from the walls and bound the man's hands behind his back, fixing them with a large bolt he hammered into the ground behind him. Even striking the hammer against the bolt seemed to be easier with his newfound strength, and the bolt was flat against the ground in one clean strike.

Once Agrimal was bound, Rynestian returned to Twann Laster-Reaver's side, and each of them stood before the pale, thin man.

Agrimal's head rolled from side to side after he had been propped up to a sitting position. Low and wordless grumbles tumbled forth from him, but nothing that Rynestian could discern.

"Perhaps I should do something to wake him, General-Master," Rynestian said after a moment. "I am afraid he may not wake for some time if we leave him be."

The Eodisian soldier leaned forward to inspect the unconscious man. "Yes, I think you are right, forge-master. You seem to have done a real number on him with those gauntlets of yours."

Rynestian grunted as he stepped away. He saw out of the corner of his eye that the General-Master held his short spear ready to strike at the man, just in case. Rynestian wondered if the Eodisians had been told of what the man had seemed to do with the fire that still engulfed the village.

He went to the quenching barrel on the opposite side of the forge and filled a nearby bucket with the liquid. It seemed a shame to waste the concoction to wake this man, but drawing fresh water from the well would take far too long. The answers this man could provide could potentially save thousands of lives in Eodisia and elsewhere.

He returned to the side of the General-Master, holding the bucket firmly in both hands, poised to strike. Twann gave him a nod, and Rynestian splashed the contents of the bucket onto the pale man.

With a start, Agrimal awoke sputtering. He strained against his bindings. He was able to move a few inches forward before the chains caught against the bolt, and he was held in place. His mouth opened in a vicious snarl as he stared up at Rynestian, seemingly ignoring Twann Laster-Reaver completely.

After struggling against the chains for a moment, Agrimal's body sagged, and his head hung so his shaggy white hair covered the majority of his face.

"Who are you?" Twann asked. "And under whose command do you attack our lands?"

For a long moment, Agrimal did not reply. Eventually, a sickly cackle echoed from deep inside the bound man that rose until it was reduced to a harsh cough that left a splatter of blood on the floor, nearly reaching Rynestian and Twann's boots.

"You should have killed me, sky rat," Agrimal said in a harsh whisper. His voice still held the sick joviality it had before their battle, when the fires had parted for him and followed his every command.

Rynestian dropped down to his haunches to put his face close to Agrimal's. "I thought the same, but I showed you mercy. More likely than not, you did not deserve it, but I gave it to you all the same. I still may change my mind if you don't give us any answers."

Agrimal released another short laugh before replying, "You will have nothing from me. I have failed, so either you kill me, or I will be killed some other way. But one stronger than I will replace me, and Eodisia will submit to the will of Those Who Serve, if not today then another."

"Eodisia will not bow to anyone, not while I still draw breath," Twann declared, kicking the bloodied dirt toward Agrimal.

Still, Agrimal paid him no mind, and he turned his head up to stare directly into Rynestian's eyes. He held his strange too-wide smile, made all the eerier but the trails of blood streaming from each side of his mouth. "How... How did you do it, sky rat? You know you did not have the strength to beat me. Were you holding back the whole time? While your friends all died around you? *How?*"

Rynestian stumbled back. Regaining his composure, he turned to the General-Master. "I don't think he will be providing us any answers, General-Master. Do what you wish with him. I would like him removed from my forge."

"Understood, forge-master. I will take him with the other prisoners back to the capital, where our questioners will have another go at him."

"You really should have killed me," Agrimal muttered, his voice low. "Soon the end will come for all who stand against us, no matter how you writhe or wriggle to escape."

As Rynestian and Twann stared down at the captured man, a searing heat ripped past Rynestian's right shoulder. He fell to the side just in time as a pillar of living flame snaked through the air toward Agrimal.

Agrimal stretched his mouth wide open with a final demonic laugh as the pillar of flame plunged into his throat. The man's body swelled as the fire consumed him, deforming beyond human contortions.

Rynestian, realizing what was about to happen, scrambled to his feet and ran out of the forge, stopping only to help the General-Master up to his feet as well. The pair of them dove from the entryway just as Agrimal and the forge erupted in flame. They were each blown several yards forward and hit the ground hard.

As he connected with the ground, Rynestian felt the full effect of the day's fighting, all his injuries, and all the pain he had been pushing to the back of his mind.

The edges of his vision blurred. The last sight he saw before losing consciousness was the Desqen Forge in flames.

Chapter 33

SHADOWS OF THE SKY

The night after the battle beneath the Sky Island, Tylanna and the other surviving members of the Night Blades made camp on the northern side of the mountain range. Some of the fighters were still not entirely convinced that the island would not fall, despite any explanation the captain or Tylanna tried to offer.

Whatever members of Those Who Serve that were not killed in the fighting escaped. They had started retreating the moment the Wing Warriors – that was what the Helanáian warriors with the strange contraptions on their backs had called themselves – arrived on the battlefield. The few that were captured offered little to no information; they all seemed more scared of whoever had given them the orders to tear down the Sky Islands than the armies of Helanái and Artani combined.

Among those that escaped were the Maiden Rhiannon and the other ritual casters, that or their bodies could not be identified. After the ritual ended, it was discovered that Vistari had been killed by being forcibly joined into the ritual by Rhiannon's Madness. Tylanna had asked that her body be buried alongside the fallen Night Blades.

Captain Pahlio had forfeited the prisoners to the Helanáians as an act of goodwill and had received tremendous thanks for their efforts in delaying the ritual long enough for them to arrive. Several of the Wing Warriors had returned up the newly formed Sky Bridge with the prisoners, and those who remained joined the Night Blades at their camp for a night of celebration.

Though the tone in the camp was one of merriment, Tylanna could not help but grieve all that were lost. Far less than half of the Night Blades that had entered the valley survived. While they had emerged victorious on the day, this was no victory in her eyes.

Presently, she sat beside a fire which she had been stoking with a charred stick. She stared down at her mismatched boots, one of which she had received from a Wing Warrior who noticed she had lost one of her own in the fighting. The two boots could not be more different, one a thick black metal, the other a lightweight leather series of straps. She wondered how different the two nations really were when they sat separated by only a few miles of sky.

"There you are, Tylanna!"

Captain Pahlio's voice cut through the general revelry that surrounded her and drew her out of her thoughts.

She saw him part ways with one of the Wing Warriors and walk towards the fire. His smile faded from his face when he saw her expression, which she had no doubt was grim. He sat down next to her and gazed into the flames.

"I know your first battle can be difficult," he said, his voice filled with a seriousness that seemed almost unfamiliar coming from him. "And I will not promise that they will get easier. But what you accomplished today was incredible. Think of all you saved with your actions!"

"And what of those I did not save?" Tylanna asked, her voice trembling, "What of our fallen comrades who will never see another day?"

"They were prepared to die for what they wanted to protect, just as you or I were. Think not of what they lost, but what we now must protect for them. The vow of a Night Blade does not end with death."

Tylanna poked at the fire a few times with her charred stick. As she leaned forward, she felt the hilt of Darkender press against her side, and she thought of all she had cut down in the frenzy of battle. She looked to her captain before speaking.

"Pahlio...erm, Captain, during the fighting, there was a point where it felt as if I had completely lost control of myself, and my blade was guiding my every action. I fear the power too great for me to control."

Pahlio drew his gaze from the fire and stared so deeply into her eyes that she had to look away. "No, Tylanna, I think you may be the only one powerful enough to control a weapon so mighty. I fought alongside you today, and I know that the sword did little but aid what skill you already possessed. You credit yourself too little."

Desperate to change the subject from flattering remarks, she interjected with a question, "What of Nuwitzwe? Has he recovered yet?"

Pahlio nodded. "Yes, some time ago. Like a fool, he went right back down the mountainside into the valley. I offered to accompany him in case there were any enemies still lurking behind, but he refused. He often likes to do this after battles, says he attempts to have one last moment with our fallen."

"That sounds nice," Tylanna said, wondering if doing so would bring her any peace. "I think I would like that as well."

"It is not as pleasant as it seems. Though he often skirts around a straight answer when I try to find out more about the Banéhûl magic, no part of the process seems enjoyable. Even with his advanced mastery over manipulating the Banéhûl Leyline energy, the result is rarely what he initially was seeking, and the cost is always greater. He carries such a heavy burden."

Tylanna stared harder into the flames, wishing that she did not have to sound so childish every time she spoke.

Behind them, a single set of hooves clattering up the mountain range sounded through the night, and the raucous sounds of celebration died down as the lone rider approached.

Pahlio spun to his feet, his hand resting on his remaining sword. Tylanna followed him towards the direction the sound was coming from.

Several of the other Night Blades dropped into formation around them, though admittedly some of them had consumed far too much ale to be handling weaponry, but one never could choose when a fight would happen.

Captain Pahlio ran in front of the others to peer over the mountainside and held his hand aloft, his hand clenched in a fist. “Hold! Lower your weapons.”

The Night Blades begrudgingly lowered their steel, though the tension in the air did not dissipate at their captain’s word. After several tense moments of quiet aside from the clopping of hooves, the rider crested the side of the mountain. Though the emblem was different, the rider wore Night Legion armor. They drew their horse to a halt and removed their helmet, golden hair falling to the woman’s waist.

“I bring word from Captain Nero Leor of the Night Legion! Is your captain present?” the rider cried out in a clear, loud voice.

“I am here!” Pahlio exclaimed as he rushed to the rider's side, offering her a hand as she dismounted.

"I am glad to see you well, Captain Pahlio. Your father and all of the other captains are rushing here with full force to assist you in the coming battle. I left but a few hours before they were meant to depart."

The rider's feet hit the dirt, and she drew herself up, and Tylanna was surprised to see that she stood at least a head taller than Pahlio.

"Well, my lady, there will be no need for their help in battle," Pahlio said with a sense of familiarity and a mischievous grin that made it clear he knew this soldier. "With the help of the Helanáians that join us here tonight, the devious plot to bring down the Sky Island has been stopped. The battle already belongs to the Night Blades!"

With that, the camp erupted into cheers, and those who had jumped up to fight were able to relax.

Tylanna still stood ready, listening to Pahlio's conversation with the woman.

"I will send a rider to meet my father and the other captains," Pahlio told the woman with a laugh, "if there are any still sober. We will hold a meeting of the twelve captains when they arrive. There is much I must tell them of our new enemy. We owe everything to the Helanáians who came to our aid, and we owe much to our newest recruit, Tylanna Desqen. Or as the Night Blades have come to call her, Tylanna Golden Eyes."

She saw Pahlio point through the crowd at her, and all of a sudden, she was set upon with one of the worst headaches of her life.

Tylanna clutched her head and dropped to one knee. The woman and Pahlio rushed over to help her back to her feet.

"Tylanna, are you all right?" Pahlio asked.

"I'm... I'm fine, just a headache that came on suddenly." She rubbed her head before gently extricating herself from the pair's grasp. "It must be the exhaustion of the day finally setting in. I think I will just retire for the night."

"Do you need us to walk with you?" the woman, whose name Tylanna still did not know, asked.

"No, I will be all right. Thank you though. Thank you, Captain."

She offered a small bow before leaving Captain Pahlio's side, and he gave her a short nod to dismiss her.

Once she was far enough away from the noise of the celebration, she plopped down in one of the many tents that had been set up after the battle. She kicked free her armor until she lay on the floor in just her underclothes with Darkender on her waist. Sweat beaded her forehead, and her head swirled with thoughts that were not hers.

She would have loved to have washed before sleeping for the night, but she feared that now that she was lying down, she might not be able to get back up. The pounding in her head increased, and she stared hard at the roof of the tent. Hoping to suppress the pain in her head, she pressed her eyes shut with all of her might.

When she opened her eyes, she was standing, and her headache had vanished as quickly as it had come. Before her stretched a forest, filled with towering trees. Water rushed over her feet, and she looked down to see that a river surged beneath her, though she felt undisturbed by the flow. This appeared different than the dreams she usually experienced when she slept, in that the form she inhabited was her own.

The vision was serene and peaceful, while also somehow giving her a nostalgic feeling. She took a step forward through the water, and she realized why it all seemed so familiar.

Below her spilled a long waterfall, the very same one she had fallen from as a child. Fear seized hold of her, and she almost staggered backward, until she saw something on one of the ledges beneath her.

Sitting exactly where she had seen the blue sparrow on that fateful day in her childhood was her mother, Tritelle Desqen. She sat cross-legged, allowing the water to flow past her. Her mother looked exactly how she remembered her before the sickness had affected her so.

It warmed Tylanna's heart so to see her again, after everything that had happened. She was sitting facing the same direction as Tylanna, so she could not see her face, as it was obscured by her impressive mane of wavy hair.

Tylanna tried to call out to her, but her voice made no noise. Instead, she took another step forward and tumbled over the side of the waterfall.

She seemed to be falling slower than she had the first time, and she was able to take in all of her surroundings. Tylanna turned to look at her mother as she fell, but her hair seemed to be blown by a wind that Tylanna did not feel as it covered her face from this angle as well.

After she fell past where her mother sat, she looked to the surface of the water, where a massive serpentine creature erupted and stretched its gigantic mouth open. Powerless to do anything to stop it, Tylanna merely braced herself as the creature swallowed her whole.

Alone, in the darkness, for a moment she saw nothing. Then, she walked alongside a small woman in a flowing white dress. The woman had long white hair that was adorned with gold. She appeared not to notice Tylanna as she walked along a battlefield. Before her stood a rusted blade that had been pierced into the ground.

The small woman walked toward the sword and laid her small, delicate-looking hand on the hilt. When she did, the rust of the blade melted away. A shining black blade was revealed beneath the thick layer of rust.

Without any apparent effort, the small woman hefted the blade free from the ground and floated as a storm of darkness swirled around her. Tylanna lost sight of the woman and the blade as her entire view was obscured by darkness.

Once more she stood alone until she felt a strong breeze blowing against her. Before she could react, the wind had swept her form up, and she was flying. She flew through the clouds, weightless, before dipping below the cloud line towards the surface. Below her stretched a rolling desert landscape that she had never seen before. In fact, she had never seen any desert before, and she found it strange that the word came so naturally to her.

As she stared below, she saw the sand swirl together at one point. A hole opened in the ground, and the surrounding sand poured in freely until finally, she could see that at the center of the hole was a gigantic blade, as tall as the buildings she had seen in Aynanu before it was destroyed, wrapped in chains. The sword seemed to be absorbing all of the sand as it fell.

The wind that carried her picked up again and propelled her directly toward the tip of the upturned blade. Just as she was certain she was about to be obliterated, everything around her changed.

She fell, though only from a short distance, onto a flat surface just below her that she could not see. All around her was pitch black.

Tylanna pushed herself up to a seated position. Her dreams were not often this interpolative – they usually only followed one experience.

As she sat, a small round piece of wood floated down before her, and she accepted it as it fell into her hands. It was smooth and sturdy to the touch. As she turned it over, the wood cracked right through the middle.

When the two pieces broke apart, they crumbled as if turned to ash with no flame.

Tylanna felt that she too was crumbling. Piece by piece, she felt her whole being fading away, becoming one with the darkness.

In that moment, there was nothing.

End of Book I: Shadows of the Sky

Tylanna and Tahnir's story will continue in

Book II: The Wooden Mask

About the Author

Sean Curtis is a writer from Pittsburgh, Pennsylvania, who currently lives in Honolulu, Hawai'i. Since a young age he has possessed a fascination with all things fantasy and has been an avid reader of the genre for all of his life. He graduated from Robert Morris University in 2017 with a Bachelor of the Arts with a concentration in Film and Digital Cinema. He began writing in 2020.

Milton Keynes UK
Ingram Content Group UK Ltd.
UKHW020637101123
432322UK00018B/732